LIFE
SUPPORT

ROBERT WHITLOW

W PUBLISHING GROUP™

www.wpublishinggroup.com

A Division of Thomas Nelson, Inc.
www.ThomasNelson.com

LIFE SUPPORT

Published by W Publishing Group, a Division of Thomas Nelson, Inc., P.O. Box 141000, Nashville, Tennessee 37214.

All Scripture quotations, unless otherwise indicated, are taken from The Holy Bible, New International Version (NIV). Copyright © 1973, 1978, 1984, International Bible Society. Used by permission of Zondervan Bible Publishers.

Other Scripture references are from the following sources:
    The King James Version of the Bible (KJV).
    The New King James Version (NKJV®), copyright 1979, 1980, 1982, Thomas Nelson, Inc., Publishers.

Library of Congress Cataloging-in-Publication Data

Whitlow, Robert, 1954-
    Life support / by Robert Whitlow.
      p. cm.
    ISBN 0-8499-4374-4 (softcover)
    1. South Carolina--Fiction. I. Title.
PS3573.H49837L54 2003
813'.54--dc21   2003006222

Printed in the United States of America
03 04 05 06 07 08 PHX 9 8 7 6 5 4 3 2 1

To all who seek to glorify God
in music and song. May you enter the uncharted realms of worship
and find in reality what this book portrays in story.

*Yet a time is coming and has now come when the true worshipers
will worship the Father in spirit and truth, for they are the kind of
worshipers the Father seeks.*

JOHN 4:23

ACKNOWLEDGMENTS

THIS NOVEL WAS not written in isolation. I deeply appreciate my wife, Kathy, who was steadfast in encouragement and accurate in editing. Much thanks to Ami McConnell and Traci DePree for their great substantive suggestions and to Wendy Wood for her careful corrections.

And thanks to the many people who have been my mentors in music. Of that number, pianist John G. Elliott *(johnelliott-music.com)* gave invaluable assistance in the preparation of this book.

The female of the species is more deadly than the male.
RUDYARD KIPLING

BAXTER RICHARDSON PRIED the cork from the wine bottle and tossed it past Rena into the clear, rushing water of the narrow stream. It immediately bobbed to the surface and joined several red and orange leaves drifting unaware toward the nearby waterfall. A few feet before the waterway cascaded over the edge of the cliff a large boulder squatted in the middle of the stream and caused the water to divide in two. It then plunged over the precipice in equal explosions of foaming white that many years before had inspired the name Double-Barrel Falls. Seventy-five feet below, the stream splattered onto several large boulders before it coalesced and continued its journey through the forest toward Lake Jocassee, a cold mountain reservoir that on a clear day could be seen as a hint of blue at the edge of the horizon. Rena Richardson had visited the secluded spot many times, but it was the first trip to the area for her husband Baxter, a sandy-haired, South Carolina coast-dweller with light brown eyes and an easygoing smile.

Baxter filled two clear plastic cups with the deep red liquid and set them on a flat rock in the autumn sun. He emptied his backpack and carefully positioned the rest of the food on a paper napkin beside the wine. The bread had been sliced by a chef at an expensive bakery where they'd bought it early that morning in Greenville. A light wind stirred the air. Rena ran her fingers through her blonde hair and pushed some wayward strands away from her pale blue eyes. She was a month past her twenty-fifth birthday. Baxter, a year older, sliced the soft cheese into chunks with a small knife while Rena watched in silence.

The young couple were alone in the clearing at the top of the water-fall. It was the first hike of their marriage, and they'd not seen another person during the three-mile trek from the trailhead. Soon, as October began, the trees would fully bloom with fall colors, and the number of hikers and tourists coming to the area would increase. This afternoon Baxter and Rena had the wilderness to themselves.

"I'm sorry I didn't bring a white tablecloth or silver candlesticks," Baxter said. "Too much weight for a hike."

Rena didn't answer. She'd been quiet all day. While Baxter strolled along the well-worn path, her thoughts revisited secret images of pain more familiar to her than the bends and twists of the trail. The scars of her soul rivaled the depth of the gorge below them.

Baxter handed her a cup of wine. "What do you want to toast?" he asked.

Rena looked past her husband to the place where she and her brothers had camped with her stepfather. She spoke with an accent that revealed a hint of her Appalachian Mountain roots.

"To the death of childhood monsters."

Baxter gave her a puzzled look. "That's a strange toast. What do you mean?"

"It fits," she responded simply.

Baxter shrugged. Holding up his cup, he proclaimed, "To the death of childhood monsters. Send them over the edge, never to return."

They touched cups and each took a sip.

The bread was chewy and the cheese soft, but even average fare tastes better in the woods after a hike. Baxter quickly drank a cup of wine and poured another. Rena nibbled a piece of bread but wasn't interested in food or drink.

She stared past Baxter. Glimpses of scenes from the past demanded her attention like a pack of wild dogs.

———

Her stepfather, Vernon Swafford, stood at the edge of the cliff with his back toward her as the sun descended behind the distant hills. He was a tall, broad-shouldered man with black hair swept back and held in place by hair tonic that smelled like stale vinegar. The smoke from his cigarette floated up above his head and lingered for a second before being dispersed by the breeze that blew across the ridge.

Thirteen-year-old Rena crouched in the shadows, trying to find the courage in her teenage soul to leap forward and push him over the edge. She rubbed the back of her leg and felt the tender spot that remained from the last time he'd taken off his belt to teach her a lesson. Her brothers were inside the tent, arguing in loud voices. Their noise would mask her footsteps. She inched closer. Her stepfather flipped the cigarette into the gorge and then immediately took out another one. Rena waited until he lit the fresh cigarette and took a deep drag.

It was her chance. She rose to her feet and took two quick steps. It would be over in a matter of seconds, and she would be free.

"What do you think you're doing, Rena?" Vernon Swafford's low voice stopped her in her tracks. His back was still turned toward her.

"Uh, nothin'," she stammered.

He turned sideways, and Rena could see the glint of evil in his eyes.

"Come over here and don't try to run away. If'n you do, it will only be worse on you later."

Hanging her head, Rena walked slowly forward. When she was within arm's reach, he grabbed her by the back of her cotton shirt, flung her around, and held her out over the edge of the cliff. Rena looked down into the deepening shadows of the gorge and tightly closed her eyes in anticipation of the feeling of falling through the air. Her shirt began to rip. She cried out, and at the sound, her stepfather grabbed her hair with his other hand and set her back on the stony ground. Rena's knees buckled, and she almost fell forward over the edge.

"Be careful," he said with mock concern. "You don't want to fall. It would be an awful mess for someone to clean up."

———

"I didn't realize how hungry I was until I started eating," Baxter said, oblivious to his beautiful young wife's thoughts. "Being outdoors gives you a big appetite. Do you want any more wine or bread?"

Rena shook her head.

"What's wrong with you?" Baxter responded in frustration.

Rena turned away. "Don't ask."

Baxter reached out and grabbed her arm. "Talk to me! I brought you here because you wanted to come, and then you clam up and act weird about it!"

Rena recoiled and jerked her arm from his grasp. "Don't touch me!"

Baxter's eyes flashed with anger, and Rena saw reflected in her husband's gaze the same malevolent glare that had threatened her in the past. Too much alcohol always brought out the worst in her stepfather, and Baxter's countenance betrayed a companion darkness. Rena's eyes narrowed, and her jaw grew rigid. She was no longer a helpless child without the ability to escape and find security for the future. She stood to her feet.

"Let's go," she said.

Baxter stared at her for a few seconds before turning up his cup of wine and draining it. Any other words would only provoke a fight. He put the remains of their food and the empty wine bottle into his backpack. Rena retrieved their hiking sticks from the place they'd dropped them near the waterfall.

"I'm going to need that stick," Baxter said curtly.

"Come and get it," Rena challenged.

Baxter stood and stepped toward her. She held the stick out toward him but didn't let go when he grabbed one end.

"I'm not interested in playing tug of war," he said.

"Do you want the stick or not?" she shot back.

Baxter pulled harder, but Rena kept a firm grasp on her end of the stick. She moved away from the falls and to her right until her husband's back was toward the edge of the drop-off, his silhouette framed against the panorama of the mountains behind him.

"That's enough, Rena," Baxter said, dropping his end of the stick. "Game over. Let's go. This is not a good place."

Rena didn't answer. Channeling all her rage and misplaced revenge into the stick, she raised it like a battering ram and lunged forward. It hit Baxter squarely in the stomach. He grunted and staggered backward until he was less than two feet from the edge of the cliff. Shock and surprise flashed across his face. His eyes filled with fear.

"No!" he shouted.

Abandoning all pretense of sanity, Rena screamed at the top of her lungs and charged again. The stick glanced off Baxter's chest, moved upward, and gouged a deep swath along the side of his neck. Rena lost her balance and crashed forward into her husband as he teetered on the edge of the cliff. In a last desperate act of survival, he stretched out his right hand and scraped it down Rena's left forearm. He grasped her fingers with his hand for a split second, gave her a frantic look, then slipped over the edge into nothingness. Rena fell to her hands and knees.

Breathing heavily, she listened.

No screams. No sounds. Just the roar of the waterfall plummeting toward the rocks below.

We are betrayed by what is false within.
GEORGE MEREDITH

DRESSED IN A CONSERVATIVE blue suit with a white, silk blouse, Alexia Lindale scribbled a final note on her legal pad. Known as "Alex" since childhood, the petite attorney with short, dark hair and green eyes took a quick sip of water as she waited for Judge Garland to nod in her direction.

"Ms. Lindale, you may conduct your cross-examination of the witness."

Alex was representing Marilyn Simpson, the estranged wife of Gregory Lamar Simpson, a real-estate developer who was seated in the witness chair. Alex's shoes tapped lightly on the polished wooden floor of the courtroom as she walked slowly to a spot in front of the jury box.

"Thank you, Your Honor," she said in a high-pitched voice that was a shade girlish. She then focused her attention on her adversary.

"Mr. Simpson, how old were you when you met your wife?"

"Seventeen or eighteen."

"Had you graduated from high school?"

"No, we started dating during our senior year. "

"And you testified on direct examination that you were married in August a few months after high-school graduation. Is that correct?"

"Yes."

"Where did you spend the first four years of your married life?"

"In Chapel Hill, North Carolina."

"Why were you living in North Carolina?"

"I was a student at the University of North Carolina."

"Was your wife also in school?"

"No. She worked."

"What type of work?"

"Uh, she had several different jobs. Mostly clerical."

Alex retrieved a stack of papers from the corner of the table where Marilyn Simpson sat watching.

"Did she work more than one job at a time?"

"Occasionally. She liked to stay busy."

"Were you also working?"

"No, I was concentrating on my education."

Alex looked down at the top sheet of paper. "Was one of her employers a law firm in Chapel Hill—Little, Goodman, & Greer?"

"I think so. I don't remember the exact name."

"Did she also work three nights a week as a convenience store clerk?"

"Uh, yes, for a while."

Alex's eyes flashed with a hint of green fire. "Would it surprise you to know that I have employment records showing your wife worked a combined average of fifty-seven hours a week at the law firm and the convenience store for more than two years?"

The witness shifted in the chair. "That sounds like too much, but I remember we bought a new car and needed to make the payments."

Alex took a step forward. "Would you like to review the employment records for yourself?"

"No," he responded quickly. "If the records are accurate, the math should be simple. But she didn't work as much when we started our family."

"When was your first child born?"

"My junior year in college."

"And was she pregnant toward the end of your senior year?"

"Yes, with our second child."

"Did she continue working?"

"Only at the law firm."

"Forty hours a week?"

Simpson looked toward his lawyer, an older attorney named Byron Smith. Smith didn't offer any help, and the witness ran his finger along the inside of his collar.

"Whatever the records show. I don't remember if it was a full-time job or not."

"Did she work outside the home after you graduated from college?"

"Some. It took a while to get my business off the ground, and then she stopped working. Even though I've had a few tough years recently, she hasn't worked in years. I wanted her at home with our kids."

"How long has she been completely dependent on your income?"

He looked up and mentally calculated the passage of time. "About ten years."

"Have you had another child during that time?"

"Yes."

Alex put the employment records on the table and slid a thick folder to a place where it would be handy.

"Mr. Simpson, you testified that for the past three years you've received all of your income from Simpco, a real-estate development company. Is that correct?"

"Yes."

"What does Simpco do?"

"We identify locations for gas stations, obtain options on the land, and market the properties to major oil companies."

"How many parcels of land have you sold in the past three years?"

"Eight. That's why my income has only been around $40,000 a year. I gave Marilyn copies of my business tax returns and asked her to provide them to you."

Alex gave the witness a slight smile. "Thank you for your cooperation, Mr. Simpson. I have carefully reviewed each one."

Alex opened the folder and took out a single sheet of paper.

"Are you familiar with a company called Nesbitt Enterprises?"

"Sure, they are a competitor of ours. They do the same thing we do except on a much bigger scale all over the country. They also develop shopping malls."

"Do you have any ownership interest in Nesbitt?"

"No."

Alex handed the sheet of paper to the court reporter who marked it as an exhibit. She then showed it to Greg Simpson's lawyer, who put on his glasses, made a few notes, and passed it back to her. Alex moved a few steps closer to Simpson but did not show him the sheet of paper.

"Are you the same G. L. Simpson who is listed as a partner with Nesbitt in an LLC developing a 200,000-square-feet shopping mall in Phoenix, Arizona?"

"That's not directly with Nesbitt."

"Is it part of Simpco?"

"Uh, no."

"What do Nesbitt's records show as the value of your interest in the LLC?"

Simpson squirmed in his seat and stared at the sheet of paper in Alex's hand before answering. "I'm not sure."

Without showing him the document, Alex returned to the folder and took out another document, which was marked as an exhibit. After showing it to Simpson's lawyer, she handed it directly to the witness.

"What does this page from the minutes of a corporate meeting of Nesbitt's directors indicate as your contribution to the Phoenix project?"

Simpson looked down at the paper and didn't answer.

"Take your time, Mr. Simpson," Alex interjected. "I want you to be sure about your answer."

Simpson cleared his throat. "Two parcels of land worth $450,000."

Alex picked up the first sheet of paper and handed it to the witness. "And what is the estimated value of your share at the beginning of this fiscal year?"

"$925,000. But that's highly speculative."

"Would you be willing to transfer your interest in the LLC to your wife as part of the property division in this case and let her bear the risk of loss?"

Simpson's face grew red. "Who told you—," he sputtered.

Byron Smith stood to his feet. "Objection, Your Honor."

"On what grounds?" the judge asked.

"May we approach the bench?" Smith requested.

"Yes."

Alex joined Smith in front of the judge.

In an intense whisper, the older lawyer began, "I didn't know about this—"

"Because his client didn't tell him," Alex responded dryly. "He probably didn't tell him how he was able to buy two pieces of real estate worth $450,000 on a $40,000 a year income."

"Can we take a break so I can talk to my client?" Smith asked.

The judge frowned. "Ms. Lindale has him on cross-examination."

"Then can we have a session with the court in chambers?" Smith asked.

"That's fine with me," Alex said.

The judge raised his head. "Very well. Court will be in recess for fifteen minutes while I consult with the attorneys. Mr. Simpson, you may leave the witness stand but may not consult with anyone."

Alex gathered the files from her table. Marilyn Simpson leaned forward. "What's happening?" she asked.

"They're on the run and want the judge to help them out of it. I'll be back in a few minutes."

The two lawyers followed Judge Garland from the courtroom to his chambers. The judge took off his robe and hung it on a hook behind the door.

"Alright," the judge said. "What do you want to discuss?"

Smith began, "Your Honor, Ms. Lindale's allegations regarding my client's financial status were not revealed in pretrial discovery. I need a continuance to review the records she is using to cross-examine Mr. Simpson."

"Did you ask her to provide this information?" the judge asked.

"Yes, I requested all documents supporting her client's claims for child support and alimony."

The judge looked at Alex. "Your response?"

Alex opened one of her folders. "The request for production of documents states 'all financial, personal, or business records of the party which in any way support her claims for child support and alimony.' The request is for Mrs. Simpson's records, not those of her husband. I furnished her records to Mr. Smith within the time required by the rules; Mr. Simpson's decision not to provide his attorney with his records was not my responsibility."

"Let me see," the judge responded.

Alex handed him the information. Both lawyers waited while the judge quickly read the filings.

"Very well," he said. "I'm going to allow Ms. Lindale to proceed with her questioning."

Smith hesitated and then looked at Alex.

"What do you want?" the lawyer asked.

Alex was ready. "One-half of his interest in the LLC together with another $250,000 in cash. Child support of $2,000 a month per child through college with comprehensive health insurance and payment of four years' tuition at the South Carolina average for private institutions at the time each child begins matriculation. Alimony of another $7,500 a month for five years or until my client remarries, whichever comes first, and total indemnification for any unpaid taxes on returns through the current tax year."

The older lawyer's face flushed. "My client doesn't have that kind of cash or income flow. There had better be plenty of room for negotiation."

"Not at this point." Alex patted the folder in her lap. "Tell him I know about KalGo and see if he agrees."

Forty-five minutes later the judge dismissed the jury and put the terms of the agreement on the record with the court reporter. There had been no further negotiation. Greg Simpson had raised a white surrender flag rather than face further dissection of his secret business dealings. When Simpson capitulated, Alex agreed that the court reporter need not prepare a transcript of anything except the terms of the settlement. There would be no hot trail for the IRS to follow. Alex walked triumphantly from the courtroom. Marilyn Simpson joined her.

Alex turned to her client. "I'll prepare a property settlement, alimony, and child support agreement consistent with what was stated in court and send it to your husband's lawyer by the first of next week."

"Can he back out of it?"

"Not without risking jail for contempt of court. The basic terms of the agreement are on the record in front of the judge. It's all out in the open now."

Greg Simpson and his attorney exited the courtroom and brushed past Alex and Marilyn without speaking. Her face sad, Marilyn watched her soon-to-be ex-husband as he retreated in defeat.

Alex noticed and asked, "What is it?"

"Did I do the right thing?" Marilyn asked.

"Of course," Alex responded curtly. "You're getting a good settlement for yourself and your children. Your husband made his choice when he filed for the divorce."

"I know, but it doesn't feel as satisfying as I thought it would."

Alex softened. "It's impossible to put a price tag on a broken relationship, but it will feel better when you get the checks every month and don't have to go back to work at a convenience store. I've seen too many women who didn't seize the opportunity to get what they deserved and lived to regret it."

"I'm sure you're right." Marilyn sighed. "I'm just hurt. Knowing he intended to hide all that money even when he was under oath made me wonder what else wasn't right in our marriage."

Alex didn't answer. Her private investigator was sure Greg Simpson had a mistress in Savannah but couldn't connect the dots before the case was called for trial. Without proof, Alex didn't burden Marilyn Simpson with rumors of adultery. Clients who suspected their husbands of infidelity often told Alex that not knowing the truth was worse than having their suspicions confirmed; however, when incriminating photographs left no doubt of unfaithfulness, the women's reactions to the stark reality of betrayal always exceeded their previous concerns. When fully exposed, the face of evil is always worse than imagined. In Marilyn Simpson's case, adultery wouldn't have made a difference. Alex knew modern-day divorce proceedings focused on money, not morality.

Lawyer and client parted in front of the courthouse. Marilyn walked toward a blue minivan. Alex unlocked the door of her silver BMW and put the thick folder that contained the Simpson file in the passenger seat.

The afternoon weather in Santee was the type natives loved and tourists avoided. It was cold enough that the summer's insect horde was no longer poised to feast on every inch of exposed human flesh and too cool for visitors to splash in the ocean that lay five miles to the east. Alex had a native's perspective. The death of the insects grown fat on the flesh of hundreds of thousands of people who flocked to the Grand Strand every year was a welcome event. The cooler weather also didn't keep Alex out of the water; it beckoned her to spend more time on the marsh and in the ocean.

Growing up, Alex had lived in four states and two foreign countries, but her favorite place on earth was the South Carolina coast. The five years her family lived in Charleston had been the happiest of her life. So during her second year of law school at the University of Florida, she spread out a map on the kitchen table in her tiny apartment and drew a line fifty miles up and down the East Coast with Charleston in the middle. The line became the area where she focused her job search.

Because her grades were not good enough to open the door to a prestigious Charleston law firm, she began exploring opportunities in smaller communities where female lawyers would have been an anomaly thirty years before but now occupied a recognized niche in the legal field, especially in domestic relations practice. Many women embroiled in a divorce were fed up with men in general and wanted a female attorney to represent them when litigating with deadbeat husbands. With her strong sense of justice and willingness to represent the underdog, Alex quickly developed a reputation as a divorce specialist who had a knack for ferreting out information that obtained a better result for her clients. When Marilyn Simpson's pain subsided, she would tell her friends about her lawyer's exploits, and the steady flow of clients into Alex's office would continue.

Alex had clerked for Leggitt & Freeman in Santee during the summer following her second year in law school. Pleased with her work, the firm had offered her a job before she returned to Gainesville for her final year of study. Six years later at the age of thirty-two she was on the verge of attaining partnership status. Alex's monthly draw as a partner would be less than her current salary, but she would have the opportunity to share in the larger pie of the firm's total revenue when it was divided each December. Prestige as a partner was an additional, intangible benefit.

It was a three-minute drive from the courthouse to her office. Leggitt & Freeman occupied a single-story, cream-colored stucco building set amid palmetto trees and surrounded by large clumps of dune grass. Everything about the office was designed to create an image of stability and prosperity. A branch bank stood across the street and a fancy café was a few doors down. Banks, boutiques, restaurants, and real-estate offices had proliferated in the area as development spread inland from the crowded coastal area. Santee was too far from the beach to advertise itself as an oceanside resort, but local business leaders had found a lucrative and less messy alternative to hordes of ill-tempered tourists—golfing communities.

They were everywhere. Fields that had been farmed by tenant farmers for generations now boasted million-dollar homes overlooking lush fairways. People with accents as homogenized as those of TV actors and actresses shopped at new stores owned by national chains. There were retirees from the northeast who viewed the price of large homes in South Carolina as a bargain and people from other areas of the South who had dreamed of living near the beaches where they had vacationed when their children were small. Wherever they came from, the new residents bought homes in the golfing communities. Some actually played golf, but most just wanted to live in a relaxed, upscale environment.

Alex opened the front door of the office and stepped into the reception area. Except for sea scenes on the walls, the waiting room didn't reflect anything about the coast. A deep red, oriental rug was surrounded by leather couches and chairs. On one wall hung high-quality photographs of all the partners who had worked at the firm since it was founded by Mr. Leggitt's father before World War II. Each man's name was engraved on a small brass plate on the bottom of the frame. It was an unusual feature, more suited to a boardroom than a law office, but Mr. Leggitt's father had started the tradition, and like most traditions, it had developed an inertia that perpetuated the practice. Once she became a partner, Alex's picture would join the others—the first woman on the wall.

Alex's office was on the back side of the building. Her secretary was Gwen Jones, a slightly overweight woman in her fifties who dyed her hair a reddish brown, always dressed in bright colors, and kept a perpetual tan. At the sound of Alex's footsteps, Gwen looked up in surprise.

"What happened?" she asked. "I didn't expect to see you until after the jury went home for the night."

Alex responded with a small, triumphant smile. "We settled it. Marilyn is set for life."

"Congratulations!"

"Thanks. It felt good. Up to the last minute, I wondered if Greg Simpson had an escape hatch, but he was busted in open court. Do you have time to type the settlement documents if I dictate them this afternoon?"

Gwen pointed a ring-bedecked finger toward Leonard Mitchell's office. "L. M. loaded me down with paperwork for a deal he's trying to put together. I don't know when he needs it, but he acted like it was a rush job. Do you want me to talk to him?"

"No," Alex responded.

Alex often faced resistance when she asked the partner to set aside his work so Gwen could help her on an urgent matter.

"It will be easier to do it myself."

Alex went into her office and shut the door. The exposé of Greg Simpson's hidden business dealings had been one of the more dramatic triumphs of her career. It wouldn't be reported in the local newspaper, but by the end of the week the legal community would be buzzing with the result. Simpson was a sleazy cheat, but it's rarely possible to neatly unravel a web of deception. Alex didn't have a complete picture of Simpson's involvement with KalGo, but after the exposure of the Nesbitt deal, Byron Smith wasn't willing to call her bluff. The questions in court were routine; the hard work had been the behind-the-scenes investigation.

Alex had personalized her office with items collected from all over the world. It was like a mini-museum. On one end of her credenza crouched a primitive sculpture of a roaring lion she'd bought in Tanzania. On the other end rested a hand-painted tray from the Yucatán Peninsula in Mexico. An intricate tapestry from Greece adorned one wall, and a collage of photographs of Alex in front of famous buildings across Europe decorated another. Most of her early travels were with her mother. Lately, she'd been sojourning on her own. After the hectic pace of life at the office, she longed for times of prolonged solitude.

For more than a year, a picture of her former fiancé, Jason Favreau, had occupied the place of highest prominence on the front corner of her desk. Jason, a tall, dark-haired engineer, shared enough common denominators with Alex that most computer dating services would have predicted a storybook romance. Both had international pedigrees: Alex's mother was a Russian who defected to the United States in the 1960s and married a man from Ohio, while Jason's father was a Frenchman who married a woman from California. Jason was fluent in French, and Alex spoke passable Russian. They both loved to travel, read, swim, and listen to classical music.

Shortly after their engagement, Jason went to Marseille to supervise a large construction project. Ten weeks passed with excruciating slowness until Alex was scheduled to fly over for a five-day visit. The night before she was to leave, Jason called and told her not to come. One of his father's cousins had introduced him to a French girl, and they were in love. Two months later, they married and moved to Quebec.

After her tears dried, Alex tore up Jason's picture and scattered the pieces in the ocean, but a measure of pain remained. Having experienced betrayal and misplaced trust, her empathy for her jilted clients increased, and she poured herself more fiercely into her work. Her daily diet of divorce work soured Alex's taste for romantic relationships, and her mother was worried that she'd be an old maid. Alex deflected her comments with statements that she was too busy for men and needed time to forget what had happened. In any event, the sampling of suitable men in Santee for a woman like Alex was sparse.

She turned on her computer. A fast typist, she was almost through with the first draft of the Simpson agreement when the light for an interoffice call came on and the phone buzzed. It was Mr. Leggitt.

"Alex, I heard about your exploits in court today," the senior partner said. "Can you come to my office? I have something important to discuss with you."

"Yes, sir. I'm finishing up the agreement. I'll be there in a few minutes."

Alex smiled. Her marriage to Jason Favreau hadn't worked out, but her partnership with Leggitt & Freeman was about to be consummated.

3

Confused and filled with murder and misdeeds.
THOMAS KYD

RENA CRAWLED TO the edge of the cliff and looked down.

It was a long way to the boulders at the bottom of the gorge, and the chance that a person could strike the unforgiving rocks and live to tell about it was negligible.

Baxter's body was in plain view. He'd fallen directly below the spot where she peered over the edge and come to rest with his back arched over a smooth, tan boulder. His right leg was twisted in an unnatural manner that left no doubt it was broken. His face was turned away from her as if looking downstream toward the place where the water regrouped and entered the woods. Straining her eyes, she tried to detect any hint of life in her husband's broken body. Nothing moved except the water cascading into the valley below. Human beings have an amazing capacity for survival, but a skier hitting a tree with a fraction of the same impact wouldn't live to the bottom of the slopes.

Spray from the waterfall was splashing on her husband's clothes. It would have been chilly to a conscious person sitting on the rock, but it was apparent Baxter didn't feel anything. Wherever people go when they die, Baxter Richardson had made a quick, unexpected journey. Rena didn't believe in a hereafter. It was all she could do to endure each day.

She sank down with her face against the cool rock and sobbed with a mixture of shock at what she'd done and relief that it was over. The childhood monsters she'd mentioned to Baxter didn't hide in the woods near the top of the waterfall. They lived as memories of the years she spent after her mother's death with Vernon Swafford in a ramshackle house where her worst tormentor sat across the dinner table from her and threatened her with death if she ever told anyone the truth. During those years of pain, what should have been a sharp line between fact and fiction blurred and sometimes Rena didn't know what was real and what was nightmare.

When she was fifteen, her stepfather was arrested and put in jail for thirty days after a barroom brawl. Left alone, Rena ran down the road to a store and called her mother's older sister in Spartanburg. She waited an hour until her Aunt Louise arrived in a dilapidated car, which to Rena looked like a heavenly chariot. They hurriedly collected Rena's meager personal belongings and fled.

Rena told Louise a fraction of her story, but it was enough to convince the local juvenile court judge to issue a restraining order prohibiting Vernon Swafford from further contact with her. Upon his release from jail, her stepfather ignored the court order and appeared one night at Louise's front door. Rena hid in a closet while Louise called the police from the phone in the kitchen.

Outside, her stepfather yelled in the darkness, "Rena! Git your things and come outside! You don't want to make me come in there and fetch you!"

Rena peeked out the door of the closet and saw his burly silhouette as Swafford passed by the window in the moonlight. She crouched lower and held her breath. The voice grew more insistent. He began to swear—a sure prelude to greater threats of violence.

"Rena! I'm tired of waiting! Git out here now!"

Rena heard a bottle crash against the side of the house. The front door rattled as he tried to turn the doorknob and then it shook under the dull thud of his boot as he attempted to kick it open. The locks held, and the wood didn't splinter.

It grew silent outside, and a glimmer of hope came into the closet. Her tormenter had given up and gone away. She strained to hear the sound of his truck backing down the gravel driveway. Seconds passed like minutes.

Then a gunshot shattered the stillness, and Rena knew it was her night to die. Her aunt screamed. Rena opened the door of the closet and began walking slowly toward the living room. It would be better to end her life quickly than continue in the torment of anticipation. Before she reached the room, sirens filled the air as the police arrived. Louise saw Rena and screamed for her to lie down on the floor. Her stepfather shot wildly in the air several times before he was disarmed. He went to prison for five years.

But Vernon Swafford's threats weren't held captive by prison bars. They were locked within the dungeon of Rena's mind. Over the following months Louise did the best she could to salve Rena's wounds, but all she had were band-aids. Rena needed major, reconstructive surgery.

So, Rena stuffed the traumas of her childhood deep into the crevices of her soul and learned to pretend. Her grades went up, and she received a college scholarship. Outward circumstances improved. Inside, she remained dark and twisted. Nightmares choked out any hope of peaceful sleep. Classmates labeled her moody, but her good looks insured a level of popularity with boys and envy from girls. Attracting the attention of males was not a problem but building an enduring relationship was an impossibility. Nothing lasted. She had a bottomless mistrust of men. At the first sign of stress, Rena bolted or reacted with emotional violence that scared off her current suitor.

She talked to a counselor in college; however, the well-meaning man only knew how to unpack a person's internal baggage, not what to do with the dirty laundry it contained. She avoided contact with her stepfather after his release from custody, but past torment stalked her along paths of fear. Only an iron will kept her from insanity.

Until now.

Rena took a deep breath and felt a weight lift from her chest. Killing another person was a drastic step, but at the core of her being she knew she had acted in self-defense. Eventually, her rich, young husband would have tired of her and thrown her away or begun his own cycle of abuse. She stood and brushed a few specks of dirt from her knees as the calm after the storm entered her soul. She would never have to trust in a man again. Baxter's money would insure security for the future. She could survive without needing anyone's help and perhaps find a measure of happiness.

She carefully cleaned the area where they had eaten their light supper and began to compose the story to tell when she returned to civilization. Baxter had already provided a logical explanation for his unfortunate slip and fall from the wet rocks. Analysis of his blood would reveal the presence of enough alcohol to impair balance and judgment.

When everything was back to normal, Rena turned away from the waterfall. It would take more than an hour and a half to hike back to the expensive new SUV they had driven to the mountains. She followed the path through the low trees and bushes that grew in scattered patches of dirt between the rocks near the top of the waterfall. When she reached the bottom of a rough, earthen stairway cut into the side of the hill, she looked up and prepared to make the ascent toward a life without fear.

Then she remembered.

The keys to the SUV were in Baxter's pocket. She stopped, and an overwhelming dread swept over her. She whirled around and looked back down the path toward the waterfall. The calm that had enveloped her after sending Baxter to his doom evaporated, and she knew a terror that made cold sweat prickle her skin. A phantomlike figure flashed past the corner of her right eye, and she quickly turned again, half expecting to see her stepfather come creeping out of the bushy forest. She stared intently at the shifting shapes of the leaves in the wind. A gentle breeze swept through the trees and made her shudder. The whisper of the wind carried the sound of faint, mocking laughter.

"He's dead!" she cried out.

It was like one of her nightmares, only this time she was awake. Visions of Vernon Swafford were joined by images of Baxter, battered and bloody, coming slowly, relentlessly to exact his revenge. She heard another rustle in the leaves and spun around. A long black snake was moving through the dry leaves at the bottom of the stairs. Rena jumped away, and the snake froze, its tongue flitting in and out as it tried to discern the nature of the creature that had blundered into its domain.

Rena fled from the snake and her thoughts back toward the waterfall. She didn't stop running until she reached the edge of the cliff and stood wavering at the place where Baxter had slid over the precipice. Panting, she inched forward. She could jump into space and in seconds join

Baxter in oblivion. That would be the cure of all ills. Her foot dislodged a small rock that slipped over the edge and bounced down past Baxter's body. She watched the rock until it disappeared from view. Her mind burned with the question of whether she should follow it or not. It would be over so quickly.

"No!" she shouted.

The sound of her voice arrested the suicidal impulse. Suicide was always an option, but not now. Only when cornered and without hope of escape would she take her own life. Taking a deep breath, she stepped away from the cliff. She'd fought too hard for survival to surrender. She had to give her new freedom a chance. She knelt down, splashed her face with water from the stream, and then considered her options.

It was at least ten or twelve miles from the trailhead to a major highway where she could flag down a motorist. She might encounter someone before then, but there was no guarantee. It would be nightfall before she could reach civilization. The thought of being alone in the dark caused a spasm of fear to return.

"No," she repeated.

Fear retreated. Her other option was to get the car keys from Baxter's pocket. Across the stream was a path that wound its way to the base of the falls. She had used the trail many times. It would take about thirty minutes to walk to the bottom and retrieve the keys from Baxter's pocket, but the thought of touching her husband's dead body caused her to inwardly recoil. She bit her lip and stared toward the distant hills. Suddenly, she had a revelation that changed her mind.

She had to go down the trail to Baxter's body. The natural thing for her to do when her husband fell would be to rush to his aid. Any other response would raise suspicions. Rena had no intention of attempting CPR on a corpse, but an act of concern as an element of her story would allay any hint of wrongdoing.

Walking a few yards upstream from the waterfall, she stepped across the stream on exposed rocks and then hurried along the top of the ridge toward the place where the path veered downward into the valley. A dense grove of small trees crowded the trail, and she had to push aside whiplike limbs. One slender branch lashed back and stung the right side of her face, almost striking her in the eye. Rena put her hand to her cheek and felt something wet. When she looked at her hand, it was red. The limb had opened a cut. She moved her tongue to the side and encountered the salty taste of her own blood.

She dabbed the cut with the bottom of her shirt but then remembered the napkins Baxter had brought for their snack. Slipping off her backpack, she found one and applied firm pressure to the cut. She hoped it wouldn't leave a scar. Rena's complexion was as clear as that of a magazine model, and she considered it one of her best features. In a few moments the bleeding slowed. The small gash wasn't serious; there was no danger of a scar. The fresh wound would, however, add additional authenticity to her frantic scramble down the rocks to help her husband.

Continuing along the trail, she came to the fork that led down into the valley. Turning right, she began the descent. The trail was not a distinguishable path but a series of rocks that kept hikers from sliding out of control. Several times she sat down and scooted from one rock to another. Her pants got dirty and her legs were scratched by sharp rocks and prickly bushes. As a little girl, she'd remembered the descent as a giant outdoor junglegym. Today, there was nothing pleasant about it. When she reached the bottom, she looked up the way she'd come. Climbing out would be strenuous but in some ways easier than the scramble down.

No clearly defined trail led to the base of the waterfall. Rena skirted boulders and climbed over rocks and fallen trees. Baxter wasn't the only thing that had crashed over the cliff. Several large trees had toppled over, plowed past the smaller growth at the top of the cliff, and rolled down the hill. One huge tree blocked her advance and required a detour into the woods.

For several minutes, the only sounds she heard were her own breathing and her shoes striking the ground. She stopped twice and listened for the sound of the waterfall. The second time, she heard the faint roar of the water. Scrambling to the top of a larger than normal boulder, she saw the two streams of water that gave Double-Barrel Falls its name. Her heart started pounding—not from exertion, but from what awaited her. She willed her heart to slow down, but it refused to obey. It grew louder until the thumping in her chest competed with the sound of the waterfall.

She caught a glimpse of Baxter's body. It was on the far side of the stream. Spray from the waterfall made the bare rocks slick, and she had to use her hands and feet to creep along. The water deepened to a few inches, and she slipped in the cold water and soaked her feet. Moving away from the main channel of water into the woods, she found a place where the stream spread out and crossed to the other side. When she emerged from the woods, Baxter's body, partially hidden by boulders, was less than thirty feet away.

Rena stopped. She had to compose herself enough to endure the next few minutes. There was room for murder in her heart, but she wanted to keep a distance between herself and her victim. She didn't kill Baxter with her hands; she used the impersonal buffer of a walking stick. The final blow when she crashed into him had been involuntary. She simply lost her balance, and this made what happened more accidental than intentional.

Rena settled on a strategy. She would slip up to the body, reach in Baxter's pocket for the keys, and return to where she now stood. All that would change within the controlled window of time would be the location of the keys to the vehicle. Everything else would remain the same. Baxter had no more capacity to harm her than the boulder on which he rested. Taking a deep breath, she walked out of the shady woods into the light. Tiny rivulets of water made the footing treacherous. When she rounded the last large boulder, she found herself looking directly into Baxter's face.

His eyes were open. Rena screamed.

The sound echoed off the rock walls and for a split second competed with the roar of the waterfall above her. Rena clamped her hand over her mouth. Baxter didn't budge or alter expression. She stepped back, preparing to flee, and then stopped. Her husband's eyes didn't see. His eyelids were open because that was their position at the split second they received their last command from his brain.

Rena's attempt to detach herself from the surroundings had failed, but she still needed the keys. Keeping her gaze downward to avoid another confrontation with Baxter's unseeing stare, she stepped forward. She could see his body from the corner of her eye. He was lying on his back on top of a medium-size boulder without any outward signs of blood or trauma except his twisted right leg and the gash on the side of his neck. From the angle of his foot, the ankle or leg was broken, but no bones poked through the surface of the skin. The splashing water she'd seen from above had almost soaked the right side of his clothing. His arms were splayed out on either side. Water was dripping from the fingers of his right hand.

Careful not to touch Baxter's skin, Rena reached out her hand and patted the right front pocket of his shorts. She could feel the keys through the wet cloth. She slipped her hand into the pocket and retrieved the keys. Backing quickly away, she slipped on the wet rocks near the body and fell, hitting the left side of her head so severely that she saw stars.

Dazed, Rena felt the area of her temple that had collided with the rock. The small knot would go with the cut on her face and the scratch on her arm. More battle scars. Moving carefully, she retreated to the woods. She had the keys but also the memory of Baxter's face. Though blinded by death, the look in his eyes stayed with her.

She crossed the stream and retraced her steps. She missed the path up the cliff but came to a dead tree that looked unfamiliar and realized she'd gone too far. It was only a few yards back to the place where she could scramble up to the main trail. She passed the waterfall without looking down again at the body, and by the time she reached the earthen stairway, her internal history of the day's events was being rewritten.

Her husband, Baxter Richardson, had died in an unfortunate hiking accident. She repeated the sentence over and over as she hiked away from the falls. As she did, her mental images of the last moments at the top of the falls underwent a steady transformation. Baxter had finished his third or fourth glass of wine and playfully wandered to the edge of the precipice. She warned him to stay back.

"Baxter, please be careful. People have fallen and died here."

He looked over his shoulder and laughed. "Not me. Don't worry. It's such a magnificent view."

"Step away. You've had too much to drink."

"Don't be silly. Come stand beside me. The leaves are more brilliant along the high ridges to the west."

Rena increased the level of anxiety in her voice. "No! Let's go."

"Look. I'm not even close to the edge."

Baxter took a step forward. His foot slipped. He swayed back and forth for an instant in an effort to regain his balance. If not for the influence of the wine, he might have been able to do it.

Rena screamed, "No!"

And her husband disappeared from view.

Yes, it was all a very tragic accident.

4

A lawyer shall not represent a client if the representation of that client will be, or is likely to be, directly adverse to another client.
CANONS OF ETHICS, RULE 1.7

ALEX'S BOSS, Ralph Leggitt, had inherited 100 percent of his father's ownership interest in Leggitt & Freeman and 50 percent of his father's legal ability. In his late fifties, Mr. Leggitt was a short man with a fringe of gray hair that surrounded his bald head like a broad sweatband. He'd entered the stage in life when men often start losing weight, and he bought new suits each year to accommodate his shrinking waistline. The contrast between himself and Mrs. Leggitt, a very large woman who loved anything chocolate, was growing greater by the year.

Although he wasn't a talented lawyer, Ralph Leggitt had business savvy, and years before Alex joined the firm he had stopped practicing law to devote his time to business interests. Leggitt was an adept deal-maker and ended up with an ownership interest in many of the businesses the firm represented. As the companies prospered, the lawyer benefited in two ways: the value of his ownership share increased and the law firm generated income by performing more legal services. It was a neat arrangement. His close connection with the corporate entities in his little empire occasionally strayed beyond the bounds of legal ethics but nobody complained. One of his favorite expressions was, "No harm, no foul."

Alex approached the door of the senior partner's office.

"He's waiting for you," Leggitt's secretary said briskly. "Go on in."

Alex opened the door and entered the largest room in the building. Ralph Leggitt liked to have meetings in his office, and the space was large enough to accommodate a massive walnut desk with two side chairs at one end and a cherry conference table with seating for ten at the other.

The result was an impressive layout that advanced the lawyer's reputation as a man who could make money happen. Many deals involving huge sums had been negotiated and formalized within the generous confines of Leggitt's office.

The senior partner was behind his desk. He looked up when Alex entered.

"Have a seat," he said. "Word of your dismemberment of Mr. Greg Simpson has traveled fast."

"Yes, sir."

Alex was surprised Leggitt knew the name of the man involved in the case. He rarely expressed interest in the clients she represented, only in the money she deposited in the firm bank account when her bills were paid.

"Who told you about it?" she asked.

"Oh, I received a call about the time you returned from the courthouse."

Alex was puzzled. "From Judge Garland?"

"No. Vinson Killoran contacted me. Do you know him?"

The name was vaguely familiar, but Alex couldn't place it. "No, sir."

"I'm surprised. It's my understanding you know a lot about KalGo Corporation."

Suddenly, Alex realized that Ralph Leggitt hadn't congratulated her on her victory.

She spoke slowly. "I didn't find out very much except that Mr. Simpson had business connections with KalGo that he didn't reveal to his wife. I don't know all the details, but he was receiving large sums of money from the company for consulting work; however, no consulting services—"

Leggitt interrupted, his countenance grim. "I don't want to hear your theories about this man's consulting work. My concern is ethical. Did you do a conflicts check when you took the case?"

"Of course. I ran a search on Gregory L. Simpson and his business, Simpco. We've never represented either him or his company. I didn't check KalGo because I didn't find out about it until shortly before trial. All I know is that it's based in Texas." Alex paused, but her mental wheels kept turning. "Do we represent KalGo?"

Leggitt's eyes narrowed, and he leaned forward in his chair. "We did until about an hour ago. They were planning a major coastal development in the fifty to sixty million dollar range. This firm was going to handle the legal work, and I was going to serve on the board for a subsidiary corporation that would oversee local operations."

Alex's face was a shade paler. "With Greg Simpson?"

"I don't know about that, and it doesn't matter at this point. Can you tell me why you didn't do a conflicts check on KalGo once the name surfaced in the case?"

Alex spoke rapidly. "I couldn't imagine that anything Simpson was involved in would be connected with this firm. He lies to everyone who will listen to him talk for five minutes."

Leggitt bristled. "That doesn't answer my question."

Alex swallowed and slowed down. "No, I didn't check it. I was zealously representing my client and didn't think about it."

"Your little area of practice is not what floats this boat, and you have to check out everything the women you represent tell you—"

"This wasn't based on what my client told me," Alex interrupted. "I discovered the information on my own."

"Which doesn't help your case with me," Mr. Leggitt shot back. "Admit it, Alex. You dropped the ball. According to Killoran, Simpson owns a piece of the corporate pie and our knowledge of KalGo's affairs is protected by the attorney-client relationship. You'll probably be getting a motion to set aside the agreement you reached in the case based on allegations that you used privileged information to gain an unfair advantage in negotiations."

"How was I supposed to know about that?"

"By checking for KalGo on the firm's conflicts system. That's what I did."

Mr. Leggitt slid a piece of paper across his desk toward her. Alex picked it up and scanned down the column of names. It was a computer printout of the firm's clients. A file for KalGo had been opened shortly before Marilyn Simpson hired Alex in the divorce case. Mr. Leggitt was right. Once a conflict surfaced, Alex was bound to withdraw from the divorce case based on the firm's prior representation of the company.

Even if the situation wasn't known at first, she had an obligation to investigate a conflict of interest once it became a possible issue. There was one tiny loophole that might get her off the hook.

"Is Greg Simpson mentioned in the records here at the office?" she asked.

Mr. Leggitt patted a file on the corner of his desk. "Yes. Do you want to see for yourself?"

Alex shook her head. She was beaten.

"What am I going to tell Marilyn Simpson?" she asked.

"To get another lawyer. And I suggest that you be a lot more careful. The future of this firm is based on attracting top business clients and making them happy. That hasn't happened today, and I'm holding you responsible."

At that moment it was easy to see what had happened, but as Alex picked her way forward in search of evidence in the Simpson case it hadn't been so crystal clear. She decided to try another angle of post-mortem justification.

"Mr. Leggitt," she began, but the look in the senior partner's eyes stopped her. "Uh, I'm sorry. I'll be more careful."

"Alright. But I'll have to bring this up at the next partners' meeting. You have cost the firm a considerable sum today, and this will have to be considered when discussing your future role here. I'll explain what you did the best I can, but I'm not sure how the others will respond."

Her triumph turned into a fiasco, Alex slunk from the office. She was used to building on victories, not trying to recoup after a defeat. She felt sorry for herself; she felt sorry for Marilyn Simpson. The woman's next lawyer wouldn't have the element of surprise in ambushing Greg Simpson, and the businessman could use the intervening time to construct a better labyrinth of deception to conceal his true financial resources. As she walked down the hallway, her embarrassment turned into anger.

She passed Gwen's desk without speaking and slammed the door to her office so hard that the frame containing her collage of European travel pictures tilted to one side. The settlement documents in the Simpson case mocked her from the tray of her laser printer. Alex picked up the papers and threw them in the trash can. On the desk in front of her chair was a motion faxed to her by Greg Simpson's lawyer while she talked to Ralph Leggitt. Sure enough, Byron Smith wanted to set aside the agreement reached in front of the judge based on "unethical use of confidential information obtained by opposing counsel."

Alex sat down in her chair and picked up the bone-handled dagger from Kenya she used as a letter opener. As she passed the dagger back and forth from one hand to the other, her anger turned inward. She was mad. First at herself for being so focused on blowing up Greg Simpson's deceit that she didn't consider the possibility that the businesses she uncovered might have links to Leggitt & Freeman. But she was also mad at Ralph Leggitt. Alex had made a mistake, but the real reason for Mr. Leggitt's rebuke was pure, narrow-minded greed. The canons of ethics were a hypocritical rationale for a self-serving motive. All the senior partner cared about was having his slice of every pie the firm baked.

Alex put the dagger back in the top drawer of her desk and dialed Marilyn Simpson's number. It took more than forty-five minutes to explain what had happened. Twice, her client started crying, and Alex had to wait until Marilyn regained her composure before continuing. Alex didn't want to cry; she wanted to bite a nail in two. She gave Marilyn the names of the only two local divorce lawyers whom Alex respected. Hopefully, one of them would be willing to take on the case and straighten out the mess.

When she hung up the phone, Alex looked at the clock on the wall. It wasn't time to leave for the day, but she was emotionally exhausted. Her anger and frustration were spent. Preparing for the trial had been enough; coping with the aftermath was worse. She put a file that she needed to review in her briefcase so she could look it over at home. She had an important hearing on the following week's court calendar and had a lot of work to do.

She stopped briefly at Gwen's desk.

"I'm gone for the day. I need a swim and a bubble bath."

"Do I need to call a repairman to fix your door?"

Alex glanced over her shoulder. "Was it that loud?"

Gwen nodded. "What happened?"

Alex leaned against the wall and sighed. "Mr. Leggitt called me into his office and chewed me out. Marilyn Simpson's husband is involved in a business the firm represents, so I'm going to have to withdraw from the case."

"Oh, no! Will he be able to weasel out of the agreement?"

"Probably. I've already received a fax from Byron Smith. He's filing a motion to set it aside."

Gwen frowned. "That stinks," she said. "Marilyn is a nice woman."

"Yes, and I feel terrible about it. I've had enough of the law for today."

A moment after Alex left, Leonard Mitchell came out of his office and saw her turning the corner at the end of the hall.

"Where is Alex going?" he asked Gwen. "It's not time to go home."

Gwen quickly diverted his curiosity with a question.

"Do you want me to use the same restrictive covenants in Kettle Creek Estates and Bent Tree Country Club?"

"No. I need to tweak them a bit. The power of the architectural control committee at Bent Tree is going to be slightly different."

Alex lived fifteen minutes from the office. After paying off a small student loan, she had saved enough money to purchase a lot overlooking a coastal marsh. Two years later she built a modest but stylish house with a mortgage that wouldn't sink her in debt like bricks in tidewater mud.

She drove south on Highway 17, the main roadway that connected the coastal communities, until she reached a narrow, roughly paved road with a crooked sign that read "Pelican Point Drive." A developer had intended the road to be the main access point for a small, exclusive community, but two bad investments in other projects sent him into bankruptcy, and no bulldozers had rumbled down Pelican Point. Alex bought her lot directly from the bankruptcy court trustee and took her chances on the property's future. With the general increase in land prices along the coast there was little risk that the tract would be turned into a mobile home park. When it eventually filled with expensive homes, the value of Alex's house would skyrocket.

She drove a half-mile to the edge of the marsh and turned left on an unmarked byway covered with broken seashells that crunched under the tires of her car. Her house was the only dwelling on the road. It was an isolated spot without friendly neighbors, but Alex wasn't afraid. In the spring and fall she occasionally slept on her screen porch in a Pawley's Island hammock. It was like camping out at the beach without the hassle of sand in a sleeping bag.

Many people who moved to the coast wanted to live directly on the ocean. Local residents often preferred the marshes. In the backwater areas there was less chance of devastation from hurricanes and storm tides, and the marsh offered a subtle variety of life. The ocean left nothing to the imagination; the marsh reserved its beauty for a careful observer. The marsh had moods. The grasses and reeds responded to the slightest breeze. The ebb and flow of the tide gave texture to the picture God painted. And a sunset over the marsh dared all competitors.

Birds, crabs, fish, and other creatures made homes in the marsh. Herons, egrets, and even an occasional alligator were familiar neighbors. Channels intersected the marsh in every direction. Alex had a flat-bottomed boat with a tiny motor. She didn't like to fish, but she would navigate the channels at high tide, cut the engine, and quietly drift through the reeds. During those moments she felt very small in the midst of a big universe.

The design of Alex's house maximized its proximity to the wetlands. It was built on tall concrete pillars covered with stucco, and she parked her car underneath. The living room featured a large picture window through which she had an unobstructed view of several hundred yards of marsh and the barrier island that served as a buffer to the ocean beyond. The kitchen was on the opposite end of the house from the porch. It jutted out slightly to accommodate a glass-walled breakfast nook that seemed to hang in the air. It was a great spot for a cup of coffee in the morning but tended to get too warm in the late afternoon. Also on the main floor were a guest bedroom to the rear of the house and a den that Alex used for storage. A wooden deck extended across the rear of the house. It was often covered with birdseed from the feeders Alex put up. Containers of red liquid for hummingbirds stood at opposite ends of the deck.

The entire upstairs was devoted to the master suite and another guest bedroom. It was a third the size of the downstairs area and from the outside gave the house the look of a gray top hat. When Alex sat up in bed, she could see the marsh, and she often woke up with the sun streaming through the windows.

Alex walked up the stairs to her front door. During the drive home, her remaining anger had simmered into a malaise mixed with a touch of depression. As soon as she opened the front door, she was greeted with unfeigned exuberance by Boris, her three-year-old black Labrador. The dog was unaware of the facts of the Simpson case or the tongue-lashing Alex had received from Ralph Leggitt. His affection was unconditional. Alex grabbed the dog's head between her hands and lowered her face so he could lick her nose.

"I love you, too," she said. "Even if you forget to do a conflict of interest check."

She opened the door, and Boris ran down the steps. Alex kicked off her shoes and walked across the living room into the kitchen where she was greeted by Misha, her silver Persian cat. Misha welcomed her by stretching her body and rubbing Alex's leg. Alex leaned over and stroked her pet's head and back.

"Did you have a rough day?" she asked sympathetically.

Misha answered with a deep-throated rumble.

"It's tough lying in your bed and sleeping in the warm sun, isn't it?"

The cat slipped away from Alex's hand and ran to the back door that opened onto the deck. Alex let her out, and a few birds scattered at the cat's appearance. They needn't have bothered. Misha wasn't interested in hunting wild game. She preferred the tasty food in her dish and didn't expend the energy necessary to stalk one of Alex's feathered guests. Boris scrambled down the steps to the sandy soil below. Misha followed at a more sedate pace.

Alex watched a ruby-throated hummingbird finish a quick drink and zoom away to a resting place in a nearby live oak tree. By having a feeder at each end of the deck she'd been able to attract four birds. The dominant male in the group, a robust little fellow, couldn't guard both feeders at once, and there was a place for the other birds to enjoy a sip. Alex walked over to the railing and looked to the west. It was close to 5 P.M., and the sun was descending rapidly toward the horizon over the tops of the trees along the coastal highway. A few cirrus clouds high in the sky promised a nice sunset in an hour or two.

Safe within the refuge of her home, Alex moved from emotion to analysis. Some mistakes in a law practice produced immediate and short-lived consequences. Others had a longer shelf life. The Simpson case would probably fall in that middle range. Marilyn Simpson would have to hire another lawyer, and Alex might become a witness required to testify that she had not relied on privileged information in cross-examining Greg Simpson or negotiating with his lawyer. It would be an embarrassing scenario in front of Judge Garland, who respected Alex's legal ability and ethical integrity.

In addition, there might be a complaint filed by Simpson's lawyer with the state bar association. Alex grimaced. The notification letter would be circulated among the lawyers at Leggitt & Freeman, and the other attorneys would self-righteously shake their heads at her indiscretion while ignoring worse violations that lurked in their own filing cabinets. A volunteer member of the local bar committee would conduct a cursory investigation, and Alex would have to write a letter of explanation. In the end, a bureaucrat in Columbia would send out a generic warning admonishing her to be more careful in the future. The experience would be unpleasant from start to finish.

Misha pattered up the steps and waited at the door for Alex to let her in. The cat had an uncomplicated, carefully ordered life. She ate when hungry, slept on her own schedule, and enjoyed a regular back scratch. Panting loudly, Boris joined her. He was wired for adventure, and if he could talk would have told Alex what he saw at the edge of the water in run-on sentences. Her pets always had a way of soothing Alex's nerves and giving her perspective. She patted Boris's head.

"Let's go inside for a drink of cool water."

5

Begot of nothing but vain fantasy.
ROMEO AND JULIET, ACT 1, SCENE 4

THE REPEATED RUSHES of adrenaline that had coursed through Rena's veins over the past hour were gone, and the climb up the trail from the waterfall proved more strenuous than she had anticipated. Breathing heavily, she stopped at the top of the ridge and wiped away the perspiration that had beaded on her forehead. Suddenly, a sharp pain shot through the upper left side of her chest, and her hand went to the area over her heart. A heart attack was not part of her plan. She leaned against the smooth trunk of a young tree and waited for the pain to diminish, but it increased. Her left arm began to tingle.

Rena closed her eyes, and her mind returned to the shadow world where her connection with reality teetered as unsteadily as Baxter at the edge of the cliff. She saw herself, pale and unmoving, lying in the newly fallen leaves. Rescue workers came on the scene and rushed over to her. One man knelt down and put his fingers on the side of her neck for several seconds and then looked up at his companions and shook his head. She could hear their voices.

"She's gone. No pulse."

The man in charge of the rescue squad spoke. "It looks like she came up the path from Double-Barrel Falls. Her husband may be down there somewhere. Three of you take out her body, and the rest of us will search for him."

Rena saw herself gently lifted in the arms of the three pallbearers who laid her gently on a stretcher that would serve as her woodland bier. She would be viewed as a heroine. A woman who died trying to climb out and find help for her husband.

Behind her closed eyelids, Rena could hear her heart beating in veto of a heart attack. She made herself breathe slowly, hoping the chest pain would pass. Still leaning against the tree, she waited. Minutes ticked by. Finally the pain retreated, and Rena took a deep breath. She was not going to die. The discomfort she'd felt was probably just a complaining muscle. The images of her death faded. She was in good physical condition, and her body recovered quickly from strenuous exercise. Her heart rate returned to normal, and she resumed her march to the parking lot at the trailhead.

After the steep ascent, the trail was generally flat as it ran along the ridge line. Over and over as she walked along, Rena rehearsed the words she intended to use when asked about the day's events. She had to be appropriately distraught to match expectations of a grieving bride, yet sufficiently circumspect to avoid statements that might implicate her in her husband's death. Natural sympathy would be her ally, factual guilt her foe. She knew everything depended on maintaining a simple theme: It was all a tragic accident. There was nothing she could have done to prevent it.

Distracted by her thoughts, Rena tripped over a root and stumbled forward. When she looked up and blinked her eyes, she saw Baxter standing ten feet away in the middle of the path. He was smiling, and his eyes showed the kindness reserved for their most intimate moments. He was wearing the same khaki shorts and cream-colored shirt he'd put on when they'd left the hotel in Greenville early that morning. Rena quickly glanced down at his right leg. There was no sign of a break or the cut on his neck. How he had beaten her back to the trailhead was incomprehensible. Baxter extended his left hand toward her and opened his mouth to speak.

Rena screamed.

At the sound of her voice the apparition disappeared. Shaking, Rena frantically inspected the shadows cast by the surrounding trees. Her mouth was dry, and she licked her lips. She didn't believe in ghosts. Baxter was a man of the earth and had no power to return except as a memory without influence beyond the world of her mind. She took several deep breaths, determined to reinforce the wall between fact and fiction. The thought that her husband might visit her again in a form less friendly than the kind face in the path sent a second cold shiver down her spine.

"No!" she called out.

Again, she inspected the shadows. Seeing nothing, she moved forward, running past the spot where Baxter had blocked her way without glancing behind her shoulder. She didn't slow down until she reached the last small rise in the trail. Panting heavily, she climbed the hill and descended through a grove of oak and poplar trees. Coming around a large oak tree she saw the parking lot and the black SUV. Relieved, she leaned over and rested her hands on her knees.

The sight of the vehicle had a calming effect upon her. The forest was a place where the line between the seen and unseen worlds grew blurry. The SUV was solid proof of civilized reality. Rena took the hardearned keys from her pocket and pressed the remote button to unlock the car. The vehicle chirped once, flashed its lights, and acknowledged its new master. She opened the door and got inside. The feel of the cool leather was soothing to her aching legs. She turned on Baxter's cell phone. It was still reading out of service. Starting the engine, she pulled out of the parking lot in a cloud of dust. Baxter had used the GPS system as a navigational aid to find the trailhead. Rena didn't need it and flipped it off.

Four miles down the gravel road, she glanced at the phone and saw that she could make a call. Pulling over to the side, she shut off the engine. It was a big moment—her first contact with the outside world. Once more, she practiced her lines and then punched 911. She knew the call would be recorded. An older woman's voice answered after one ring.

"Mitchell County 911."

"This is Rena Richardson," she said rapidly. "My husband and I were hiking at Double-Barrel Falls. He slipped and fell into the gorge. I'm afraid he's dead."

Her voice was much more shaky than when she practiced. Rena wasn't sure if it made her sound sincere or unequivocally established her guilt.

"Slow down, dear. Where are you now?"

"I'm on the forest road 49. I ran back to the car and drove until I could get a signal to make a call."

There were a few seconds of silence. Rena twirled a strand of her hair.

"I've located the road in the state recreational area," the woman said. "Where is your husband now?"

"His body is on the rocks at the base of the waterfall. I tried to revive him, but I'm—" Rena hesitated. Then in a voice that cracked with a sudden rush of emotion she said, "afraid that he's dead."

"Are you injured?"

"Nothing except for cuts and bruises."

There was another moment of silence. Then Rena could hear the woman talking on a radio, dispatching police and emergency crews to the area.

"I've called for help. Do you need medical care?"

Before she could say no, Rena felt nauseated and slightly dizzy.

"I'm sick to my stomach."

"You may be in shock. Don't try to drive any farther. Wait for the medical personnel to come to you. You think you're four miles from the parking area for the trail?"

"Yes."

"Let me read back the phone number that is appearing on my screen."

Rena listened with her hand over her mouth.

"Yeah, that's it."

"We'll call you if we have trouble locating you. Do you need to stay on the line with me?" the woman asked.

Rena was getting sicker by the minute. She didn't want to hear another human voice. She wanted to be left alone.

"Uh, no."

Rena clicked off the phone and leaned her head against the seat. She cracked open the window. By sitting completely still and taking deep breaths, she could take the edge off the nausea. She closed her eyes and saw an ambulance scream around the curve and stop. Two workers jumped out the back and rushed over to her.

"Are you okay?" one asked anxiously.

Rena raised her head feebly. "Don't stay here. Go find my husband."

"Where is he?"

It took all her strength to sit up enough to gesture with her hand. "He slipped and fell at Double-Barrel Falls. I'm afraid he's dead."

"But what about you?"

Rena's head fell back against the seat.

"Never mind me. Help him."

Rena was impressed by her unselfishness. It would be a good idea to send the first ambulance that arrived on up to the trailhead—a sacrificial gesture that would look good in the report filed by the EMT personnel. Something hit the roof of her vehicle with a loud thud and jarred her. She opened her eyes and saw a green walnut the size of a tennis ball rolling down the front windshield. She was still alone in the woods. It would be at least fifteen to twenty minutes before anyone arrived. She closed her eyes and returned to her selfless fantasy.

After giving her pets fresh water, Alex looked at the clock and decided she had time for a swim before supper. She changed into a competition-style, one-piece, red swimsuit and put her other gear in a beachbag. When Boris saw that Alex was wearing the swimsuit, he ran immediately to the front door and started barking.

"Is this your favorite outfit?" she asked him as she slipped on a windbreaker that was hanging on a hook by her front door.

Boris scratched the door. When she opened it, he ran down the steps so fast that he was at the bottom waiting before she turned the key in the door.

The temperature of the ocean had already begun to drop as fall advanced toward winter. A few hearty Canadians still splashed in the surf fifty miles north at Myrtle Beach, but almost no local residents ventured into the ocean farther than necessary to make a good cast into the surf.

Alex's boat, a lightweight aluminum craft on a small trailer, was underneath her house. She kept it locked with a thick, rusty chain wrapped around one of the stucco pillars, but it would be a desperate thief who considered the ancient watercraft a worthy object. It was only 150 feet from her house to a place where she could easily slide the boat into the marsh, and it was easier to pull the trailer by hand than hitch it to her car for a ten-second drive.

Alex was wearing an old pair of dock shoes that had been seasoned by the salt water and marsh mud. Digging her heels in the sandy soil, she was able to get the trailer moving. Once it was rolling all she had to do was maintain a constant speed to the edge of the water. Her biggest challenge was keeping Boris away from her feet. When the boat reached the first strands of marsh grass, she expertly turned it so that the engine was pointed toward a small canal. She pushed the boat forward and then released the latch that held it on the trailer. Lifting up the tongue of the trailer, she held on to a rope tied to the bow of the boat as the stern slid into the water.

Boris didn't need coaxing. He bounded into the boat as soon as Alex pulled away the trailer. His feet made loud scratching sounds as he ran back and forth from the engine to the bow. Alex pushed the boat into the water and hopped in it at the last second. Stepping over a single seat, she sat on the gunwale beside the motor. The engine could be started with a key, and in a few moments, she was guiding the boat along watery paths as familiar to her as a sidewalk in town.

It was a zigzag route through the marsh to the barrier island. Boris took up his position as figurehead, madly barking at the mullet that jumped from the water on both sides of the boat. The silver sides of the fish flashed against the dark water. Alex smiled at the dog's antics and wondered what he would do if one of the slender fish jumped out of the water and landed in the boat.

The barrier island was owned by the state of South Carolina. Only two hundred yards across at its widest point, the one-mile strip of sandy beach was too narrow for commercial development. It existed at the whim of the ocean and feared nothing except the sea. A major hurricane could cut it in two in a night, or a shift in offshore currents could erase it in one hundred years. Alex was simply glad it existed for her. Plans were made to build a causeway from the mainland to the southern end of the island so people without boats could walk on the pristine sand. Alex hoped the funding for the causeway went into repaving a road somewhere else.

She steered the boat toward a spot at the northern end of the island. The last twenty yards of her journey were through open water where the ocean met the marsh. The front of the boat bumped into the muddy sand on the landward side. Boris leapt through the air onto the shore and disappeared over the top of the sand dunes. Alex tossed out her beach-bag and pulled the boat halfway onto the dry ground. She carried a rope tied to the boat's bow across the sand to a clump of scruffy bushes and wrapped it around the largest bush.

Alex trudged up a rise fringed with dune grass and stopped at the top. This was always one of her favorite moments. The human eye and mind are incapable of grasping the vastness of an ocean, but Alex liked to try. A breeze blew from the northwest, and the water beyond the surf was decorated with narrow white caps. This was not going to be like paddling across a suburban swimming pool. Alex walked to the edge of the water and emptied the contents of her beachbag. Rarely did she see anyone else on the island and never in the evenings. She was as alone as Robinson Crusoe. Boris splashed into the surf and then ran back to her.

"How is the water?" she asked.

In answer the dog shook himself and let her feel the spray.

"Cold," Alex responded.

She slipped a black wet suit over her swimsuit. From October until the beginning of May she felt more comfortable with an extra layer of insulation between herself and the cool water. She put her goggles on top of her head and walked into the water. The waves broke against her. The tide was coming in. Boris stayed close by her side and was soon plowing through the water with his head sticking up and nose pointed slightly skyward. On land, the dog was an undisciplined adolescent. In the water, he was obedient and under control. When the water reached waist level, Alex dove through the next wave and stood up. Her hair was slick against her head. She slipped the goggles into place and swam through the next wave into the water beyond the surf.

A small woman, Alex swam slowly yet powerfully. She'd spent four years on swim teams as a teenager and competed in the distance races. She rarely won but always finished. Boris plowed along a few feet from her right shoulder. If he strayed too far away, Alex could call out, "Heel!" and he would return to his place by her side.

Alex turned south and swam parallel to the beach about fifty yards from the shore. Timing her breaths to avoid mouthfuls of salt water wasn't easy, and the swells caused her to swing back and forth. Progress was slow. However, Alex knew not to flail against the water in frustration but rather to coexist with it. Once she adjusted to the rhythm of the waves, she began moving forward.

Alex enjoyed the risk and danger inherent in swimming alone in the ocean. The greatest threat to her safety wasn't a shark that mistook her for a struggling fish but riptide currents. Three times in the past she had entered a riptide zone and felt the ocean reach out with irresistible strength to draw her into its deep embrace. The first time she had had to fight the urge to turn toward the shore and exhaust herself in a vain attempt to return to land. Her mind had obeyed that day, and she had not given in to her instincts. She had continued swimming parallel to the beach as the riptide carried her rapidly out to sea. Boris had kept his focus on his mistress and stayed by her side. Then, just as suddenly as it had begun, the current had abated and abandoned its attempt to capture her. When Alex had looked at the beach, she guessed that they were more than three times the usual distance from shore. She had rolled onto her back, looked up at the stormy sky, and laughed. She had fought the ocean and won.

Today, choppy waves were her only obstacles. After thirty minutes in the water, she turned toward the beach. When the ocean was calm, she would swim the entire length of the island, but today she stopped toward the middle. She body-surfed on a few waves as she neared the shore. Boris swam ahead and rolled in the dry sand. When Alex stood up in the shallows, the evening breeze was cool on the parts of her body not covered by the wet suit. Boris greeted her.

"You're the best swimming buddy in the world," Alex told him. "If I ever get a cramp, will you pull me to shore?"

Boris ran splashing back into the edge of the surf. Sea rescue was not listed on his résumé.

Alex walked north along the edge of the water and looked for undamaged treasures. The beach offered a paltry selection of shells, most of them broken into small fragments before reaching the shore. Because she came so often, Alex could be picky. Today, she didn't find anything worth taking home to deposit in the large glass bowl in the center of her kitchen table.

By the time she returned to the place where she'd left her beachbag, the sunset she'd anticipated from her deck stretched across the sky. The high clouds were a vibrant red tinged with pink. She took off the wet suit, dried herself with a yellow beach towel, and then played tug of war for a few minutes with Boris. Back in the boat, Boris lay quietly at her feet as they crossed the marsh. Alex enjoyed the final chapters of the sunset. By the time she rolled the boat into its resting place, the clouds had lost their color and darkness was falling.

6

Shake off this downy sleep, death's counterfeit.
MACBETH, ACT 2, SCENE 3

THE FIRST VEHICLE to reach Rena was not an ambulance. It was a police car. She heard the siren before the vehicle, raising a cloud of dust, came into view. Except for the flashing blue lights on top, the yellow-and-brown cruiser could have been mistaken for a city cab.

A short, overweight, completely bald man got out of the car. He was dressed in a white shirt without a tie and wrinkled green slacks. When he came closer, Rena could see that he was disfigured by a deep scar that began above his left eye and continued up his forehead. The reddish color of the scar contrasted with the adjacent white skin and made the man look like he'd survived a scalping by hostile Indians.

Rena opened the door to get out. When she did, her nausea returned with a vengeance. Gagging, she leaned over and got sick on the gravel roadway.

The man waited until she stopped gagging then spoke in a deep, slow-moving voice. "Take it easy, Mrs. Richardson. I'm Detective Giles Porter with the Mitchell County Sheriff's Department. The deputy in the car is checking on the location of an ambulance."

In spite of her condition, Rena pointed up the road toward the parking lot for the trail and croaked, "Don't stay here. My husband fell off a cliff."

"We know. A helicopter is on its way and should arrive in a few minutes. It will get to him long before we could. We're here to take care of you."

"A helicopter?" Rena asked as her strength began to return.

"Yes. We have an airborne rescue squad that serves this area of the state. It's headquartered in this county."

Immediate validation of the detective's words came as a helicopter roared over their heads. It was painted white with a green logo on the side.

Porter pointed upward. "They should be at the falls in a couple of minutes. There is a landing area not far from the bottom. It would take us over an hour to get there on foot."

Rena closed her eyes. "It's no use. My husband is dead."

"Are you sure?" the detective asked with concern.

Rena nodded. "I tried to revive him. He didn't have a pulse and was already getting cold by the time I reached the bottom of the falls to help him."

"I'm sorry. It's a dangerous place, but don't try to talk about it now."

"We'd been married less than a year," she added weakly.

The officer in the patrol car opened the door and called out, "If she can ride in the car, the ambulance is going to meet us at the end of the road. They had to bring in a unit from the other side of the county."

The detective stepped closer to Rena.

"We'll put you in the back of the patrol car and take you to the hospital. You need to see a doctor yourself."

At the mention of a ride in the back of the police car, Rena shrank back. This was a trick. The grotesque looking detective wanted to put her in the back of the vehicle and take her to jail. The thought of involuntary confinement in any form prompted another wave of nausea. She put her hand over her mouth.

"Are you going to get sick again?" Porter asked.

Rena closed her eyes to shield them from the detective's gaze. She knew that the wrong expression on her face could be her downfall. There was something disturbing about the detective. His eyes, especially the left one beneath the scar, seemed to be probing for something, attempting to look within her. She struggled to shake her fear.

"Could someone drive my car?" she asked. "I can lie down in the backseat."

The detective paused then turned toward the deputy who was standing outside the patrol car, talking on the radio.

"I'm going to drive her vehicle!" Porter yelled. "See if the ambulance can meet us at Henderson's Store."

Rena moved shakily to the rear door. The detective reached out to steady her. It took every ounce of Rena's will power not to snatch her arm away from the detective's grasp. He opened the door for her, and she slid into the backseat and lay down. The deputy in the patrol car turned on the siren and took off in the lead.

Porter followed at a fast pace down the gravel road. Rena bounced up and down as she lay on her back. She looked out the opposite window. In some places the limbs of trees met and turned the gravel road into a green tunnel. She began to feel better but didn't sit up. She wanted to avoid any encounters with the detective's eyes looking at her in the rearview mirror. Eye contact could encourage conversation, and conversation could lead to questions. Too many questions could become interrogation, and interrogation could lead to a murder charge. She kept her mouth shut and rehearsed her lines.

The sound of the tires on the gravel road suddenly stopped. They had reached a paved highway. Still following the wailing siren of the patrol car, they sped at a much faster speed for a few more minutes and then pulled off the roadway and stopped. Porter turned in his seat.

"An ambulance will be here in a couple of minutes."

Rena sat up.

"Which hospital are they taking me to?"

"Mitchell Regional. It's our local hospital. If they can't handle a situation, a patient is sent to Greenville."

Rena took a tissue from a small box on the seat beside her. She wasn't crying, but dabbing a tissue to her eye would be a good gesture. She made sure the detective saw her.

"And my husband? Where will they take him?"

"He will go to Mitchell Regional, too."

Rena wanted to force a tear but nothing came. Crying on cue had never been her strong suit. She quickly tried to think of something sad but nothing came to mind that could produce a tear. Her bad memories were wells of anger not sorrow. She was spared further conversation when a red-and-white ambulance turned into the parking lot. Two medical workers rushed out of the vehicle. Though she didn't need assistance, Rena decided it wouldn't look right to experience a miraculous recovery.

She let herself be led slowly to the ambulance where she lay down on a stretcher in the back. The EMTs scurried around her, poking, prodding, and checking her vital signs.

Giles Porter's face appeared. "I'll see you at the hospital."

Rena closed her eyes.

The ride to the hospital took fifteen minutes. Rena didn't see or hear any sign of the helicopter when they rolled her into the emergency room entrance. She had an IV in her arm, and an orderly whisked her into a treatment room. A handsome young physician shone a light in her eyes and carefully moved her arms and legs. Rena dutifully answered his questions. The doctor set his clipboard on the corner of the bed.

"I don't think there is any need to send you to x-ray. There's no indication of broken bones."

Rena touched the bruise on her head and winced.

The doctor noticed and continued, "You may have a slight concussion, but I think the nausea you experienced was due to mild shock at what happened to your husband. The bump on your head is a bruise, but I don't see any evidence of intracranial injury."

"When can I leave?" Rena asked. "I need to contact my husband's family. They don't know what happened."

"Just a few minutes. I'll send a nurse in to take out the IV. I'm very sorry about your husband's accident."

Hearing the doctor use the word "accident" was comforting. Rena lay on the bed staring at the ceiling while she waited for the nurse. Suddenly, she sensed someone standing in the doorway behind her head. Rena didn't turn her head. It wasn't a nurse. A nurse would have immediately entered the room to remove the IV. The presence didn't come into the room, but stayed still, watching her.

Her woodland encounter with Baxter flashed through Rena's mind. If he manifested in the busy hospital, how would she suppress the scream necessary to banish him? The encounter with her husband's ghostly specter had been almost as bad as the dead gaze on his face at the bottom of the waterfall. She groaned in frustration. The person at the door spoke in a low voice that didn't sound like Baxter.

"Could I talk to you for a minute?"

Rena recognized the voice. It was the scar-faced detective. He stepped into the room and stood close to the gurney. From his position, he could see her, but she couldn't see him unless she turned her head.

Rena groaned louder. "I feel terrible," she said. "I think I'm going to be sick again."

"Oh, the doctor told me you were going to be released. Do you want me to get him?"

Rena didn't answer. She was going to have to talk to the police sooner or later. Perhaps her sympathetic status on the gurney with an IV in her arm would encourage the troublesome man to make it quick.

"No, if I lie still, I'll be okay."

"I know this is hard for you but tell me what happened."

Rena shut her eyes to conceal the truth that lay embedded in her soul and repeated verbatim the lines she'd rehearsed as she walked along the trail.

"I'd camped in the area when I was a little girl and wanted my husband to see it. We left Greenville this morning and hiked down the trail to the waterfall. We spent some time enjoying the view from the rocks. No one else was around. Baxter had put a bottle of wine along with some bread and cheese in his backpack. We ate a snack, and Baxter drank most of the wine. When we got ready to leave, he wanted to take one last look. He stepped too close to the edge and lost his footing on the wet rocks. I was a few feet away but couldn't do anything. He slipped and fell. It was a tragic accident."

Rena stopped. It was the end of her story. It sounded much more mechanical than when she'd rehearsed it in her head, but at least she'd been able to repeat it verbatim. She waited for the detective to thank her and leave, but he didn't say anything. She turned her head to see if he was still there. He was looking down at her with an expression that was neither friendly nor hostile. He let the silence linger until Rena felt that she really might get sick.

"Is that all?" he asked.

Rena closed her eyes again and tried to keep her voice calm.

"What do you mean?" she asked.

"Is that all you remember?"

"Uh, I looked over the edge. That's when I saw he was dead. I'd rather not talk about it anymore."

"Of course. I know you're upset, but whenever there is a death, I have to file a detailed report. Unfortunately, your husband isn't the first person who has died up there. Since I've been with the sheriff's department three other people have slipped on the rocks and been seriously injured or killed. The park service should post signs warning people to stay back."

"I'm not going to sue anybody," Rena blurted out. She immediately regretted saying anything that sounded so mercenary.

"That's not why I mentioned it. I didn't think you would be thinking about that at a time like this."

Rena tried to regain control. "I don't want to think. It's all such a shock. I haven't even called his family with the news."

The detective stepped back. "I'd better leave you then. Could I have your phone number in case I have other questions when I'm preparing my report?"

Rena couldn't think of a good reason to deny his request. She didn't want him calling her cell phone so she gave him the number for their house in Santee. The detective didn't write down the number.

"How are you going to remember it?" she asked.

"I'm good with phone numbers. I've had a lot of practice. I'll note it in a file when I get back to my office."

The detective took out a business card and laid it on the bed beside her arm.

"I'm very sorry about your husband. Here's my card and the keys to your vehicle. It's parked near the ER entrance. The helicopter has probably arrived by now. I've been inside waiting to talk to you and haven't been in contact with them. Someone at the triage desk can give you the information you need about the body. I assume you'll want to have him taken to your hometown. If I can help you in any way, please let me know."

With the end of the interview in sight, Rena became gracious.

"Thanks," she said. "You've been a great help."

The detective stepped to the door. Then he stopped and turned toward her. "Oh, how did you get the scratches on your face and arm?"

Rena touched her face and felt the dried blood. "When I was running down the trail to the bottom of the falls, a limb slapped me. I also have a knot on my head where I slipped and hit a rock near my husband's body."

"Did it knock you out?"

"No, but it dazed me for a second."

"Was that before or after you gave your husband CPR?"

Rena quickly analyzed her answer and couldn't see a reason to pick one time over another.

"After. I was so upset, I wasn't careful."

The detective moved farther out of the room. "Of course. I hope you're going to be okay. Don't forget to call if I can help you."

Rena nodded and closed her eyes. The image of Baxter's face as he lay on the rock at the base of the waterfall played on the movie screen behind her eyelids. Every time she erased it, the scene returned as soon as her guard was down. Giving up, she opened her eyes and turned her head to make sure the detective was gone.

Giles Porter was standing less than a foot from her bed.

"What do you want?" she demanded indignantly. "I've told you everything that happened!"

"Oh, I'm sorry. I didn't mean to upset you. I wasn't sure if you were awake. It's my report. I forgot to ask your address and social security number."

Rena gave him the information. Once again the detective didn't take a note. He moved closer to the door, but Rena held no hope that he was really leaving.

"Is there anything else?" she asked.

"No. I have everything I need from you. I'm very sorry about the accident."

A nurse brushed by the detective and came into the room to take out Rena's IV. The detective watched for a second and then left without a parting question. The nurse finished, and Rena sat up on the edge of the bed. She put the keys to the SUV in her pocket and dropped Porter's card in the trash receptacle. Going to the triage station, she asked about the helicopter. It hadn't arrived yet. Transporting Baxter's body was taking longer than she had expected.

Rena found her vehicle and sat inside to wait for the helicopter. She hoped she wouldn't be asked to identify the body. The last thing she needed was another image of Baxter to stalk her future.

While she waited, Rena telephoned Baxter's father at a number where she was sure he wouldn't be there to answer. Fifty-eight-year-old Ezra Richardson was at the office and could be reached on his private line, but she didn't want to talk to him in person. Not yet. A message that didn't require immediate explanation would be the way to break the news of his younger son's tragic accident. Her father-in-law lived alone in a massive house near the eighteenth green of the best golf course in the area, but since his wife's death from cancer five years before, he spent most nights in a suite adjacent to his office. His work had always been his mistress; now it was his wife as well. Rena called his home phone number. Her voice cracked with emotion.

"This is Rena. There has been a tragic accident. Baxter got too close to the edge of a cliff on our hike and fell." She held the phone away from her mouth for a second as if trying to regain her composure. When she did, she had a sudden change in plan. "Please call me. I'll have my phone with me at all times."

She couldn't report Baxter's death to an answering machine. That wouldn't look right. Only the government could send a notice of death in a cold, impersonal way. It was better to lay the groundwork of bad news in a voice message and finish the job when Ezra called back. She put the key in the ignition and turned it to accessory power so she could listen to music in an effort to calm herself while she waited for the helicopter. There was a knock on the window. Rena jumped.

It was Giles Porter.

Rena pushed the button that lowered the window. Without trying to hide her irritation, she asked, "What is it now?"

The green-and-white helicopter came into view. Porter pointed to it.

"I was in my car and heard the pilot call in on the police band. They're not landing here. They're taking your husband to the trauma center in Greenville. He's alive."

7

True worshipers will worship the Father in spirit and truth.
JOHN 4:23

TED MORGAN READ the last page of the book and set it on the wooden lamp stand beside his chair. He rubbed his eyes and ran his fingers through curly brown hair that was beginning to show streaks of gray along the edges. It was quiet inside the small, white frame house that served as the parsonage for the part-time music minister at Sandy Flats Church. The curtains moved slightly in front of an open window that let in the cool night air tinged with the salt smell of the ocean that lay a few miles to the east. The salt air refreshed the inside of the house but attacked with silent fury the peeling paint on the outside. The church trustees had stopped by after supper and told him it was time to scrape off the old flakes and put on a new coat. That meant by next week Ted would be on a ladder with a paintbrush in his hand.

A walnut regulator clock on the mantel struck the hour. Beside the clock was a picture of Ted's daughter, Angelica, when she graduated from Juilliard. She still lived in New York and played the viola in chamber music ensembles while waiting to land a job with a major orchestra in the United States or Europe. Angelica shared her father's broad brow and deep brown eyes, but her hair was black and straight like that of her mother. She didn't blame either one of them for the divorce that irrevocably divided the family when she was a little girl.

Ted had been awake since before dawn that day, but he wasn't sleepy. He paced back and forth across the room. He wanted to live in the world where the book had taken him—a place where miracles happened as part of everyday life and the atmosphere of whole towns was charged with the manifest presence of God. But his experience mocked his desire. Sandy Flats Church barely kept equilibrium between living souls coming in the front door and dead bodies departing out the back to the ancient cemetery behind Ted's house. The words he'd read about extraordinary revivals in South America had stirred him. The same ocean touched the coasts of South America and South Carolina. Why couldn't the same mighty rushing wind blow onto these shores? Wasn't Jesus Christ the Lord of the whole earth?

There was only one remedy for the discontent he felt.

Putting on a lightweight jacket, Ted went outside. It was dark. A strong night breeze swept off the ocean, and clouds were building as the warm air above the water clashed with the cool air over the land. A midnight storm was brewing. The breeze parted the long strands of dune grass that guarded the entrance to the crushed-shell parking lot in front of the sanctuary. The church didn't need a fresh coat of paint. Preservation of the beautiful building with its narrow, pointed windows and ornately crafted steeple was the highest priority of religion for many longtime members of the congregation, and the trustees kept the church in pristine condition. Ted had spent many hours repairing everything from leaks in the plumbing to a crack in the pulpit.

The church had a rich heritage. Before the Revolutionary War, Francis Asbury preached from horseback to local settlers less than a hundred yards from where Ted lived. The high watermark of the church's history came in the 1850s, when Sundays found the sanctuary packed with hundreds of people who attended the morning services and stayed most of the afternoon for dinner on the grounds and additional preaching. Many members of the congregation from that era lay buried in the church cemetery beneath live oaks covered with Spanish moss. Others died in Civil War battlefields to the north and west.

It was a short walk from the front door of the old parsonage to the brick steps leading up to the church. The senior pastor, John Heathcliff, lived in a newer house two miles away; however, instead of tearing down the old parsonage, the congregation used it as part of the compensation package for a minister of music. Ted was hired because he had two valuable skills—he could play the piano for the Sunday service and perform maintenance work on the church buildings during the rest of the week.

He unlocked the door to the sanctuary and went inside. The bare wooden floors creaked as he walked down the center aisle past dark pews hand-planed by nineteenth-century craftsmen, then worn smooth by generations of church members sliding in and out on Sunday mornings. Outside, storm clouds partially concealed the moon. Still, the dim light penetrated through the narrow, stained-glass windows and created a faint glow without strength to cast a shadow. Ted didn't turn on any lights. He wasn't bothered by the dark and knew where he wanted to go. He made his way to the front of the room where the piano waited behind a low altar railing.

Ted sat on a piano bench in front of a magnificent Steinway more suited for a concert hall than a rural church building. He opened the cover for the keyboard. No light shone on the ivory keys, but it didn't matter. Ted's connection to the piano was not based on sight. The eighty-eight keys were as much a part of him as the fingers that touched them, and he knew their sounds more intimately than his daughter's voice. He closed his eyes. Although frustrated by the atmosphere of spiritual impotency that surrounded him in that sanctuary each week, Ted knew that the remedy for his negative feelings was not to bang out a demand toward heaven. The presence of God is wooed, not coerced, and tonight he began with notes of quiet reflection intended as an invitation. He didn't say a prayer; he played one.

As often happened, the music took Ted to a place he hadn't planned to go. He came to the sanctuary to ask for revival and healing power. Instead, the invitation led to a musical oasis where his heavenly Father reminded him of his divine love. From that spring, all living water flowed, and the rippling of the notes brought a sweet peace into the room and to Ted's soul. The balm of Gilead is gentle, not strident, and the notes expressed in music the endless compassion of the God who loves his children with an eternal love. Tears pooled in Ted's eyes, and two matching drops rolled slowly down his cheeks. No matter the dryness of the spiritual landscape around him, this refreshing flowed in the presence of the Lord.

Ted blinked back the tears. Usually, he played with his eyes open as he stared into the darkness. Sometimes, glimpses of light flashed by the corner of his vision as unseen messengers gathered to watch and wonder. Occasionally, he played with his eyes shut and enhanced to the fullest his sensitivity to the sounds produced by his hands. But always, from beginning to end, it was a spontaneous composition never heard before nor reproduced again. It was a new creation and flowed from the depths of the musician's spirit to the place where anointed music goes.

Ted could change from one key to another as effortlessly as a landscape artist selecting a different color. The sounds began to build. He transitioned to the deep-throated notes of the lower octaves. He stayed for several minutes in the lower range and let the call build in intensity. Ted had learned not to hurry from one theme to the next and sustained the suspense until the urge to move higher became irresistible. When his hands finally climbed up the keyboard, the sound exploded as the entire range of the piano's capabilities was fully revealed. Nature answered with thunder from a distant lightning strike. Ted lost himself in the music and found himself in the manifest presence of God—the place where all the praise of a lifetime is not enough.

An hour later the last note softly soared away. Ted let out a deep breath and lifted his hands from the keyboard. His burden lifted. His petition set free.

8

A persistent vegetative state or other condition
of permanent unconsciousness.
S.C. Code 44-77-50

Driving to work in the morning, Alex turned on a local radio station and learned about Baxter Richardson. The news report was short on details.

> *A member of a well-known Santee family, Baxter Richardson, was seriously injured while hiking yesterday with his wife in the mountains near Greenville. Richardson was airlifted from the area by helicopter and taken to Greenville Memorial Hospital, where he is listed in critical condition.*

Ezra Richardson was one of Ralph Leggitt's biggest clients. Alex didn't do any legal work involving Mr. Richardson's business holdings, but she'd heard that Ralph Leggitt often filled in the blanks on his daily time sheet with a single entry: "Richardson—General Matters." Two hundred thousand dollars in annual legal fees to the local businessman was as certain as the monthly phone bill. The peripheral benefits reaped by Leggitt from minority ownership interest in some of Richardson's ventures were not included in law firm revenues.

Alex hadn't been invited to Baxter and Rena's wedding, but everybody in town was familiar with the details. Five hundred carefully selected guests from Charleston, Georgetown, Santee, and other areas of the coast came to celebrate the wedding of Ezra Richardson's younger son. The bride and groom stood under a flower-draped gazebo at the family's summer house overlooking the Santee River. Rumor had it Rena Richardson's dress cost fifty thousand dollars.

Ralph Leggitt made it to the third row on the groom's side of the open-air seating and had a picture of Ezra and himself standing beside the wedding gazebo. Alex had seen the photograph at the Leggitts' home during the firm Christmas party.

Alex parked in her customary spot in the back corner of the parking lot near a palmetto tree. Gwen stopped her before she went into her office.

"Did you hear about Baxter Richardson?" the secretary asked.

"Just a blurb on the radio about a hiking accident. Do you know any details?"

"Mr. Leggitt was on the phone with Mr. Richardson first thing this morning, so he probably has the full story. He asked the partners who were here to come into his office. Leonard and a couple of the others are in there now."

Gwen opened the middle drawer of her desk. A black wire ran from a tiny radio to her ear. "I'll let you know the news."

Alex smiled. "So if you type a letter that has the weather forecast and the tide schedule in the second paragraph, I'll know you were listening to the wrong ear."

Gwen lowered her voice. "This is huge news. If Baxter Richardson dies, can you imagine how rich his widow will be? She's in her mid-twenties and would be set for life."

"Gwen, that's morbid."

"When you get to be my age, you'll learn that men are fickle, and a girl's best friend is a big bank account."

Alex didn't argue. Her primary job for her clients was to accomplish what Gwen believed.

"Anyway," Alex said, "the radio said he was in critical condition. People usually get better when they say that."

Gwen scooted back in her chair. "You never know. I want to stay on top of it."

Alex went into her office and listened to her voice mail messages. Marilyn Simpson had called. Her husband had issued a stop payment on a check he'd given her for groceries, and her finances were in shambles. She'd called the two lawyers Alex suggested and neither of them would take her case. Grim-faced, Alex wrote down the pertinent information from the call. She had to get Marilyn a lawyer first thing. She was about to pick up the phone and call a well-known divorce attorney in a nearby community when the phone buzzed. It was Leggitt.

"Alex? Are you there?"

She pushed the talk button. "Yes, sir."

"Come into my office."

Alex walked down the hallway. After her experience the previous day, it felt like a return to the school principal's office. She knocked and entered. Four of the partners were sitting around the conference table. A speakerphone was in the middle of the table.

Apprehensive, Alex sat beside Leonard Mitchell, who was eating a doughnut and skimming the *Wall Street Journal*. On the other side of Leonard was Kenneth Pinchot, the firm's senior litigator. Pinchot, a tall, distinguished attorney with carefully combed gray hair, always wore expensive suits with a silk handkerchief in the front pocket of his jacket. Looking slightly bored in response to required attendance at an early morning meeting, he nodded in greeting to Alex and took another sip of coffee. Across the table from Pinchot was Bruce Fletchall, Ralph Leggitt's alter ego and the lawyer who did most of the work for which the senior partner took credit. Bruce, a bookworm attorney who wore thick rimless glasses, was squinting at some documents and making notes on a legal pad.

"Did you hear about Baxter Richardson?" Leggitt asked Alex.

"Only the radio announcement about a hiking accident. What happened?"

"He fell down a cliff near a waterfall outside Greenville. He's in a coma with head and spine injuries. Ezra flew up last night in his plane and talked with Rena at the hospital. I'm going to phone him in a few minutes and wanted you to work through some documents with us."

Relieved that the meeting was not about her foibles of the previous day, Alex relaxed.

"What kind of documents?" she asked.

Leggitt took the papers from Bruce and slid them across the table to Alex. The top sheet read *Last Will and Testament of Baxter Norris Richardson.*

Leggitt continued. "This was prepared by Dennis a couple of weeks before he left. It's short and to the point."

Dennis Lipscomb, an estate-planning specialist, had worked with the firm for seven years before leaving to take a management position with the trust department of a bank in Columbia. The firm had not yet hired someone to fill his niche.

Alex flipped through the will. Because Baxter and Rena had no children, it was relatively simple. If Baxter died, Rena received everything. Testamentary transfers from husband to wife aren't subject to estate tax so there wasn't any need for fancy trusts. She couldn't imagine why there would be a problem with the will. She shifted into divorce lawyer mode.

"Was there a prenuptial agreement?"

"No," Leggitt responded. "Dennis drafted one to protect Baxter in case Rena filed for divorce, but Baxter didn't want to make her sign it. According to an e-mail in the file, he thought it would send the wrong message to Rena and told Dennis to drop it."

"Young love believes it will bloom forever," Pinchot added dryly.

"I wish some of the wives I represent had been so lucky." Alex shrugged. "Is there life insurance on Baxter's interest in the family businesses in case he dies?"

Leggitt turned to Bruce Fletchall. "That's your area."

The studious lawyer spoke in a soft voice. "There are several older agreements. We were in the process of changing them, and Baxter was scheduled to come in next week to sign several new ones. All of the buy-outs signed before the marriage provide for payment to various Richardson companies if Baxter dies."

"How much insurance?" Alex asked.

Fletchall rubbed his left temple while he ran mental calculations. "Around twenty-five million."

Alex was stunned. "For a minority interest?"

"Yes."

"And how much would Rena get outside the business holdings?"

"Standard stuff—the house, personal belongings, and any personal insurance Baxter was carrying."

"How much would that be worth?"

"A couple of million, and she would inherit his interest in companies not subject to buyout. The new buyouts would have given her over twenty million, but Baxter never signed them."

"Bad timing on the accident from Rena's point of view," Alex replied.

Ralph Leggitt answered, "Maybe, but that's not the problem. Baxter is still alive, and we don't have a fight between Rena and the family over the assets of an estate. The immediate concern is control of Baxter's medical care. In addition to the will, Dennis prepared a health care power of attorney that gives Rena the right to make decisions about Baxter's medical treatment. Dennis didn't cross-check other Richardson files"—Leggitt paused and looked over his glasses at Alex—"a disturbingly common problem here at the firm. If he had, he would have discovered that Baxter had previously given his father authority over his affairs in a durable power of attorney."

"Which wasn't revoked after the marriage," Bruce added.

Alex had a working knowledge of powers of attorney because they often came up in the divorce cases she handled. A health care power of attorney allowed a person to designate someone to direct his or her medical care in case of a serious illness or injury. A durable power of attorney was a much broader document that gave the holder the right to manage a person's legal affairs even if the person who signed it became mentally incompetent.

"Doesn't the health care power of attorney take precedence over a durable power of attorney in the area of medical decisions?" she asked. "The specific grant of authority should override a general one."

Fletchall shook his head. "You have logic on your side, but not the Code of South Carolina. Under the current law, a durable power of attorney that grants authority over health matters trumps a health care power of attorney and gives Ezra the right to call the shots on medical care. There is also a declaration of desire for a natural death signed by Baxter."

"What election did he make?" Alex asked.

Fletchall slid a single sheet of paper across the table. "He wants the minimum effort allowed by law to keep him alive."

Alex read the statutory language.

If I am in a persistent vegetative state or other condition of permanent unconsciousness,

_____*I direct that nutrition and hydration BE PROVIDED through any medically indicated means, including medically or surgically implanted tubes.*

BNR_____*I direct that nutrition and hydration NOT BE PROVIDED through any medically indicated means, including medically or surgically implanted tubes.*

Alex stared for a couple of seconds at Baxter's signature at the bottom of the sheet. When the young man had signed the paper four months previously, he had done so without a clue that before his next birthday his instructions might be a sword of Damocles hanging over his head.

"Does he meet the criteria?" she asked.

Leggitt shrugged. "We don't know. Ezra hasn't talked in detail with the doctors. If Baxter isn't going to come out of the coma, it doesn't matter what Ezra or Rena wants to do, and the conflict over control of medical care is moot. Baxter has already issued orders to terminate life support."

Bruce Fletchall spoke. "Here's a copy of the health care power of attorney and the durable power of attorney."

Alex quickly scanned the health care document. It contained the standard language used by husbands and wives and reflected the trust implicit in the marriage relationship. One of the first things Alex did for her clients in divorce cases was revoke any outstanding power of attorney and remove any control the estranged spouse had over life-and-death issues. She picked up the durable power of attorney. It was thicker than all the other documents combined.

"Don't try to read the durable power of attorney now," Leggitt said. "It's extremely broad in its scope. Ezra made Baxter sign it as soon as he turned eighteen. It gives Ezra the ability to do everything Baxter could do—buy, sell, borrow, transfer stock, and dictate medical care. He didn't want Baxter running wild without the ability to rein him in by controlling the money. As far as I know, Ezra never used it. Baxter has worked in the family business for several years now, and although he isn't a brilliant entrepreneur, he hasn't given his father any trouble."

"The medical provisions are on page thirteen at the bottom," Fletchall added.

Alex's mental wheels were turning while she listened. "Who wants to disconnect Baxter from life support?"

Leggitt and Fletchall both spoke at once, "Rena."

"Why?"

Ken Pinchot wrinkled his patrician nose. "That's easy. She wants him out of his misery or out of her way. Take your pick. I vote for number two."

Leggitt shrugged. "It's not that simple. We've been discussing the situation, and I've talked with Ezra. We want you to go to Greenville. You're a woman who knows how to convince women to trust you. Get inside Rena's head and find out what she's up to. Ezra doesn't want to take action with the durable power of attorney unless he thinks Rena is trying to hurry up an inheritance."

Alex's guard went up. "But it sounds like there's already a conflict of interest between Rena and Mr. Richardson. If he is going to use the durable power of attorney Baxter signed before the marriage to transfer property out of Baxter's name, there is going to be a lawsuit. I don't want a repeat of yesterday."

"That was stupid, Alex," Leonard blurted out. "Why didn't you—"

Leggitt cut him off. "The conflict in this situation is still theoretical. We'd like to keep it that way. Your job is to help our client—the entire Richardson family."

Alex was skeptical.

"This is your chance to really do something significant for the firm," Leggitt continued. "If we can help the Richardsons through this difficult time, it will help our overall relationship with them. Ezra still sends part of his business to the Rollins law firm in Charleston, and I'd like to get it all. This is a great opportunity for you."

All Alex saw were land mines.

"We believe you're the one to handle this," Pinchot added in a serious tone of voice. "That's why we brought you into the partners' meeting."

"What if it blows up?" she asked.

"You can only do your best," Fletchall said quietly. "I'm not sure it will work myself, but I don't see any better options at this point."

Everyone was silent for several moments. Still uneasy, Alex wanted to say no but couldn't see how to refuse without appearing grossly insubordinate.

She spoke slowly, "Okay, I'll see what I can do."

Leggitt gave her a congratulatory smile. "Good. We'll send you up in a private plane. Be ready to leave in ten minutes. I'll call Ezra and recommend that he avoid any contact with Rena until you are on the scene to mediate any problems."

Alex hurried back to her office with a folder containing copies of the documents from Baxter's file in her hand.

"Gwen!" she called. "Come in here."

"Did they chew you out again?" the secretary asked belligerently. "If they did, I think—"

"No, it wasn't about me," Alex interrupted. "It's the Richardson situation. I'm leaving town in ten minutes to go to the hospital in Greenville. Call the people on my appointment calendar and reschedule for early next week."

Gwen paused. Then she added in a matter-of-fact voice, "It's the money. The poor, young wife wants the money, and the Richardson family is trying to squeeze her out."

Startled by Gwen's accuracy, Alex didn't immediately respond. Her secretary had been married three times—once widowed and twice divorced. She knew both men and in-laws.

"Well?" Gwen insisted.

"Not exactly," Alex replied hesitantly. "Listen, I don't have time to talk. I have to leave in a few minutes."

"You don't have to tell me," Gwen said with satisfaction. "The truth is written all over your face."

After Gwen left the office, Alex stopped to make sure she wasn't forgetting anything. She saw the open phone book on her desk and remembered Marilyn Simpson. She wrote down the phone number for the other lawyer on a slip of paper and put it in her purse so she could call while driving to the airstrip.

Returning to Gwen's desk, she asked, "What am I forgetting?"

"Don't let them mistreat the girl. Her husband is dying, and someone will need to stand up for her."

"You're impossible," Alex responded. "If Mr. Leggitt heard you say that, he'd send you out the door. I'm on a peacekeeping mission."

"He doesn't scare me, and you're a warrior, not a diplomat. You're in your natural element in the heat of battle, not sitting around trying to get everyone to agree to a group hug."

Alex grinned. "I hope you're wrong about this one."

"I'm not. When will you be back?"

"I'm not sure."

"If you have to spend the night, I'll check on your pets. Is the key in the same place?"

"Yes. On top of the lantern by the front door. Thanks."

9

Remember him—before the silver cord is severed.
ECCLESIASTES 12:6

DURING THE SOLITARY drive from Mitchell County to Greenville Memorial Hospital, Rena's emotions raged unchecked as she alternatively screamed in frustration and cried in sorrow. Second thoughts and regrets about what she had done crept to the edge of her consciousness, but she furiously fought them back. The consequences of admitting guilt were more abominable than the prospect of living with secret sin.

As she neared the hospital, she wiped her eyes with a tissue and checked her appearance in the mirror on the sun visor. At least she had the visage of a grief-stricken wife. She pulled into the parking lot but didn't immediately get out of her vehicle. The sun had set and darkness was at hand. There was still the opportunity to run. Vanishing into the night had an anonymous attraction; remaining created the risk that she would spend the rest of her life in a prison cell—or worse.

She opened her purse and counted several hundred dollars in cash. But how far would that take her? She wasn't an Eric Rudolph who could disappear into a remote wilderness and frustrate the efforts of men and dogs to track him down. Instinctively, she knew that any effort on her part to become a fugitive would be short-lived. She would be caught within minutes of the first time she used her credit card, and by running away she would abandon any chance to salvage the life of safety and security she'd risked so much to obtain.

Back and forth, the debate raged.

In the end, Baxter vicariously persuaded her to enter the front doors of the hospital. She remembered the look of death on his face as he lay broken at the base of the waterfall. She shuddered again at the thought of his unseeing expression, but the image gave her hope that her husband was incapable of telling the police what had happened. If she ran away, Rena would be found guilty in absentia. By staying, she could influence events.

When she walked into the ICU waiting room, Giles Porter was there to greet her. At the sight of the detective, Rena's resolve disintegrated, and the urge to turn and flee returned with a vengeance.

"I should have offered to drive you," he said.

"Uh, that's okay," she managed. "How is Baxter?"

"I talked briefly with a nurse. All I know is that he's unconscious and listed in critical condition. They've taken him to the operating room."

Rena sighed with relief. The first hurdle was passed. Baxter was not giving interviews to scar-faced detectives.

"Are you going to stay?" she asked.

"I'll be glad to hang around for a while if you need me."

"No!" Rena said sharply. "That's not necessary."

The detective touched the scar on the top of his head. The gesture made Rena feel squeamish. It was a subtle threat sending a subliminal message— *tell me what you know, or you'll end up with one of these across your skull.*

"I'll be going," the detective said. "If I can help in any way, let me know."

"No, thanks," Rena said as civilly as possible.

She started to turn away and then remembered Baxter's father.

"Wait," she said. "Could you contact my husband's father in Santee? I left a message on his answering machine but didn't tell him what had happened. There are other numbers where it may be possible to reach him. It's too painful for me to talk to him yet."

The detective nodded. "Of course. What's his name and the numbers?"

Rena gave the contact information for Ezra. Once again, the detective made no effort to write down any of the data.

"I'll try to contact him as soon as possible," he said. "I hope your husband makes it."

After the detective left, Rena approached a male hospital employee who was monitoring ICU visitation. The young man was sitting behind a desk in a corner of the waiting area. A clipboard rested on the desk in front of him.

"I'm Rena Richardson," she said. "They told me at the entrance to come here and wait for news about my husband. He's in surgery."

"Was he in the ICU unit prior to surgery?"

"No. He was in an accident and came to the hospital in a helicopter."

"Okay, then he's not on my list. I'll let you know as soon as he's brought to a room." Rena sat down in a gold vinyl chair with wooden arms. Fatigue returned, but it was impossible to get comfortable. She made an effort to doze for a few minutes; however, whenever she closed her eyes, she replayed images from the edge of the cliff. By refusing to die, Baxter had doomed her to ongoing connection with him. His death grip remained. She flipped through a few stale magazines but couldn't focus on the words and pictures, which portrayed a world that seemed so phony when compared to the harshness of her reality.

It was almost midnight when the desk clerk answered a phone call. Then he looked in her direction and called her name.

"Mrs. Richardson!"

A few seconds of sleep had finally come to her shortly before he spoke, and Rena awoke with a start.

"No!" she said in a loud voice that caused the other people in the room to give her a puzzled look.

Coming to her senses, she walked to the table.

"They called from the nurses' station," the young man said. "Your husband came up from the recovery room a few minutes ago and is in a room. You can go back and see him."

Her heart pounding, Rena opened the door and went into the ICU area.

The patient rooms were clustered in a circle around an open area where nurses constantly monitored the condition of the patients. She walked up to the nurses' station. A young nurse looked up from a chart, and Rena introduced herself. The woman's face immediately registered concern.

"I'm sorry about your husband," she said. "He's in room 3824. Dr. Kolb, the neurosurgeon, had to go into another surgery and won't be here for a while. I'll go with you."

Rena followed the nurse toward the door. She wasn't sure how she should or would react to the sight of her husband. The nurse slowly opened the door. Rena held back slightly. As the nurse moved to the side, Rena stepped forward and reluctantly renewed contact with her husband.

Baxter was lying on his back with his eyes closed and was surrounded by tubes running to all four points of the compass. His chest rose and fell in rhythm in response to a ventilator that was inflating his lungs via a tube inserted into his nose. The machine made a slight hissing noise that immediately grated on Rena's nerves. A heart monitor was emitting a low-level beep, and an EKG of his cardiac function played across a small screen on the wall behind his head. His broken right leg had been set and immobilized in an air cast. An IV was attached to the back of his left hand.

Rena stared. It was Baxter but then not Baxter. His skin was a pale yellow, and his eyes were sunk into his skull. She shook her head. It was a pitiful sight. He would have looked better in a casket. At least a mortician could have applied a fake tan that mimicked the effects of the sun after a day on the golf course.

Something else was different, but she couldn't put her finger on it. It wasn't just the high-tech apparatus. It was more basic. Then she realized the change. Baxter's hair was parted on the opposite side. Rena wondered if he had been mistaken about the location of his natural part for his entire life. She instinctively stepped forward to brush it back but recoiled at the thought of touching the corpse. The nurse misinterpreted her gesture.

"You can touch him," she said. "Just avoid the life support apparatus. He's in a coma."

"A coma?" Rena said. She quickly looked to see if Baxter responded to the sound of her voice.

He didn't move a millimeter.

"Yes. The doctor will explain what's happened, but your husband is better off unconscious at this point."

"Is he going to wake up?"

The nurse touched Baxter's arm. "Dr. Kolb will give you the details. Most of your husband's chart is still at surgery, so I don't know much more myself. I'll leave you alone. I'm sorry but visits are limited to five minutes every hour."

The nurse left, and Rena took inventory. She was surprised at how calm she felt. Baxter's immobility lessened the immediate threat. A twinge of the remorse she'd felt at the cliff and during the drive to the hospital returned, but she pushed it away. She blinked quickly as she moved closer to the bed and watched herself reach over and unplug the ventilator. An alarm sounded but no nurses came rushing into the room. Baxter's chest heaved a few times, but the electrical impulses from his damaged spinal cord could not command the lungs to function in regular sequence. His unassisted efforts to maintain life were as futile as trying to start a car with a dead battery. It was over in a matter of seconds. Baxter was at peace. He would never awaken to accuse her.

Rena stepped away from the bed and returned to the real world.

She sighed. The hissing noise of the ventilator cried out to be silenced. She put her hand on the tube that ran from the machine to her husband's mouth and bent it shut for a couple of seconds. Nothing happened. No alarm. Perhaps that would be the way. An interruption of the flow of oxygen without turning off the machine. She squeezed again and held it longer.

"Please don't try to adjust the breathing tube," a voice said.

Rena jerked back her hand. An older, African-American nurse carrying a blood pressure cuff had entered the room.

"I know it's hard to see him like this, but you shouldn't touch the equipment," the nurse said. "Are you his wife?"

Rena nodded. "Yes. Do I need to leave?"

The nurse gave her a compassionate smile. "No, I'm just going to check his vital signs, then you can finish your visit. Even though a patient is unconscious, we encourage family members to spend time with their loved ones. You never know what effect your presence may have on him."

Rena moved to the end of the bed and watched the nurse efficiently perform her duties.

"His blood pressure is normal, he has a slight fever, and his heart is strong," the nurse concluded. "His vital signs have stabilized."

"That's good," Rena responded woodenly. "You're not going to write down that I tried to adjust his breathing tube, are you? I don't want to get in trouble."

"Of course not. I know you meant well, but it's better to call us if you think there is a problem. That's why we're here."

When the nurse left, Rena sat in a chair staring at the heart monitor while the sound of the ventilator continued its relentless assault against her future. Baxter was tethered to the earth by thin threads of plastic that served as artificial conduits for breath and nutrition. For all practical purposes, he was dead, and the best way for her to cope would be to classify him as a nonentity. If he were not truly human, it would be easier to contemplate the best method to sever the cord and set him free.

———

Ralph Leggitt was right when he said that Alex had a lot of experience handling difficult matters for distraught women. The situation facing Rena Richardson was different from a divorce, but the dynamics would be the same. As Alex drove to the airport, she planned her basic strategy. She would patiently listen to the young woman pour out streams of relevant and irrelevant information, identify the important data, and summarize options without painting a picture that was too rosy or too bleak. Only when she'd won the client's trust would she offer strong advice. By that point, most of her clients were ready to heed it.

Alex used her cell phone to set up an appointment for Marilyn Simpson with another attorney, then she called the office and asked Gwen to relay the information to Marilyn. She clicked the phone off as she pulled into the parking lot for the airport.

The Santee airport had no commercial airline service. It catered to businesspeople, golfers, and individuals who wanted to learn how to fly. Alex went into the small metal building that served as the fixed base operation center. This was new territory. She had never flown in anything except commercial jets.

An older man with thinning black hair and wearing a stained white T-shirt leaned against a counter, reading a magazine and smoking a cigarette. The scruffy figure looked out of place at an airport. A radio tuned to the local flight frequency crackled in the background.

"I'm a lawyer from Leggitt & Freeman," Alex said. "Someone from my office called to set up a flight to Greenville."

The man put out his cigarette. "Preflight's all done. I'm ready when you are."

Alex followed the pilot through a door to the aircraft ramp behind the building. On his way out, he grabbed a shirt with "Jack Link Air Service" embroidered on it and slipped it on over his stained T-shirt.

"Are you Mr. Link?" Alex asked as they walked across the asphalt.

"No, I found the shirt abandoned in the pilots' lounge in Des Moines. My name is Mo Reynolds."

The plane was a single engine Piper Warrior with seating for four. As they approached it, Alex glanced down and could tell that one of the two tires on the landing gear was low on air. Before she could say anything, Mo pulled an air gauge from his shirt pocket and checked the pressure.

"We need a shot of air in that tire. I'll get the compressor and be right back. Can I trust you not to jump in the plane and take off without me?"

He left without waiting for an answer. Alex stayed beside the plane, wondering what else was wrong with it. The pilot rolled out an air compressor and put some air in the sagging tire.

"We're set," he said. "You can sit in back, but there is more room up front."

"Where do you recommend?" Alex asked.

Mo smiled. "The best seats in the house are always in the front row."

Mo stepped up onto the wing and opened the door on the passenger side of the aircraft. It was set up as a trainer with full controls on both sides. Alex reluctantly followed and plopped down in the front passenger seat. To her relief, Mo went through a preflight checklist before starting the engine.

"You know, lawyers put Piper out of business," he said. "They filed so many lawsuits every time an idiot would crash a plane into a mountain and get killed that the company went under. It's getting harder and harder for me to find spare parts."

"I've never sued Piper," Alex reassured him.

Mo glanced at her out of the corner of his eye. "Yeah, most of the lawsuits were in the '60s and '70s. I doubt you were born then."

The pilot started the engine, which roared to life and shook the little cabin. He backed off the throttle and taxied away from the building.

"Hold your breath and exhale when I take her up," he said with a grin.

They rolled forward to the end of the runway and Mo announced his intention to take off over the radio. There was no response.

"Is anyone listening?" Alex asked.

Mo shrugged. "Probably not until we get to Columbia."

He revved the engine and released the brakes. The small plane accelerated and lifted smoothly into the air.

"That wasn't too bad," Alex said without thinking.

"That's cause you were breathing right."

They climbed to 8,500 feet, and the temperature in the cockpit dropped. Alex put on a sweater and began to relax. It was a clear day and there was nothing to obstruct their view. The countryside from the coast to Columbia was flat and rural. Much of it was farmland devoted to soybeans or corn, but there were also large tracts of trees planted by lumber companies. Alex particularly enjoyed the airborne perspective of the streams and rivers that divided the landscape. A river follows the path of least resistance in seeking a way to the sea, and the twists and turns of waterways were much more apparent from the air than when standing on the ground.

"Do you want to fly it?" Mo yelled over the sound of the engine.

Alex looked at the flight controls in front of her. They were barely moving. Once they were in the air, Mo nonchalantly used a couple of fingers on his left hand to steer the aircraft. Alex had been careful not to touch anything and had kept her feet close to the seat.

"Does that cost extra?" she asked.

Mo smiled. "No, it's on the house. Don't worry about your feet. Just take the control wheel. Try to keep the plane level on the horizon and maintain the same compass heading and altitude."

"Where's the compass?"

Mo pointed to the silhouette of the plane on the directional gyro.

"That's all?" she asked.

"Yeah. Just try not to overcompensate. It doesn't respond like a car. Everything is a delayed reaction. Just keep it on this heading."

Alex reached forward and took the controls. Everything was fine for the first fifteen seconds, but then the plane shifted slightly to the left. She gradually corrected and waited. The plane tilted farther to the right than it had been to the left. She moved the controls a little bit more. The plane was gently rocking back and forth in the air. Alex laughed.

"Take it back. If we keep this up, we'll pass over both Columbia and Atlanta."

Mo took the controls and brought the plane level. "Not a bad effort. You didn't lose altitude."

"It's a finer touch than I thought. Don't have a heart attack. I'm not ready to solo."

The pilot put his hand to his chest. "I've got a few more flights in here before I go in for another triple bypass."

Alex wondered if he was telling the truth. As they approached Columbia, Mo called approach control. Within a few minutes, Alex spotted the state capitol building and the stadium where the University of South Carolina played its home football games. On Saturday afternoons in the fall it would be filled with garnet and black. Small hills began to dimple the landscape as they continued toward the northwestern corner of the state. Many people from Charleston and the coastal areas thought the rest of South Carolina was devoid of personality. Alex generally agreed.

Greenville shared an airport with Spartanburg. Its official name was the Greenville-Spartanburg International Airport, but it didn't serve foreign nations, only other states like Georgia and North Carolina. Air traffic was light, and they were cleared by the tower to descend to the runway. Mo set the plane down as casually as a farmer dropping a disk harrow in spring soil. There was one bump, and then they quickly slowed down.

"Be sure to check the overhead bin for your personal belongings and don't unbuckle your seat belt until we reach the terminal," he said with a grin. "There won't be anyone available inside the concourse to direct you to your next flight because we don't have any other employees. I hope you had a pleasant trip."

Alex smiled. "It was fine. I've never flown in a small plane before."

"Somehow that doesn't surprise me. When are you going back?"

"I don't know my schedule. I'm going to see someone at the hospital."

"Let me know if I can fly you in the future. You need a few more lessons before we practice recovering from stalls and spins."

They taxied near the terminal, and Alex climbed out. By the time she reached the main building, Mo was already moving back toward the runway.

Still questioned me the story of my life.
OTHELLO, ACT 1, SCENE 3

RENA ARRIVED AT the ICU waiting area around 9:30 A.M. after a few hours of fitful sleep at a nearby hotel. She recognized several familiar faces from the night before, but her father-in-law's wasn't among them. Ezra Richardson had finally arrived at the hospital after Rena met with Dr. Kolb at 2 A.M. Usually in total control of himself and those around him, Ezra was obviously disoriented and struggling to come to terms with the terrible news about his younger son. Rena repeated her rote version of the accident and gave a summary of the doctor's gloomy assessment of Baxter's condition. However, when Rena suggested the merciful thing to do might be to terminate life support, the older man's eyes blazed, and she beat a hasty retreat while he stayed at the hospital. She hoped that after her father-in-law heard Baxter's prognosis directly from the doctors he would see the situation in a different light.

Rena approached a perky young woman who was monitoring ICU visitation.

"I'm Rena Richardson. How is my husband, Baxter, doing this morning?"

The young woman picked up a clipboard, read down a list, and flipped it over. A puzzled look came over her face. Rena's heart skipped a beat as the truth hit her. Baxter had died during the night, and they'd moved him from ICU to the morgue. The young woman started over at the top of the list. Rena was both ecstatic and upset. She was glad that Baxter had breathed his last, but mad at her father-in-law for not notifying her. It was the height of rudeness for Ezra not to leave her a message on her cell phone that Baxter had died. It was already midmorning, and she needed to get busy with the funeral arrangements. She would let him know how she felt as soon as she saw him.

"Here it is." The young woman interrupted the flight of Rena's thoughts. "I missed him the first time."

"Oh, he's alive?" Rena asked.

"Yes. Do you want to see him? I can let you go right back."

"Is anyone with him?"

"I just came on duty, but if he had a visitor with him, it would be marked on this sheet."

"Okay."

Rena didn't want to spend pointless time viewing Baxter as the machines put him through his morning paces, but expectations demanded at least a cameo appearance. When she entered room 3824, it was exactly as she'd left it the previous night. Baxter hadn't moved a millimeter. Even the IV bag seemed to be at the same level. It was a world of suspended animation. Rena didn't linger at Baxter's bedside, but stepped into the small bathroom to inspect her appearance.

There were dark circles under her eyes from lack of sleep. The knot on the side of her head was hidden by her hair, but it was tender to the slightest touch and had made it hard to sleep on her left side. The scratches on her face were slightly inflamed. She hadn't covered them with makeup. They were her red badges of courage, the proof that she had scrambled heedless of her own safety into the rocky ravine to try to save her husband.

After a final glance at Baxter, Rena returned to the waiting room, where a familiar silhouette was sitting in a chair, reading a newspaper. She stopped and stared in disbelief. It wasn't Ezra Richardson. It was the hideous detective who had told her Baxter was alive. Giles Porter turned, and before Rena could avoid his gaze, their eyes met. The detective stood and casually walked over to her.

"I was able to contact your father-in-law," he began. "Has he arrived?"

Rena did her best to be civil. "Yes, thanks for calling him. He came in late last night. He'd been out of town on a business trip and had to fly in from Baltimore."

The detective nodded. When he did so, it gave Rena a clearer view of the scar on the top of his head. It grew redder as it progressed across his skull and then split into smaller, pale tendrils.

Rena felt suddenly dizzy and had to sit down. She closed her eyes for a second.

"Are you okay?" the detective said.

Rena didn't look up. "Uh, very tired."

The detective sat down beside her. When he did, Rena could hear the clink of metal against the wooden arm of the chair. She didn't know if it was handcuffs or a gun.

"How is your husband this morning?" Porter asked.

"No change," Rena managed. "He's in a coma and on life support. He may be totally paralyzed."

The detective shook his head in sympathy. "Do the doctors think he's going to recover?"

"It's fifty-fifty. I haven't talked to them this morning. I was supposed to be here for a meeting." Rena looked at her watch. "They may be waiting for me in one of the consultation rooms. I'd better be going."

When Rena stood, the detective did, too, and blocked her path.

"I don't want to hold you up too long," he said, "but I have a few more questions for you."

Rena felt her face flush. "I told you everything I know yesterday."

The detective didn't move out of the way. "It's been my experience that the day after a tragedy people remember more information because the immediate shock has subsided."

Rena shook her head. "I'm still in shock and having you harass me doesn't help."

Porter gave her a patient look. "Mrs. Richardson, I'm not trying to harass you, but I have to do my job when there has been a death or serious injury in Mitchell County. If you can answer a few questions, I'll be on my way."

Rena was tired of the detective's badgering and considered brushing past him, but in the split second she had to decide what to do next, she remembered that Giles Porter was a man. Manipulating men was not new to her. She turned from sour to sweet.

"Okay," she replied with a tired smile. "I'll talk to you for a few minutes. I'm sorry I've been rude."

Porter put his hands in his pockets. "No need to apologize. You have every reason to be upset."

The detective looked past Rena as if searching for the right question. When he spoke, it was on the same topic he'd asked her about before.

"Tell me what happened at the waterfall."

Rena rewound the memory tapes she'd developed during the hike away from the falls. The tapes were still intact, and her words tracked verbatim what she'd told Porter the previous day. Porter listened impassively. When Rena finished what she thought was a satisfactory answer, he asked another question. Rena's resolve to be sweet began to melt under the heat of the detective's probing. Every answer led to another question. Rena began to fidget.

———

Alex got off the elevator. A sign on the wall directed her to the ICU waiting area. She pushed open the door and saw an expensively dressed young woman with blonde hair talking in an animated way to a medium height, pudgy man wearing a brown, wrinkled suit and green tie. Alex walked quickly over to her.

"Excuse me," Alex said, "are you Rena Richardson?"

Startled, the woman shifted her eyes from the man to Alex.

"Yes."

Alex extended her hand. "I'm Alexia Lindale, a lawyer with Leggitt & Freeman in Santee. I'm here to help you."

"You're my lawyer?" Rena asked.

Alex repeated her instructions. "Our firm represents you and your husband's family. We learned about the accident, and I came up to help."

Alex turned toward the bald man and saw the scar on his face. The detective spoke first.

"Ms. Lindale, I'm Detective Giles Porter with the Mitchell County Sheriff's Department. I made the initial contact with Mrs. Richardson and helped transport her to our local hospital for medical care while a helicopter flew her husband here to Greenville."

Alex shook the detective's outstretched hand.

Rena turned toward Porter and spoke with an edge in her voice. "That's enough questions for now. My husband is on life support, and I have some difficult decisions to make without the distractions of being interrogated. I told you everything I know yesterday."

"I'm not interrogating you, Mrs. Richardson," Porter said in a slow voice. "But I have a few more questions to ask before I file my incident report."

Rena shook her head. "You've already asked a lot more than a few questions. I need a break. I can't think straight."

Hearing the tension in Rena's voice, Alex stepped in. "Could it wait, detective? I haven't had a chance to talk with my client."

The detective touched the place over his left eye where his scar began. "I'd like to finish my investigation so I don't have to make another trip. I only have a few more questions."

"That's what he always says," Rena interjected.

"What kind of questions?" Alex asked sharply.

"About Mrs. Richardson's conduct after her husband fell."

"I can't remember anything else," Rena said. "I told you everything yesterday and again today. Leave me alone! I don't want you in my face every time I turn around!"

"I'm not trying to be difficult, Mrs. Richardson, but I have a job to do."

Alex spoke. "Is she under criminal suspicion?"

Porter looked directly at Rena when he answered. "Maybe."

Rena's face went white. "No!" she shouted.

Alex stepped back. The hospital worker sitting at the desk glanced up. Porter didn't budge.

"You can't do this to me!" Rena cried out. She grabbed Alex's arm. "Please, help me!"

Since totally focusing her practice on divorce cases, Alex hadn't handled any criminal cases, but she knew Rena Richardson was in no condition to answer questions about anything. She touched Rena's shoulder.

"Please, go sit down. I'll be with you in a minute."

Rena fled across the room to a chair where she buried her head in her hands.

Alex faced the detective. "What's going on here?" she demanded.

"Just doing my job. Mrs. Richardson made statements about the incident that are inconsistent with the facts."

"What kind of statements?"

"I'd rather not go into that right now," Porter responded dryly. "I don't see any benefit to talking to you if your client isn't going to talk to me."

Alex felt a flush of anger at the man's attitude. Porter gazed back impassively.

Alex spoke in a soft but intense voice. "I'm going to advise my client not to answer any more questions at this time. She's obviously distraught. If you give me your card, I'll call you later so we can discuss the matter more fully."

Porter took out a card and handed it to her. "Suit yourself. But I want to talk to her, not you."

Alex handed the card back to the detective. "Then here's your card. I won't be calling you. There's no sense in wasting our time in a pointless discussion."

Porter shook his head. "No, keep it. May I have one of yours?"

Alex passed one to him. He glanced at it and put it in his shirt pocket.

"You know, Mrs. Richardson has been hiking in those woods all her life," Porter said. "She didn't tell me, but I found out that her maiden name was Callahan. After her mother died, she lived with her stepfather in a bend in the road called Nichol's Gap."

Alex didn't respond. There was something inherently accusatory in the way the detective spoke. He made it sound as if growing up in Nichol's Gap with the name Callahan was a criminal act. Alex could understand why Rena Richardson didn't want to talk to him.

"I hope your client's husband makes it," he continued. "He took quite a fall. He's lucky to be alive. If he comes around, I'd like to talk to him."

"That will be up to him."

Porter straightened his tie, but it remained crooked. "I hope you'll suggest that the family keep a close watch on Baxter. He's been through a lot. He may be in a coma now, but the human body has a remarkable way of coming back. I'd hate for anything to stand in the way of a full recovery."

"I'm sure the family will see that he receives the best medical care available."

Porter nodded. "Of course. I'm sure they will."

As soon as the detective left, Alex went over to Rena. She was still crying.

"I'm sorry about that," Alex said.

Rena spoke through sobs. "That horrible man has been bothering me ever since they found me on the road in the forest. I know I shouldn't have yelled, but the past twenty-four hours have been a nightmare, and I couldn't take it anymore. " She dried her eyes. "What did you tell him?"

"To leave you alone. You can tell someone like him the truth, and he would make you think it was a lie. I can see why he upset you."

Rena looked up and dried her eyes with a tissue. "That's exactly how I felt. I told him exactly what happened, but he wanted to twist it around and make me think I was lying." Rena's chest heaved one more time, and her voice trembled. "Is he going to arrest me?"

Alex wanted to reassure the young woman without making any guarantees. "I don't know, but I think he's just fishing for information. Was anyone else with you and Baxter on the hike?"

"No."

"Did you see other people?"

"No. The trail was deserted."

Alex thought for a moment. "He's suspicious because that's his job, but you probably don't have anything to fear. If he comes back, don't talk to him. He'll just try to twist your words."

Rena rubbed her eyes. "Okay. I'm so glad you came when you did. I need somebody I can trust."

"That's one reason that I'm here."

Alex waited for Rena to regain her composure.

"Has your family been to the hospital?" Alex asked.

"What about my family?" Rena responded sharply.

"The detective said you grew up in this area. He said your maiden name was Callahan."

Rena's eyes grew wide in fear. "Did he contact my stepfather?"

"He didn't say. He mentioned a place called Nathez Gap."

"Nichol's Gap. It's where I lived until I was fifteen." Rena put her head back down in her hands. "My mother died when I was eleven, and my stepfather is a horrible man. I haven't seen him in years. I didn't even let him know I was getting married, and he doesn't know where I live."

Alex could imagine a few things that would make Rena want to sever all contact with her stepfather. She looked at the young woman with increased sympathy.

Rena's tears threatened to return. "Do you think the detective will tell my stepfather where I am?"

"I'll give him a call and tell him not to reveal any information about you. If need be, I'll seek a court order for your protection."

Rena sniffled. "Thanks." She wiped her eyes again and then looked up with a new fear in her eyes. "Don't tell Baxter's father either. Baxter made up a story about my past so that his father would accept me. It would be a disaster if he knew the truth."

Alex hesitated. One of the land mines she'd feared was at her feet. She chose her words with care.

"Everything between us is confidential and protected by the attorney-client privilege. That means I won't repeat it to anyone. Your father-in-law is also one of our clients, but the information about your family is not related to our representation, so I won't repeat it to him or anyone in my firm."

Rena sighed. "Okay. That makes me feel better."

Alex wanted to ask more questions but stopped. Rena Richardson's present stress was bad enough without dredging up additional memories from the past. She took out the folder with the documents she'd brought from Santee but left it unopened in her lap. Rena needed space, and Alex gave it to her. The young woman sat with her eyes closed for several minutes while Alex kept guard. Rena opened her eyes.

"How long are you going to stay?" Rena asked.

"I don't have a set schedule. Do you know when Mr. Richardson is coming to the hospital?"

"No, we didn't talk about it last night. He was so upset when I mentioned unplugging Baxter's life support that I left the hospital. I don't want to lose my husband, but when I see him lying in bed kept alive by machines, it seems cruel not to let him go."

"What did the doctors tell you about his condition?"

"The one in charge told me that Baxter was paralyzed from the neck down and might not wake up."

From the forlorn look on Rena's face, Alex decided that Ken Pinchot's snide remark about Rena wanting to end her husband's life to collect a lot of money didn't have the ring of truth.

"Do you remember the doctor's name?" she asked.

"It was Dr. Kolb, or something like that. I think he's a neurosurgeon."

"Did Mr. Richardson hear this?"

"No, but I told him, and it made him mad. I'm afraid he will try to intimidate me about what to do, but Baxter is my husband."

Alex nodded. "We'll discuss everything when he gets here. Maybe I can help the communication between the two of you."

"He should be here soon. He knew the doctors wanted to meet with us this morning."

"It might be good if I could talk to him beforehand. Do you have his cell phone number?"

"Yes. I can't use my phone in the hospital, but they will let you call from the desk."

Alex wrote down the number and walked over to the attendant's desk and obtained permission to use the phone. She faced Rena as she dialed the number. Before the phone started to ring, the door opened and a man entered the room with a grim look on his face. He walked directly toward Rena. Alex put the receiver back in its cradle.

Ezra Richardson had arrived.

11

No one can serve two masters.
MATTHEW 6:24

HE WAS OF medium height, in his late fifties, with thinning but carefully groomed brown hair liberally sprinkled with gray. Alex immediately noticed his eyes. They were dark and intense, giving him the type of expression that communicated a person who was used to getting his own way. He was wearing a casual shirt and dark slacks. Alex moved toward Rena as he spoke.

"How is he?" Ezra asked Rena. It was more of a demand than a question.

"The same," Rena answered.

Alex stepped forward and cleared her throat. "Mr. Richardson, I'm Alexia Lindale with Ralph Leggitt's office. I flew up this morning."

Ezra faced Alex and gave her a quick inspection.

"Why didn't Ralph come?" he responded sharply. "I talked to him this morning and thought he would make the trip himself. What is he doing that is more important than helping my family at a time like this?"

Alex stepped back before the unforeseen attack. She'd thought Ralph Leggitt had told Mr. Richardson that she was coming. Alex didn't have a complete answer she could give in front of Rena and inwardly fumed at her boss for putting her in such an awkward position.

"Uh, I'm sure he tried to reach you. The partners met this morning and decided it would be best for me to come." She held out the folder she'd taken from her briefcase. "I've brought the documents that affect Baxter's care. I'm sure there is a conference room where we can talk."

"What documents?" Rena asked. "Baxter wanted me to make decisions about his care."

Alex stepped back toward the attendant. "Is there a small conference room we can use? Maybe the place where doctors talk with family members?"

"Go out in the hall and turn right. There are two rooms on the left. Use either one of them."

Before either Ezra or Rena could protest, she led the way into the hall and down the corridor to a wooden door with a small sign that identified it as "Family Consultation Room A." Alex flipped the sign underneath to "occupied," and they went inside. It was a windowless space, smaller than Alex's office and bare except for a simple table surrounded by six chairs. Alex sat at the end of the table with the unopened manilla folder in front of her. Ezra and Rena positioned themselves on opposite sides of the table.

Alex spoke. "Before we get started, I need to tell you that I'm here to help both of you." Facing Ezra, she said, "Mr. Richardson, our firm does a lot of work for you, and we've also provided legal services to Baxter and Rena."

Ezra Richardson grunted. "I want you to tell Ralph Leggitt that I don't appreciate him sending a second-string lawyer up here. This is a lot more serious situation than some of the business deals he's dropped everything to attend."

"I like Alexia," Rena blurted out. "She's already helped me a lot."

"Really?" Ezra asked with raised eyebrows. "Am I coming in late to this discussion? I'd like to know what's already been covered."

"Please, Mr. Richardson," Alex interjected. "We haven't discussed anything about the documents your son signed. I waited for you."

"Alright, let's have it," the older man said. "Explain the durable power of attorney to Rena. Ralph told me it took priority over everything else Baxter signed."

"What are you talking about?" Rena asked.

Alex was determined to be systematic. "There are several relevant documents. I'll start with the most recent ones."

Alex pulled out the declaration of desire for a natural death. In her haste to leave Santee, she'd forgotten to make extra copies. It was awkward reading the words upside down and positioning it so both Rena and her father-in-law could see it.

"This form has the highest priority because it indicates Baxter's own wishes. If he's in a persistent vegetative state or permanently unconscious, he does not want to be kept alive and requests that all feeding tubes and IVs be withdrawn. To trigger this document two doctors must certify that Baxter's condition is irreversible and death will occur within a short time once life-sustaining procedures are disconnected."

"Why is my name on it?" Rena asked.

Alex pointed to a line at the end of the document. "Baxter had the right to designate someone to revoke the declaration. He chose you."

"How do you revoke it?" Ezra asked.

"Anything that shows intent to do so. It can be torn up or crossed out with a pen."

Ezra pushed the papers toward Rena.

"We'll start there. It's time to cancel this absurd thing. Tear it up, Rena."

Rena picked up the declaration. The young woman's hand trembled, and the papers shook slightly.

"No," Alex began. "That won't—"

"Keep out of this!" Ezra barked at her. "This is none of your business. Rena, do it now!"

Alex persevered. "It won't do any good to tear it up. The original is at our office in Santee. This is only a copy."

"What incompetence!" Ezra sputtered. "How did you expect to get anything accomplished without the right documents?"

Alex remained calm. "I'm here to explain everything to both of you. Tearing up the copy is ineffective, but Rena could sign a statement revoking the declaration if that's what she wants to do."

"Alright," Ezra responded. "Write something legal on a sheet of paper and let's do it. This meeting will not go forward until Rena cancels this insane death wish. I don't believe Baxter knew what he was doing when he signed this ridiculous piece of paper."

Rena looked at Alex. "Should I do what he says?"

Alex kept her voice soft. "You can, but you don't have to."

Ezra's face grew red. "Don't let this lawyer convince you to ruin your future! If you want to be a part of this family, you'll do as I say."

"I'm not sure," Rena said. "Baxter and I talked about this and decided what we wanted to do. My paper says the same thing."

"It was a mistake. Don't make another one," Ezra said grimly. "Be careful how you choose, Rena. It will have consequences for the rest of your life."

Rena dropped her gaze and stared at the table. Alex wanted to re-enter the conversation but couldn't come up with a way to do it. They sat in silence. Finally, Rena spoke in a steady voice.

"I'd like to hear everything before I make up my mind. Please give me a few minutes to understand the whole picture. I'll listen to everything you want to say. I only want us to do the right thing."

The angry expression on Ezra Richardson's face lost its edge. Rena might be from a backwoods bend in the road, but she demonstrated an amazing knack for split-second diplomacy with her high-powered father-in-law. Alex wanted to cheer.

"Alright," Ezra grunted. "Get on with it."

Alex didn't hesitate. "As I mentioned, two treating physicians must concur that life support is futile. Until that happens the provisions of the declaration don't apply. Rena mentioned that one of the neurosurgeons doesn't hold out much hope that Baxter will wake up. At least one more doctor would have to concur. I suggest that all the physicians involved in Baxter's care be consulted so we can get a consensus opinion."

Rena frowned, but Alex continued. She took out another bundle of papers.

"Baxter also signed a health care power of attorney selecting Rena to make medical decisions if he was unable to do so. There are several options to choose. The one he initialed states: *GRANT OF DISCRE-TION TO AGENT. I do not want my life to be prolonged nor do I want life-sustaining treatment to be provided or continued if my agent believes the burdens of the treatment outweigh the expected benefits. I want my agent to consider the relief of suffering, my personal beliefs, the expense involved and the quality as well as the possible extension of my life in making decisions concerning life-sustaining treatment.*"

"Expense is not an issue," Ezra said. "He has great health insurance, and we can pay for the best care in the world."

Alex waited for Rena to respond, but she didn't say anything, so she continued. "There is also a statement regarding tube feeding. *With respect to Nutrition and Hydration provided by means of a nasogastric tube or tube into the stomach, intestines, or veins, I wish to make clear that I do not want to receive these forms of artificial nutrition and hydration, and they may be withheld or withdrawn under the conditions given above.*"

Alex looked up from the paper.

"Before the health care power of attorney becomes effective, two physicians have to certify that a patient can't act on his own. Baxter is in a coma so there's no question that his condition satisfies the requirements for Rena to step in and direct Baxter's medical care."

"What are the conditions?" Rena asked.

"The first part I read about the burdens of treatment outweighing the expected benefits. The agent named in the power of attorney has the authority to terminate food and fluids."

"That's what I want—," Rena began.

Alex shook her head. "Except there is another power of attorney signed by Baxter before you were married. It is a durable power of attorney, which grants your father-in-law extensive powers that were not terminated by your marriage or Baxter's current incapacity. The law in South Carolina gives a person named in a durable power of attorney a higher priority than the holder of a health care power of attorney unless the health care power of attorney contains a clause revoking any previous grant of authority."

"Huh?" Rena asked.

"The health care power of attorney doesn't specifically cancel the control over medical treatment Baxter gave to his father in the power of attorney signed before your marriage."

Rena's face was ashen. "You mean, I can't do what Baxter wanted? But he's my husband."

"Baxter's wishes in the declaration of desire for a natural death must be considered, but Ezra's power of attorney overrides the one you obtained."

Ezra picked up the declaration and held it out toward Rena.

"Does that answer your questions? I refuse to let a group of doctors decide whether Baxter will live or die. I listened to them when my wife was dying and regretted it ever since. As long as there is a heartbeat, I want to fight for my son's life. I'm asking you to revoke this piece of paper that is hanging over Baxter's head."

Rena closed her eyes for several seconds. Alex wondered if she was praying. She opened her eyes, picked up the durable power of attorney, and looked directly at her father-in-law.

"Before I answer, I have a question for you. Are you willing to tear up the power of attorney that gives you so much control over my husband's life? If Baxter could speak, that's what he'd ask you to do."

Ezra sputtered for a moment before saying, "No, of course not."

"Then that's my answer, too."

It was a stalemate. Alex glanced from Ezra to Rena. The young woman broke off eye contact with her father-in-law and faced the lawyer.

"What now?" she asked.

"I suggest we meet with the doctors," Alex said. "I understand there was to be a meeting this morning anyway."

Ezra abruptly pushed his chair from the table. "We can talk to them, but I will not consent to any efforts to end life support."

Alex didn't argue. There was no benefit in expressing a lay opinion about Baxter's medical status. His condition sounded critical enough to trigger the declaration, but Alex didn't want to antagonize Mr. Richardson by making an observation that might prove wrong.

"Let's go back into the waiting room and try to find out when we can have a meeting," she suggested.

Rena immediately got up and walked to the door. Her father-in-law lagged behind. Alex didn't know whether to rush after Rena or stay with Ezra. The older man touched her arm.

"What is your plan? How are you going to take care of this situation?"

Alex glanced toward the door. Rena was not in sight. Alex spoke in a low voice.

"Mr. Leggitt asked me to come to Greenville because I spend most of my time representing women in divorce cases. He thought I would be able to communicate with Rena and help your family get through this crisis. I think your daughter-in-law trusts me."

Ezra moved so close to Alex that she could feel his breath on her cheek when he spoke. "Should I trust you?" he asked.

Alex tried to step back, but there was no place to go. "Yes. I'm not here trying to take sides. That wouldn't be ethical. My job is to be a mediator."

Ezra spoke in a low but intense voice. "In the midst of mediating remember that my son's life is at stake, and I don't want to see him die. Your boss told me the durable power of attorney gives me control, and I intend to use it in every way possible. If I think you're trying to help Rena terminate Baxter's life support, you'll regret it. Is that clear?"

"Yes, sir."

Ezra backed away and Alex slipped past him into the hallway. Rena was not in sight. When Alex entered the ICU waiting area, Rena was talking to the attendant at the table.

"Most doctors have already made their rounds this morning," Rena said. "So it may take a while to get them together, but she's going to work on it and let us know in a few minutes."

"I'm going to step outside and smoke a cigarette," Ezra said. "Don't begin any discussion until I return."

"Yes, sir," Alex responded. "I need to go outside myself. I'll be back in a few minutes."

Alex wanted to escape the pressure she felt in the presence of Ezra and Rena and analyze several legal questions that had come to mind while the Richardsons were sparring with one another. She needed to get alone and think. She walked out the front door of the hospital and paced up and down the sidewalk. Ezra was nowhere in sight.

Ezra and Rena were her responsibilities, but she also found herself thinking about Baxter. She didn't know Baxter Richardson, but the profound sadness of his condition was inescapable. Alex wasn't sure what she thought about terminating life support. Ending pointless suffering for someone you love made sense. Wanting to hold on to a son you'd thought would outlive you was hard to condemn.

On the horizon loomed several dark clouds that held the threat of legal thunderstorms. If Rena refused to revoke the declaration of desire for a natural death, Ezra might use the durable power of attorney to transfer all Baxter's property out of his son's name and decimate Rena's inheritance. Only Baxter's death would end his father's control. In response, Rena would have an equitable argument that Ezra's use of the durable power of attorney should be enjoined by a court because Baxter's last will and testament gave all his estate to his wife.

Alex took out her cell phone. She needed to call Ralph Leggitt for direction. She dialed the number, and the morning receptionist answered.

"This is Alex. Is Mr. Leggitt in his office?"

"Yes, but he's on the phone."

Alex hesitated. "Could you slip him a note that I need to talk to him immediately?"

"You know he hates that sort of thing."

"This is a real emergency."

"Okay, but if I get chewed out, you'll have to do something nice for me."

The receptionist put Alex on hold for a couple of minutes before she came back on the line.

"He put his hand over the receiver and told me to tell you he was talking to Ezra Richardson. Then he wrote something on a scrap of paper and gave it to me."

"What does it say?"

"It says, 'E.R. is the client.'"

Alex swallowed. "Okay. Thanks."

12

Deceive not thy physician, confessor, nor lawyer.
GEORGE HERBERT

MULLING OVER HER new marching orders, Alex returned to the waiting room and sat next to Rena, who was gingerly touching her left
temple.

"My head is killing me," Rena said. "I hit it on a rock when I was trying to help Baxter. Do you have anything for pain?"

Alex took a small bottle of pills from her purse and handed it to Rena,
who took out two and swallowed them without water.

"I wish I could trust my father-in-law, but I can't," Rena continued.
"He didn't want Baxter to marry me. Before I came into the picture, he
had picked out a skinny girl from a rich family in Georgetown as his
future daughter-in-law. Do you think I did the right thing in refusing to
tear up the paper in the conference room?"

Alex avoided a direct answer to the question and focused on what lay
ahead.

"The only thing that matters now is to meet with the doctors and
find out what they recommend about Baxter."

"What if they don't agree?"

Alex didn't answer. She had considered that exact scenario while riding the elevator up to the ICU floor. It was another reason why the same
lawyer would likely have trouble representing both Ezra and Rena. A disagreement among the doctors could spill over into a court fight between
the family members and a battle royal of expert witnesses with the comatose Baxter in the middle.

Alex needed to tell Rena about the pitfalls ahead of them, but the young woman was fragile, and Alex didn't want to hurt her. She searched for the right words. Abandoning women in distress cut against the grain of Alex's nature. Before she could decide how to begin, Ezra returned to the room. He caught Alex's eye and gave her a knowing nod.

"Any word on a meeting?" he asked.

"No," Rena answered. "You know how doctors are. Everybody has to wait for them. We could be here for hours."

Alex decided to lobby for faster action. She walked over to the desk and waited while the young woman there finished talking on the phone. The attendant spoke first.

"That was Dr. Berman on the phone. They plan to discuss the patient's status in Conference Room B in a few minutes."

"Thanks."

Alex relayed the news.

"Good," Ezra said. "I'm going to the conference room." He looked at Alex. "Would you like to join me?"

Alex hesitated. "I'll be there in a minute. I need to discuss something with Rena."

Ezra's face showed his irritation, but he turned and left.

Alex had to tell Rena that she wouldn't be able to represent her. Losing Alex as a lawyer would be a minor hit compared to the other blows that had rained down on the young woman in the past twenty-four hours.

"Rena, do you remember when I told you that my law firm sent me here to represent the Richardson family?"

"Yes. And I should have thanked you more for stepping in to help me," Rena said gratefully. "I don't know what I would have done without you this morning. You didn't take sides, but with you in the room, I could think about what to do without being afraid of Baxter's father. He tried to intimidate me, but it would have been much worse if you hadn't been sitting at the table. I appreciate it very much."

"Uh, yes, but—"

The young woman at the desk called across the room. "The doctors are waiting for you in the consultation room."

Rena stood. "Let's go."

Alex found herself looking at Rena's back. Picking up her briefcase, she followed.

———

Consultation Room B was larger than Room A. Rena's mouth was dry as she walked down the hall, and she stopped for a quick drink of water from a fountain. She followed Alex into the room. Five physicians with their names embroidered on their white coats were examining an image on a large light box on the far wall. Ezra was in the middle of the crowd. When Rena and Alex came into the room, everyone turned around and conversation ceased. A middle-aged doctor with dark hair, a large nose, and bushy eyebrows stepped forward and introduced himself to Rena and Alex. To Rena, he looked more like a comic book character than a physician.

"I'm Peter Berman, one of the neurosurgeons treating Mr. Richardson."

Dr. Berman identified the other doctors in the room. Included in the group was an orthopedic surgeon, a neurologist, a pulmonary specialist, and an internist. After they all sat down at the table, Dr. Berman turned to Rena.

"I believe you met my partner, Dr. Kolb, last night," he began. "He's getting some sleep this morning and couldn't be here. The rest of us have discussed your husband's status and reviewed the results of the tests conducted thus far. At this time he is in a coma due to cerebral edema or swelling of the brain. As I'm sure you know, a coma is an unconscious state; however, not all comas are alike. There are different levels of unconsciousness, and there are recognized guidelines that rate the degree of brain impairment. As soon as he was admitted to the hospital, your husband was evaluated according to the Glasgow Coma Scale. It's a test that gauges reactivity of the eyes, verbal response, and motor control. Each of the three categories is assigned a number based on the level of unconsciousness and degree of dysfunction. A score of fifteen is a mild injury; a score of three is the most serious rating short of death."

Rena listened carefully, waiting for the opportunity to ask the ultimate question.

The doctor opened a folder in front of him. "His initial score was an eight, which is the upper end of a 'severe' head injury."

"Does that mean he's going to die?" Rena asked in a plaintive voice she hoped expressed the proper level of remorse at the prospect of Baxter's imminent demise.

"No."

Rena's face fell.

"And this can change, can't it?" Ezra interjected.

The doctor nodded. "Of course. The intracranial pressure or ICP that induced the coma is unstable. When I checked him this morning, I still gave him an eight even though there might have been a slight deterioration in his involuntary eye response. We are still in the first forty-eight hours since injury—the most critical phase of medical intervention."

Rena tried to keep her expression impassive, but under the edge of the table she was wringing her hands. Like the legalese of the documents Alex had brought from Santee, the convoluted medical terminology was an enemy, not a friend.

"That's why we are primarily focusing on the head injury at this time," the doctor continued. "Unless the ICP is reduced we may lose him, so we have created as controlled an environment as possible. He was breathing on his own when admitted to the hospital, but we put him on a ventilator to regulate his respiration and stabilize his blood pressure. He is receiving medication to diminish ICP, and we have the option of surgery to further lessen the pressure."

"Do the surgery if it will help," Ezra responded and then quickly glanced at Alex. "I can authorize it, can't I?"

The doctor spoke before Alex could answer. "Neither Dr. Kolb nor I recommend surgery at this time. The additional trauma of the procedure might push him over the edge."

"Don't say that!" Rena blurted out.

"I'm sorry, but it's a very serious situation," the doctor continued. "There are no known medications that will shorten the duration of a coma. In fact, we are giving Baxter drugs to make sure he remains temporarily unconscious. Any movement at this point could create more problems."

"What about internal injuries?" Ezra asked.

"That's the good news," Dr. Berman replied. "Apparently, he slid part way down the rockface of the cliff and didn't land on the rocks following a free fall. He has a broken right leg, but it was a clean break and has been set. He has some scrapes and abrasions; however, except for the spine and head injury, no serious internal damage."

"Will the paralysis be permanent?" Ezra asked.

"I've reviewed the situation; however, I'm going to let Dr. Graham, who is a neurologist, address that aspect of your son's condition."

Dr. Graham, a young, handsome, blond-haired doctor with bright, blue eyes turned on the light box, slid a sheet of film into place, and took a retractable pointer from his coat pocket. Rena immediately liked him.

"Let me show you some pictures from the MRI performed last night. This is a view of Mr. Richardson's neck or cervical spine. He has what we call a tetraplegia between the C-4 and C-5 levels of his cervical spine. A tetraplegia is an injury to the spinal cord that results in total loss of all motor and sensory function below the level of injury."

The doctor changed images and pointed to a place where there was obvious misalignment of the vertebrae. Even Rena, who didn't have a good view of the light box, could tell that the spine was damaged.

"This is from a CT scan that gives a better visualization of the bony anatomy of the spine. You can see there is evidence of a cervical fracture at the C-4/C-5 levels. There is also evidence of injury at C-3/C-4; however, the extent of damage is less clear. The location of injury is very important because the nerves that exit the spinal cord at each level control different bodily functions. A tetraplegia between the C-3 and C-4 levels terminates a person's ability to breathe on his own. If Mr. Richardson had suffered the same damage at C-3/C-4 as he did at C-4/C-5, he would not have survived long enough to make it to the hospital. An injury at C-4/C-5 causes quadriplegia, but the patient can usually breathe without permanent need for a ventilator. The difference in status can be measured in millimeters."

Rena inwardly groaned. It wasn't fair. Tiny random movements of Baxter's body as it plummeted over the cliff had been the difference between life and death.

The doctor looked at Ezra. "You asked if his paralysis is permanent. Loss of function does not mean that the spinal cord has been severed. It can be caused by a contusion to the cord or by compromise of blood flow to the injured area. Based on our physical examination and the objective evidence from the MRI and CT scan, the spinal cord is not cut, but the damage is severe. If he survives, the chance of recovering any meaningful use of his arms and legs is not more than 10 percent."

"What about speech?" Rena asked anxiously.

Dr. Berman answered. "That's more difficult to predict. The CT scan of the brain revealed what we suspected. Your husband has a diffuse injury that affects many parts of his brain. Thinking, speech, memory, taste, and other functions could all be affected. We have no clear idea at this time. However, damage to the region that serves one of these purposes doesn't mean total loss of them all. The brain cannot form new cells, but the remaining areas can take over some of the activity of those that are damaged or destroyed."

Rena didn't hide her frustration. "I thought you were going to tell us whether life support should be terminated. I don't want my husband to continue to suffer on a tiny whim that he might get better without any realistic chance that he would be more than a vegetable. Neither of us wanted to be kept alive by machines." She gestured toward Alex. "Our lawyer has a piece of paper Baxter signed that says he wants to die with dignity."

Dr. Berman's eyebrows came together in a clear expression of concern. "We face these situations on a regular basis and have to give advice based on legal standards in documents like the one you mentioned. But we're in the first stages of evaluating your husband's condition and don't recommend termination of life support at this time."

Rena glanced around the room, hoping for signs of disagreement. None surfaced. Even the handsome Dr. Graham offered no support.

"Can you provide everything he needs at this hospital?" Ezra asked. "I'm willing to pay whatever it takes to send him anywhere in the country."

"In terms of critical care, it's better to leave him here," Dr. Berman said. "Our protocol is consistent with any major hospital in the country. Transferring your son to another treatment center would involve too many risks. Down the road, I might suggest a specialized facility but not now."

"Is there anything else that can be done for him?" Ezra asked.

"No. We have to wait and see," Dr. Berman answered. "One day at a time."

After the doctors left, Ezra pushed his chair away from the table and spoke to Rena.

"Dr. Berman wasn't nearly as pessimistic as the neurosurgeon you talked to last night. We're going to beat this thing."

"Did we hear any good news?" Rena asked. She held up three fingers on her right hand and touched each one with the index finger on her left hand. "Baxter is in a serious, life-threatening coma, he's paralyzed from the neck down, and he has unknown, possibly extensive damage to his brain."

Ezra was magnanimous in his temporary victory. "But each day he survives increases the possibility that he'll get better. He's young and in good health. As soon as the doctors let me, I'm going to move him to a place where he can receive the best care available. You need to be more positive." Ezra glanced down at his watch. "Visitation is in a couple of minutes. I'm going back to the waiting room so I can go in to see Baxter. Are you coming with me, Ms. Lindale?"

"No, sir. Since I'm not a member of the family, I don't want to intrude on your time with Baxter. I'll keep Rena company."

Ezra locked eyes with Alex. "Very well. I hope you have a productive talk."

When the older man left the room, Rena put her head down on the table. Everything was crumbling around her. She needed help but wasn't sure where to find it. She heard Alex tapping her fingers on the table. The female lawyer was a fighter. Intuitively, Rena sensed that Alex wanted to come to her aid, but she wasn't sure how to irrevocably win her over and bind her to her cause. Suddenly, in the midst of the darkness behind her eyelids, Rena had an idea. It was so bold she suspected it might work. Rena's best decisions were always made on the spur of the moment.

———

Alex waited. Not sure if Rena was crying, she knew it wasn't a time for an ill-chosen word. If Baxter survived, he would be completely dependent on Rena for the rest of his life, and Alex was certain that taking care of a helpless invalid was not what Rena Callahan signed up for when she walked toward the flower-draped gazebo in her expensive wedding dress. "In sickness and in health" was a nice sentiment for a bride and groom with no fear of tomorrow worse than a common cold. It took on a new meaning when one spouse was as badly injured as Baxter.

"What do you think?" Rena asked in a muffled voice without raising her head.

Alex wasn't sure what she meant. "You heard the doctors. Wait and see. That's all anyone can do."

Rena lifted her head, and Alex could see she wasn't crying, just profoundly sad.

"I'm not sure that's an option," Rena sighed. "I feel like I'm under a death sentence. I can't live like this."

It was a selfish statement, but Alex didn't feel critical because it mirrored her own thoughts moments before. She spoke slowly. "I know the future is difficult to consider, but you have to live one day at a time. It's too soon to know anything for sure. If you let your mind race into all the things that could happen, it will drive you crazy."

Rena looked up at the ceiling and gave a short laugh.

The sound startled Alex. "Did I say something funny?"

Rena's anger and frustration suddenly boiled to the surface, and she banged her fist on the table. "This is not fair!"

Alex quickly glanced toward the door. Ezra had closed it when he left the room. They were alone.

"Situations like this are hard to—"

Rena interrupted her. "You told me that everything I tell you is confidential, right?"

Still holding out hope of a successful mediation for a woman in trouble, Alex couldn't bring herself to completely cut the cord.

"Uh, yes."

"And you want to help me?"

"Yes, if I can."

"Do you want to know what really happened at the waterfall?" Rena asked. "I swore to myself that I'd never reveal the truth, but I've got to talk to you about it."

"Wait, maybe you should—"

Rena leaned forward and spoke in a low, but intense voice. "Baxter tried to push me over the edge of the cliff. That's how I got the cut on the side of my face and the knot on my head." She pulled back her hair so Alex could see the purplish bump. "We fought, and he hit me in the head with a rock. I staggered backward and lost my footing. He grabbed me and tried to drag me to the edge, but I pushed him away with my legs. He lost his balance and fell."

Shocked, Alex asked, "Why would he do that?"

Rena shook her head. "I've been wracking my brain trying to figure it out. Maybe he had a girlfriend and wanted to get rid of me. Maybe he decided that he didn't really love me. I don't know. He'd just taken out a huge life insurance policy on me, but he didn't need to murder me to collect money. Baxter has plenty of money. Unless he wakes up and tells me, I'll never know the answer."

Still stunned, Alex asked, "Why didn't you tell the truth to the police?"

Rena sighed. "I thought he was dead, and it was easier to say it was an accident than explain what really happened. Baxter is from a rich family. If something happened to him, people would accuse me of killing him to get his money. That's why the scar-faced detective bothered me so much. I think he knew I was lying."

Alex studied Rena's face while she talked and couldn't see any obvious sign of deceit. Eye contact was good. No body language that suggested deception. Tone of voice that was fearful but firm. Overall, it was the most coherent the young woman had been about anything since Alex met her.

"Maybe," Alex said, "but now you're the subject of a criminal investigation, and the truth needs to come out. If what you say is true, Baxter committed the crime, not you."

"Do you think the detective will believe me?" Rena asked. "Or my father-in-law? Will he believe that his son tried to kill me?"

Alex's mind raced in three directions at once. There were medical issues about Baxter's care, the danger of criminal charges against Rena, and a possibility the young woman didn't realize—Ezra Richardson could gut Baxter's property by using the durable power of attorney.

"I've got to think this through," Alex said.

"Please, that's what I want," Rena pleaded. "Then tell me what to do."

The two women walked back to the ICU waiting area. Ezra was in Baxter's room, and they sat in a corner by themselves. Alex continued mulling over different aspects of the situation. Baxter's attack at the waterfall made Rena's willingness to end her husband's life understandable. She hadn't spoken in terms of revenge, but at some point Rena might exercise her influence for vengeance. It was a sensitive issue.

Rena interrupted Alex's thoughts. "You won't tell anyone else what I told you about Baxter, will you?"

Alex knew the information was shared with a clear expectation of attorney-client privilege. It was as impossible to undo as unscrambling an egg.

"Yes; however, I won't be involved as the primary attorney in this situation. Mr. Leggitt is the one who handles your family's legal matters."

Rena frowned. "I've never met him and don't want him to know what I told you."

Alex hesitated, but at its core, the privilege was personal to her, not to the law firm.

"Then I won't tell him or anyone else in the firm without your permission."

"Thanks," Rena said with relief. "Like I said. I need someone I can trust."

13

Be still before the LORD and wait patiently for him.
PSALM 37:7

ALEX STEPPED INTO the hallway and called Ralph Leggitt. She tapped her foot nervously on the shiny floor while waiting for the call to reach the senior partner's office.

"What's happening?" Leggitt asked brusquely.

"An uneasy truce. I was able to stick to our first game plan and assist the Richardsons as the family lawyer. They had a few tense exchanges, but there is no open conflict. The doctors are calling the shots."

Alex quickly summarized the discussion of the legal documents and the meeting with the physicians.

"I've been here several hours since we met with the doctors and don't think anything else is going to happen," she concluded.

She stopped talking and listened to silence. Ralph Leggitt was either thinking or preparing to explode.

"Okay, that's fine," he said. "It may not come to war. It sounds like you've done all you can do at this time. Come back to Santee."

"How do I travel?"

"I'll have my secretary hire another private flight. It should be arranged by the time you reach the airport."

Relieved, Alex put her cell phone in her purse. She returned to the ICU waiting area and gave her contact numbers to both Ezra and Rena. As she drove to the airport in her rental car, she decided the best course of action would be for Ralph Leggitt to deal directly with Ezra Richardson. If called upon, Alex could step in and hold Rena's hand, but the Richardsons needed a group of attorneys to advise them. There would be safety in numbers.

The pilot who flew Alex from Greenville to Santee wore a clean white shirt and dark tie. His company owned a bigger plane than Mo Reynolds, and she shared the passenger cabin with two businessmen who were going to play golf at Litchfield the following day. They tried to engage her in small talk, but Alex wasn't interested. She let the roar of the engine silence any attempt at conversation.

It was late afternoon when she landed in Santee, and Alex didn't return to the office. She'd given enough of herself to the cause of Leggitt & Freeman for one day. She drove home and changed into comfortable clothes. Sitting on her screen porch with a glass of wine in her hand, she watched the dance of the marsh grass in the evening breeze. Misha purred in her lap, and Boris lay quietly at her feet. She let the cleansing wind from the ocean wash over her soul.

Rena's secret was a heavy burden. The young woman faced staggering problems, and Alex felt drained by her contact with her. Alex stayed on the porch until the air grew cool. She emptied her glass a second time, but the relief she sought didn't come. Evil had come to her sanctuary, and there was no barricade to keep it out. She went to bed and had fitful dreams without resolution.

The following morning Gwen greeted her in a conspiratorial tone.

"How did it go?"

In the light of a new day, Alex managed a smile. "The sisters held together."

"I knew you wouldn't disappoint me. Is the husband going to make it?"

"Don't know. The first couple of days are the most critical. He passed one hurdle, but his condition is terrible. He's in a deep coma and probably quadriplegic. If he wakes up, there is the possibility of serious brain damage."

"They never give any details on the radio," Gwen said with frustration.

"You know to keep it quiet," Alex reminded.

"Of course," Gwen sniffed. "I know the rules."

Alex leaned against the secretary's desk. "I'm feeling a lot of pressure and don't want to step out of bounds. It's different from the typical situation. The stakes are higher than usual."

Gwen nodded. "Someone's life is hanging by a thread."

"Yes. I guess that's it."

Alex picked up a stack of phone messages from the corner of Gwen's desk and began to leaf through them.

"Did anything horrible happen while I was gone?" she asked.

"No. It was a quiet day. Marilyn Simpson hired the lawyer you suggested. I'll copy the file and send it over to him this afternoon."

"That's good."

"And Barbara Kensington gave me the name of a character witness for her case."

"Who is it?"

Gwen raised her eyebrows. "A minister."

Alex groaned. Clergy and priests uniformly testified about their parishioners in glowing terms that frequently contradicted other evidence so dramatically that the ministers' credibility slid to the bottom of the scale with their testimony ultimately ignored by the judge.

"You know that's no good," she said.

"He's not a preacher. He plays the piano and leads the choir. Barbara says he also does remodeling work on the side."

"A musical Jesus figure," Alex grunted. "Does he walk on water?"

Gwen smiled. "You'll have to ask him. He works at Sandy Flats Church on McBee Road. He's usually there in the late afternoon."

"Do you have a phone number?"

"Only for the church."

"Call and see if I can meet with him this afternoon on my way home. It's not far out of my way."

"Will do. And Bert Nixon called. If I had to guess, he has tickets to a classical music thing in Charleston and wants you to go with him on Saturday night."

Bert Nixon was a successful young stockbroker who thought it worthwhile to invest time in Alex. They'd gone out for dinner twice in the past two months, but Alex wasn't sure she wanted to buy what Bert was offering. She raised her eyebrows.

"That is quite a detailed guess. Are you talking about the woodwind ensemble from Houston that's in town for a couple of performances?"

Gwen grinned. "Hey, you should be flattered. Bert's obviously trying to fit into your mold, so he can spend time with you. He is very polite and friendly when he calls. I like '60s beach music, but if a man like him wanted me to listen to an oboe for a couple of hours, I'd say yes."

Alex took the slip with Bert's phone number on it. "I'll think about it. You know, I leave for France the following day, so it may not work out."

"Don't break his heart without a good reason," Gwen admonished. "Oh, you also have a voice mail from a possible new client."

"Who?"

Gwen resumed her conspiratorial voice. "Eleanor Vox."

Alex's eyes grew wide. Mrs. Vox was a very wealthy older lady from a conservative, well-established family.

"She's getting a divorce?" Alex asked.

"The deputy sheriff served her with the papers while she was playing bridge and drinking tea with her friends. It must have caused a big stink. She's coming in tomorrow."

"Did she tell you any background information?"

"Don't they all? Nothing unusual. Her hubby has a girlfriend young enough to be his daughter. Eleanor found out and confronted him. He said he would straighten up and fly right. The next thing Eleanor gets is the summons from the clerk of court. The complaint was signed before she busted him, so it was already in the works before he promised to repent."

Insuring a steady flow of new business was always at the top of her agenda, so before sorting through her mail or thinking about Bert Nixon, Alex called Eleanor Vox. Mrs. Vox was a stiff upper lip aristocrat who didn't break down in tears. She succinctly answered Alex's preliminary questions and scheduled an appointment for the following morning. It would be a good case. Mr. Vox would probably be able to keep his thirty-six-foot sailboat, but he might have to live on it and put off retirement for several more years. Eleanor should get the house, her diamonds, the newer Mercedes, a hefty alimony check, and all the money her rich father had left her.

Alex spent the rest of the day catching up on her correspondence and returning business-related phone calls. In the back of her mind, she thought about Ezra and Rena and wondered if the Richardson case was going to raise its head and bite her. When she made it past lunch without receiving a summons from Ralph Leggitt to come to his office, she began to relax. At 3 P.M. she buzzed Gwen.

"Am I going to the church? I didn't see it on my calendar."

"Sorry. I forgot to enter it on your computer. It's at four o'clock. The minister's name is Ted Morgan."

Alex continued processing the files piled on her desk until she saw only her blotter. The disturbing feelings she'd experienced after her day in Greenville dissipated by the time she walked out of the office and got in her car. It was a warm afternoon, and she rolled down the windows. As she pulled out of the parking lot, she called Bert Nixon on her cell phone. He wasn't available so she declined his invitation to the concert in a nice way on his voice mail. Bert was okay, and Alex appreciated his willingness to please her, but she wasn't sure the real man underneath was someone who could hold her interest.

The route to the church took her through a cross section of the Santee area. It was a jumbled mix of rich and poor. She passed well-manicured entrances to gated communities built next to concrete block houses with more sand than grass in the front yards. Pockets of poverty were being squeezed out by the spread of prosperity, and those who needed cheap housing were migrating to the western part of the county.

Many of the poorer inhabitants filled low-paying jobs on the coast or at the golf courses. Every morning busloads of workers left for Myrtle Beach where they cleaned motel rooms or washed dishes all day. Others stayed close to home and worked as maids and groundskeepers. Unemployment was low, but underemployment at subsistence wages was rampant. A steady influx of immigrants kept the labor pool overflowing.

Sandy Flats Church was located near the two-lane highway built over what had once been the main thoroughfare along the coast for the Indians and early settlers. Alex turned into the driveway for the church. It was a picturesque building often featured on postcards of local places with historical interest. Two enormous live oak trees stood as sentinels close to the road. The stately trees framed the beauty of the building. The white structure had narrow, stained-glass windows and ornate molding along the rooflines that reminded Alex of a gingerbread house, although not as ornate. Azalea bushes skirted the front of the building, and dune grass surrounded the parking lot.

Alex stopped near the front entrance. A small black sign on an iron post pointed around the corner to the church office. She followed a brick path to a small white building constructed behind the sanctuary and connected to it by a short covered walkway. When she opened the door, a bell gave a quaint tingle, and she entered a small waiting room containing a single green leather chair and a matching sofa. A skinny, middle-aged woman with half-frame glasses and short brown hair looked up from an antique desk.

"May I help you?" she asked.

"I'm Alexia Lindale. I have an appointment with Rev. Morgan."

"About a wedding?"

"I wish," Alex said in an attempt at humor that was immediately lost on the church secretary. "It's about a divorce case. I'm a lawyer."

The woman looked down her nose at Alex. "He's in the sanctuary."

Alex chuckled to herself as she walked between the latticework that served as open walls for the covered walkway to the sanctuary. She suspected there would be further interrogation of Rev. Morgan by the dour-faced woman after Alex left. She went into the foyer through a side door. Her nose immediately caught the smell of well-oiled wood and the slight mustiness that is unavoidable in buildings more than two hundred years old.

Then she heard the music.

Alex stopped and listened. Within a few measures, she knew it was from *The Italian Concerto* by Bach. The sound that traveled through the wide opening between the sanctuary and the foyer had a richness and depth exactly like the recording she'd listened to the previous week.

Bach's genius was undeniable and, when expertly performed, often revealed new facets of intricate beauty far beyond what the composer could have produced on a harpsichord.

Alex loved classical piano music. She'd taken piano lessons as a child but never progressed beyond watered-down versions of Mozart sonatas. However, her limited talent didn't prevent her from developing an enduring appreciation for the scope of the piano's musicality. In law school, she listened to Rachmaninoff while studying casebooks or marking legal outlines with a yellow highlighter. Friends whose musical preferences were popular songs that repeated the same three guitar chords over and over accused her of being stuck-up. Alex was unmoved. She jokingly maintained that the intricacies of classical music prepared the human brain for the complexities of the law. But her real motive had no secondary rationale. She loved music because it was the greatest form of beauty created by mankind. Others might like art or poetry. Alex chose sound.

She set down her briefcase, took a few steps forward, and peeked around the edge of the opening for the sanctuary. A middle-aged man with curly brown hair was sitting in front of a grand piano. His head leaned forward as he bore down on a climactic passage. There was no music on the stand before him. Alex drew back. She had no sense of reverence for a church building but held in awe the sounds coming from the piano. To intrude was out of the question. She sat in a small chair against the wall of the foyer, closed her eyes, and pretended she was in a symphony hall. Barbara Kensington's case could wait.

When the last notes faded, Alex wanted to stand up and applaud. She stepped around the corner.

"Bravo!" she called out. "That was magnificent!"

The man looked toward her. He was wearing a simple blue shirt and blue jeans. He took a pair of glasses from the front pocket of his shirt and put them on.

"May I help you?" he asked.

"I'm Alexia Lindale."

"Ted Morgan. Tell me how you like this."

The pianist launched into a variation on the wedding march that featured an enhanced prelude and extra frills in the bridges between repetitions. Startled, Alex walked down the aisle that separated the two narrow banks of pews. As she drew closer, she saw that the music minister definitely looked more like a musician than a preacher. His slightly disheveled hair was sprinkled with gray, and he had a few permanent furrows in his forehead. He had a finely shaped nose and wore wireframe glasses that gave him a studious look. He cocked his head slightly to the side as he played.

"Would that work?" he asked.

"It's great, but I'm not getting married. I'm a lawyer who needs to talk to you about Barbara Kensington."

Ted tapped the side of his head with his fingers. "Oh, I thought you were the woman who wanted to talk to me about the music for her wedding."

Ted stood and extended his hand. Alex shook it and felt calluses across the top of his palm. She remembered Gwen's comment that the minister also worked in construction.

"Sorry for the misunderstanding," he said.

"My wedding day hasn't come," Alex responded. "But when it does, I know who I want to play the wedding march. I was in the foyer listening to *The Italian Concerto*. I've never heard it performed in person."

"You recognized it?"

"Yes, I was listening to it on a CD several days ago."

The minister nodded in approval. "What did you think of my rendition? I know there needed to be more contrast in dynamics."

Alex shook her head. "I'm not a critic, but I thought it was perfect. How did you learn to play like that?"

"I took lessons and practiced."

Alex laughed. "Me, too, so I know there's more to it than that."

Ted smiled. "There is, but that's a long story."

Alex touched the shiny black top of the piano. "That's quite a piano for a small church."

"It's a Steinway 'B,' a seven-footer built in Hamburg in 1919. It doesn't belong to the church. It's mine."

"It's beautiful. Where did you get it?"

"In Romania."

Alex removed her hand from the piano. "I do have a criticism about the way you played the wedding march. People will be more interested in your playing than watching the bride walk down the aisle. No woman wants to be upstaged at her wedding by a seven-foot piano."

"I can do it straight."

Ted began again and played in a ponderous manner that suggested the music was slightly beyond the upper end of his ability. He stopped and looked at Alex.

"How was that?"

"Too typical. Something in between should work."

"Over the years, I've learned to adapt to a lot of situations." Ted closed the cover over the keyboard.

Alex wanted to ask a follow-up question, but reminded herself why she had come. She sat down, opened her briefcase, and took out a legal pad.

"Can I ask you some questions about Barbara Kensington?"

"Sure."

Forty-five minutes later, Alex left with two sheets of handwritten notes and several question marks in the margins. Ted stayed behind in the sanctuary. He knew the young lawyer was dissatisfied with his answers to some of her questions. He'd refused to follow obligingly the path she'd marked out for him.

"I'll testify about Barbara's strengths as a mother," Ted told her. "But if her husband's lawyer asks me about her weaknesses, I'm not going to cover for her."

"Does the same apply to her husband? Will you talk about his weaknesses, too?"

"If you ask the right questions, and I know the answers."

"Will you appear without being subpoenaed?" Alex asked.

"Yes, but please give me as much advance notice as possible."

"Of course," Alex said efficiently as she put her legal pad in her briefcase and snapped it shut. "Thanks for talking to me. I'll be in touch."

Ted watched the lawyer leave, not knowing how radically he had departed from the stereotypical mold for ministers. To her credit, Alex didn't bristle or bluster when he disagreed with her that the Kensingtons' marriage could be saved with the right combination of willingness to change by both parties and input from a skilled counselor, but he suspected she wouldn't contact him about the court date. He was a loose cannon she wouldn't want rolling around on the deck of her case.

Ted's perspective about divorce was not solely the product of his theological training. Carved on his heart were wounds from the disintegration of his own marriage many years before. His wife had hired a female lawyer who attacked Ted with zest and made his life miserable for several months. The sharp pain of those days was gone, but he still felt an occasional deep ache, and nights were still often lonely no matter how many had passed by in solitude. Intellectually, he believed the love of God filled all voids. In practice, his beliefs and feelings didn't always agree.

The afternoon sun had dipped below the trees, and the sanctuary filled with silence for the evening. Ted heard the church secretary's car drive across the parking lot. The prospective bride who was going to talk to him about her wedding hadn't shown up. He could have been mistaken about the day of her appointment and would have to check the church calendar in the morning. Keeping a detailed schedule was not his strong suit.

Ted sat quietly on the piano bench for several minutes, letting his thoughts meet the spiritual mood of the moment. It wasn't a game of hide-and-seek with God, but there was truth in the admonition to wait patiently for the Lord. The object of Ted's spontaneous playing was not merely to create a pleasant sound within the parameters of music theory. He wanted to play with purpose. Sometimes the notes reflected the desire of his own heart; at others they glorified him to whom all praise is due. But always, Ted played for an audience of One.

The seed of a sound began to vibrate in Ted's spirit. He smiled. A seed was enough. From it could grow the planting of the Lord. His hands touched the keys, and his spirit rode the notes as they soared from a small spot on earth into the limitless expanse of the heavens.

Full well the busy whisper, circling round, conveyed the dismal tidings.
OLIVER GOLDSMITH

ALEX TURNED ON the stereo in her bedroom and put in a compact disk. Listening to Ted Morgan play the piano had put her in the mood for a musical evening. She had an extensive collection of performances by Russian pianists Sergei Rachmaninoff and Ignacy Paderewski. Their early recordings had been digitized and improved through modern technology so that she could listen with greater clarity than a 1960s music lover who owned a stereo system costing thousands of dollars.

Looking through her collection, Alex found the composition by Bach that Ted had played at the church and loaded it into her machine. The pianist on the recording played it slower than Ted, but she liked the minister's interpretation better. Bach was a religious man, and it made sense that someone who worked in a church would have a superior understanding of the composer's true intent.

As she listened, Alex thought about the music minister. Without question, Ted Morgan was a paradox—a man whose remarkable talent lay hidden in Santee like a pearl oyster in tidal mud. Alex was intrigued by him, not in a romantic way, but by the presence of sensitive genius wrapped in a package with callused hands.

She would not ask Ted to come to court. His testimony might prove to be a hindrance to her agenda for Barbara Kensington, and Alex didn't win by taking risks. She strictly adhered to the legal maxim "never do anything that might hurt your case more than it helps it."

Misha pattered up the stairs, jumped onto Alex's bed, and curled up in a furry ball. Boris didn't budge from his cedar bed in a corner of the living room downstairs. The dog's sensitive hearing didn't translate into an appreciation for fine music. His ear was more attuned to the sounds of wild creatures creeping along the ground outside the house or Alex's voice announcing that it was time for a swim.

Alex replaced Bach with Rachmaninoff and closed her eyes while the performer serenaded her with *Rhapsody on a Theme by Paganini, Op. 43*. It was an amazing composition. The complete work contained thirty-four variations, but Alex's favorite was number eighteen, a short but incredibly beautiful melody that took the listener from quiet intimacy to rapturous heights of grandeur. When it was over, she turned off the music and turned on her computer. It was time to do the final research for her upcoming trip to France.

Alex loved to travel; however, her decision several months before to visit the Provence area of southern France had a secondary purpose. She wanted to prove to herself that Jason's ability to hurt her had ended. She wasn't sure how she would feel when she arrived in Marseille, but she was determined that when she left, she would be free from the last emotional links to her former fiancé.

She had located several villages with charming places to stay off the beaten path and narrowed her top choices to four spots where she made reservations. She would be traveling in rural, non-English-speaking areas but knew enough French to avoid starvation and ask for directions.

Time slipped by as she looked at computer-generated pictures of vineyards, horse-drawn carts, and quaint inns. Misha was fast asleep at the foot of the bed. Alex yawned and went downstairs to let Boris go outside for a few minutes. She stood on the deck in the dark and listened to the dog crashing through the underbrush behind the house as he followed an interesting scent. It was comfortable outside. The temperature didn't drop rapidly at night along the coast because of the stabilizing influence of the water. She let Boris romp a few extra minutes before calling him. He came running up the steps.

"What did you find?" she asked.

Panting an unintelligible answer, Boris followed her back into the house. The dog's world of invisible smells offered unique challenges as he thrashed through the marsh. For Alex, the unexplored realm of her emotions awaited her in the picturesque villages of Provence.

———

Needing a break from the tension of the ICU waiting room, Rena spent most of the morning at an expensive spa and salon near her hotel. During a vigorous workout on a treadmill, she ran as fast as she could to escape the mental tormentors that trailed her like hungry wolves. Afterward, she received a massage. As she lay on the table, some of the tension bound in her muscles flowed out of her body for the first time since she and Baxter had hiked to the waterfall. She then sat in a sauna in an effort to let more of the stress caused by her current dilemma seep from her pores. The exercise and massage helped her relax, but the multiple problems she faced from Baxter, Detective Giles Porter, and Ezra were too great for a sauna to solve.

Rena feared Baxter. He was a living corpse whose resurrection could cause her death. Thoughts about Giles Porter made her stomach queasy. The detective might be bluffing about criminal charges, but she'd seen too many crime shows on TV in which evidence from an improbable source cracked an impossible case. Ezra was a shrewd businessman who had the money and connections to harm her.

When she arrived at the hospital, Ezra wasn't there. Instead, she saw Dr. Kolb. The older neurosurgeon, a tall, distinguished-looking man with white hair and kind brown eyes, greeted her as he walked through the ICU waiting area. He was dressed in light green operating room garb.

"How is Baxter?" she asked.

"Come with me into ICU," the doctor replied. "I'll get his chart, so we can talk for a few minutes."

She followed the physician through the door to the ICU nurse's station. Rena could see Baxter's motionless legs through the open door of his room. Dr. Kolb picked up a chart that had already grown to two inches thick and began flipping through it.

"There hasn't been any improvement in his Glasgow Coma Scale rating, which is still at eight. That disappoints me."

Rena quickly quoted language she'd memorized when reading copies of the documents Alex had provided to her before leaving Greenville.

"Does that mean he's in a persistent vegetative state from which he might not recover?" she asked.

The doctor turned toward her with a puzzled look on his face. "No. It's simply too soon to make a judgment about his long-term status, but there is good news. His acute injuries didn't kill him, he has lived through the first twenty-four hours, and we have established a stable environment that will allow the body to regroup. Of course, bad things could still happen."

"What kind of bad things?" Rena asked, trying not to sound hopeful.

"We're guarding against several possibilities. He could have a seizure due to swelling of the brain, and he is at risk of infection that could cause pneumonia."

Rena thought for a moment. "And there's no way to know if he'll ever wake up."

"That's right, and from what we've seen so far, I would be surprised if it happened soon. He would have to fight through the trauma of the injury and the effects of the medication he is receiving. Once we taper off the drug that keeps him sedated, we'll be looking for signs of returning consciousness."

"Can he hear us now?"

"That's debatable. Most people in comas remember nothing, but you should still be careful what you say. Recently, I had a comatose patient who suffered a severe head injury in an automobile accident. Her chances of survival were slim, and while she was unconscious, her family discussed the funeral arrangements in her hospital room. The patient surprised all of us when she woke up a week later and told them she didn't approve of the type of flowers they planned to drape over the casket. Today, she's in a rehabilitation facility. So I recommend that you avoid any negative comments when you're with your husband."

Rena bit her lip in frustration. All the doctors talked in circles and told her things she didn't want to know. She'd hoped Dr. Kolb would be different. The doctor closed the chart and continued.

"He may exhibit activity that looks inconsistent with unconsciousness: sounds, agitation, and slight movements. If he moves his arms or legs, notify someone at the nursing station immediately. Because of the severity of his spinal cord injury, any voluntary or involuntary movement of his upper or lower extremities would be very significant. In the next days and weeks our goal will be to assess more accurately the damage done and whether it's permanent. Then I can answer your questions about the future."

Rena sighed. It was hard to face the possibility that Baxter might have a future.

Dr. Kolb handed the records back to a nurse. "Let the staff know if you need to talk to me or Dr. Berman."

Dr. Kolb turned away, and Rena walked slowly into Baxter's room. She didn't know what to do. Waiting was not an option. The benefits of her self-indulgence at the spa hadn't lasted past her conversation with Dr. Kolb. She could feel the muscles in the back of her neck begin to constrict.

Baxter's appearance revealed no visible change from the previous evening. He was lying on his back with his chest rising and falling in clockwork rhythm. The same tubes circulated fluids in and out of his body. His hair was still parted on the wrong side. Anger against him rose up in her. While she was suffering waves of anxiety and fear, Baxter was oblivious to all the problems he was causing and sleeping peacefully in what Dr. Kolb called a stable environment.

Then Rena had an idea.

She pulled a chair close to her husband's head. There was risk involved, but it provided a bookend to the story she'd planted in Alexia Lindale's mind about Baxter's attack at the waterfall.

"Hi, sweetheart," she began. "It's me."

Baxter showed no sign of hearing. His eyelids didn't flutter. His head remained motionless. Rena reached out and touched her husband's hand. It felt cool and unnatural. She drew her hand back but leaned close to his ear.

"You've had a bad accident. You slipped near the edge of the rocks where we had our picnic. I held the walking stick out to you, but you couldn't hold on and fell over the edge. You had too much to drink, dear. I should have said something but didn't want to ruin our day together. You had an accident. It wasn't anyone's fault."

Rena paused.

"It was an accident. It was an accident," she repeated the words several more times.

She watched closely for any sign of response. Nothing.

"You're in the intensive care unit of a hospital in Greenville. We're doing all we can for you. You have good doctors. Your father is here. Your brother, Jeffrey, should be coming soon."

Baxter's chest rose and fell in obedience to the commands of the ventilator.

"You may have some bad dreams but don't think about them. You've had an accident. That's all."

Rena leaned closer until her lips almost touched Baxter's ear.

"Remember one thing, darling. I love you very, very much. All that matters is our love for each other."

Baxter's head moved slightly. Startled, Rena sat up straight. Maybe Dr. Kolb was right.

Leaning forward, she continued with greater confidence, "Yes. All that matters is our love for each other. It was an accident. It was an accident."

15

But now commandeth all men every where to repent.
ACTS 17:30 (KJV)

ALEX ARRIVED EARLY at her office so she could spend extra time organizing her schedule. She'd written "France!" in large letters across her calendar for the days she'd be gone. Leaving for vacation wasn't as easy as walking out the door with her passport and airplane ticket in her hand. It involved predicting what might go wrong in her cases and trying to postpone any fires until she returned. Judge Garland had granted her a blanket excuse from court in her pending cases as protection against other lawyers filing a sneaky motion while she was out of town.

After lunch, Ralph Leggitt's secretary buzzed her office. "He'd like to see you in his office in fifteen minutes."

Alex glanced at her appointment schedule. It was an hour until her initial appointment with Eleanor Vox.

"Okay. I'll be there in a minute."

She finished dictating a memo and then walked down the hallway. She suspected the only topic on the older lawyer's mind would be the Richardson situation. Alex had survived the trip to Greenville unscathed, but she still believed the situation was a time bomb. There would be an explosion, and she didn't want to be standing within range of the legal shrapnel when it happened.

Leggitt's secretary was on the phone but motioned for her to go inside. The senior partner was sitting behind his desk, signing a stack of checks. He looked up when she entered and skipped any preliminary banter.

"Did Ezra seem satisfied with your help?" he asked.

Alex sat down. "I think so. He may have wanted me to be more partisan on his behalf, but I think in the long run it helped the situation that I didn't come across as his lawyer. Rena trusted me, and that helped avoid a blowup."

"Give me a more detailed summary of everything that happened."

When Alex finished, Leggitt asked, "Did you see Baxter?"

"No, it's family members only, but it's as bad as reported. He is in a coma and probably quadriplegic. The neurosurgeon described the situation as 'wait and see.'"

Leggitt tapped the edge of the desk with his fingers. "Did Rena talk to you about the accident?"

Alex hesitated. She'd not anticipated any questions except about the doctors and Rena's response to the various documents that affected Baxter. She would have to tread carefully.

"She mentioned it briefly."

"Was Ezra there when you talked to her?"

"No. They probably discussed it before I arrived. What did Mr. Richardson tell you?"

"No details, just something about Baxter slipping and falling down a cliff onto some rocks."

"That's what Rena told me."

Leggitt shook his head. "It's a shame."

Alex changed the subject to avoid further probes about Rena. "Don't forget, I'm leaving for France on Sunday and will be gone five days."

"Yes, I saw the e-mail a few weeks ago."

"Since I won't be available, someone else should take over communication with the Richardson family, especially Rena."

Leggitt looked over his glasses at her. "Trying to get out of the case?"

Alex was blunt. "Yes. It still makes me nervous. Rena believes she has an attorney-client relationship with me, yet you made it clear that Mr. Richardson is the client. They were getting along when I left Greenville, but there's no guarantee for the future."

Leggitt put his hands together underneath his chin.

"Rena has to be handled carefully," he said. "Even under current circumstances, if something happens to Baxter, she could end up owning a sizable piece of Ezra's empire."

Alex leaned forward in her chair. "Unless Mr. Richardson uses the durable power of attorney to wipe out Baxter's assets, leaving Rena nothing except insurance proceeds."

"Does she suspect that might happen?" Mr. Leggitt asked sharply.

Alex shook her head. "Not yet. I didn't mention it to her. It would have been contrary to promoting cooperation."

"Good. We don't want her hiring separate legal counsel, and unless an open dispute flares up, we'll maintain the status quo with Rena until you get back."

"Does Ezra accept the fact that Rena has an attorney-client relationship with me?"

"He's satisfied, and so am I."

Alex could tell Leggitt was not going to change his mind about her involvement with Rena.

"Okay. I'll call Rena and let her know that I'm going out of town. Who should she contact while I'm away?"

"Bruce can serve as your backup. Will we have any way to reach you?"

"I'm going to the Provence region in southern France. There may be Internet access in the local inns, but I doubt it."

"Alright," he said. "Let's hope nothing major happens."

"Yes, sir."

Alex left, unaware of the contents of the Richardson subfile on Ralph Leggitt's desk.

Alex had a good meeting with Eleanor Vox. Gwen brought a small pot of tea into the conference room, and except for the topic of conversation, the meeting had the appearance of a young woman visiting with her aunt. Alex kept a box of tissues available in case the tears flowed, but Mrs. Vox had progressed beyond tears to anger mode. The fury of an aristocratic southern lady is as lethal as a poisoned mint julep.

"Hubert is an idiot," the older woman said through tight lips. "I made him stop picking his own stocks years ago. Without my money, he'd still be peddling debit life insurance from a storefront office."

"So, you don't think he's hidden any significant assets?"

Mrs. Vox sniffed. "He only thought he controlled the money in the family. I know ten times more about our financial status than he does. I was willing to stay with him, but just in case, I prepared for civil war."

"I hope you're right," Alex said dubiously. "Did you bring the records I requested?"

Mrs. Vox handed Alex a thick manilla envelope. Alex pulled out the paperwork and quickly glanced through it. It was perfectly organized.

"This is excellent," she said as she continued scanning the information. "This will save me a lot of time."

"Honey," the older woman said, "if born in a different era, I'd be sitting where you are."

Later that afternoon, Alex got in her car to drive home and listened to a recording of Tchaikovsky's *Concerto no. 1 in B-flat Minor.* She thought again about Ted Morgan's prodigious talent. On the spur of the moment, she turned onto McBee Road. Upon reaching the church she parked in the same spot near the front door of the sanctuary. When she entered the foyer, she heard the music.

Alex looked at her watch. It was later than the previous time she eavesdropped on the minister's solitary practice session. As before, she didn't go into the sanctuary but sat in a small chair that had been her concert seat the previous day. On the walls of the foyer were several tarnished plaques listing the names of benefactors long since departed and forgotten by even local residents. Through the opening into the sanctuary came sounds from the soul of a deceased foreign composer whose fame still circled the globe.

It was Rachmaninoff, another Russian whose music she knew well, but it took her a few moments to remember the title. Then she recalled the composition as one of the *Études Tableau,* an intricately beautiful melody interlaced with moments of great tension. Thundering cadences in the lower octaves were answered by brilliant and sumptuous sparkles of crystal clarity in the upper range. At heart it was a characteristically Russian piece whose moments of intense sadness reflected the tragic history of the Russian people. The music spoke of joyful reunions, touched by poignant pain, and although the composer wrote the piece during a different era, the emotions it expressed fit today's world just as well.

When the last note faded, Alex was suddenly nervous. Deciding it would be better to admit her presence than be found out by accident, she looked into the sanctuary.

"Bravo again!" she called out.

Ted Morgan, dressed in stained carpenter's overalls, looked up and squinted. He took his glasses from a pocket in the front of his overalls and put them on.

"Ms. Lindale, come in! I hope another member of the church hasn't filed for divorce."

Alex walked down the aisle and held up her hands. "No briefcase, today. I stopped by, uh . . ." She hesitated, searching her mind for the truth. "Because I hoped you were playing the piano. Is it okay that I eavesdropped?"

Ted gave her the same smile that had set her at ease the day before. "Only if you can name that tune in four hundred notes?"

"It was one of the *Études Tableau* by Rachmaninoff."

Ted nodded in approval. "Ms. Lindale, you get an A in music appreciation. You weren't bluffing when you said you loved classical piano music."

Alex sat down on the front pew nearest the piano. "Call me Alex. I especially like Russian composers and pianists. My mother grew up in St. Petersburg."

"A beautiful city."

Alex's eyes grew wide. "Have you performed there?"

Ted laughed. "Not exactly. I visited two years ago as part of a mission outreach to a summer camp."

"Mission outreach?"

"I helped with a summer camp for children sponsored by a Christian ministry in Florida. I played the piano for the meetings."

"Did you give any concerts?"

"Twice in the evenings I played for the adults. The Russians take great pride in the genius of their composers, so it helped their attitude toward the camp when I performed their music. When did your mother come to America?"

"She was a soccer player who defected when the Soviet national youth team was touring the United States in the 1960s. She met my father in college at Ohio State."

"Do you speak Russian?" Ted asked.

"*Da*. My accent isn't the best, but I can communicate. We visited relatives five years ago, and I had a good time practicing Russian with them while they tried out their English on me."

Alex glanced around at the church. Its inner beauty was different from the architecture on the outside. The most striking interior feature was the stained-glass windows. Ted noticed her glance.

"Would you like a tour of the church?" he asked.

Alex's previous visits to old churches had been hurried events when she was on a trip to England the summer after her first year in law school. She wasn't particularly interested in religious buildings but didn't have a reason to decline the minister's offer.

"Sure," she said.

Ted left the piano bench and walked down the aisle to the middle of the room. Pointing to the stained-glass window at the left rear of the sanctuary, he said, "Each window shows a miraculous event in the ministry of Jesus. Usually, stained-glass windows depict his birth, death, resurrection, and ascension, but the artists who created these focused on his actions. The first one is the wedding feast at Cana where Jesus turned water into wine."

Alex followed Ted until they stood beneath the window. The colors were muted because the afternoon sun was shining on the opposite side of the building, but Alex was impressed by the obvious attention to detail. The windows weren't a modern kaleidoscope quilt of roughly cut shapes but a glass painting that relied upon natural light to bring it to life. In the first window, the bridal couple and the celebrating guests were prominently portrayed in the foreground. Jesus stood to the side.

"He's not the center of attention," Ted said. "At the time of the miracle, no one knew what he had done except his mother and the servants who took the water turned into wine to the man in charge of the wedding."

Alex studied the window. "Since he started with water was the wine a Chablis?"

Ted chuckled. "The only detail in the Bible is that it was the best wine served at the feast."

They went around the room. There were eight windows in all. Blind eyes were opened; food was multiplied; lepers were cleansed. Ted casually talked about the events as if they had happened the week before on the streets of Santee. He wasn't stuffy, and Alex decided that with some coaching, he might be a good witness after all. They stopped on the opposite side of the sanctuary from the wedding at Cana.

"This is my favorite," he said. "The healing at the pool of Bethesda. The man in the picture had been paralyzed for thirty-eight years before Jesus healed him."

"A paraplegic?"

"Yes."

The scene featured a man lying on a mat spread on a stone pavement and looking up at Jesus. Other less distinct figures joined the two figures around a small pool of water. Alex thought the window was one of the duller images. In the upper right-hand corner, there was a second, smaller scene of the man walking up the steps away from the pool with his mat rolled up on his shoulder.

"Why is this your favorite?" she asked.

"Step closer," Ted told her. "Stand directly under the window so that your line of sight follows that of the man on the mat. This is the perfect time of day to do it."

Alex walked between two pews. The afternoon sun brilliantly illuminated the colors without overwhelming them. When she was in position directly under the window, she looked up into the face of Jesus. His eyes were like brownish gold fire focused directly on her.

She caught her breath. "How did they do that?"

"I don't know. It's a remarkable perspective."

Alex stepped back, then forward—in and out of the attention of the stained-glass figure. "There is just a small spot where it happens."

Ted joined her in front of the window. "Of all the other sick people around the pool, only one saw the face of Jesus in a way that brought healing."

"I'm not sure what you mean," she said.

"Faith and the presence of Jesus is the recipe for miracles."

Alex didn't respond. The stained-glass window was a clever piece of art, but it didn't prove anything about life today. Maybe something happened when Jesus looked at people during his life on earth, but it ended when he died. Ted moved on. The last picture was an apocalyptic scene in which a vast throng of people streamed toward a glorified Christ who stood with his hands outstretched in blessing.

"That's the redeemed at the end of the age," Ted said. "They are totally restored and healed. No cancer. No heart disease. No depression. No sin."

"You can't see their faces," Alex observed.

"Because their focus is on Jesus."

Alex shook her head. "I don't like it. It makes Jesus Christ the consummate egotist who wants all the attention on himself. I liked him better at the wedding."

Immediately, Alex wished she'd kept her thoughts to herself and avoided offending the minister. It was like telling a doting mother her only child was a self-centered brat.

"I'm sorry," she added. "I didn't mean—"

"Of course, you did," Ted interrupted her. "But it's understandable. This is Jesus glorified. Until you see his beauty for yourself, it's impossible to imagine the basis for the attraction. Jesus doesn't seek adoration because he's insecure. He receives it because he's worthy."

Alex didn't understand how it was possible in the present day to see Jesus, but she was impressed by the way Ted, like a skilled expert witness, handled her objection without getting flustered.

"Thanks for the tour," she said.

"One more stop," Ted said. "You need to see the church from the pulpit."

Ted led her to the front of the sanctuary to an elevated pulpit made of very dark wood. The preaching area could only be reached by climbing four steep steps in the rear.

"Climb up," he said.

Alex climbed the steps and entered the small circular area. A large Bible was open on the lectern in front of her. She surveyed the expanse of the room. The pulpit was the bow of a ship with the pews like waves lapping against the hull.

"I like it up here," she said. "It's different from standing in front of a jury box. It makes me think I have something important to say."

"That's the point. Try it out."

"What do I say?"

"Preach whatever you think God wants the people in the pews to hear."

Alex thought for a moment. Then she pounded her fist on the side of the lectern. "Men! Repent or suffer at the hands of the ultimate Judge!"

She looked back at Ted. "How was that?"

"Short and to the point but limited to the male segment of the congregation. What would you say to the women?"

"Women?" she asked with raised eyebrows. "They don't need to repent."

Ted smiled. "I've met a few of those women, but I didn't know you were one of them."

"Okay, give me a second." Alex scanned the empty pews. "Women! I warn you! Hear the voice of experience! Document everything because your lawyer will need it later. Look out for yourselves because no one else will do it for you. And never, ever trust a man!"

16

To sit in darkness here hatching vain empires.
PARADISE LOST

RENA APPEARED appropriately distraught, although for reasons other than the fact that her husband lay paralyzed in a coma. She'd spent so many hours at the hospital that the ICU waiting room with its vinyl furniture and pea green walls had become her prison cell. The orderly who sat at the table and monitored visitation was the guard on duty, and Ezra the cellmate whose every habit was designed for maximum irritation. Baxter's status remained unchanged. He had survived the first forty-eight hours, but no one knew whether he was on death row or serving a life sentence in suspended animation. Rena had no choice but to wait for the arrival of Jeffrey, Baxter's older brother. Jeffrey was an unknown variable whom Rena wanted to influence in her favor. If he became an ally, there might be a chance to sway Ezra.

Jeffrey Richardson had been in California on a business trip when he received the phone call from his father about his brother's accident. He immediately prepared to return to South Carolina; however, Ezra vetoed his plans and told him to finish his business. Baxter was unconscious, and there was no reason for a silent vigil around a hospital bed in hope for a fleeting good-bye. So Jeffrey sat through a day of meetings with a real-estate developer in San Diego and then flew to Greenville via Atlanta.

Ezra wasn't in the ICU waiting area when Jeffrey arrived at the hospital. Rena saw her brother-in-law and burst into tears. Jeffrey quickly came over to her. Rena stood, buried her head in his broad right shoulder, and sobbed.

"Am I too late?" Jeffrey asked in alarm. "Is he dead?"

Rena didn't respond until her weeping subsided. "It's worse," she sniffled. "It would be merciful if he did die. It's so terrible."

Jeffrey gently rubbed her back. "But my father said the first two days were the most critical."

Rena pulled away slightly but remained in Jeffrey's arms. "He wants to believe there's hope, but when you see Baxter, you'll know what I mean. I need your help in talking to your father. We can't keep avoiding the decision about continuing life support."

"I knew it was bad, but I didn't—"

"You need to see him for yourself," Rena interrupted. "He's only allowed one visitor for five minutes every hour. I went back a half an hour ago, but we can ask if they'll make an exception for you since you just got here."

"Where's my father?"

"He went outside to make some phone calls and smoke a cigarette."

Rena introduced Jeffrey to the attendant who monitored visitors. A minute later Jeffrey was with his brother. Five minutes later he emerged with his face a shade lighter. He sat next to Rena.

"I see what you mean. I wouldn't want to be kept alive like that by machines. His skin is so pale and washed out. It was eerie—as if he's already gone."

Rena nodded. "And I don't think it's right to make him artificially linger like this."

"What do the doctors say?"

Rena tried to keep her voice calm yet emphatic. "They talk in circles and tell us to wait and see, but it's not right. A decision needs to be made."

"Has my father talked to the doctors?"

"Not without me there, too. I've tried to stay here so we could meet with them together."

Jeffrey glanced toward the door leading into the hallway. "How long has he been gone?"

"I'm not sure, but he should be back shortly."

Several minutes later they were still waiting.

Jeffrey looked at his watch. "Business must go on," he said. "That's why he told me to stay in California yesterday. We're about to close a big deal with a developer in San Diego who wants to expand to the East Coast. I'm going to look outside for him. Where would he go to smoke?"

"Probably near the hospital entrance."

"Okay. Wait here."

Ten minutes later Jeffrey returned.

"I couldn't find him and called his cell phone. He left the hospital and returned to the hotel to review some documents that were being faxed about the deal I worked on in California. He won't be back for several hours."

Rena sank down in the chair. "I'm beat."

"Have you eaten anything today?"

"No. I haven't been very hungry," she answered forlornly.

"Let's get something. You need to take care of yourself."

Rena perked up a little bit. "Okay, there's a cafeteria in the basement. I ate a salad there the first day Baxter was here."

"No, somewhere nicer. You need a break from this hospital."

Rena hesitated. She wanted Jeffrey as an ally but didn't fully trust him. Things were going nicely, but there was a lot of Ezra in him.

"I don't want to go too far."

"You know Greenville, don't you?"

"Yes."

"You choose."

It was beginning to rain when they exited the building. They walked under a causeway to the parking deck, and Rena led the way to the black SUV.

"We'll take Baxter's, uh, my car," Rena said. "You drive."

"Okay. Tell me where to go."

Rena gave directions. It was about ten minutes to the café she had in mind. As they drove, she glanced sideways at Jeffrey. Four years older than Baxter, he resembled his brother but was better looking with a well-defined nose and a chin that jutted out in a masculine line. His eyes made up in intensity what they lacked in softness. According to Baxter, Jeffrey always had a girlfriend but never took the step into commitment. His current companion was a gorgeous redhead about the same age as

Rena. She had arrived on the scene about the same time as Rena's wedding to Baxter and based on past history was approaching the end of her shelf life.

"Did Baxter get his eyes from your mother?" Rena asked when they stopped at a red light.

"Uh, I guess so. I've never thought much about it. Ever since we were little boys, people have said we look alike. I can't see it myself."

"Anyone could pick you from a crowd and put you in the same family."

Rena turned her attention back to the street scenes. The clouds overhead were thick and black, and the rain made everything outside blur together. When she turned her head toward Jeffrey, he wasn't there.

Baxter was behind the wheel. He was peering forward, focused on driving in the rain.

Rena gasped, and Jeffrey quickly looked in her direction.

"What's wrong?" he asked.

The sound of Jeffrey's voice was enough to break the spell; however, Rena took a deep breath before answering.

"I don't know. Seeing you healthy and Baxter at death's door is a shock. I guess talking about the similarities in your appearance brought that home to me."

They pulled into the parking lot for the restaurant. The rain poured down in sheets, so he drove as close to the door as possible.

"Do you have an umbrella?" Jeffrey asked.

Rena looked in the backseat. "Only one. You use it. I'll run for the door."

Jeffrey reached into the backseat and handed the umbrella to Rena. "Take it. A little water won't hurt me."

Rena walked the few steps to the door. Without the umbrella, she would have been soaked. When Jeffrey appeared, his head was dripping wet.

"Get a table while I go to the restroom and dry off," he said.

When Jeffrey appeared, Rena noticed that he had parted his hair on the same side as the comatose Baxter. Perhaps that, together with the discussion of the brothers' common physical traits, had triggered the disturbing reappearance of her husband in the SUV. Rena had decided Baxter's appearance on the trail when she was walking back to the parking lot was a product of the stress of the moment, not a recurring phenomenon. Jeffrey's cell phone chirped, and he answered it.

"Yes, I saw Baxter, and I'm taking Rena to get a bite to eat."

He listened for a few moments.

"That's right. Twenty-two million and not a dime more. Our cut is 15 percent as a developer's fee. If the contract says anything else, don't sign it. I'll see you at the hotel. Bye."

"Your father?"

"Yes. He's at the hotel. One of us has to go back to Santee in the morning."

"Can you stay and let him go?" Rena pleaded. "It has been so stressful being around him."

Jeffrey looked down at her with a curious look in his eyes. "Maybe."

They were seated at a small, round table for two. The restaurant was as authentically French as anything Greenville, South Carolina, could boast. They sat in ornately designed wrought-iron chairs painted white. The owner was an Algerian who had lived many years in Paris before coming to the United States. The waiter brought them water with a twist of lime in wineglasses.

"This is what I needed." Rena sighed after she took a sip. "I haven't been able to think about myself since the accident."

"Are you hungry?" Jeffrey asked.

Rena looked at the menu. There were four different quiches, an assortment of delicately seasoned pastas, three soups, and a variety of meat pastries with flaky crusts.

"I am now," she said.

Rena selected a quiche and soup. Jeffrey opted for a meat pastry. He quickly scanned the wine list and ordered a bottle.

"Baxter would have done that differently," Rena said. "He'd have found out if the wine steward was here and called him over for a long conversation before making a selection."

"He's the expert. I think the differences are exaggerated."

Rena took another sip of water. "You know, Baxter drank almost a whole bottle before he fell. We were sitting on some rocks near the water-fall, and he was wobbly when he stood up. I told him to be careful. If only—" She stopped.

Jeffrey shook his head. "Even a whole bottle shouldn't have made him drunk. Baxter can drink four glasses and still walk a straight line."

"Maybe it was drinking after hiking for a couple of hours that caused the alcohol to have a greater effect on him."

Jeffrey nodded. "I hadn't thought about that."

"He wasn't used to much exercise."

"Yeah, he resents it when we can't drive the golf cart directly to the ball and have to walk from the cart to the middle of the fairway."

The waiter brought the wine, held the bottle so Jeffrey could inspect the label, and then poured a small amount into a glass. Jeffrey sampled it and nodded.

"The hike was my fault," Rena continued sadly. "He wanted to see a waterfall I'd told him about. It's a beautiful place. I've been there many times since I was a little girl."

"Has anything bad happened there before?" he asked.

"What do you mean?" Rena asked sharply.

"Have other people fallen and injured themselves?"

Rena relaxed. "Yes, but there weren't any signs warning people to stay away from the edge."

Jeffrey shrugged. "That shouldn't be necessary. Anyone should know to stay away from the edge of a cliff. Did he slip on some wet rocks?"

"I think so. After he finished the bottle of wine, he stepped too close to the edge and lost his footing. I tried to save him, but it was too late." Rena held out her left arm and pointed to the deep scratch marks. "I tried to grab his hand, but it slipped down my arm. He was there one second and gone the next. It all happened so fast, there was nothing I could do."

Rena's eyes were dry, but she thought it would add pathos to the story if she touched her right eye with her napkin. Telling the story to Jeffrey had been her best performance thus far.

Jeffrey saw her and asked, "Do you have something in your eye?"

Rena's voice cracked when she answered. "The beginning of a tear.

The shock of the accident is beginning to wear off, and I'm beginning to grieve. I think watching Baxter continue to suffer is worse torture than dealing with his death."

Jeffrey reached out and touched her hand. "I'm sorry. For all of us."

Rena looked into his eyes with gratitude for a moment and then lowered her gaze.

Jeffrey withdrew his hand and spoke more sternly. "But I'm also upset with Baxter. I can't believe he was so reckless. When I saw him today, I felt pity for him, but I'm also angry that he wasn't more careful."

Rena put her napkin back in her lap. "I've gone through the same thing. Look at my situation. I've not been married a year, and my husband is paralyzed in a coma because of one foolish step. It doesn't seem fair."

The waiter brought their meal. It was delicious. Rena particularly savored the soup, a creamy spinach concoction that felt smooth in her mouth and caressed her taste buds. Since meeting Baxter, she'd become accustomed to the benefits of wealth, and she was determined never to return to the generic canned soups of her childhood. While nibbling the fluffy quiche, she glanced at Jeffrey. It felt odd sitting across the table from her brother-in-law without Baxter present. The brothers occasionally spent time together in social settings; however, Rena's impressions of Jeffrey were formed more by Baxter's comments than her own observations. Seeing Jeffrey now, she had to admit that he had a strength Baxter lacked and a decisiveness that communicated security. A stray thought crossed her mind that she had married the wrong one of Ezra Richardson's sons.

"Have you thought any about the future?" Jeffrey asked softly.

Rena was surprised that Jeffrey had picked up her thought. A widow isn't propositioned at her husband's funeral. And Baxter wasn't even dead, yet. She leaned forward.

"What do you think?" she asked.

Jeffrey spoke in a matter-of-fact tone. "If Baxter survives, where will he go for ongoing medical help? I know there are good facilities in Atlanta, and there might be something suitable in Charleston. I guess a lot depends on his mental condition if he comes out of the coma. If he can think and talk normally, he can tell us what he wants to do."

Rena swallowed nervously and shook off her misunderstanding of Jeffrey's intentions toward her. The specter of Baxter in a rehabilitation facility—alert and talking to Detective Giles Porter was her greatest fear. The pleasant sensation the luncheon had evoked evaporated like cotton candy in a child's mouth. Her stomach felt suddenly queasy.

"Oh, I haven't given it much thought," she answered. "I've been focused on the immediate situation and haven't considered the future."

Jeffrey poured another glass of wine for both of them. "Yeah, I guess talking about wine stewards and playing golf made me think Baxter may come out of this, but I know we have to be realistic."

"And find a doctor we can trust. The ones I've met are giving us the runaround," Rena reiterated.

Jeffrey leaned back and folded his arms. "I have a fraternity brother in Richmond who is doing a residency in neurosurgery. I could contact him. He'd give us a straight answer." Jeffrey stared past Rena's shoulder. "Of course, there's the chance Baxter won't wake up. Lying in a hospital room with tubes everywhere is not living."

Rena pressed forward. "You're right, and every time I see him I'm more convinced that it's wrong to sustain his life artificially. You know, it's weird, but we'd prepared for this very situation."

"What do you mean?"

"Several months ago, Baxter and I had an appointment with a lawyer in Santee and signed a declaration of desire for a natural death, making it clear we didn't want to be kept on life support in case of a serious injury. Baxter also gave me a health care power of attorney so that I could decide the treatment to approve in situations like this one."

Jeffrey nodded. "Yeah, I wouldn't want anyone to have that kind of control over my life. Of course, it's different with you and Baxter. You're committed to one another."

"For as long as we both shall live, until death do us part," Rena responded piously. "But there is a problem with your father. When Baxter was eighteen, he signed power of attorney—"

"Giving my father control of everything," Jeffrey interrupted.

Surprised, Rena asked, "Did Baxter talk to you about it?"

"No, but my father mentioned it last night on the phone. I had to sign one when I was eighteen," Jeffrey said. "A couple of years later, I went to a lawyer in Charleston and revoked it."

"What did your father do?"

Jeffrey shrugged. "He doesn't know. He probably thinks it's still valid, but my attorney in Charleston knows what to do if it ever comes up."

"I wish Baxter had thought ahead," Rena said bitterly.

"How do you know he didn't? I told him what I'd done a few months before you were married."

Rena sat up straight. "What did he say?"

"That he would look into it. Whether he did or not, I don't know."

"Did you give him that name of your lawyer in Charleston?"

"Yeah, he knows him. We've gone sailing together several times."

"Could I call him and find out if he talked to Baxter?"

"Sure. His name is Rufus Grange, but he goes by Rafe. He's a trial lawyer, but he helped me out because he'd been with us on the boat. Do you want his phone number?"

"Yes. I also need to talk with the woman attorney from Santee who flew up and met with us. I liked her a lot."

"Who is it?"

"Alexia Lindale."

"Does she work for Leggitt & Freeman?" Jeffrey asked.

"Yes."

Jeffrey frowned. "I've heard about her. She handles a lot of divorces. She nailed a friend of mine last year, and he had to give his wife twice what he offered before trial."

"What's wrong with that?" Rena asked. "He was probably going to rip her off."

The frown was replaced with an impish grin. "Probably. Women usually stick together, but anybody who works for Ralph Leggitt is in my father's back pocket. That's why I went to Charleston for legal advice. Leggitt & Freeman is okay for business matters, but for personal protection, I want my own attorney."

"But Alexia told me everything we discussed was confidential."

"It is until the lawyers have to pick sides. If her firm has to choose between my father and you, who will they pick?"

Rena's face flushed. "She mentioned a possible problem but told me I could trust her."

Jeffrey gave her a cynical look. "Don't be naive. I've never met a lawyer who wasn't looking out for themselves first and the client second. Male or female doesn't make any difference."

"Then I don't know who to trust."

Jeffrey took a sip of wine. "You can trust me."

Rena looked into his eyes but couldn't see beneath the surface. "Why?"

"We have more in common than you suspect."

"What do you mean?"

"After seeing Baxter, I agree it would be cruel to keep him alive by artificial means."

Rena's heart leaped. "Does that mean you will talk to your father about ending life support?"

Jeffrey nodded. "Yes. At the right time."

17

The aim of forensic oratory is to teach.

CICERO

GWEN BUZZED ALEX.

"Prince Pinchot wants to see you," she said.

Before working for Alex and Leonard Mitchell, Gwen had served as Kenneth Pinchot's legal secretary. She had jumped at the chance to switch, even though it meant working for two lawyers instead of one.

"Is that what you called him when you worked for him?" Alex asked.

"You don't want to know what I called him behind his back."

"Okay, tell him I'll be there shortly."

Alex smiled. Pinchot's arrogant confidence rubbed Gwen the wrong way. Alex could tolerate an egotistical lawyer if he or she backed it up by superior performance in the courtroom. She'd assisted Pinchot in several trials. He was meticulous in preparation and calm and thoughtful when questioning a witness. His methods occasionally lulled enemies into letting down their guard—a lapse they later regretted.

The senior partner stood in the hall outside his office as Alex approached. Pinchot wore professionally tailored suits with a monogrammed shirt and silk tie. His idea of casual dress at the office was a sport coat and tie. Today, he was wearing a banker's gray suit.

"Alex, can you spare a couple of hours? I'm in the second day of a trial, and a witness can't make it, so I'm going to have to use a deposition we took several months ago. My paralegal was going to read the answers, but she's gone home with a fever."

"Yes. What kind of testimony?"

"I'll tell you as we go."

They walked down the hall and out the door. Pinchot drove a new Mercedes. Alex waited for him to open the door for her. She'd learned that the older lawyer was insulted if he wasn't allowed to play the gentleman's role.

"You're a witness to a will," Pinchot said as he started the car's motor. "There was a caveat filed by the children of the first wife against the children of the second wife. They claim undue and improper influence by wife number two in favor of her children. Both wives predeceased the man."

"Where is the witness to the will?" Alex asked.

"That depends on your belief in the hereafter," Pinchot replied dryly. "She died a few weeks after we took her deposition. She was a secretary at the law firm that prepared the second will."

"Which group of children do we represent?"

"Wife number two's brood."

Pinchot turned the corner onto the street that led to the courthouse and continued. "The two children of the second wife receive 80 percent of the estate, and the four children from the first wife split the remaining 20 percent."

"Ouch."

"You'll understand when you read the deposition transcript. You'll have a few minutes before you're called to the witness stand."

The most common instance of reading a deposition occurred with the testimony of doctors who didn't want to sit in court until called to the witness stand. Reading lay testimony was less frequent.

"How old am I?" Alex asked.

Pinchot grinned. "Sixty-eight. You've been a legal secretary for forty-five years."

They parked along the street. City leaders wanted to encourage people to come to the downtown area, so there weren't any parking meters.

For generations, the courthouse in Santee had reflected the poverty years of the South Carolina coast that lasted without significant interruption from 1865 to 1939. A painting of the old courthouse, a one-story building built with dirty brown bricks similar in color to the ones used by the ancient Egyptians, still hung in the main lobby of the newer building. The burst of manufacturing activity that swept across the region during World War II broke the bondage of economic slavery, and shipyards and military installations brought high-paying jobs to the area.

Then the tourism boom that began in the 1960s carried the Low Country to a level of prosperity not known since cotton and rice sat on the wharves of Charleston. The old courthouse was demolished without regret in the 1970s and a structure erected that reflected the architecture of the prosperous coast. Built to look older than it was, the imposing building was faced with sandstone and had a red tile roof.

Alex and Pinchot walked through metal detectors that were unplugged and unguarded. The local sheriff's office only sent deputies to the security checkpoints on busy court days. The rest of the time the two courtrooms on the main floor were unprotected from terrorists; however, the greater dangers to the public safety were from hotheaded exhusbands and the friends of criminal defendants. It wasn't unusual for the deputies to confiscate a wickedly long knife or two during a two-week term of court.

The trial was in the smaller of the two courtrooms. It was a long, rectangular room with a high ceiling and plaster walls painted a pale yellow. Fake columns stood in the corners for decoration. The jury box was to the left and featured fixed chairs that both swiveled and rocked. The judge's bench, made of dark walnut, stretched across the front. Most divorce trials were held in this courtroom, and Alex liked the acoustics. The larger courtroom was reserved for serious criminal matters and major civil suits.

Alex sat behind the bar and began skimming the deposition while Pinchot and the attorney on the other side prepared for the afternoon session. Pinchot's clients, a man and woman in their early thirties, were seated with him. At the opposite table sat a younger lawyer with four middle-aged people clustered around him. Judge Garland entered and everyone stood.

"Are you ready for the jury to come back in?" the judge asked.

Pinchot spoke. "We need to discuss use of a deposition in lieu of live testimony. The witness is now deceased."

The judge looked toward the other attorney, a young man about Alex's age whom she didn't recognize.

"Any objection, Mr. Harrison?"

"Your Honor, I was not representing my clients at the time this deposition was taken, and it was conducted before additional information came to light that raises serious questions about the credibility of the witness who was deposed. To allow the deposition to be read into the record without an adequate opportunity for cross-examination would be seriously prejudicial to my clients."

"Mr. Pinchot?" the judge asked.

Pinchot cleared his throat and stepped from behind the table.

"Judge, I appreciate Mr. Harrison's dilemma; however, there was nothing to prevent the caveator's previous lawyer from conducting a thorough investigation prior to the deposition of the witness. Furthermore, at the time the testimony was given, it was clearly stated on the record that the deposition was being taken for discovery and any other purposes allowed by the civil practice act. That includes use of the deposition at trial if the witness is unavailable."

"Were those the stipulations?" the judge asked the younger lawyer.

"Yes, sir. But it was assumed that the witness would be available for trial."

"She's not," the judge replied curtly, "and I'll allow the deposition to be read."

"May I interpose objections to the testimony that were not made at the time of the deposition?" Harrison asked.

"Yes, I'll give you that latitude so long as you don't abuse it. Bring in the jury."

After the judge gave an explanation about use of deposition testimony to the jury, Pinchot called Alex to the witness stand. Her mission was to become Mrs. Helen Jacklett. After several background questions, Pinchot cut to the heart of the issue.

"Mrs. Jacklett, do you remember the day that Mr. Keiffer came into the office to sign the will that has been marked as Exhibit A?"

"Yes, sir," Alex answered. "It was in the spring shortly before Easter."

"Did you have any personal acquaintance with Mr. Keiffer prior to that time?"

"Oh, yes. He had been a client almost as long as I'd worked at the office. We were on a first-name basis and had talked hundreds of times over the years."

"Based on your contact with him during the months prior to signing the will, how would you describe his mental state?"

"Sharp as ever. He was a very successful businessman, always on top of what was going on. Even after he retired, I think his company called him in as a consultant and—"

"Objection," Harrison said. "Hearsay and lack of personal knowledge."

"Sustained."

"Begin at line 25," Pinchot said.

Alex glanced down the page. "He called me several weeks before changing his will and told me he wanted to redo his estate plan. I didn't ask him why, but he mentioned several reasons."

"What were those reasons?"

Harrison was on his feet. "Objection, Your Honor. That would be double hearsay. Neither Mr. Keiffer nor Mrs. Jacklett is available for cross-examination on this information and the testimony is therefore unreliable and prejudicial."

Judge Garland compressed his lips. "Gentlemen, approach the bench."

The lawyers stepped forward. Alex knew what was about to happen but leaned close to listen.

"Mr. Harrison," the judge said in an intense whisper, "if Mr. Keiffer were still alive, we wouldn't be trying this case. His mental state during the time the will was prepared is the issue on trial, and I've already ruled that the testimony of this witness on this question can be presented by deposition."

Pinchot spoke up. "I'm sure Mr. Harrison is aware of the law, Your Honor. His objection was for the jury, not the court."

"Your Honor," Harrison began, "if you allow—"

The judge interrupted in a voice that Alex suspected carried all the way to the jury box. "Mr. Harrison, your objection is overruled, and if you make another objection on similar grounds, I will consider sanctions against you and your clients. Is that understood?"

The young lawyer's face flushed. "Yes, sir."

"Proceed."

Pinchot stepped back and spoke to Alex. "Please, answer the question."

"He told me that the children of his first wife had depleted the assets of the inter vivos trust he'd established for them during a gambling trip to Las Vegas, and he wanted to change his will to leave most of his property to the children of his second wife."

"Did he mention how much money was lost through gambling?"

Alex saw Harrison squirming in his seat, but he kept his mouth shut.

"More than $200,000 during a Christmas vacation attended by all four of the children."

"Did he give any other reasons for changing his will?"

Alex looked toward the jury before she answered. "Yes, he mentioned that two of the children of his first wife wouldn't let him see his grandchildren. He wasn't even sure if the presents he sent the grandchildren on their birthdays were being delivered."

Several jurors looked toward Harrison's clients and frowned. The witness then described in detail the events surrounding the signing of the will. Pinchot's questions brought the jury into the room with Mr. Keiffer. He then moved to the events surrounding the signing of the will.

"Did Mr. Keiffer express a clear understanding of the natural objects of his affection?"

"Yes. He named all his children and talked about each one. He expressed regrets about the conduct of the older children but still wanted to leave them something from his estate."

"Was Mrs. Keiffer present at the will signing?"

"Yes."

"What did she say?"

"She told him to do whatever he wanted to do."

"Did she try to influence him in any way to favor her children?"

"No. Not at all."

The cross-examination of the witness in the deposition by the other side's first lawyer was inept and only reinforced the direct testimony. Alex had read ahead enough to know that it would be fun to repeat the responses; however, when Pinchot finished, Harrison stood and said, "No questions, Your Honor."

Alex returned to her seat and listened to Pinchot conduct his direct examination of one of his clients, a woman who lived in Brunswick, Georgia. It was classic Pinchot. The client cried at the right time when talking about her father and avoided sounding like a greedy child. Pinchot knew better than anyone how to bring the focus of the jury onto his client. His direct examination questions floated softly across the courtroom without being intrusive. Harrison's cross-examination was valiant but didn't shake the witness's credibility. When the woman stepped down, Alex tapped Pinchot on the shoulder.

"You're winning. I'm going to walk back to the office," she said.

The older lawyer was busy making notes and didn't turn around. "Go ahead."

Alex stepped into the afternoon sun and looked up into the blue sky. She always learned something from watching Ken Pinchot. He didn't call the other lawyer a shyster for knowingly interposing a lame objection; he aimed the judge in the right direction and watched him blast him. And he didn't seek to be the constant center of attention when his case was better served by bringing the jury's focus onto his witness.

Alex could conduct a good direct examination, but she wasn't sure she could have exercised the same restraint when dealing with an improperly manipulative lawyer on the other side. As she walked back to the office, she carefully filed the day's lesson in her mind.

Fair stood the wind for France.
Michael Drayton

Rena wanted Jeffrey to talk immediately with his father about terminating Baxter's life support. Jeffrey counseled restraint as they walked from the parking deck to the hospital.

"Be patient," he said. "I have a lot of experience dealing with my father. No one can read his moods better than I can. If I sat down with him now, it would only cause him to harden his position. We don't even know if a decision is going to be necessary."

"But in the meantime, Baxter continues to suffer," Rena responded with frustration.

Jeffrey stepped closer to her and spoke softly. "Rena, calm down. Baxter doesn't know what's going on. You heard the doctors this morning. He doesn't feel anything. His condition is critical but stable."

Rena glanced away and stood still with her arms firmly folded. "Maybe, but I can't go on like this indefinitely."

Jeffrey touched her arm. "It won't. When the time is right, I'll speak up."

After Jeffrey left, Rena stayed outside the hospital and sat on a bench near the entrance. From her vantage point, she could watch people leave without being noticed herself. She dialed the number for the lawyer from Charleston who had helped Jeffrey cancel the power of attorney. She identified herself as Baxter's wife and asked for Rafe Grange. In a few seconds, a deep, southern voice came on the line.

Rena told him what had happened to Baxter. With each telling her twisted version of the events at the waterfall became more convincing.

"I'm very sorry," the lawyer responded with obvious concern. "How can I help you? Although I know Jeffrey better, I consider your husband a friend."

"It's about the power of attorney that Mr. Richardson made Jeffrey and Baxter sign when they turned eighteen. Did Baxter ever ask you to help him cancel it?"

There was silence on the other line for several seconds. Rena began to wonder if it had been a mistake to call. There was no guarantee that the Charleston lawyer wasn't connected with her father-in-law.

"Uh, hello," she said. "Are you still there?"

"Yes, sorry. I was checking my computer for a file. I remember talking with Jeffrey about a power of attorney, but I don't show any contact with Baxter. I never opened a file in his name. Do you want me to check with the other attorneys in our office?"

"Did any of them know Baxter?"

"I'm not sure, but I can find out."

Rena gave him her cell number and hung up. The sky grew darker in concert with her mood. Rafe Grange was a dead end, and based on Jeffrey's comments, she wasn't sure she could rely on Alex Lindale. As she brooded, Ezra came out of the building and lit a cigarette. Rena stayed in the shadows. When he disappeared into the parking deck, she went back into the hospital to continue her solitary vigil.

———

The Friday before her departure for France, Alex arrived at the office at 6 A.M. Attorneys didn't take vacations, only prolonged continuances from work that had to be done when they returned. Eight hours later the wooden surface of her desk was bare except for her blotter, the brass cup from Madagascar that she used to store extra pens, and a pale green stone paperweight from Peru. After a week's absence, Alex knew that mail would be stacked across the front of the desk like paper battlements awaiting her assault. She walked from her office to Gwen's desk.

"What am I forgetting?" she asked.

"Plane tickets, passport, camera, sunscreen?" the secretary responded. "I think it's sunny in southern France. Don't forget an extra suitcase in case you meet the perfect man and want to bring him home as a souvenir."

Alex smiled slightly. "Everything is covered except the extra suitcase. You know one reason for the trip is to get rid of any remaining emotional baggage from Jason."

"Which means you'll have room for the right man on the return flight. If you don't want to bring someone back for yourself, look for me."

"You trust me to find the right one?"

Gwen shrugged. "You can't do any worse than I have for myself. Just make sure he picks up his dirty clothes and speaks English with a romantic French accent."

Alex grabbed a piece of paper from Gwen's desk and pretended to take notes. "The accent I can handle, but how am I supposed to find out about the dirty clothes?"

"You're a lawyer!" Gwen exclaimed. "It should be easy compared to some of the dirty laundry you uncover for your clients."

Alex held her pen at ready. "Very clever. Any age requirements?"

Gwen thought for a moment. "About the same as me or slightly older. I don't want to have to break in a younger man."

Alex put the cap back on the pen. "Consider it done," she said.

Gwen patted the stacks of files Alex had deposited on the floor beside the secretary's desk.

"Oh, and you forgot to stop dictating. Between you and Leonard, I have enough work to make my fingers raw from typing."

"I'll buy you some expensive French hand lotion."

"That would help."

"And don't worry about my dictation. There's nothing lengthy. It's mostly correspondence to delay things until I get back. Open my mail. If anything looks urgent, ask Ken Pinchot what to do."

Gwen made a face. "By the way, what happened in the case you helped him with the other day?"

"The other side fired their lawyer an hour before closing arguments. It was a mess. The judge wouldn't let them delay the trial, so they took a voluntary dismissal. I think it will go away. No attorney in their right mind would accept them as clients. Ken had the case nailed down tight."

Gwen looked down at a list on her desk. "Where are your pets staying?"

"With a lady named Pat who has a small kennel on Highway 17. Boris loves it; Misha hates it. I'm taking them to her as soon as I get home."

"Okay. That's it. Go, before someone calls. Have a great trip."

Alex was walking down the hall when the receptionist buzzed Gwen. "Is Alex there? She didn't pick up the page to her office."

Gwen waited until Alex turned the corner before answering. "She's gone and won't be back for a week."

"It's Rena Richardson. Did Alex leave any instructions if she called?"

Gwen looked again at the stack of files. "Maybe, but I won't know for a few days. Take her number and tell her Alex is out of the country. If I find something in my dictation about Rena, I'll call her myself."

———

It was dusk when Alex arrived in Marseille via Charleston, Atlanta, and Paris. She'd practiced her French with an Italian woman on the short flight from Paris but was tired and their accents didn't mesh.

Alex didn't experience any sadness during the flight, but when she stepped through the gate at Marseille, she had a sharp twinge of regret. A handsome man with a joyful smile on his face and a bouquet of fresh flowers in his hand should have been waiting for her. Walking rapidly along the concourse next to impersonal strangers who were oblivious to her existence was not the way she'd dreamed of arriving in southern France. Alex let a tear escape her right eye and pressed on.

She spent the first two nights in Aix-en-Provence just north of Marseille. She learned that the picturesque city was founded by the Romans as a military outpost in 122 B.C. For Alex, it was a place to lay down her weapons, get in touch with herself, and think about what life had taught her.

As a litigator, Alex had to maintain a sharp emotional edge because she never knew where the next blow would fall against one of her clients, and it always took her a couple of days away from the office to relax.

Aix-en-Provence was a perfect resting place. She dozed late the first morning in one of the softest beds she'd ever slept in. Surrounded by six white pillows and an eiderdown comforter, she felt as if she were sleeping in the clouds. The inn where she stayed was on a side street, and the only early morning sounds that came through the window of the second-story room were the friendly greetings of people on the street below. Because the townspeople spoke so rapidly, Alex couldn't distinguish the words, and any concerns they expressed didn't disturb her dozing.

She ventured out in the early afternoon for a leisurely walk. Because she was alone, she set her own pace and visited the Roman ruins and a famous local university. The age of buildings in Europe always had an effect on her. Two-hundred-year-old structures in America are often placed on the National Register of Historic Places. In southern France, a two-hundred-year-old house was in robust middle age and attracted no particular attention. She walked across the stone floor of the Roman court. No women attorneys donned white togas to argue in Roman courts, and Alex was glad she'd been born long after the stones were freshly hewn from the quarry. As the first female partner at Leggitt & Freeman, she would push the liberation of women a tiny step forward in her corner of the world. She was alive at the right time.

Provence has two seasons: July/August and the rest of the year. During the two summer months, it is difficult to find a vacant table at a restaurant, the inns are full, and the roads crowded with tourists. During the rest of the year, clerks in the stores pause to chat, tractors are as common as cars, and a meal that lasts less than two hours is considered a quick bite to eat. Alex knew a late fall visit there would give her unhurried days of exploring and quiet evenings of dining.

The first evening, Alex ate a leisurely dinner at a restaurant recommended by the owner of the inn. Toward the end of the meal, a handsome man about her own age approached her and offered to share a bottle of wine with her. He had kind, friendly eyes, and she accepted. He was a businessman from Marseille who had lived for almost a year in Seattle. Through tentative conversation that kept them laughing at misunderstandings, they talked about life in America and France.

"May we take you places you've never been before?" he asked as he filled her wineglass with the last drops from the bottle.

"What places?" Alex asked.

"Where Cézanne looked when he painted his famous paintings. No tourists see the places I know. We can have a meal on a sheet. What do you call it?"

"A picnic."

"Yes. We will bring the wine and cheese and bread."

The invitation made Alex feel feminine and attractive but not stupid.

"No, thanks," she said.

The man's passionate appeal for her to reconsider his invitation was denied, but he left with a good-natured twinkle still sparkling in his eyes. Walking back to the inn, Alex wondered if she had made a mistake.

The next morning she ate an ephemeral pastry for breakfast and rode a bicycle into the countryside. Beyond the bounds of the city lay a picturesque rural area whose soul was revealed in the works of the impressionist painter Paul Cézanne. She had no guide but didn't need one to enjoy the views of haystacks and hedgerows.

Each day, Alex went shopping. In Aix-en-Provence, she bought a straw hat in the town market. The second day, she spent more than an hour in a tiny, unorganized dress shop that made up in style what it lacked in selection. She found a sleek dress with a French flair that she wore when she went out for dinner. No one intruded on her quiet meal, and she remained alone with her thoughts.

From Aix-en-Provence, she went to the Camargue, a marshy delta area west of Marseille and home to *les chevaux,* the horses who roamed in semiliberty along the coast and splashed through the blue waters of the Mediterranean. It was Alex's first chance to see the French cowboys who guarded the herds. The men were like colorful gypsies on horseback, quite different from drab, unshaven cowboys of the American West. She picked one out for Gwen and took his photograph. The man came over to her, and they had a halting conversation in French. Alex didn't have the vocabulary to conduct a cross-examination in French and couldn't determine if he picked up his dirty socks and scraped the mud from his boots before entering the house.

She spent the night in Les Baux-de-Provence, a small village surrounding the ruins of a medieval castle, and stayed at L'Oustau de Baumanière, a place frequented by both Winston Churchill and Elizabeth Taylor. It was very expensive, but Alex had planned to splurge.

She ate leg of lamb cooked in a salt crust and boiled squab with cous-cous topped with tomato vinaigrette. The wine cellar boasted ninety thousand bottles. Many were local; others were imported. Alex learned that "imported" meant the producing vineyard was more than fifteen miles away.

One sunny morning she was sitting at a street café in Beaucaire Tarascon, drinking a cup of coffee and trying to decipher a French newspaper. The news couldn't hold her interest so she folded up the paper and simply watched the people passing by. In a few minutes, a small boy and girl, each no more than six years old, came down the street holding hands. The love and trust between the two children was so pure and innocent that Alex couldn't take her eyes off them until they rounded a corner. It was a living memory richer than any photograph could capture.

The next day she drove to Saintes-Maries-de-la-Mer, the main town in the Provence region. It was the end of the bullfighting season there. Although no bulls are killed in French arenas, the sport was too close to cruelty to suit her taste, so she avoided the town's arena. Instead, she went for a long swim in the calm waters of the Mediterranean. The water felt good, but she missed Boris's black head plowing through the water beside her.

The small hotel where she was staying featured a sweeping panorama of the water. That afternoon, she sat alone on the terrace as the sun descended and said good-bye to Jason Favreau for the last time. All the towns she'd visited were places they'd planned to see together. She'd kept her end of the bargain but had to connect the dots of her journey with one line instead of two.

Leaving the terrace, she walked down a narrow stone path to the water. The small waves gently touched the shore. Alex took off her sandals and stepped into the edge of the water. A graceful sailboat was leaving the nearby harbor. As it caught the evening breeze, the crew released a huge spinnaker that billowed out and caused the boat to move quickly toward the horizon.

Alex's thoughts followed the boat as she considered her own future. She was plowing through life and needed a new sail filled with a burst of wind to send her speeding toward her destiny. She exhaled and cleared her lungs for a new breath of air. She wasn't sure what the future held, but she wanted to run before it with a fresh breeze driving her forward.

Alex spent her final day in Provence near Avignon. One of the main attractions of the area was a stone church built in the twelfth century. When she walked into the cool, dark interior, she thought about her recent encounters with Ted Morgan at Sandy Flats Church and wondered what he would think about the ancient structure. Today, no exquisite piano music beckoned her when she passed through the narthex into the sanctuary. The church was quiet as a tomb, and she missed the vibrancy of Ted's music. Several ornate stained-glass windows offered muted light. Alex approached one that depicted Jesus walking on the water and tried to find the place where his eyes would gaze into hers. She moved back and forth but never made contact with the image.

She arrived in Marseille with several hours to spare for a final shopping spree. In an art shop, she found an eighteenth-century watercolor portrait of a Frenchwoman who bore a remarkable resemblance to herself. It was more expensive than anything Alex had bought and would be hard to transport on the plane. She hesitated as she stood before it. A young female clerk came over to her, glanced at the portrait, then looked at Alex.

"*C'est vous,*" she said with surprise.

Alex laughed. "*Non. Je suis American.*"

"Okay," the clerk said. "I speak English."

"Who is she?" Alex asked.

"I do not know. I will ask Monsieur Benoit."

Alex watched the clerk speak rapidly to a middle-aged man with a well-trimmed goatee. The man gestured and pointed in several directions. The clerk returned.

"He says it is a woman who lived in a big house. On the waterfront. She was a member of the royal family of Monaco and married a rich merchant."

The storekeeper could be lying, but any resemblance to royalty is flattering. Marriage to a rich merchant also had a nice ring to it, and the woman probably sailed about the Mediterranean in a yacht with bunches of billowing white sails.

"I'll buy it. Box it up so it can be taken to the airport."

Alex spent the flight from Paris to Atlanta curled up in her seat. There was a vacant space next to her, and she was short enough that she could tuck her legs beside her and rest. She closed her eyes and relived her favorite scenes from the week. Top billing wasn't won by a picturesque landscape or the exquisitely decorated interior of one of the quaint inns. It was the simple, uncomplicated moment of the two children who loved each other.

The plane landed in Atlanta and dumped her into the massive bustle of the Hartsfield Airport. It was a shock to her system after adapting to a slower pace of life that wasn't always pushing forward to the next event. She had a two-hour layover until her flight to Charleston. While she waited at the gate, she called the voice mailbox for her number at the office. It was Sunday afternoon.

The computerized voice announced, "You have seventy-four saved messages. Press one if you want to listen to your messages."

Alex hung up. Calling the office had been a mistake; listening to the messages while she sat in the airport with no resources to respond would be compounding her error. Gwen said she would take care of any emergencies. Whether she did or not, nothing could be done until Alex walked through the door on Monday morning.

She arrived home too late to pick up Boris and Misha from the kennel. Dark and lonely, her house waited for her at the edge of the marsh. The night air was cooler than when she'd left for France. She unpacked her suitcases and found the perfect place for the portrait on the wall near the front door. While Alex was hammering a nail to hang the picture, the phone rang. She ran into the kitchen and glanced at the receiver. The caller ID flashed unknown.

"Hello," she said.

A weak, female voice said, "Alex? Is that you?"

From the few indistinct words Alex couldn't determine the identity of the caller.

"Yes," she responded. "Who's calling?"

"Rena Richardson. I've been trying to reach you for over an hour."

The feeble voice didn't match Alex's memory of Baxter Richardson's wife.

"If I'm in trouble, will you help me?"

"What's wrong?" Alex asked.

"I'm at the Greenville County jail."

Magistrates may punish by fine not exceeding five hundred
dollars or imprisonment for a term not exceeding thirty days,
or both, all assaults and batteries and other breaches of the peace.
S.C. Code 22-3-560

Shocked, Alex asked, "What are you doing at the jail?"

"It's Ezra's fault. He's using the power of attorney Baxter signed before we were married to take money out of our checking account. I called the bank and found out that I have less than a thousand dollars left. When I confronted Ezra at the hospital, he refused to talk to me, and I lost my temper. I slapped him, and someone called hospital security. They took me to a room in the basement of the building and locked the door. I calmed down in a few minutes, but they refused to let me leave. Ezra must have called the police because two policemen came to the hospital."

Rena's voice grew stronger as she continued to talk. "One of them put handcuffs on me and threw me in the back of a patrol car. It was humiliating. A detective wants to ask me some questions, but I refused to talk to him until I could talk to my lawyer."

"Where are you now?"

"I'm sitting in a room by myself. I think it's one of the places where lawyers meet with their clients."

"Can anyone hear you?"

"No. I shut the door."

Alex slid a writing pad across the kitchen counter and picked up a pen. "How hard did you hit him?" she asked.

There was silence for a second. "It made a noise and stung my hand."

Rena had an athletic build. Alex suspected she could deliver a significant blow if she wanted to do so.

"Did he fall down?"

"Uh, no."

"Or try to hit you back?"

"No. The orderly in the ICU waiting room got between us. Everyone was yelling and stuff. I'm not sure what happened until they dragged me to the elevator and took me to the basement."

"Have you seen Ezra again?"

"No."

Alex turned and leaned against the kitchen counter. She knew there was a plausible basis for outrage against Ezra. Whether it justified a punch was debatable, but she had little doubt that Ralph Leggitt was helping Ezra Richardson transfer Baxter's property into hidden places so Rena couldn't touch it. A joint checking account would be the tip of the iceberg. The senior partner's actions put any continued representation of Rena by Alex at odds with the firm's involvement with Ezra. Alex could only give one response to Rena's request for help. She spoke as firmly as possible.

"Rena, you have to get another lawyer. If you and Ezra are at war, my law firm can't be involved. I wanted to help your family work everything out, but I can't represent you in a dispute with your father-in-law. In the meantime, don't talk to the police until you can retain another attorney."

Alex was not prepared for the sound that came through the receiver. It was a wail that made the hair stand up on the back of her neck. The only thing she could compare it to was the cry of a wounded animal.

"Rena?" she asked sharply.

"No! You are the only person who knows the truth!" Rena cried out, her voice broken and hysterical. "Please don't abandon me! You've got to help me!"

Alex bit her lip. It was hard to resist a woman's cry for help, but she had no choice. She wracked her brain for a solution.

"Calm down, so you can listen."

She waited until Rena's sniffles subsided.

"This is a bit outside the rules," Alex continued, "but I'll help you find a lawyer. I had a case against a firm in Greenville. I know they have some good lawyers. I'll call someone in the morning and try to arrange an appointment."

"No!" Rena responded emphatically. "You told me you were representing me, and I trusted you! You can't dump me on someone else!"

"I'm not dumping you," Alex protested. "I can't represent both you and your father-in-law. I have no choice but to send you to another attorney. Our firm can't be involved in a dispute between the two of you."

"Is your law firm helping Ezra rob me?"

Alex winced and evaded the question. "I've been out of the country and haven't talked to anyone at my office. I'll look into the situation first thing in the morning."

"But what do I do now?" Rena asked with renewed desperation. "I don't want to go through what happened with that awful detective who harassed me after Baxter fell. He came by the hospital two more times this past week."

Alex stood up straighter. "Did he try to talk to you?"

"No, except to ask how Baxter was doing. But I know he's trying to come up with something against me. The second time that he showed up Ezra was in the waiting room. They went outside, and Ezra didn't come back for almost an hour."

Alex started to ask Rena more questions about Ezra but stopped. The more she talked, the greater Rena's expectation that an attorney-client relationship existed between them.

"Okay, where is the detective?"

"In another room. He let me use my cell phone to call you."

"Tell him I want to talk to him."

Alex heard a heavy door shut and then the sounds of a radio dispatcher talking to patrol officers.

"Here he is," Rena said.

A deep male voice said, "Detective Vinson Lilley. Who am I talking to?"

"This is Alexia Lindale. I'm a lawyer in Santee where Mrs. Richardson lives."

"Are you her attorney?"

Alex looked at the ceiling before answering. "Yes. Has she been charged with anything?"

"Not yet. I want to take a statement from her to determine probable cause for an assault and battery charge. She refused to talk to me until she could contact you."

Alex was skeptical. The detective probably wanted an incriminating statement from Rena that would only bolster what he had already decided to do.

"Have you interviewed anyone else?" she asked.

"Yes, I spoke with the two hospital security officers who removed Mrs. Richardson from the ICU waiting room, and I took a statement from the complainant, Mr. Ezra Richardson."

Alex couldn't believe Ezra would try to turn a face slap into a criminal charge. If he was doing what Rena suspected, he deserved to be slapped.

"Is Mr. Richardson pressing charges?" she asked.

"Yes."

"Did he tell you that my client's husband is in a coma with a broken neck?"

"He informed me that his son is a patient in ICU."

"What did Mr. Richardson tell you about the incident?"

"That information is part of my investigation."

"Which is not an answer to my question," Alex responded sharply. "What did Mr. Richardson tell you precipitated the incident?"

"Ms. Lindale, I've told you enough already, and I'm not going to let you cross-examine me about my investigation of this case. No charges have been filed against your client, and I want to give her the chance to offer an explanation before I decide what to do. Either she answers my questions or I proceed based on the evidence I already have."

Alex had heard enough. "Please put Mrs. Richardson on the line."

In a few seconds, Rena asked, "What do you think?"

"Walk away from the detective so we can talk." Alex waited until the sound of the police dispatcher in the background faded. "Did you hear his side of the conversation?" she asked.

"Yes."

"Most of the time it's a mistake to talk to the police. I think it's likely that he has already decided to file an assault and battery charge against you. If that's the case, there is no use giving him additional information."

Rena's voice rose higher. "But what if they put me in a cell? I can't imagine being locked up! I'd go crazy!"

Keeping her voice calm, Alex asked, "How much cash do you have in your purse?"

"About $300."

Alex did a quick calculation and summoned back bits of information about the criminal process she'd picked up in the past. As a young associate she had handled a few indigent criminal cases for people who couldn't afford a lawyer.

"Any assault and battery charges will be a misdemeanor because there wasn't any serious threat of injury. That means your bond to leave the jail will be a thousand dollars or less. Any bondsman will make your bond the amount you have in your purse. Most of them will even take credit cards."

"I have a fifty-thousand-dollar limit on my card, and I'm not close to being maxed out on it."

"Good," Alex responded. Then she realized Ezra might have canceled the card. "Have you used the card today?" she asked.

"At lunch."

"Okay. I'll tell the detective that you're not going to talk to him. He'll probably issue an arrest warrant for you."

"Will they fingerprint me and take my picture?" Rena asked anxiously.

"Yes, but I'll ask them to leave you in the booking area until a bondsman can get you out. Is there a phone book available?"

In a few moments, Rena said, "Yes. There is a pay phone down the hall. The phone book is hanging by a chain."

"Look up bail bondsmen in the yellow pages."

Alex waited until Rena said, "Here it is. The pages are all wrinkled, and the bottom half is torn out."

Alex suspected the yellow page listing for bail bondsmen was far more popular at a jail than the phone number for pizza delivery.

"Pick out three names and write down the phone numbers so you can call them if you need to."

Alex could hear Rena muttering to herself. "AAA Bonding Co.—

twenty-four-hour service, Eastside Bonding and Pawnshop. Here's one I don't want to use," she said.

"What is it?"

"Porter Bonding Company. That's the name of the other detective."

"It can't be the same guy. He works in a different county, but that would be a huge conflict of interest for a police officer to own a bonding company. Write down the number or find one more."

Hearing herself say "conflict of interest," Alex rolled her eyes. She was getting in deeper with Rena's problems. Her number one item of business the following day would be to extricate herself from the Richardson situation after she confronted Ralph Leggitt about Ezra's actions. The senior partner had ultimate ethical oversight, but as an associate, Alex couldn't avoid bringing it up.

"That's it," Rena said. "I have it all down. What do I do?"

"Once you know the amount of the bond, phone one of the companies and tell them where you are and the amount of your bond. They'll ask some questions about payment and take care of everything from there. You'll be out in a couple of hours."

"Okay. I'm taking the phone back to the detective."

"What's his name again?" Alex asked.

"His nametag says 'Lilley.' Like the flower only spelled differently."

"Detective Lilley, here," he said.

"I've discussed the situation with my client, and she doesn't want to give a statement. Please don't ask her any more questions."

"Suit yourself. Without anything to contradict the complainant's account of what happened, you've given me no option. I'm going to issue a warrant."

"Will you let my client wait in the booking area until a bondsman can get there?"

"There are a few chairs in the hallway. She can sit there for thirty minutes. If no one shows up by then, we'll take her back to the cell block."

"And what will her bond be?"

"That's up to the magistrate. Anything else? I've got paperwork to do."

"That's all. Let me talk to Mrs. Richardson."

The phone was handed off one more time. Alex could hear Rena snif-fling again.

"I can't believe Ezra is doing this to me," she said. "What have I done to hurt him or his family? I should be the one trying to put him in jail for stealing from Baxter and me."

Alex was not going to be drawn into another cycle of conversation for which there was no answer until morning light.

"Just call the bondsman as soon as you can," she said. "I'll be here the rest of the night if anything else comes up. I'll try to find you another lawyer tomorrow, or you can try to contact one yourself."

"I don't know any lawyers," Rena answered in a pouting voice. "And if you're going to dump me, what about Ezra?"

Alex hesitated. Rena would have the right to force Leggitt & Freeman to withdraw from representing Ezra in any areas of potential conflict. Because Baxter was involved in so much of the family business, that wouldn't leave much territory where Ralph Leggitt could continue to harvest massive legal fees.

Alex spoke slowly. "I will bring everything to the attention of my boss and recommend that we don't get involved."

"Are you going to tell him what I told you?" Rena asked in alarm. "You promised that you wouldn't do that!"

"You're right. That is confidential. Period."

Alex could hear Rena exhale.

"Okay," she said. "I'm going to call the bondsman."

Alex put down the phone. She felt sorry for Rena. First, her husband tries to kill her. Then her father-in-law pillages her property. The young woman was going to need two legal armies: one to defend her from groundless criminal accusations and another to attack her father-in-law before he booted her out into the street. But Alex could not let her natu-ral sympathies rule her ethical response to the situation. Rena would have to find help from another source.

Alex poured a glass of wine and sat down in a beige leather chair in the living room, but it was impossible to relax. Rena's phone call had shocked her like ice water that jarred her senses. Reentry into the legal arena should have been more gradual, but life's problems don't follow a predetermined script. Alex tried to revisit in her mind's eye the enchanted places where she'd spent the past week, but the inn at Saintes-Maries-de-la-Mer seemed as illusory as the picture of a medieval castle in a children's book of fairy tales. She sipped the wine, but it was a poor substitute for the nectars of southern France.

Eventually, the fatigue of her travels crept over her, and her eyelids grew heavy. The phone didn't ring, and she concluded Rena Richardson was not going to spend the night at the Greenville County jail. Alex yawned. She'd not asked Rena about Baxter but assumed his condition was unchanged. It just wasn't fair. Baxter slept while the effects of his attack on his wife caused his family to collapse into a pile of rubble. Alex trudged slowly up to bed and hoped for pleasant dreams as the antidote for harsh reality.

I charge thee, fling away ambition: by that sin fell the angels.
HENRY VIII, ACT 3, SCENE 2

WHEN THE ALARM clock sounded the next morning, it took Alex a few seconds to reorient with her surroundings. She groaned and burrowed under the covers. She should have allowed an extra day to cope with jet lag before returning to the office. She stumbled downstairs and brewed an extra strong cup of coffee, which she drank in the kitchen while watching the white mist that covered the marsh begin its retreat before the rising sun. It would have helped if Boris had been available to greet the day with his unrestrained exuberance. His example as he bounded down the steps for his morning run put a positive spin on life. She called the kennel and made arrangements to pick up her pets later that afternoon.

When she pulled into the law firm parking lot, she noticed that Mr. Leggitt's car wasn't there. Gwen had come into work early to help ease Alex back into her routine.

"Good morning!" Gwen said cheerily. "Bon voyage!"

Alex managed a weak smile. "That's what you say when someone is leaving, not when they return."

"You know what I mean. How was the trip?"

"Wonderful. As soon as I get my pictures developed, I'll give you an armchair summary. The scenery, the places I stayed, the food—everything was perfect."

"And the perfect man?"

Alex shrugged. "I brought the suitcase back empty, but I also left behind the last links to Jason. I'm ready to go on."

"Good. Did you meet anyone I might like?"

Alex perked up and leaned forward. "Yes. There was a cowboy who herded wild horses on the shores of the Mediterranean. I took his picture one afternoon on a hill overlooking the water. I didn't see a wife in sight."

"How old was he?"

"Old enough, but not too old. He had a close-cut beard that was sprinkled with gray and eyes as blue as the sea. We talked for a few minutes. I couldn't understand everything he said but gathered that he was in charge of that area of the coast. His English was limited to hot dog and Coca-Cola."

Gwen nodded. "I'll take him. We can eat hot dogs and drink Coke every night."

Alex chuckled. "It would be a challenge for a French cowboy to tame you."

Gwen pretended to be hurt. "I'm not that hard to manage. It takes a gentle hand."

Alex stepped over to the door of her office and peeked inside. The mound of mail was not as high as she'd anticipated.

"The mail isn't too bad," she said to Gwen. "What have you done with the rest of it?"

"Nothing," Gwen replied, pulling a box from underneath her desk. "The junk mail is in here. I thought it would help if all you had to look at today was the important stuff. You can decide if you want to order fruit or candy for Christmas presents later in the week."

"Thanks. Any fires burning?"

Gwen shook her head. "Everything was calm. You did a good job before you left, and I didn't have to talk to Ken once." She lowered her voice. "Rena Richardson phoned you several times. I think Baxter is still hanging on to life by a thread. I'm not sure what's going on with the rest of them."

"Nothing good," Alex replied. "Rena phoned me at home last night from the Greenville County jail. She slapped Ezra, and he had her arrested."

Gwen gasped. She sat on the edge of her seat with her eyes opened wide while Alex related the previous night's phone call.

"I talked to Rena once," Gwen said, "but she didn't want to give me details about anything. I don't think she trusted me even though I told her I worked for you."

"She has reason to be suspicious."

Gwen nodded. "If her father-in-law is doing what she said, he ought to be drug through the mud in the newspaper."

"It may come out in the open but not through us," Alex said. "I need to talk to Mr. Leggitt this morning. Do you know anything about his schedule?"

"No, but I can find out." Gwen buzzed Leggitt's secretary and then said to Alex, "He'll be in about ten-thirty. He had to meet someone for breakfast in Georgetown."

Alex called the law firm in Greenville on Rena's behalf and left a message. Picking up the bone-handled dagger she used as a letter opener, she opened her mail in reverse order. The longer she was away from the office the more likely a problem might develop, and the latest correspondence would reveal it.

Nothing leaped from the pile to bite her. Marilyn Simpson's new lawyer sent her a blind copy of his letter of representation with the words "Thank you for the referral" handwritten on the bottom of the sheet. The lawyer on the other side of the Eleanor Vox case had released a deluge of paperwork in response to Alex's initial salvo. Other cases were moving down the river of divorce and spawning letters, pleadings, notices of hearings, trial calendars, and motions. Alex organized everything in separate stacks across her desk. She was halfway through the papers and making good progress when Gwen buzzed her.

"Mr. Leggitt is here. He stopped in to see Leonard for a few minutes and then went to his office."

"Have I gotten a call from any lawyers in Greenville?"

"No."

Alex's heart began to beat slightly faster. It wasn't going to be easy confronting the senior lawyer at the firm about the Richardson matter, but she had no other option. She picked up the folder she'd taken to Greenville and walked down the hallway. Leggitt was on the phone but motioned for her to come in and sit down while he finished his conversation.

"That's right," he said. "The only way they'll be able to get access to the waterway is through us. I talked with the folks in Georgetown this morning, and they're on board. I had a memorandum of agreement in my briefcase, and they all signed it before we left the table. Working together we can quadruple the price for the boat ramp. I haven't run the final figures, but we should recoup 90 percent of our investment before we sell a quarter of the lots."

Alex glanced at Leggitt's desk. She didn't see any sign of a file with "Richardson" typed on the folder. The senior partner listened for a few seconds before continuing.

"They can sue us, but it won't do any good. We are in an impregnable position and have no legal obligation to grant an easement. They wouldn't join with us when they had the chance, and now they'll pay. In the long run, this is going to be better for us anyway."

When he hung up, he smiled at Alex.

"You know Zack Crosland don't you?"

Alex remembered him. He was an overweight man who wore a thick gold chain around his neck and didn't button the top buttons of his shirt. His wife was a woman twenty years younger who married him for all the wrong reasons.

"I represented his third wife in their divorce," she said.

"Did he have any money left after you worked him over?"

"Yes. I did the best I could, but my client wasn't the best candidate for sympathy."

"He's going to part with a lot of it now. Otherwise, he's stuck with a useless tract of land near the Intercoastal Waterway."

Leggitt glanced down at his calendar.

"I have to leave in a few minutes. How was your trip?"

"Good. I recommend it if you ever decide to take a vacation."

Leggitt shook his head. "Taking my wife to a place where neither of us can communicate with the locals is not my idea of relaxation." He picked up a folder that he'd set on the credenza behind him. "I guess you're here because of the conflict of interest problem."

Relieved that he mentioned it first, Alex said, "That's why I wanted to talk to you as soon as possible. We have to do something."

"It's a no-brainer," he said. "You need to drop the client immediately. There is no way this firm can represent Eleanor Vox. You weren't aware that her husband, Hubert, was a silent partner in the Dune View golf development because his ownership interest doesn't show up on the firm list of clients. He called me upset after you filed an answer, but I reassured him that you would be out of the case as soon as you returned."

Alex's mouth dropped open. "Uh, I was referring to what has happened with Rena and Ezra Richardson. She called me last night from the Greenville County jail and told me Ezra is using the durable power of attorney to transfer Baxter's property out of his name."

It was Leggitt's turn to register surprise. "What was Rena doing at the jail?"

Alex repeated the gist of the conversation. Ralph Leggitt shook his head. When Alex finished, he tapped his pen on the surface of his desk.

"So you told her to get another lawyer?" he asked.

"Yes. In fact, I told her the firm would have to withdraw from representing either one of them. She has shared confidential information with me, and Mr. Richardson has talked with you. We can't help him gut Baxter's estate at Rena's expense or help her fight her father-in-law over use of the power of attorney."

Leggitt's eyes narrowed. "Why did you tell her we had to withdraw from representing Ezra? Didn't you get my message when you called from Greenville? I specifically told you that Ezra Richardson was our client. If you did something to misrepresent the situation to Rena, that was contrary to my instructions."

Alex felt her face flush. She spoke slowly in order to keep control.

"Initially, you told me our client was the Richardson family. I went to Greenville to try and be a peacemaker and that's what I did. My interaction with Rena gave her the impression that I was there to help her as well as Ezra, and she told me things with a reasonable expectation of an attorney-client privilege."

"What sort of things?"

It was a moment of decision. Alex immediately saw her two choices. She could tell all and please Ralph Leggitt or refuse and suffer the consequences.

She hesitated. "Are you sure you want to know?"

"That's why I asked you. Stop this foolishness and tell me what Rena said."

Alex stared at the front edge of Mr. Leggitt's desk. In a few seconds the whole plan played out in her mind. Ralph Leggitt had shielded himself from accusation by sending her to Greenville while he stayed in Santee and plotted with Ezra the best method for depleting Baxter's assets. The senior partner was a sorry lawyer but a master manipulator. It had been a ploy from the first meeting. She looked up from the edge of the desk into Leggitt's eyes before answering.

"No."

Leggitt's voice rose in volume and pitch. "What did she tell you? Tell me now!"

Alex shook her head. "No. She shared it in confidence. You've made it clear that Ezra is your client, and I won't reveal what she told me."

Leggitt stood up. He was a short, unimpressive looking man, but he was also Alex's boss. His face was red, and at that moment he appeared to tower over her. He started to speak, then checked himself and sat down.

His voice softer, he said, "Alex, you have a good future here. This is not a field to die on."

"Then don't make me. I'm not going to add one mistake to another."

"Are you sure?" he asked.

Alex heard the hint of retreat in his voice. She had called his bluff. Her law practice generated a steady stream of income that yielded a consistent profit to the partners of the firm. Ralph Leggitt liked money too much to throw that away.

"Yes," she nodded.

Leggitt tapped the top of his desk with his pen. Alex waited.

"You're fired," the senior partner said matter-of-factly. "Clear out your desk and leave the office within the next hour. Do not take any files with you until we have conducted an inventory."

Alex was shocked. "But—"

Leggitt cut her off. "There's no room for further discussion. I'm sorry for your decision, but you left me no other choice. The past few weeks have shown the basic incompatability of your practice with the main business of the firm. Simpson, Vox, now this. It would have ended sooner or later."

He stood up, stepped to the door, and opened it. Still numb, Alex rose to her feet. As she walked blindly down the hall to her office, she heard the receptionist page her on the building intercom. Eleanor Vox was on line six.

Alex ignored the page.

When she reached Gwen's desk, the secretary pulled a letter from the printer and said, "Mrs. Vox just called. I put it into your voice mail."

Alex didn't respond for a few seconds, and Gwen looked up. At the sight of Alex's face, she asked, "What happened?"

Alex glanced at the door to Leonard Mitchell's office. It was closed.

"Mr. Leggitt fired me," she said flatly. "He told me to clean out my desk and leave the office."

Gwen gasped. "No!"

Alex's voice began to regain its intensity. "I have to leave immediately, but I'm not going to abandon my clients. Run a printout of my active cases with phone numbers and addresses. I'll need to contact my clients over the next few days and sort out what I'm going to do."

For the first time since she'd known Gwen, the secretary was speechless.

"He said it was inevitable," Alex continued. "My practice doesn't mesh with the firm's primary emphasis."

"That's ridiculous!" Gwen sputtered. "It had to do with Rena Richardson, didn't it?"

Alex nodded. "That's the immediate reason for the blowup. But I can't talk about it."

Before Gwen could get up a head of steam, Alex retreated into her office, closed the door, and leaned against it. She'd never been fired in her life. Since her first job as a sixteen-year-old clerk in a women's dress shop through part-time work during college and law school, she had always received nothing but praise and promotion from her supervisors. She was a lifelong overachiever who conquered every obstacle. Until now.

She glanced around her office. She'd taken a lot of pride in creating a workplace that reflected herself. Most first-time visitors remarked about the variety of items on display, and Alex often took time to tell at least one story about a picture or artifact. In a few curt sentences, Ralph Leggitt had demolished everything she'd built over the past six years. Now, there was nothing left to do but pack up her trinkets and put them in the trunk of her car.

When she opened her office door to get some empty boxes from the copy room, Gwen turned around, and Alex could see that she'd been crying.

"Gwen, don't do that."

"If I don't cry, I might march down to Ralph Leggitt's office and stab him with your letter opener! I've worked with a lot of lawyers, and you're the most decent, honest attorney I've ever known. You care about your clients; you know what you're doing on your cases—"

"Please, stop!" Alex interrupted. "I appreciate you, too, but this is making it worse. I need to get out of here so I can decide what to do."

Gwen bit her lip. "Okay."

"I'm going to get some empty boxes. Please print out the information I need about the clients."

The copy room was on the other side of the reception area. As she passed through the room, Alex looked at the pictures of the lawyers hanging on the wall. She'd done everything right to advance along the partnership track at Leggitt & Freeman except compromise her ethical convictions. The space she'd reserved for herself would go to someone else. If a woman ever became a partner at Leggitt & Freeman, it wouldn't be Alexia Lindale.

Hope deferred makes the heart sick,
but a longing fulfilled is a tree of life.
PROVERBS 13:12

BY THE TIME Alex had packed her first box and carried it to her car, the news of her termination had rippled from one end of the law firm to the other. Several secretaries looked away when she walked by. Others met her gaze with a shake of the head or a quiet word of sympathy.

Leggitt's paralegal came by her office and told her not to take any files from her office. Alex ignored her. She knew the rules. All her clients had signed an agreement for legal representation with Leggitt & Freeman; however, Ralph Leggitt couldn't prevent a client from following Alex if she went to work for herself or with another firm. The state bar prohibited restrictions against a client's freedom to select a lawyer, and so long as Alex paid the correct percentage of the fee earned to Leggitt & Freeman, her former employers couldn't complain.

On her second trip to the car, Alex passed the open door of Ken Pinchot's office. The litigation partner was on the phone, and she heard him laughing. The sound was a harsh reminder that life went on at the firm for others even if hers was ending. Returning to her office, she noticed that Leonard Mitchell's door was closed, and she asked Gwen if he knew what had happened. The secretary nodded.

"Mr. Leggitt sent an e-mail to the partners as soon as you left his office."

"How do you know?" Alex asked.

Gwen shrugged. "I went in on Leonard's screen name and read it. I know his password."

"What did it say?"

"Nothing much. Just that he had terminated you and would provide the details at the firm lunch on Wednesday."

Every Wednesday, the partners ate a catered meal in Ralph Leggitt's office. Alex suspected the meetings were a mixture of fraternity bull session and board of directors meeting.

"Do you have the list of clients ready?" she asked.

Gwen handed Alex a large, flat envelope. "It's all in here. There is another copy for Mr. Leggitt. Is he going to contact the clients and try to get them to stay with the firm?"

Alex shook her head. "I don't think anyone here wants my clientele, but I'll have to let them know something soon. Keep the correspondence organized until I make up my mind."

"Where are you going now?"

"I'm going to pick up my pets and go home. After that, I don't know. What do you think I should do?"

Gwen was silent for a moment. "I don't trust my thoughts."

"Me, either."

Alex put the last box in the trunk of her car and looked back at the building where she'd spent most of her waking hours since moving to Santee. She remembered her first day as a nervous young attorney who didn't know how to enter a client number in order to operate the copy machine until Gwen came to her rescue. It was the beginning of their friendship. Much had happened since that day: her first deposition, dictating letters without writing a rough draft, her first jury trial, the congratulations of other attorneys when she won a big case. Most of the significant events of the past six years had been intimately connected with the people in the office that had been at the center of her universe. Now, it suddenly looked small.

Alone in the privacy of her car and shielded from curious eyes, Alex waited for tears but none came. She wasn't the type of woman who made herself cry. She drove out of the parking lot without glancing in the rearview mirror. Like the ship in the Mediterranean, it was time to sail in a different direction.

She called the kennel and listened to an answering machine message that Pat would be unavailable for at least two hours. With time on her hands, Alex drove slowly through the center of Santee and thought about her future. She approached the courthouse. She saw two familiar faces: a young lawyer recently hired by another firm in town and an older woman employed at the clerk's office. Alex wondered when and how they would find out that she was no longer working for Leggitt & Freeman. The legal gossip network in Santee was faster than a computer modem, and within twenty-four hours scores of people would discuss what had happened to her. She took little comfort in the fact that within a week her firing would be old news, and another item would take its place in the information pipeline.

As she passed the courthouse, she considered picking up her pets and driving to her parents' condominium in Cocoa Beach to lick her wounds. Because she represented so many women who needed emergency legal care, a long grieving period wasn't possible, but a temporary respite would be understandable. However, she quickly rejected the idea of a trip to Florida. Her parents had their own lives, and Alex was too old to run home with a skinned knee.

She turned down a side street where two other law firms were located. A Charleston firm seeking to tap into the deepening stream of money flowing into the area had rented an older building and turned it into an elegant office. The Charleston group's presence made Ralph Leggitt nervous, and it would be a twist of the knife if she joined them. The other law firm was a group of three young male lawyers who had launched out on their own a couple of years before. They might want to add a woman with a healthy client base to the mix. Alex knew she would have options, but what she needed was direction.

She drove away from town toward Highway 17. When she reached McBee Road, she turned toward Sandy Flats Church. It was earlier in the day than the times when she'd wandered into Ted Morgan's practice sessions, and the sanctuary would be a quiet place to think.

When she pulled into the church parking lot, she saw Ted Morgan on a ladder, painting the trim of an old, white house on the property. He saw her and waved. Seeing his face made Alex smile. She needed contact with a decent human being.

"Another masterpiece?" she called out as she stepped from her car.

"In the works," he answered.

Ted climbed down the ladder. He was wearing white painter's overalls with a collection of colors from different jobs.

"Are you still practicing the piano?" she asked.

Ted nodded. "Yes, I suspect it's like law practice. You never get it exactly right." Alex didn't want to discuss the law and decided on a quick exit.

"I'm sorry to interrupt. I'll be going. I don't want to keep you from your work."

Ted wiped his face with a red bandanna that he took from his back pocket.

"No. I'm thirsty and ready for a break. Would you like some lemonade?"

Alex hesitated. Ted didn't wait for an answer. "Come inside," he said and walked toward the front door.

Alex slowly followed him into the old house. The wooden floors creaked under her feet. The plaster walls were painted in pale pastels.

"For about a hundred years this was the parsonage where every pastor of the church lived," Ted said. "The senior minister now lives in a house in the Dune View community."

"I'm familiar with it. Nice area."

"Yeah, but this house has its charms. Have a look around while I wash up."

Alex entered the living room. It was Spartan and functional, not surprising for a bachelor. On the mantel above the fireplace she saw a picture of a young woman leaning against a tree. She stepped closer for a better look. If it was the minister's daughter, the young woman's mother contributed the most to her appearance. The eyes and hair were dark and the cheekbones high, but the mouth and smile were taken directly from Ted Morgan.

Ted stuck his head around the corner. "Do you want to help me make the lemonade?"

"Sure."

The kitchen was at the rear of the house. There was a bank of windows over the sink that gave a panoramic view of the church graveyard. Alex looked outside while she washed her hands.

"That's a happy scene," she said. "Rows and rows of tombstones."

"Only if you don't like graveyards."

"Do you like them?"

"Not in a morbid way, but this one has so many old graves that I don't think about the fact that the people are dead. I'm more interested in finding out how they lived when they were alive."

Alex dried her hands with a towel. "Are any famous people buried here?"

"A former U.S. senator and at least twenty men who fought in the Civil War. The soldiers' tombstones list their rank and regiment even if they died many years after the war ended. There's also the tombstone of one of the earliest missionaries to the local Indians. He and his wife lived along the Santee River in the 1720s."

Alex dried her hands with a towel. There was a large bowl filled with lemons on the counter. Ted handed a knife to Alex.

"Start cutting them in two while I set up the juicer. We'll need about six or seven."

"Do you always keep so many lemons on hand?" she asked.

"Usually. I drink it year round."

While Alex sliced the lemons, Ted opened a cabinet door and took out the juicer. He plugged it in and pressed a lemon over a device that spun around rapidly until the juice ran into a trough and down into a container. When all the juice was collected, he poured it into a pitcher filled with ice and water. He took out a canister of sugar and dumped in two generous scoops.

"Don't ask me how much sugar I'm putting in," he said. "It's better not to think about it. The end result is what counts."

He took two cut-glass tumblers from a cabinet and poured a glass for Alex and himself. He handed one to Alex then held his up in the air.

"To Russian composers," he said.

"And those who play their music," Alex responded.

They clinked glasses, and Alex took a sip.

"This is good," she said. "The last time I drank something like this was at my grandmother's house in Ohio. She was like you."

"She loved lemonade?"

"No, she was religious. She went to church all the time."

A small, rectangular wooden table stood against one wall of the kitchen. Ted sat at one end and Alex at the other.

"Is that a picture of your daughter in the living room?" Alex asked.

"Yes. She's twenty-two now and living in New York. She graduated from Juilliard and plays the viola."

"With the New York Philharmonic?"

Ted laughed. "Maybe someday. She is doing ensemble work and looking for a job with a symphony somewhere in the U.S."

"And her mother?"

"Lives in California. We've been divorced for many years."

Alex took a sip of lemonade and wondered what about Ted Morgan would convince a woman to divorce him. He seemed like a nice man, but male flaws emerge as surely as a daily growth of beard. She thought of another question but stifled it. She was a guest in Ted's home, not cross-examining him on the witness stand. She took another drink and wondered what to talk about since the minister apparently wasn't going to hold up his end of the conversation.

"I just returned from France," she said. "I visited an old church with stained-glass windows. It was a beautiful place, but none of the windows had a figure who looked directly at me."

Ted smiled. "Interesting."

Alex looked at her glass. If she took a few quick gulps, she could be on her way. She raised the glass and took a long drink. The tart juice made the edges of her tongue tingle. She raised it again and drank until the remaining ice cubes touched her lips. The last drops were sweet with extra sugar.

"Thanks for the lemonade," she said.

"You're welcome."

Alex stood up. Ted stayed seated and leaned back in his chair.

"Before you leave," he said, "do you want to tell me why you came by the church?"

"Oh, I was going to spend a few minutes alone in the sanctuary."

"Come anytime. Is everything okay?"

"Yeah, of course."

It wasn't a big lie, but immediately Alex felt guilty. The minister had been kind to her and deserved the truth.

"Actually," she continued slowly, "I lost my job this morning and didn't have any place to go for a couple of hours. I was going to sit in the sanctuary and try to sort through what happened."

Ted knit his forehead and looked at her with compassion. "I thought you were upset but didn't know why," he said.

"Really?" Alex asked in surprise. "I didn't think it was obvious."

"Sometimes I can tell when a person is troubled. It's like a note out of tune."

Alex felt tears suddenly welling up in her eyes. She'd been stoic when leaving the office, but in the presence of the minister her sorrow rose to the surface. She wanted to weep and pour out her heart to Ted Morgan at the same time.

"I'm sorry. This isn't like me."

Ted stood. "Why don't you go to the sanctuary? That's why you came. We can talk later if you want to. I'll be painting the house for the rest of the afternoon."

Alex nodded and turned away before the first tear ran down her cheek into the corner of her mouth in salty contrast to the lingering sweetness of the lemonade. Her vision blurry, she grabbed a handful of tissues from a box in the living room as she fled from the house.

Her feet crunched across the broken seashells of the church parking lot. Inside the sanctuary she let the hot tears flow unhindered. She didn't sob. It wasn't hysteria. It was a release of pent-up feelings by a woman who had made emotional restraint one of the bulwarks of her personality. She sat on the pew nearest the piano and let the disappointment flow from her eyes. Spending the rest of her legal career in close proximity to Ralph Leggitt and Leonard Mitchell would not have been occupational bliss, but she had devoted six years of her life toward achieving a goal that was now impossible to attain. Disappointment was inevitable.

By the third tissue, she began to calm down. Drying her eyes, she looked around the sanctuary. It was a quiet and beautiful place. Ted Morgan and others like him felt at home here; she was still a stranger. But even as a stranger, she felt welcome. Her impulsive decision to stop by the church had been right. She needed a place of peace and protection, a sanctuary where her feelings could be released in safety.

And Ted Morgan was a rarity—a good man. She needed the nudge he provided to release the pent-up dam of her feelings, and she sensed that even now he stood on guard outside to protect her time alone in the sanctuary. She barely knew Ted, but he'd already shown more concern for her as a person than anyone at Leggitt & Freeman except Gwen. The minister showed more facets than musical talent.

Her thoughts shifted. Ted Morgan cared, but what about God? Did the Almighty have an opinion about what had happened to her in Ralph Leggitt's office? Did he have an interest in the direction she took in the future? Was Jesus any more alive than the bones of those buried in the nearby cemetery? Alex knew the basics of Christianity via osmosis through American culture and contact with her grandmother in Ohio, but she had never seen the relevancy of faith for herself. Perhaps it was time to give it more serious consideration.

Standing and moving to the aisle, she inspected the stained-glass windows. The miracles depicted were for desperate people without any other options. Alex wasn't desperate, just drained and frustrated and empty. She didn't need a miracle, just a new direction for her ship. If the answer for her future was in the church, she wasn't sure where to look for it.

She approached the window in which Jesus was healing the man at the pool of Bethesda. Keeping her eyes on the face of Jesus, she moved closer until she stood directly beneath him. She inched to the left and came within the range of his gaze. When she did, recognition came.

It was the same look of kindness she'd seen in Ted Morgan's eyes at the kitchen table.

The world uncertain comes and goes.
RALPH WALDO EMERSON

AFTER POSTING A two-hundred-dollar cash bond, Rena left the jail by taxi and returned to her hotel. She tried to contact Jeffrey, but he didn't answer at home or on his cell phone. Emotionally exhausted, she went to bed but was unable to sleep. At 3 A.M. she stared at the ceiling and considered calling Giles Porter to confess to the attempted murder of her husband. Maybe then the enormous weight that threatened to crush her chest would be lifted, and she could get some rest. However, after two hours of sleep, she awoke with a measure of strength restored and resolved never to admit wrongdoing. She had acted in self-defense. Her nighttime thoughts were unreliable guides summoned by the stress of the past twenty-four hours. Tossing back the covers, she called room service and ordered breakfast.

Rena didn't want to return to the hospital and run the risk of another encounter with her father-in-law. While eating a poached egg, she phoned Leggitt & Freeman. Alex was in a meeting. She waited half an hour, tried again, and was told that Ms. Lindale would be out of the office for the rest of the day. Frustrated, Rena searched in vain for the slip of paper on which she'd written the lawyer's cell phone number. When she couldn't find it, she called Leggitt & Freeman again, only to be told by the receptionist that Alex's personal information was not available. Rena slammed down the phone. Jeffrey had been right. Anyone who worked for Leggitt & Freeman could not be trusted when Ezra was on the scene. Alex had carried through with her threat to dump her and had lied when promising to help her find other representation.

Rena opened the yellow pages of the Greenville phone book to the attorney section. Page after page of multicolored advertisements promised expert legal help for everything from accountant's malpractice to zoning disputes. Most of the lawyers specializing in criminal law emphasized expertise in DUI cases. Rena narrowed her choices to four women lawyers. Two of them handled medical malpractice and criminal cases. The other two represented people who were injured on the job and criminal cases. Rena dialed the first number.

"Jenkins & Lyons," the receptionist answered.

"I'd like to talk to Patricia Jenkins," Rena said.

"May I ask who's calling?"

"Rena Richardson."

"What type of problem do you have?" the receptionist asked.

"Uh, I'd rather talk to a lawyer about it."

"Is it a civil or criminal case?"

Rena wasn't sure about the differences. "I've been charged with assault and battery, and my father-in-law is stealing my money with a power of attorney that my husband signed before we were married."

"Please hold."

Rena waited for several minutes and listened to five cycles of an advertisement that told about million-dollar verdicts the firm had won against doctors and hospitals. Rena was impressed. Finally, the receptionist returned.

"Ms. Jenkins is out of town for the rest of the week. May I take your number and have her call you back?"

Rena hung up. The next two calls were equally fruitless. On the final call, she spoke with an attorney named Ann Moser. She listened as Rena told her about the assault and battery charge.

"What is the date set for the hearing?" the lawyer asked in a voice that rasped with the hint of long-time cigarette use. "It should be on the bottom of the pink piece of paper they gave you at the jail."

Rena had put the sheet on the nightstand. She picked it up and looked at the bottom.

"I can't read it. The date didn't come through clearly."

"Call the jail and give them the number of the case. They will tell you the hearing date. Then get back in touch with me. Do you have any money?"

"Uh, I think so."

"What do you mean?"

Rena told her about the power of attorney.

The lawyer grunted. "That's not my field. If you hire me on the criminal case, I'll help you find someone else to fight your father-in-law."

"Thanks," Rena responded. "I'll be in touch."

Rena put a star by the number for Ann Moser. She sounded like a tough attorney. And she had no connection with Ezra Richardson.

Throughout the day Rena grew increasingly restless. She was both drawn to and repulsed by Baxter. She wasn't sure why. Early in the afternoon she called the ICU waiting room. A young man answered the phone. Rena didn't identify herself.

"Do you know Mr. Ezra Richardson?" she asked.

"Yes."

"Is he there?"

"No. He left about an hour ago."

Rena fidgeted with the phone cord. "Are you sure you know him?"

"Yes. I was on duty when he checked in."

"And he's gone?"

"Yes."

Rena hung up and paced back and forth for a few minutes. Then she left for the hospital.

Ezra was not in sight when she peeked through the door of the waiting room. Her head slightly bowed, she approached the attendant. It was a different person from the young man on duty when she was arrested, and he showed no sign of recognition and gave no instructions to bar her from the ICU area. Relieved, she signed in and went back to Baxter's room. He was alone with no nurses in sight.

Rena had begun to notice subtle yet tangible changes in Baxter's condition. He was in reasonably good shape before the injury, but his flesh was already beginning to turn flaccid. A nurse had told her the human body rapidly loses muscle tone when totally immobilized. Rena gingerly poked Baxter's upper arm with her index finger and it yielded passively to her touch. He was as weak as a baby. She wondered if the outward deterioration was mirrored by a breakdown of her husband's internal organs. It was a question she'd not yet asked the doctors.

In the midst of her monotony and boredom at the hospital, Rena had kept up her unrelenting propaganda campaign. Hundreds of times she had whispered her revised version of the events at the waterfall into Baxter's left ear. She renewed her chant.

"It was an accident. Your fall was a tragic accident. You stepped too close to the edge and slipped. I tried to save you but couldn't. I love you very much."

Baxter never gave any visible sign of assent or disagreement, but once Rena became fixed on a plan, she could display dogged determination in carrying it out.

After her visit with Baxter, she drove a few blocks from the hospital to a place that served cappuccinos. She sat sipping her coffee when her cell phone rang. It was Jeffrey.

"Where have you been?" she asked in frustration. "I've been trying to reach you."

Her brother-in-law spoke rapidly. "Don't be mad at me. I know what my father is doing with Baxter's money, and I don't agree with him. I just drove into Greenville and want to talk to you about it."

"Did you know he had me arrested?"

"Arrested!"

"That's right."

"What happened?"

Rena told him about the events of the previous night. She concluded by saying, "They took my picture, fingerprints, everything. It was horrible. I didn't leave the jail until midnight."

"Where are you now?" Jeffrey asked.

"A few blocks from the hospital. I was afraid to come, but I've seen Baxter every day since the accident and didn't want to miss. Your father left before I got here and hasn't been back, so I didn't run into him."

"He's on a flight to Baltimore for a meeting in the morning," Jeffrey replied.

Rena felt a wave of relief.

Jeffrey continued. "Listen, there's more going on with the power of attorney than the money in your checking account. I need to see you."

"What are you talking about?"

"How soon can you meet me at the hospital?"

"A couple of minutes, but why can't we talk over the phone?"

"I'd prefer to see you in person."

Rena hesitated, but Jeffrey was her only possible source of information about Ezra's plans.

"Okay, I'll see you in the ICU waiting room. But it will take a lot to convince me that you're being sincere."

"That's why we need to talk. Don't blame me for what my father is doing. That's totally his deal, and I think it's wrong."

Rena's mind churned as she walked to her vehicle. She was suspicious of Jeffrey's motives. He'd abandoned her after their meal together at the French restaurant, and it didn't make sense that he would side with her in a dispute with his own father. She opened the door and slid into the driver's seat. She was so distracted by worry and anxiety that she didn't see the man sitting in the rear seat of the SUV until she looked in the rearview mirror before backing out of the parking space.

It was Baxter.

He had a tube in his nose and a malevolent glare in his eyes. Rena gripped the steering wheel and screamed. At the sound of her voice Baxter lingered for a split second—just long enough to give Rena a look that told her he wasn't fooled by the lies she'd been feeding him as regularly as the drip of fluids from his IV bag. Baxter knew the truth, and it was buried so deep within him that only the grave would destroy his ability to reveal it.

———

After leaving Sandy Flats Church, Alex picked up Misha and Boris at the kennel. Boris was wild with excitement when he saw her. Although not as exuberant, Misha was no less glad. She rubbed against Alex's leg in welcome and curled up in the passenger seat for the ride home. Boris jumped into the backseat and ran from one window to the other. Alex was envious of her pets. They didn't know or care about her employment status. As long as they had food and water in the bowls in the kitchen, they were content.

"I'll take care of you," Alex reassured them as they drove down the coastal highway. "Doggy bones and cat snacks are still at the top of my grocery list."

It was odd getting home in the middle of the afternoon. Alex let Misha and Boris go outside while she called her parents with the news of her job loss. Her mother offered words of sympathy and invited her to come to Florida for a few days to relax, but Alex turned her down.

After she hung up the phone, Alex walked onto her porch and looked at the marsh. A pleasant breeze wafted in from the ocean. Several white egrets flew low over the reeds. The tide was going out, and the black mud glistened in the sun. It would be hard to leave her seashore enclave so soon after returning from France. She needed to stay in Santee and sort out her future.

It had been almost two weeks since she'd gone for a swim in the Atlantic. Alex put on her swimsuit and packed her beachbag. Boris ran in excited circles as soon as he realized her plan and bounded down the steps in front of her. She pulled her boat to the water. Soon she was navigating through the canals toward the barrier island.

The expanse of blue sky filled her vision. Nature began to work its magic. Alex loved every nuance of the marsh, and the unrestrained optimism in Boris as he stood proudly wagging his thick tail in the bow of the little boat was so infectious that a glimmer of joy returned to Alex's world.

The scene in Ralph Leggitt's office no longer received top billing in the theater of her mind. Her legal career had taken a major hit, but it wasn't as severe as it would have been a few years earlier. Her law practice and personal confidence had grown so that if she decided to join another firm or open her own office, she knew she could do it. She stepped onto the sand of the beach with renewed assurance.

In spite of the slight breeze, the water was calm, and she swam farther down the island than usual. Boris stayed close by her side. A leash was mandatory on land, but a word sufficient in the water. Before turning toward the beach, Alex flipped over and floated on her back for a few minutes while Boris swam around her. She watched a sea gull dive into the water no more than twenty feet away. It came up swallowing a fish.

When they reached the shore, Boris shook himself and started racing back and forth from the edge of the water to the top of the dunes. Alex almost never saw him run out of energy. At home on land or in the water, the black Labrador was bred for strength and stamina. Squeezing the excess water from her hair, Alex scampered after him. Boris looked over his shoulder and laughed at her with his eyes. Several times he slowed just enough for her to touch his back and then sprinted away before she could grab his neck and hold him still.

When she reached her beachbag, Alex gave up the chase, sat down on the sand, and closed her eyes. In a few seconds she heard panting, and Boris licked her hand. She opened her eyes and patted his head. He sat down beside her, and they gazed out to sea together. She scratched the favorite spot under his chin, and he craned his neck higher.

"Thank you," she told him. "You remind me of things I need to remember."

He looked at her with happy eyes.

At home, Alex fixed a cup of hot tea. Misha came into the kitchen and curled up in her basket in the corner while Alex boiled the water and put a tea bag in a mug. She turned on her stereo and let her soul steep in the sounds of Prokofiev.

As the fishes that are taken in an evil net, and as the birds that are caught in the snare; so are the sons of men snared in an evil time.
ECCLESIASTES 9:12 (KJV)

STILL SHAKEN FROM her encounter with Baxter in the car, Rena walked into the ICU waiting room. Jeffrey was waiting for her. He was wearing a dark suit but had unbuttoned the top button of his shirt and loosened his tie.

"Do you want to see Baxter before we talk?" he asked.

"Not again!" Rena said more forcibly than she intended.

"Why not?"

"Uh, it's been a stressful day."

"Let's go somewhere and talk."

"I need a drink of water," she said.

Rena brushed a stray strand of hair from her face. The similarity in appearance between Baxter and Jeffrey was not helping her mental state. The water fountain was in the hall. When she pushed the button, the arching stream of water reminded her of the waterfall. She closed her eyes and drank.

When she returned to the waiting room, Jeffrey was talking with Dr. Berman. The neurosurgeon was dressed for the operating room.

He nodded to Rena. "Mrs. Richardson, I'm glad I caught you. Let's go to one of the consultation rooms so we can talk in private."

Rena and Jeffrey followed Dr. Berman to the conference room where Rena and Ezra had crossed swords with Alex in the middle. This time, Rena and Jeffrey sat on the same side of the table. The doctor looked at Rena.

"There has been a slight reduction in the intracranial swelling in your husband's head; however, that doesn't mean he's about to wake up. In fact, I don't see any signs that he is regaining consciousness."

"What about his brain activity?" Jeffrey asked.

"He is not what people call 'brain dead.' He is in a coma, but I would not yet describe it as a persistent vegetative state."

Rena worded her question carefully.

"How long would a coma have to last before it could be called a persistent vegetative state?"

"There is not an exact measurement. Doctors disagree."

"What about you?" Rena persisted.

The doctor shook his head. "I'm not ready to commit myself. The severity of damage to your husband's neck complicates everything. Based on my review of all the tests conducted, there is no doubt that he is paralyzed from the neck down. I'm sorry to have to tell you this, but even if he comes out of the coma, he will not be able to move his arms and legs. In addition, the paralysis makes him more susceptible to other conditions: urinary dysfunction, respiratory infection, even bedsores can cause serious, life-threatening problems. The greatest danger is pneumonia; second is non-ischemic heart disease."

"What is that?" Rena asked.

"An unexplained heart attack. The neck injury greatly increases the possibility that an underlying heart condition might manifest in a heart attack. A cardiologist examined him this morning and found no obvious signs of problems with his heart, so that danger may not be so great. Respiratory problems are an unavoidable concern. We're watching him closely for any sign of infection."

"Could you take him off the breathing machine?" Jeffrey asked.

"Not yet. He was able to breathe on his own before we inserted the ventilator; however, at this time I'm not sure he could survive without it. In the meantime, we don't want him struggling to breathe. His body must be able to focus on recovering from the coma."

Rena squirmed in her seat. "What are we supposed to do?"

"Other than visit him, not much. It's a wait and see situation."

The doctor rubbed his eyes. "Any more questions?"

Rena couldn't think of anything that wouldn't sound homicidal. Jeffrey spoke.

"Are all the doctors in agreement about waiting?"

Dr. Berman rubbed his eyes. "The majority opinion is to maintain the status quo. Dr. Kolb and I requested a consultation with a neurologist who works a lot with seriously brain-injured patients. Dr. Draughton is less optimistic about the patient's recovery."

"What did he suggest?" Rena asked quickly.

"To stop the ventilator if that's what the family wants to do. If your husband can't breathe on his own, he would die."

Rena caught her breath.

"Would my father have to be involved in that decision?" Jeffrey asked.

"Yes. The chart indicates that Mr. Richardson has a power of attorney."

"I do, too!" Rena blurted out. "And I'm his wife."

The doctor rubbed his chin. "I realize there are legal issues that may have to be sorted out. If everyone involved can sit down and talk—"

"That's not an option," Rena interrupted.

Dr. Berman's face became grim. "Then I don't have anything else to tell you at this time. We will continue to monitor your husband closely and let you know if anything changes for better or worse."

"How could we reach Dr. Draughton?" Jeffrey asked.

"He is with Horizon Neurology here in Greenville, but he also sees patients in Spartanburg and Anderson."

After the doctor left, Rena and Jeffrey stayed in the consultation room. Rena wanted Jeffrey to make the first move.

"What do you think we should do now?" she asked.

"Contact Dr. Draughton."

"What would you ask him?"

Jeffrey paused. "The longer this goes on without any change, the more I'm convinced it's cruel to keep Baxter alive with machines and tubes. If Dr. Draughton is the expert in treatment of serious head injuries, I'd like to know why he wants to unplug the ventilator. If he gives me a good reason, it's time for me to talk to my father."

"I think so, too," Rena said with satisfaction. "We have no business trying to play God with Baxter's life. In my heart, I know he wants to be set free."

"But there are other factors that affect what my father is willing to do," Jeffrey added. "After our lunch, I talked with Rafe Grange in Charleston. Did you try to call him?"

"Yes. He never did any work for Baxter."

"Too bad. Rafe told me a power of attorney is only valid as long as a person is alive. It's automatically revoked at death. After that, it's worthless. That means it may be harder to convince my father to let Baxter go than I thought."

Rena suddenly realized the implication of Jeffrey's words and her eyes grew wide with indignation. "That's sick! Your father would try to keep Baxter alive just so he could use the power of attorney to steal money from our checking account!"

"There is much more to it than that. Let's go someplace else and talk. This waiting room is depressing, and I'd like a drink."

It was almost dusk when they left the hospital. Rena drove them to an upscale bar not far from the hospital. The after work crowd was leaving the pub, and it was too early for the evening rush. The hostess led them to a small, round table for two in a dimly lit corner.

"What do you want?" Jeffrey asked Rena. "I'm ordering a martini."

Rena avoided hard liquor. It made her giddy. "Just a glass of wine."

After a cocktail waitress took their order, Jeffrey leaned forward.

"Do you believe that I want to help you?"

Rena inspected her brother-in-law's face, but she couldn't discern his intentions.

"I don't know, but I'm here to listen."

"After you hear what I have to say, I think you'll be ready to trust me. First, you need to know that my father can use the power of attorney to transfer all Baxter's property out of his name. That includes his interest in businesses, stocks, savings accounts, and everything else."

Rena sputtered, "If he does that—"

Jeffrey interrupted. "Did Baxter have the deed to the Santee house changed so that it is in both your names?"

"Uh, no," Rena said. "I'd bugged him about it, but he hadn't done anything about it. Can your father take away the house?"

"Yes, and I'd bet he's getting ready to throw you out in the street."

Rena felt like she'd been punched in the stomach. She'd risked everything at the waterfall only to have her future snatched away from her by a stupid piece of paper. The waitress brought their drinks. Rena didn't touch hers. The anger she'd felt moments before fought with a rising hopelessness.

"This isn't right!" she said in frustration. "What am I going to do?"

"Exactly what I tell you," Jeffrey responded confidently. "Did Baxter talk about how my father has structured our business holdings?"

"Not much. All I know is that you develop property and make golf balls."

Jeffrey nodded. "My grandfather was one of the largest landowners in our corner of South Carolina. Most of the property was worthless until people started coming to the coast for vacations after World War II. Property values soared; however, instead of selling to others, he and my father began developing the property themselves. They also started manufacturing golf equipment. Everything was routine until my grandfather died about ten years ago, and my father brought in some new investors. A lot of what happens now is beyond the fringes of legality."

Rena's eyes narrowed. Ezra was mean and domineering, but she couldn't see him as a criminal.

"No way. There is too much money to be made as a regular businessman."

"Not compared to other avenues."

Rena was unconvinced. "Tell me exactly what you're talking about."

Jeffrey nodded. "Okay. Did you know that most of the golf balls and golf clubs we sell are manufactured overseas?"

"No, I thought they were made at the factory on the south side of Santee."

"Only 40 percent. Most of them come from islands in the Caribbean."

"Is it cheaper to make them there?"

"No, it's more expensive. Some of the balls sell for $10,000 a dozen. A set of custom woods and irons can top $100,000."

Rena sat up in surprise. "How could twelve golf balls be worth that much money? I'd be afraid to play with them."

"It makes sense only if it's a way to pass dirty money through a legitimate business so that it comes out clean on the other side. That's why they call it money laundering. A special group of very wealthy people have invested in Richardson Golf Equipment. They order golf equipment at outrageous prices, pay the bill, and stand at the door to receive profits from their purchase in the form of stock dividends from the company. They also funnel money into land development along the Grand Strand. My father is the local contact and visible partner. We get a cut of everything."

Rena shook her head. "I'm not following you."

"It's simple. We help people who don't want the government to know how they've made a lot of money make everything look like normal business revenue."

Rena suddenly thought of Baxter lying in intensive care. He'd never dropped a hint of the things Jeffrey was talking about.

"But Baxter never—"

"He didn't know," Jeffrey interrupted. "All he cared about was getting paid so he could play golf and buy wine. He never looked at any of the records or asked questions. He signed everything my father put under his nose."

Rena knew Jeffrey was right. Baxter hated financial details. He rarely wrote anything in his checkbook except the amount of the check. Fortunately, the supply of deposits had been unlimited, and no checks ever bounced.

"Why are you telling me this?" she asked. "If it's true, your father could go to jail. Maybe you, too."

Jeffrey didn't appear worried and ignored her question. "Even though Baxter didn't know what was going on, he owns 25 percent of everything. He has interests in offshore companies, investment trusts, limited partnerships. We recently started a huge construction project in Costa Rica. My concern is that my father may transfer Baxter's interest in the companies into his name. If he does, there is no way I can accomplish some of the goals I've been working toward for more than five years. I know he has taken a few thousand dollars from your checking account but that is nothing compared to the value of the businesses I'm telling you about."

Rena raised her wineglass to her lips. "I could go to the police. They would stop him."

Jeffrey snorted. "What would that get you beside nothing?"

Rena didn't immediately answer. Jeffrey looked into her eyes.

"And some of the people who buy expensive golf balls might become very upset with you."

Rena froze with the glass to her lips and tasted a new fear. Things had gone awry with Baxter at the waterfall, but she had always considered herself the predator. She had had no idea that large, dangerous beasts lurked in the shadows of the Richardson family. She spoke slowly.

"What do you want me to do?" she asked.

"Nothing fancy. You have to attack my father's use of the durable power of attorney. Without it, he can't gut Baxter's holdings. If you file suit, he'll back off because of concern that everything I'm telling you will come to light."

Rena suddenly saw danger from another direction.

"Who will protect me from your father?" she asked.

Jeffrey smiled. "I will. If you help me, I have close friends who will care a great deal about what happens to you. They will watch out for you better than a guardian angel."

"If I sue your father, will the lawyer in Charleston represent me?"

"He's not part of this deal, but I think it will work better if you use someone in Santee. I think you should hire the woman attorney who came to the hospital."

Rena raised her eyebrows in surprise. "Alexia Lindale? I thought I couldn't trust her because she works for the firm that represents your father."

"Not any more," Jeffrey said nonchalantly. "She was fired this morning because of you. I think she'll be more than willing to take the case."

"How did I get her fired?"

"By talking to her. She thought Leggitt & Freeman ought to withdraw from representing either you or my father because of a conflict of interest. Ralph Leggitt disagreed and terminated her."

Jeffrey's words mirrored what Alex had told her. Rena looked at her brother-in-law with renewed confidence in his credibility, but she still had questions.

"How do you know about Alexia Lindale?"

Once again Jeffrey ignored her question. "With the ammunition I give you, Lindale can get the job done. She's a fighter."

"How will I pay her? I'm broke."

"Open a new bank account. I'll fund it with all you need until this is straightened out."

"All I need could be a lot."

Jeffrey shrugged. "Not a problem. I won't even make you show me receipts."

"Will your name be on the account?"

"Of course not. Everything between us will be secret, and except for paying your legal fees, I don't care how you spend your money. I'll give you cash. I have almost twenty thousand dollars in a briefcase in the car. Be sure to make separate deposits under ten thousand so the bank doesn't have to report it to the government."

Rena's head was spinning. "What about Baxter? Everything you're talking about assumes he isn't around to protest."

"If Baxter wakes up, he won't be happy with my father for the way he's treated you and will be very willing to let me guide his decisions. His 25 percent plus my 30 percent will equal control. If he dies, then I have a new business partner."

"Who?"

Jeffrey grinned. "Do I have to get down on one knee to make a business proposal to you? If Baxter doesn't make it, you and I will be our own majority."

And we, who with unveiled faces all reflect the
Lord's glory, are being transformed into his likeness.
2 CORINTHIANS 3:18

ALEX AWOKE IN the morning and threw off her bed covers before realizing that she didn't have any place to go. She'd been so exhausted from jet lag and the emotional upheavals of the previous day's events that she'd gone to sleep at 7 P.M. and slept almost twelve hours. Falling back into bed, she pulled up the covers and closed her eyes. Two more hours of sleep would be nice, but it was no use. Consciousness had cracked open the door to reality, and her mind was churning in motion. The emotional shock of her termination had begun to subside, and she needed to consider seriously what to do. She propped up two pillows and sat so she could look out the picture window at the foot of her bed. The early morning sun was in full glory over the silhouette of the barrier island.

First on her list, she had to start making contact with her clients. The names and phone numbers printed out by Gwen were in her briefcase. Whether Alex was going to continue to practice law in Santee or not, her clients had to be notified. The window of time to decide her future was small. Client loyalty is limited to immediate service, and the curve of gratitude can quickly spike and precipitously fall.

Walking downstairs, she let Misha and Boris outside and started a pot of coffee. It was still early enough that she could catch Gwen at home before she left for the office. Alex dialed the number.

"Ms. Lindale's office," the familiar voice answered. "How may I help you?"

"When did you get caller ID?" Alex asked.

"After I got tired of answering the phone when the only men calling wanted to sell me vinyl siding for my house. How are you doing this morning?"

"I don't know. It's going to take a while to get a handle on everything. I talked to my mother, and she told me it would work out for the best. I'm sure she's right, but it's hard to see right now. Did anything else happen at the office?"

"No one quit in protest, although I gave it serious consideration."

"Don't do it. It wouldn't prove anything."

"The jury is still out. I was so mad that I didn't trust myself to speak to Leonard all afternoon. All he heard from me were grunts. One grunt was yes; two grunts was no. I'm not sure he figured it out."

"And Mr. Leggitt?"

"I didn't see him at all. I think he may have left the office right after you did and didn't come back the rest of the day. Maybe he choked to death on a chicken bone. What's your plan for today?"

"I'm going to start calling the clients this morning and give them my cell phone number. If anyone calls, you can give it to them."

"Okay. Did Rena Richardson reach you?"

"No."

"I picked up a message from her at the receptionist's desk. Do you want the number?"

Alex hesitated. She couldn't blame Rena for what happened, but many of Alex's worst problems were connected with the Richardson family. Although she was no longer an employee of Leggitt & Freeman, it could be argued that the conflict of interest still existed because she had access to Ezra's records during the course of her employment. The same rationale applied to Ralph Leggitt as to Rena if the lawyer who ultimately represented Rena raised the issue. It would continue to be a quagmire.

"Give me the number, but I'm not sure if I want to try to untangle that knot."

Alex wrote down the number.

"I dreamed about the French cowboy last night," Gwen said. "We were riding horses together bareback on a sandy beach. When will the pictures be ready? I'd like to see if he looks the same as the man in the dream."

Alex chuckled. "As you know, I was sidetracked yesterday, but I'll let you see them as soon as I can pick them up. I didn't know you knew how to ride bareback."

"Only in my dreams. I weighed about thirty pounds less, too."

"If you threw away the stash of candy in the bottom drawer of your desk, your dreams could come true."

"Stop meddling. Do you want me to do any spying for you at the office?"

"No, that's the kind of trouble neither of us needs. Take messages from the clients, and let them know I'll be in touch with them as soon as possible."

"Okay. If you decide to open your own office and hire a secretary, I'll send you a résumé."

Alex put the phone on the kitchen counter and took another sip of coffee. She thought about Gwen's final comment. Working with another law firm would be the path of least resistance. Alex could step into an established practice that would provide a guaranteed salary, health insurance, clerical support, and the thousand other things that enabled an attorney to focus on client problems without being distracted by mundane administrative matters. With six years' experience, she wouldn't be starting over, but in some ways it would be three steps backward, and with a large firm there would always be the possibility of the type of problems that caused the blowup with Leggitt & Freeman.

It was quiet in the house, and Alex realized she'd forgotten about Misha and Boris. She went to the back door. The cat was curled up on top of the deck railing where the morning sun reached around the corner of the house. Alex couldn't see Boris, but he was thrashing around in the bushes near the edge of the marsh. Alex stepped onto the deck. The wood was cool and slightly damp under her bare feet. She looked toward the tree line that ran along the coastal highway. Beyond the highway was the road to Santee.

It wasn't an obvious time for making a decision, but Alex suddenly realized what she wanted to do. Her conclusion wasn't the result of tightly woven analytical reasoning or the bottom line of a flow chart of options, but it felt right.

She would stay in Santee and open her own law office.

Freedom to do what she wanted as an attorney was sufficient reason to take the risks inherent in launching out on her own. Alex had enough money in the bank to pay her personal bills for at least six months, and any bank in town, except the one controlled by Ralph Leggitt, would give her a credit line to help with start-up expenses. She could do her own typing until she was able to ask Gwen to join her.

Alex stroked Misha's silver fur until she could feel the familiar rumble of purring under her fingertips.

"I think we should stay here, and I'll open my own office," she said. "What do you think?"

The cat's purring didn't miss a beat.

Alex spent the rest of the morning talking to clients. She tried to put a positive spin on her change in employment. One of the first people she called was Eleanor Vox. The older woman asked about her trip to France.

"It already seems a long time ago," Alex responded truthfully. "Have you been to Provence?"

"No. Hubert doesn't eat foreign food. We had trouble finding a place he liked when we went to San Francisco a couple of years ago."

"There was mail from your husband's lawyer on my desk when I returned," Alex said. "Nothing out of the ordinary. I'll forward it to you as soon as possible. However, there has been a change in my law practice. I'm no longer with Leggitt & Freeman."

"Really? You're not leaving Santee, are you?"

"No. I'm going to open my own office, but until I have a new phone number, call me on my cell phone or at home."

Alex gave her the numbers.

"When did you decide to go out on your own?" Eleanor asked. "You didn't mention it when we talked the other day."

It was a personal question, but Alex would eventually have to tell Mrs. Vox about the conflict. She went directly to the point.

"One of the reasons involved friction between my practice and other parts of the firm's business. Your case was mentioned because your husband has connections with transactions handled by Ralph Leggitt, one of the senior partners. Even though Hubert's name wasn't on our client list, I was asked to withdraw from your case."

"You left your firm over me?" Eleanor replied with obvious surprise in her voice. "I wouldn't ask you to do that."

"No. It was just the beginning of a discussion that led to a parting of ways."

"I'd hate to think I got you in trouble."

Eleanor Vox was a nice lady. Continuing to help her gave Alex immediate confirmation about her decision.

"No, it will be better for me in the long run; however, we may face a motion from your husband's lawyer to remove me as your attorney. He'll argue that I had access to privileged information that gives me an unfair advantage. Technically, it's not true because Hubert was never a client of Leggitt & Freeman, so I don't think the judge will make me withdraw."

"I hope not. I've felt better since we talked the other day. I don't want to lose you."

"Oh, one other thing. You may be contacted by someone from my old firm. Just tell them I'm still your lawyer and that should be the end of it."

"They made a big mistake when they let you leave."

"Thanks. I'll let you know about my new office in a few days."

The encouragement Alex received from her clients boosted her spirits. Woman after woman expressed her support. It was better than a testimonial dinner for a retiring schoolteacher. One person she called was a real-estate agent named Rachel Downey, a longtime Santee resident. Except for a few loose ends to tie up, her case was almost finished.

"Do you have a new office yet?" Rachel asked, after hearing about Alex's decision.

"No. Any suggestions?"

"There is a little house that came on the market yesterday two blocks from the courthouse. It's been residential rental property, and the owner is wanting to sell in a hurry."

"I'm not sure I want to buy anything. My long-term plans aren't set."

"You should consider it. The asking price is reasonable, and I'd suspect the owner would take a few thousand dollars less."

"Which street is it on?"

"King Street. It's gray with black shutters."

Alex knew the area but couldn't visualize the house. Rachel read the description from the information on the multilisting realtor service. By the end of the conversation, Alex had scheduled an appointment to view the property at three o'clock that afternoon.

She then spent several hours on the computer making projections of income and expenses. She had no experience in the business side of a law practice, but she knew that if she kept her overhead low there would be less pressure to generate revenue. Doing her own typing and hiring an answering service would keep her from having to immediately incur the weekly cost of a secretary/receptionist. She was confident that Gwen would join her, but she didn't want to offer her friend a position until she had a stable foundation. Preoccupied with her plans, she worked through lunch. She ate a cup of yogurt and called Gwen's direct line at the office.

"Anything happening today?" she asked.

"I have a list of people who called."

Alex told her about the response of her clients.

"Client satisfaction is all based on trust, and your folks know they can count on you," Gwen said. "Are you going to talk to another firm? I'm sure several would like to bring you in."

Alex took a deep breath. "No, I'm going to open my own office."

"Yes!" Gwen exclaimed. "You can do it. I've worked for sole practitioners before. It takes a special type of personality, and you have it."

"What do you mean?"

"It's the difference between the lone wolf who's left the pack and a buffalo who travels in a herd."

Alex smiled. "Are you calling me a wolf?"

"You're not a fat, lazy buffalo," Gwen replied. "That's more Leonard's speed. You have enough wolf in you to make it on your own."

"Thanks, but shake me if I start howling at the moon."

"I'll be there. Should I give my one-day notice and start next week?"

Alex laughed. "You know I want you to come, but let's wait until I get on my feet. I don't want you to miss a paycheck and suffer chocolate deprivation. I'm moving fast. I called Rachel Downey. She's going to show me a little house for sale on King Street at three o'clock. What do you think?"

"That's close to the courthouse. Would it need renovation?"

"Yes, it's been a rental house."

"Okay. If you decide to buy it, let me know and I'll bring my paintbrush."

Gwen's loyalty was more touching than all the other words of affirmation Alex had received while phoning her clients. Still emotionally fragile, she suddenly teared up.

"Uh, thanks. You're the greatest."

Unaware of Alex's reaction, Gwen continued. "Ditto. Oh, Rena Richardson called again."

Alex rubbed her eyes. "Did you talk to her?"

"Yes. She already knew you weren't working here."

"I wonder how she found out?" Alex asked. "I wouldn't be surprised if Mr. Leggitt told Ezra Richardson, but after what happened the other night, I doubt Rena and Ezra are on speaking terms."

"Do you want me to call her back for you?"

"No, I don't want you to get into trouble doing my work. I'll take care of it before the end of the day."

Later, Alex drove to town for her appointment with the realtor. Turning down King Street, she passed a convenience store and a large home that had been turned into an insurance agency. She immediately spotted the property for sale even though there wasn't a sign in front. She'd never noticed the house because it was concealed from the street by huge, overgrown boxwoods. In the middle of the small front yard were two clusters of crape myrtles that had graduated from bushes to small trees. The crape myrtles were past their late summer blooming phase, but earlier in the year the limbs would have sagged under the weight of heavy, reddish-purple blooms.

As Rachel had told her, the house was painted a light gray with black shutters. Alex's first impression was negative. The house was as neglected and dreary looking as a nineteenth-century spinster who never left her sitting room. The front door was painted the same gray as the house, and the roof was covered with black shingles. A narrow, red brick chimney climbed up the right-hand side of the house.

A skinny driveway led to a garage that was barely visible to the rear of the property. It was a typical bungalow built in the early 1950s, when living two blocks from the town's main street would have been considered convenient. Most of the retail stores that were nearby when the house was built had moved to outlying areas or gone out of business.

Rachel Downey's car was in the driveway. The personalized license plate on her sleek, pearl-colored sedan read "SOLD2U." Rachel had taken back the name of her first husband at the time of her divorce from her third one, but at the moment, Alex couldn't remember the exact reason for her rekindled affinity to husband number one. A short, jolly woman with curly hair dyed a startling blonde, Rachel had made a lot of money selling vacation property. It had been a tough fight keeping her third husband from collecting alimony. The realtor was walking in the backyard and came around the corner of the house as Alex pulled into the driveway.

"Just checking the backyard," she said in a cheery voice. "It has the potential to be a garden spot."

Alex joined her and walked to the rear of the house. Anytime a realtor used the word "potential" it meant the current condition was abysmal. Sure enough, the sun-splashed backyard was mostly dirt with a few scrubby clumps of sickly grass. A rusty tricycle was turned over beside a wooden fence that ran along the rear of the property.

"It looks ready for plowing," Alex said. "There isn't much growing that would get in the way."

Rachel waved her hand as if it were a magic wand.

"Oh, you could turn it into a delightful little courtyard by adding some brick pavers, a fountain, and a few large pots of flowers. The rest of it could go natural with pine bark and shrubs."

Alex smiled. "Okay, let's go inside."

They walked around to the front steps.

"What about the crape myrtles?" Alex asked. "I would need a sign out front so that people could find the office."

"You'd need to remove a few branches that are crowding the sidewalk, but the rest can be sculptured by trimming the bottom limbs so that the growth doesn't branch out until four or five feet in the air. The boxwoods would have to be scalped, but in a year they would come back. It would be very classy. Kind of an old English look."

Alex doubted crape myrtles grew in Devonshire but didn't argue.

Rachel unlocked the front door and continued her chatter. "The owners are a couple who live in New Jersey. The wife inherited the house from her mother. They're tired of dealing with renters and want to sell. The price might be a little high for a private residence, but everyone knows this street is going commercial. I double-checked the zoning, and you can do whatever you want except open a liquor store."

The door led into a small foyer with a wooden floor. There was a living room to the right and a dining room to the left. The inside of the house was in better shape than the backyard. The wood floors had been refinished. They walked down a hall past a bathroom to the kitchen at the back of the house. The master bedroom was behind the living room. While they walked through the house, Rachel's experienced eye picked up details that she pointed out to Alex.

"You could turn the living room into a multipurpose reception area and secretarial space. Clients could sit by the fireplace while waiting to see you, and your secretary could serve as hostess. I always thought it was a nice touch how we drank coffee or tea together when I visited your office. With a new coat of paint and the right rugs this could be even more homey."

"You make a visit to a lawyer's office sound like a social call. Most people would rather go to the dentist than to a lawyer."

"Not me," Rachel responded. "You charged more but hurt less."

"And I'm not sure I'm going to hire a secretary immediately."

"Oh, as busy as you are, it won't be long before you need help. Doesn't Gwen Jones still work for you?"

Alex didn't want to start any rumors that might get back to Gwen's bosses.

"Yes, but I shared her with another lawyer at Leggitt & Freeman, and she has a stable job with good benefits."

They stepped into the dining room. It was covered with silver-striped wallpaper that was a cousin to aluminum foil. A brass chandelier hung from the ceiling. At the sight of the wallpaper even Rachel grimaced.

"This wallpaper would have to go," she said. "But the chandelier is nice. You could position your desk under the light."

"Are you sure the dining room would be a better office than the master bedroom?" Alex asked.

Rachel nodded. "This room can be fixed up in a jiffy and would be very classy. You'd need to get it wired for your computer gadgets and bring in nice furniture. All the items you've collected during your travels would look great in here."

Seeing the house through Rachel's eyes began to spark Alex's own imagination.

"How long do you think it would take to get it ready?" she asked. "I would have to work out of my home and meet clients somewhere else until it was ready."

"It depends on who does the work. You don't need a big contracting crew to do what needs to be done. Do you know anyone who does remodeling work?"

Alex thought about Ted Morgan. "Yes."

"If he's not too busy and can get started soon, most of the work could be done in a few weeks. It's all cosmetic. In the meantime, there is a vacant office at my place. You could rent it for a month or two while the renovation is going on here."

"That would be ideal."

"I'll get a blank sales contract from the car," Rachel said.

Alex held up her hand. "Wait. Don't rush me. I can see that the house might work, but I'd like to think it over."

Rachel looked concerned. "I wouldn't wait. This place is going to sell fast. If you want it, you should make an offer now."

Alex smiled. "Are you using high-pressure sales tactics?"

Rachel feigned a hurt expression. "Never, but buying it would be a smart move. After seeing the interior of the house, I'm surprised at the asking price. It's in good shape."

Alex looked around and for the second time that day made a quick decision.

"Okay. Make an offer eight thousand dollars under the listing price."

"That's quite a drop," Rachel said dubiously.

"If the owners want a quick sale, they may bite," Alex replied. "I'll probably have to spend more than that fixing it up and want to keep my overhead as low as possible."

Outside, Alex looked at her watch. She had time to stop by Sandy Flats Church and find out if Ted Morgan was interested in a new job.

On the way she drove by Leggitt & Freeman. It was odd passing the parking lot without slowing down, but Alex held the wheel steady. Never again would she stop and check her phone messages before going home for the day. When she came back to pick up her files, it would be like visiting a house where she'd lived in the past.

No sounds of piano music greeted her when she quietly opened the front doors of the church and stepped into the narthex. Ted Morgan was not in sight in the sanctuary. She took a few steps down the aisle and the wooden floor creaked beneath her feet.

A deep-throated voice said, "Who's there?"

Alex jumped.

"Ted? Is that you?"

"No," the voice answered in even deeper tones. "This is God."

"Come out, Ted," she said. "Your impersonation of God could use some work. Is that the voice you use to scare children?"

Ted peeked over the top of a pew where he'd been kneeling near the piano.

"No, only lawyers who interrupt my prayer time."

Alex was walking down the aisle toward him and stopped. "I'm sorry. I didn't know you were praying. Should I leave?"

Ted got up and sat on the pew. "No, I was almost finished."

Alex joined him and sat sideways with her arm on the back of the bench. "How did you know it was me?"

"A guess. You've been coming by regularly."

Alex suddenly felt insecure. "Is that okay?"

"Anybody who loves music like you do is always welcome. How are you doing?" he asked.

"Better. I had a good time in here yesterday. I can't say that I prayed, but I cried a lot, and it was an opportunity to let my feelings out."

"That's healthy. Did anything else happen?"

"Yeah." Alex told him about the encounter at the window. "The expression on Jesus' face was similar to how you looked at me in the kitchen when I told you that I'd been fired. It was eerie."

Ted glanced at the window. "Is that good or bad?"

"Oh, good. I should have used another word."

Ted shifted on the pew so he directly faced her. "I hope people see a reflection of Jesus when they meet me. That's how God works. He uses people to show the world what he's like."

Alex mulled over his comment for a few seconds. "I've never thought about religion in those terms. I've connected it with going to church and believing in God."

"That's part of it, but there's much more. Faith in Jesus is the first step, but what God does in a person's life after they believe is the exciting part."

"Exciting?" Alex asked dubiously.

Ted nodded. "Yeah. It's the beginning of the adventure of faith—the chance to be fully alive."

"What do you mean by fully alive?"

Ted went over to the piano bench and sat down. He hit a few random notes. "Have you heard about the young man who fell from a cliff while hiking and is on life support in a Spartanburg hospital?"

Alex gave him a startled look. "Yes, Baxter Richardson. But he's not in Spartanburg; he's at Greenville Memorial."

"Do you know him?"

Alex paused to frame her response. "Never met him, but I'm familiar with the situation. He's in a coma, being kept alive by machines."

"That's what I heard on the radio. Do you consider that living?"

Alex thought about the medical prognosis for Baxter's future. "Only at the most basic level. It's existing, but I can't call it living."

Ted nodded. "It's the same for natural life and spiritual life. Without God, a person may be breathing and taking up space, but they're unconscious when it comes to spiritual reality. They're getting by on life support and don't even know it until they wake up."

Alex quickly saw where Ted was heading. "Is that what you're trying to do to me?" she asked with a slight smile. "Get me off life support?"

Ted grinned. "That's my job. Your eyes are starting to flutter open, and I want to encourage the process. Imagine the reaction of the Richardson family if Baxter woke up from the coma and got out of bed."

Alex wasn't sure how Rena would respond to a revived husband. "I'm sure it would be a shock," she said truthfully.

"They would be ecstatic, of course, and everyone in town would be talking about it. It would be like someone coming back from the dead. It's the same when a person becomes a Christian."

"You make it sound so dramatic," she said.

"When it's real, it is."

Alex had heard enough. After her teary session in the sanctuary, she wasn't antagonistic to Ted's comments, but they made her feel uneasy. She decided to change the subject to the reason for her visit.

"I need to ask you a question about your other profession," she said. "Would you be interested in working for me if I buy an older house in town and want to renovate it into an office?"

"Maybe. I don't do any big jobs."

"From what the realtor tells me I need a painter and handyman, not a demolition and reconstruction crew. I've made an offer on the house. If it's accepted, I'd like you to take a look and tell me what you think it would cost to do the work."

"Where is it?"

"On King Street near the courthouse. The house is about fifty years old."

Ted closed the keyboard cover. "I'll be finished painting the parsonage by the end of the week and might be interested in another job."

"Could you look at it before then?"

Ted hesitated. "Uh, okay. Just let me know, and I'll put together an estimate."

Alex stood up. "Thanks, I'll call."

Ted nodded. "I'll look forward to the adventure."

25

What authority and show of truth can cunning sin cover itself withal.
MUCH ADO ABOUT NOTHING, ACT 4, SCENE 1

ALEX HAD TWELVE messages on her answering machine. Number ten was from Rena Richardson.

"This is Rena. I'm sorry you lost your job. I had no idea Baxter's father would get you into trouble at your law firm, and I want to help by hiring you to represent me. There are several things I need to tell you, but I don't want to leave a message on your answering machine. Please call as soon as possible."

The callback number was the same one Rena left at the office. Alex wrote it down and put two question marks at the end. It might be better if Rena hired a large law firm in Charleston or Greenville to champion her cause. Wrestling with the multiple tentacles of the young woman's legal problems without the logistical support of a fully staffed office could overextend Alex's resources. She listened to the final two messages. Neither call required an immediate response. She put the phone on the kitchen counter and weighed her options in the Richardson case.

If Alex became involved, Ralph Leggitt and Ken Pinchot would be her adversaries; however, all three lawyers would have a conflict of interest because they previously served as attorneys for both sides of the warring Richardson family. For Alex to litigate against her old firm would precipitate a crisis. She could demand that Leggitt & Freeman withdraw from representing Ezra because the firm had access to confidential information about Rena. Of course, the same problem existed with Alex representing Rena in claims against Ezra. Alex didn't know very much about the Richardson family's business affairs, but Ezra couldn't be sure what Alex knew, and any reassurances by Ralph Leggitt to the contrary would be patently self-serving. This scenario would force both Leggitt & Freeman and Alex to withdraw as counsel for either side—the exact step Alex recommended in the meeting when she was fired.

Only a written waiver of the conflict of interest dilemma from both Ezra and Rena would allow all three lawyers to stay in the case. If one side balked on a waiver, it would sting Leggitt & Freeman a lot more to withdraw from representing Ezra than it would Alex to give up Rena. At the moment, the thought of causing Ralph Leggitt a high level of consternation was not unpleasant.

Alex picked up the phone and dialed Rena's number. She answered on the third ring.

"Thanks for calling back," Rena said, sounding relieved. "I'd almost given up on you."

"I've been busy," Alex said shortly. "How is Baxter?"

Rena told her about the conversation with Dr. Berman and the difference of opinion expressed by Dr. Draughton. "I know Baxter didn't want to live hooked up to a bunch of machines," she concluded. "Do you think I could make them take him off life support?"

Alex listened without comment until Rena finished. "It would be a battle of experts. If the doctors don't agree, it would be up to a judge to decide. Unless Dr. Draughton is very, very persuasive, I doubt a judge is going to grant a petition to suspend treatment if the regular treating doctors don't recommend it. Have you talked to him yourself?"

"Not yet. I wanted to discuss it with you."

"And you'd have to overcome your father-in-law's use of the medical care clause in the durable power of attorney."

"Which is why I need your help."

Alex was blunt. "Before we discuss my representation, do you believe you can make a decision about Baxter's medical care without being influenced by the fact that he tried to kill you?"

"Oh, I've forgiven him for what he did at the waterfall," Rena responded in a casual tone of voice. "All I want now is to put an end to his suffering. It's the merciful thing to do."

"You've forgiven him?" Alex asked skeptically.

"I had no choice. Baxter wasn't mentally stable, and something must have snapped. It didn't come out while we were dating, but after we married, there were times when he was so depressed that he sat in a dark room for hours without coming out. If I tried to talk to him, he yelled at me and told me to leave him alone. I called them his 'black moods' and learned to stay out of his way."

"Was he depressed on the day of the accident?"

"Yes, and the more wine he drank the worse it got. You should have seen the look in his eyes; he was totally out of his mind. Even if he woke up tomorrow, I wouldn't want to press charges against him."

Alex tapped a pen on the edge of the kitchen counter. Rena sounded like a different woman. Very calm and collected. And, if true, her willingness to forgive Baxter was remarkable.

"What about the charges Ezra filed against you?" Alex asked.

"They gave me a summons to be in court for some type of hearing."

"When is it?"

"I'm not sure. It's not clear on the ticket. I have to call the jail and find out."

"Do you want to hire me for everything?"

"Yes. I talked to a few lawyers in Greenville, but none of them made me feel as comfortable as you."

It was a familiar refrain Alex had been hearing all day from her clients, and it set her at ease. She decided to take the first step with Rena.

"Okay, before we discuss the terms of my representation, I need to explain a few things to you," Alex said.

She outlined as simply as possible the conflict of interest situation.

"I don't care that your old firm represented my father-in-law," Rena responded. "I trust you to look out for me, now."

"I appreciate your confidence, but any contract will contain a waiver of any objection based on my employment with Leggitt & Freeman."

"That's no problem. Fax it to me at the hotel."

This was going faster than Alex had anticipated. She broached the most important question—payment of attorney's fees.

"And I will also need a retainer fee to cover my initial time and expenses. How can you pay me if Ezra has taken all the money out of your checking account?"

"I have money he doesn't know about. How much do you need?"

Quoting an inadequate fee would be like jumping from the top of a tall building into three inches of water. Alex was willing to help Rena but not at the risk of her own financial hardship. Pro bono work was not the way to begin a new law practice.

"Ten thousand as a retainer," she answered. "I'll bill against that, and whenever it falls below two thousand, you will put in another five thousand."

Rena answered immediately. "I can give you seven thousand immediately and the balance next week."

Alex would know quickly if Rena was going to make good on her promises. If she didn't send the money, Alex could withdraw from the case before she was in so deep that a judge might force her to continue. She cleared her throat.

"And five thousand every time the balance goes below two thousand?" she asked.

"Yes. That shouldn't be a problem."

Alex had expected a few more questions, but Rena seemed content to trust her. A seven-thousand-dollar retainer would be a nice start to her first week as Alexia Lindale, Attorney at Law, and she could put language in the retainer agreement that protected her down the road.

Rena continued. "I want you to sue Ezra and make him give back my money. He's taken almost everything from my checking account, and I'm wondering what else he's done to Baxter's ownership in the family businesses."

Alex nodded. She'd suspected such a step by Ezra since the first meeting with the partners at Leggitt & Freeman.

"That is a distinct possibility. We can request a temporary restraining order that will stop him from shifting anything else out of Baxter's name and demand an accounting of what he's already transferred. It won't be very different from the work I do in divorce cases. Husbands often try to hide assets from their wives, and I have to find out where they're stashed."

Alex's mind began formulating theories of investigation and recovery. Most men didn't take the time to skillfully cover their financial tracks. She hoped Ezra felt secure cloaked in the legality afforded by the power of attorney and that he hadn't used any sophisticated tactics of concealment.

"You won't have to do much digging," Rena said. "I have an inside source of information that will give you what you need."

"Who is it?" Alex asked.

"I can't tell."

"It's not someone at Leggitt & Freeman, is it?"

Rena gave a short, harsh laugh. "No. Closer to the center of things than that."

Alex did a split-second analysis. To be close to the center, Rena's contact had to be one of Ezra's top businesspeople or a member of the family, possibly the older brother whose name Alex couldn't remember.

"There may be a time when you have to tell me," Alex said. "And when that time comes, I need to know that you won't hold back."

"What type of situation?"

"I don't want your contact to do anything illegal to obtain information for you."

"Oh, nothing like that will happen. My source had legal access to everything anyway."

Alex made a note on her paper. It had to be Baxter's brother. He was one of the few people who would have come to Greenville, and the trip would have given him opportunity to talk to Rena. However, Alex couldn't imagine why he would choose his sister-in-law over his father.

"In the meantime, stay away from Ezra," Alex said. "Avoid him if he comes to the ICU waiting area, and if he tries to talk to you, tell him your lawyer has instructed you not to have any contact with him."

"That sounds good."

"I'll fax you a contract in the morning," Alex said. "Mail it back to me with a check for the retainer at my home address. What's the fax number for the hotel?"

Rena told her the number. "I may bring the money to you myself. I want to come back to Santee for a few days. Baxter doesn't know I'm here, and I'm going crazy with nothing to do but go to the hospital and return to the hotel."

"That's up to you. Just make sure the doctors know how to contact you."

"They have my cell phone number. I'll let you know tomorrow if I'm coming home."

After she hung up the phone, Alex poured herself a glass of water. Rena needed a champion. She didn't deserve anything that had happened to her, and even if Alex had to eventually withdraw from the case, she could start her in the right direction.

Alex was up early in the morning. After fixing a cup of coffee, she prepared a short contract for Rena to sign. She faxed it to the hotel in Greenville and then took her coffee onto the screened porch. It was the coolest morning of the month and the mist clung closely to the warm surface of the water in the marsh. She heard her cell phone ring and walked back into the kitchen. It was Rachel Downey. The realtor's chipper voice jarred her ear.

"I hope I didn't call too early," she said.

"No, I've been working."

"I have good news. The owners of the house have made a great counteroffer. If you can add fifteen hundred to the purchase price and guarantee closing within thirty days, we have a deal. They're even willing to let you take possession and begin renovation before closing if you can pay five thousand dollars as earnest money."

Alex didn't jump with glee. "Five thousand is a lot for earnest money."

"Yes, but gaining immediate access would give you a head start in fixing it up. You could probably close one day and move in the next."

Having an office was important, but the negotiator in Alex rose to the surface.

"We're close, but not there yet," she said. "They must want to sell badly. What did their realtor tell you?"

"Nothing, but he called me back within an hour after I faxed over a copy of the proposed contract. It's obvious they want to turn it around quickly."

"I want the contractor who is going to do the renovations to look at the house. There may be something we've missed, and I don't want a serious problem to come up later that costs a lot of money to repair."

"How much time do you need? If the sellers are willing to cut their price so much, this house won't stay on the market very long. A speculator will snatch it up and sell it for a profit."

"I'll call him this morning and check his schedule. Are you going to be around so he can get into the house?"

"Yes. I'll be here at the office. This is my paperwork day."

"I'll call you back as soon as I have a time."

After Alex clicked off the phone, she looked up Ted Morgan's number in the phone book. His name wasn't listed, so she called the church. The answering machine gave her the number, and she dialed it. The minister answered in a voice that sounded sleepy.

"Ted, this is Alexia Lindale. I'm sorry if I woke you up."

"That's okay. I was up late last night."

"Do you want me to call later?" she asked.

"No. What do you need?"

"It's about the house I mentioned to you yesterday. Could you look at it later this morning?"

Alex could hear Ted yawn. "Yeah. What time?"

"About eleven o'clock would be good. I'll call the realtor so she can meet us there."

"Okay. Give me the street address."

Alex gave him the information.

Alex spent the next two hours talking on the phone and typing correspondence. She even drafted a motion to file in Eleanor Vox's case. While she was printing out her pleadings, she heard a fax coming into the machine beside her desk. It was the contract she'd sent to Rena Richardson. As the paper slowly exited the machine, Alex waited for the signature line to appear. Rena had signed the agreement and attached a short note.

I'm driving home today. Call me about a meeting. I have the ten thousand.

It was almost time to meet with Ted and Rachel Downey, so Alex didn't immediately call Rena. She laid the contract on her computer table, took out an empty folder, and typed a label: *Richardson v. Richardson.* She put the contract in the file. It was official. The first new case of her life as a sole practitioner had begun.

Rachel Downey's sedan was in the driveway of the house. Behind it was an old-model white pickup truck with several pieces of scrap lumber in the back. Alex parked along the curb. As she walked past Ted's truck, she looked in the front seat and saw a compact disk of a pianist performing Debussy.

Rachel and Ted were inside the house. Alex opened the front door and heard their voices coming from the back of the house.

"Hello!" she called out.

Rachel stuck her head into the hallway. "We're in the kitchen."

Alex joined them. Ted was wearing painter's overalls. His hair was disheveled, and some sandy dirt stuck to his left cheek and across the front of his clothes.

"I've already been under the house," he said. "There is evidence of old termite problems but no serious damage. You'll need to treat the house again as a preventative, but the foundation is solid. Inside it looks fine. I'm about to check out the attic."

There was a pull-down ladder in the main hallway. Ted grabbed the thin rope attached to the cover and lowered the ladder to the floor. Reaching into his back pocket, he took out a flashlight and quickly climbed up into the darkened area above the ceiling. Rachel and Alex could hear his footsteps overhead.

"How did you find him?" Rachel asked.

"At Sandy Flats Church."

"Is he the custodian?"

Alex thought about the music that Ted brought forth from the tips of his fingers.

"Yeah, but he's very talented."

"That's a beautiful sanctuary. It's great for weddings. My niece was married there a few years ago."

Ted reappeared at the top of the ladder and climbed down.

"You need to blow in some fresh insulation, and there have been visitors coming in through the eaves toward the back of the house."

"What kind of visitors?" Alex asked.

"Squirrels. They gnawed a hole through the wood. It's a mess, and unless you want to maintain a squirrel sanctuary, it will need to be fixed."

"Will that be expensive?"

"No. It can be done in a day or two."

They walked through the rest of the interior. Alex and Rachel talked about the work to be done before it could be used as an office, and Ted took notes on a small pad he took from one of his front pockets. They ended up in the living room. Alex turned to Ted.

"How much do you think it will cost to get it ready?"

"You want a bid?"

"No, an estimate."

Ted wrinkled his brow. "Almost everything is cosmetic. Are you going to help with the painting?"

Alex remembered Gwen's offer. "Maybe, but don't include that in your figure."

"Okay. It can all be done for ten to twelve thousand dollars in labor and materials—give or take a thousand."

Rachel's cell phone rang. She retrieved it from her purse and held a quick conversation.

"Someone else wants to look at the house in an hour," she said. "What do you want to do?"

Alex frowned. "I wanted to make a counteroffer, but I don't want to lose it."

Rachel couldn't conceal her exasperation. "Alex, the house is going to sell. If you want it, accept the offer and don't try to negotiate. It's a good deal."

Alex looked at Ted. "What do you think?"

"If you buy it, I'll make some money, so I think you should close the deal as soon as possible."

Alex smiled. "No need to cross-examine you about your bias."

Rachel's phone rang again, and she pressed the talk button. "Yes, I'm showing the house right now. Take his number, and I'll get back to you in a few minutes." She closed the cover on her phone. "That was my office about a speculator who wants to see the property. I'm not answering another call until you make up your mind."

Alex nodded. "Okay. I'll take it."

"Good," the realtor said with relief. "I have a blank contract in the car. Let's fill it out and sign it before you leave."

Ted stepped toward the front door. "I'm going back to the church. I'll talk to you later."

"Okay. We'll get together about the details. Thanks for coming by."

Standing in front of the kitchen counter, Rachel completed the contract in less than five minutes, and Alex signed it. As they were leaving, Alex stopped in the small foyer and pointed to the wall facing the front door.

"Do you think it would be tacky to hang a nice photograph of myself near the entrance?"

Those oft are stratagems which errors seem.
ALEXANDER POPE

IT HAD BEEN a couple of years since Alex graduated from the list of young attorneys who had to represent indigent defendants in criminal cases, and she felt rusty. The charges initiated by Ezra were more a nuisance than a serious threat, but Alex hated giving advice that had to be modified later because she hadn't properly researched the issues. After leaving Ted and Rachel, she drove to the courthouse. She parked along the street and dialed Rena's cell phone. There was no answer, and she left a message to return the call.

Without an office or computer terminal giving her access to a sophisticated legal research database, Alex had to fall back on an archaic method of legal inquiry—books. Located in a forgotten corner of the courthouse, the county law library was a musty reminder of the days when the printed page was the bread and butter of law office research. Finding Title 22 of the South Carolina Code, she turned to the section on "Assaults and Batteries and Other Breaches of the Peace" and read the pertinent provision.

Magistrates may punish by fine not exceeding five hundred dollars or imprisonment for a term not exceeding thirty days, or both, all assaults and batteries and other breaches of the peace when the offense is neither an assault and battery against school personnel pursuant to Section 16-3-612 nor an assault and battery of a high aggravated nature requiring, in their judgment or by law, greater punishment.

If Ezra had been a high-school English teacher, Rena would have been in big trouble; however, sneaky millionaires didn't receive any greater protection under the law than two drunks exchanging blows in a barroom brawl. The charges against Rena were barely a blip on the radar screen of the criminal justice system; nevertheless, to an ordinary person, they could loom large and ominous.

Alex spent more than an hour researching the more complicated issues surrounding Ezra's use of the power of attorney to gut Baxter's assets and impoverish Rena. Casebooks began to stack up around her at the small table where she sat. No one came into the room to disturb her. She found several cases that provided guidance but nothing directly on point. She would be charting new waters. Her cell phone lit up. It was Rena.

"Where are you?" Alex asked.

"I'm at home," she answered peacefully. "It's a relief to be away from the hospital."

"Where do you want to meet? I'm not set up in my temporary office."

"Why don't you come here?"

Without an office, Alex might be making some house calls, but she had another idea.

"I've not had any lunch. Why don't we meet at Katz's in forty-five minutes? Have you been there before?"

"Yes. I'll see you there."

Alex continued her research until it was time to leave for the restaurant, a New York–style deli that catered to northern transplants looking for a taste of home. Inside the deli she was warmly greeted by the owner, a stocky, orthodox Jewish man with an accent that made Brooklyn seem around the corner. He'd never grown comfortable calling her Alex.

"Alexia!" Mr. Katz cried out. "Where have you been? We've missed you."

Alex smiled. "In France. I've been back a couple of days."

"France! You must be starving! All those fancy soups only fool you into thinking you've had something to eat. You need some corned beef on rye to rebuild your strength."

Mr. Katz called to his wife. "Edith! Come see the world traveler!"

Edith Katz, a small woman, appeared from the rear of the restaurant with a kerchief on her head and looking as if she was about to scrub the floor of her house on the eve of Passover.

"I could have heard you in the street," she said to her husband. Turning to Alex, she smiled. "Where have you been?"

"The Provence region of southern France. It's a beautiful area. Very romantic."

Mrs. Katz punched her husband in the arm. "Do you hear that Arthur? I saw a special on TV about Provence. That's where I want to go for our fortieth wedding anniversary." She turned back to Alex. "Did you see the wild horses?"

"Yes. You'll love it. I can give you information about places to stay. Very nice."

Arthur Katz held up his hands in surrender. "Do you know how many pounds of salami I have to sell to fly across the ocean?"

Alex patted him on the arm in the same place where his wife had punched him. "I'll do my part and order a reuben."

Mrs. Katz wiped her hands on her apron. "Arthur, fix her a sandwich and make it extra nice. Don't forget to give her two big, fat pickles."

Alex sat down at a table for two. Mr. and Mrs. Katz had a few tables and chairs for those who wanted to eat in. The walls were decorated with scenes from New York. Alex's favorite was the Statue of Liberty at night. It reminded her of the freedom her mother desired so desperately that she gave up everything she knew to begin life in a foreign country.

Rena walked through the door. She had a harried look on her face. In her hand was a large, fat manilla envelope. Alex waved to her.

"I just ordered," Alex said. "Have you eaten here before?"

"You go ahead. I'm not hungry."

Rena put the envelope on the table. "Here's the money. All ten thousand."

"I'll write you a receipt after we talk. Did you find out when you have to be in court on the assault and battery charge?"

"Next Monday morning at ten o'clock."

Alex took out her PDA and turned it on. "Okay. I'm clear on Monday. I did some research this morning, and the worst thing that can happen is a five-hundred-dollar fine and thirty days in jail."

"Thirty days in jail!" Rena said in a loud voice.

At that moment, Mrs. Katz approached the table with Alex's sandwich. She put it down and quickly walked away.

"I don't think that will happen," Alex responded calmly. "It's a misdemeanor case in front of a magistrate, a lower-level judge who probably won't be a lawyer. They don't normally send someone to jail unless it is a much worse case than this one. Ezra will have to be there or the charges will be dismissed for lack of prosecution."

Rena perked up. "I can try to find out if he's going to show up."

"By asking Baxter's brother?"

Rena nodded, and Alex knew with certainty the source of the inside information Rena had mentioned.

"What's the brother's name?" Alex asked.

"Jeffrey, but I don't want him mentioned."

"No need to do that, but even if Jeffrey says his father isn't going to appear, you have to be there. The only way to avoid it would be if the charges are dropped before the hearing."

Rena slumped down. "There's no chance of that happening."

Alex thought for a moment. "Maybe. I can talk to someone at my old law firm and find out if your father-in-law has cooled down enough to dismiss the complaint. They don't know we're about to file other actions and might be willing to drop the charges." Alex took a bite of her sandwich. "This is good. Are you sure you don't want something?"

Rena shook her head. "What about ending Baxter's life support? I saw him this morning, and there is no doubt in my mind that he's getting weaker. In my heart, I've already forgiven him and said good-bye. The waiting is cruel to him and me."

Alex studied Rena's face for a second. Hearing her speak of forgiveness in person was even more startling than over the telephone. It was a remarkable personal achievement.

"How were you able to forgive him?" Alex asked. "It's hard for me to imagine."

Rena shrugged. "Every time I walk in the hospital room, I see his punishment. If I hadn't forgiven him, I would want to keep him imprisoned in a paralyzed body connected to tubes for the next forty years. I'm ready to set him free."

Alex nodded. "Okay. That makes sense. I need to talk to the doctor you mentioned and find out the basis for his opinion that it's futile to continue extraordinary life-sustaining measures. If I think he'll be a strong witness, we can file a petition to terminate the ventilator and stop artificial feeding."

Alex picked up a pickle. It suddenly struck her as odd that she was eating a robust sandwich while talking about cutting off the thin liquid stream that kept Baxter Richardson alive.

She took a small bite and put it down on her plate. "I can use the medical care power of attorney to reach the doctor," she said. "It may take me a few days to get through."

"No, it won't," Rena replied. "Dr. Draughton is expecting you to call him today or in the morning. He'll be out of town tomorrow afternoon."

"Did you talk to him?" Alex asked in surprise.

"No. I went by his office and left a copy of the power of attorney and paid his bookkeeper five hundred dollars as a consultation fee." Rena reached into her purse and took out a business card. "Here's the direct number into his office."

Alex was impressed. "Good thinking. This will help a lot."

"When will you file the case?"

"The petition will have to be filed in Greenville County because that's where Baxter is hospitalized and the doctors are located. Because Baxter is in critical condition, the case won't have to go through normal channels."

"What about stopping Ezra from stealing my property?" Rena asked. "Something needs to be done as soon as possible."

"That involves strategy and a bit of patience."

Rena raised her voice. "What do you mean? If we don't stop him, he'll get everything. I won't even be able to live in the house!"

Alex leaned forward. She didn't want Rena to lose her cool in the middle of the restaurant but had to tell her the truth. She spoke in a low voice.

"Rena, it's probably too late to stop him. Ralph Leggitt could prepare the paperwork in less than two days to transfer everything out of Baxter's name, and your father-in-law could sign the documents in five minutes. It's already happened."

"But there are things I know," Rena sputtered, "that could send him, uh, get him in trouble."

"We'll talk about that later. My first job is to get the criminal case against you thrown out. I don't want you going into another court with something like that hanging over your head. Second, we need to schedule a hearing as soon as possible about Baxter. What happens to him affects everything else. It will take all the evidence I can muster to convince a judge to override Ezra's wishes to keep Baxter hooked up to life support, especially if several treating doctors think it would be wrong to terminate extraordinary measures."

"But why can't we file everything at once?"

"That was my first thought, but I would rather ambush Ezra about his manipulative dealings at the hearing on life support than give him advance notice."

"I don't understand. When I saw my checking account balance, I knew he'd taken the money. Don't you think he knows I'm aware of what he's doing? I'm not stupid."

"No one is saying you're stupid. Think about the implications of the decision on terminating life support. As long as Baxter is alive, Ezra can use the power of attorney to control anything with Baxter's name on it. Once Baxter dies, the power of attorney dies with him. At the hearing on termination of life support, I want to show the judge that one reason Ezra wants Baxter breathing is so he can control his son's property and defraud you. In that case, Ezra will not look like a father who loves his son, but a greedy man who wants to rob his dying son and"—she paused for emphasis—"the person his son loves most."

Alex could see the wheels turning in Rena's mind. Many times she'd seen understanding dawn in clients when she explained the reasons for her legal advice.

"What if he denies doing anything?" Rena asked slowly.

"That's where your source comes in. If I file a suit attacking the power of attorney, it might take months to overcome all the barricades your father-in-law's lawyers will throw up, and the element of surprise will be gone. Do you think your source can get information showing how Ezra has used the power of attorney without letting Ezra know what he's doing?"

Rena nodded. "Probably. I'll have to check."

"If he can, that's the way we'll proceed. Beside the difficulty of proving the case from a medical standpoint, there is only one obvious problem."

"What is that?"

"If Ezra wants his son alive for the wrong reason, he can make the argument that Baxter's death will benefit you."

Rena's eyes grew wild again. "That's horrible! I'm thinking about Baxter, not myself!"

"And you're the one to persuade the judge of the truth."

"How?"

Alex looked into Rena's eyes. "Your face. Hopefully, Ezra's credibility will be destroyed, so the judge will be looking for someone in the courtroom who genuinely cares about Baxter. It will be up to you to convince the judge that the only reason you want to terminate life support is because it is the best decision for the man you loved enough to marry. You have to look at the judge with the same kind of conviction you showed a few minutes ago when you told me you've forgiven Baxter."

Rena vigorously shook her head. "No! I can't do it."

"Why not? You did a good job explaining how you feel to me."

"It's easy talking to you, but it would be impossible in front of a bunch of people. I'd go to pieces."

"We'll practice," Alex responded patiently. "Then, as soon as the hearing about Baxter's care is over, we'll file an action for a temporary restraining order to stop Ezra from using the power of attorney. We can file that here in Santee."

"I'm not sure that's a good idea. Ezra has a lot of powerful friends and probably knows the judges."

"There's no real choice. Everyone involved lives in Santee and that means the local court will have jurisdiction."

"But Baxter will still be in Greenville."

Alex had been rattling along and spouting her opinions as if discussing a hypothetical question in law school. She stopped and spoke slowly.

"At that point, Baxter may be dead, and we'll be fighting over his estate. Even if he's alive, his residence for purposes of jurisdiction and venue is here in Santee. And don't worry about the judge. There will be a different rotation of judges coming into the area in a week or so. We may get someone from Columbia or Aiken who has never heard of Ezra Richardson."

"But the people on the jury will know him."

"I did some research about that earlier today. I think a jury would likely rule in your favor because Ezra didn't use the power of attorney until after your marriage while Baxter was lying helpless in the hospital. Anyone with a conscience will consider Ezra's conduct incredibly selfish. If Baxter is dead when we go to trial, I can ask the jury to protect you as his widow from the greed of your father-in law."

"That makes sense."

Alex could see Rena calming down as her confidence in the lawyer increased.

She continued. "But there is a problem. It may be hard to get a jury involved. Legal interpretation of the validity of a durable power of attorney is up to the judge, not a jury. Only if there are questions of fact about the events that led to the signing of the power of attorney would a jury be required, and I'm not sure I can come up with any evidence of wrongdoing when Baxter signed it. The misuse occurred after Baxter became comatose—an event anticipated by specific language in the document. We may have to invoke the equitable power of the court, which puts us at the mercy of the judge."

"I'm not following you."

"Just know I'm researching the issue. We'll have time later to decide the best strategy."

Alex took a bite from her sandwich. "Do you have any other questions?"

"When are you going to call Dr. Draughton?"

Alex looked at her watch. "Tomorrow morning. I have some things to do this afternoon and need to prepare for the interview. I'll let you know how it goes."

After Alex finished eating, they walked outside to her car. Rena sat in the passenger seat, and Alex took the money from the large envelope. She'd been paid in cash before but not such a large amount. Seeing the stacks of hundred-dollar bills made her realize how much money she was charging as a retainer.

"Are you going to open another checking account?" she asked Rena.

"Yes, but just in my name."

"Where did you get the cash?"

Rena turned away and looked out the window. "Does it matter?"

Alex stopped. "It might."

"A friend."

Alex cocked her head to the side. "A very good friend?"

"Yes," Rena said with exasperation. "It was a gift from someone close to me who knows my problems. Are you going to keep it or not?"

Satisfied she'd gotten enough of the truth to appease her conscience and the code of professional responsibility, Alex said, "Yes. I just needed to ask a few questions. Please watch me count it."

Rena barely paid attention. She kept looking out the window and pulled down the sun visor to check her appearance in the mirror. Alex neatly lined the bills in stacks of one thousand dollars each across the bottom of her briefcase.

In a few minutes, she said, "Ten thousand. I'll bill my time against this amount. If I have to withdraw because of the conflict of interest, I'll refund the balance to you so you can find another attorney."

Rena flipped up the sun visor. "I don't want another lawyer."

Alex handed Rena a receipt and snapped shut the briefcase. "And I hope you don't have to get one."

Alex and Rena left in opposite directions. A blue car followed Rena; a tan van fell in behind Alex.

27

*The longest part of the journey is
said to be the passing of the gate.*
MARCUS TERENTIUS VARRO

ALEX WENT TO the only bank in Santee that wasn't partially owned by Ralph Leggitt or represented by Leggitt & Freeman. With a sense of accomplishment, she opened a business checking and trust account in the name of Alexia Lindale, Attorney at Law. She then stopped by the office of the vice president of the commercial lending department and talked to an older, gray-haired woman who looked more like a retired schoolteacher than a bank executive. Forty-five minutes later she left, confident that there wouldn't be any hitches in approving her loan to buy the King Street house for a law office.

Relieved, Alex walked out to her car. As she was opening the door, she saw Ralph Leggitt and Ken Pinchot drive by. Leggitt glanced in her direction before quickly looking away. Alex knew that soon her former bosses wouldn't be able to avoid her gaze. Rena Richardson would guarantee close contact, and she began to relish the thought of combat that would vindicate her and liberate Rena. She mulled over different lines of attack as she drove to Sandy Flats Church to discuss the house renovation with Ted Morgan.

When she pulled into the parking lot of the church, she put aside her plans of war. Once inside the narthex, she heard a succession of slow, quiet notes drifting from the sanctuary. Other melancholy tones joined them. She quietly entered the room so that she was out of Ted's line of sight and sat down in a back pew to listen. She didn't recognize the piece. It was simpler than most classical works for piano but filled with haunting pathos that could only flow from the soul of a Russian composer. Ted finished and let his hands fall to his sides.

Alex cleared her throat. "Hello."

Her voice sounded high and tinny after the deep, somber sounds that had reverberated in the church. Ted looked over his shoulder.

"How long have you been here?" he asked.

"Several minutes. I'm sorry. I should have let you know."

"It would have been polite."

Alex had grown so used to eavesdropping that she hadn't thought twice about failing to announce her presence. Unlike the time when she interrupted his prayer time, the minister seemed irritated.

"Do you want me to leave?" she asked.

Ted paused. "No. You said you were going to stop by. I should have remembered."

Alex walked to the front of the sanctuary and sat down on a pew. Ted stayed at the piano bench. The late afternoon sun was shining in the windows on the left side of the building. The serious mood of the music lingered.

"I didn't recognize the music you were playing, but it sounded very Russian," Alex said.

"Russian?"

"Yes. Who wrote it?"

"I did," Ted responded simply.

Surprised, Alex said, "I didn't know you were a composer, too."

"I'm not really."

"It was beautiful. Sad, but beautiful. When did you write it?"

Ted looked at his watch. "During the time it takes to send a message from my brain to my fingertips."

Alex's eyes widened. "It was improvisation? Yet it flowed so well. I would never have guessed you did it on the spur of the moment."

Ted tapped a few notes in sequence. "It's nothing more than applied music theory. The transitions from one key to another are second nature to me, so I don't have to think about it. I can often go where my thoughts and emotions take me."

"What were you thinking about when you played?"

Ted looked down at the keyboard and replayed a few measures of the haunting introduction Alex had heard when she first arrived.

"Regrets," he said.

Alex's next question died before it reached her lips. Ted Morgan wasn't a player piano waiting for someone to put in a quarter or a minister without feelings or problems of his own. He was a middle-aged, divorced man who lived alone in a small town in South Carolina. Her thoughts had been on what Ted could do for her as a witness, a performer, and a contractor, not whether he had any needs of his own. As far as she knew, no one properly recognized or appreciated his extraordinary talent. Seeing him vulnerable, Alex wanted to take a tentative step toward learning more about him but couldn't think of the right thing to say. It was an awkward moment.

Ted looked into her eyes and relieved the tension. "Do you want to ask me about my regrets?"

"Yes," Alex said. Then she quickly added, "But I respect your privacy. I apologize again for stopping by without a specific appointment. I wouldn't want someone barging into my office unannounced."

Ted motioned with his hand around the sanctuary. "This place doesn't belong to me."

"But the music and your thoughts do."

"True," Ted agreed. He paused before continuing. "Have you ever been married?"

Alex compressed her lips. "No. I was engaged last year, but my fiancé broke it off and married someone else a few months later. Recently, I've come to terms with it and put it behind me."

"What does that mean?"

"That I can go on with my life."

"I've tried to do that, but it hasn't happened so neatly." Ted tapped his fingers against the piano bench. "And it's been a lot longer than a year. At first, I thought it was because Roxanne and I had a child, but now that Angelica is grown there is still an ache in my heart. As a Christian, I believe my relationship with God should satisfy me, and in many ways it does, but the link between a husband and wife is unique in the universe. My wife and I became one, and the divorce cut all the way to the core of my being. Years have passed, but the regrets and 'what if's' remain. Neither time nor my faith has answered all my questions or healed my wounds."

Alex admired the way the minister could express his feelings. With all her analytical ability, she'd not been able to put words to her hurts, just tried to find a way to jettison them.

"You have more understanding about these things than I do," she admitted. "Most of my time is spent helping marriages end, not trying to figure out what went wrong or saving them. In my own situation, I think my greatest hurt was to my pride."

Ted shook his head. "Then he wasn't the right man for you."

"Why do you say that?"

"Because the link between the two of you was in the mind, not the heart."

Puzzled, Alex said, "I still don't understand."

"Our minds are offended when we're rejected. Our hearts break when we lose someone we treasure. You're right. If your primary wound was to your pride, you can go on with your life. God spared you from making a big mistake by getting married to the wrong person."

Alex remained perplexed. "I never thought God was involved in what happened between Jason and me. Neither of us gave religion very much thought. I mean, we would have been married in a church, but we never talked about religion."

A slight smile returned to Ted's face. "Just because you don't think about him doesn't mean he's not thinking about you."

The minister had a knack for bringing every conversation around to herself. Alex decided to turn the table.

"Would you like to remarry your wife?" she asked.

"That's impossible. We're completely different people now, and she's been married to someone else for fifteen years. I'm not sure how the void in me will be filled."

"Have you considered another relationship?"

Ted stood and stretched. "Of course. I've dated some, but nothing connected at the level we're talking about. What sort of woman do you think I should consider?"

"I'm not sure I know you well enough to answer that."

Ted stepped through an opening in the altar rail and stood in front of her. "Go ahead, you're a woman. I'm curious about your thoughts. Consider it a request for a professional opinion."

Alex thought for a moment then counted off on her fingers. "She should love music, not care about money, have similar beliefs, and find delight in who you are as a person."

"Do you know someone like that?"

Alex shook her head. "Sorry. None of my clients would make suitable candidates, but if one comes along, I'll send her your way."

"What about you?"

Alex flushed. "Me?"

Ted's smile widened, and he sat down on the pew beside her. "Is that beyond consideration?"

"Uh, I love music, but I'm not sure about the rest of it."

"Is it your goal in life to be rich?"

"No, but I don't believe in God the same way that you do."

"That could change," he said.

Alex was flustered. Ted Morgan had a daughter who had graduated from college. He was probably old enough to be her father.

"I'm forty-five," he said, reading her thoughts. "How old are you?"

"Thirty-two."

"So, I was in the seventh grade when you were born."

The thought of Ted Morgan at age thirteen broke the tension Alex felt. She laughed. "Thirteen-year-old boys are scary."

"I've grown out of it." Ted leaned forward with a more serious look. "Would you like to come to my house for dinner Friday night? I'm going to grill steaks."

Alex raised her eyebrows. "I've never been invited over to dinner while sitting on the pew of a church."

"Which means God is watching us."

Alex glanced up at the ceiling. "Did he tell you to invite me?"

"No, it was my idea, but I think he approves. We can eat and talk about the renovation of the house you're buying. If you like, you can bring paint and wallpaper samples."

The conversation had moved quickly from Alex's realization that Ted wasn't a musical automaton to a dinner invitation.

"How long have you been thinking about this?" she asked.

Ted looked at his watch. "Since the first time I met you and found out that you loved good music. But I wasn't sure I wanted to invite you over for dinner until you asked what I was thinking about while I was playing."

"What did that tell you?"

"That you were interested in who I am as a person."

Alex was intrigued. The minister's intuition was at least as good as her own, and none of her antennae indicated he was a predatory male. He made her feel special. His musical genius didn't demand to be the center of attention. He focused on her.

"Okay," she said. "But only on one condition."

"What?"

"I have the right to ask you anything I want, and you promise to tell the truth."

"Like cross-examination?"

"No, you're not a hostile witness, but it's hard for me to trust anyone."

"But you're going on with your life."

Alex smiled. "Yes. That's what I said."

"Do you have time for a quick Chopin?" Ted asked.

Ten minutes later, Alex left the church with a different subject on her mind than when she arrived. Ted Morgan wasn't particularly handsome. There were too many angles to his face, and his hair was more like a wire brush than a flowing lion's mane. But he had an innate goodness that couldn't be hidden any more than evil can be concealed. She'd experienced the devastation of betrayal from a man with textbook good looks. In the depths of her heart she knew that character mattered more than a handsome profile.

Alex arrived home to the usual welcoming party of Misha and Boris. She wrote herself a reminder to call Ted Morgan and offer to bring something to dinner and then retrieved eight messages from her answering machine. Sitting at her kitchen table, she returned calls and talked with clients until after six o'clock. The women she spoke with were now, more than when she worked for Leggitt & Freeman, her clients.

The aftershocks of her termination were growing less frequent. Signing a contract for the house, receiving a substantial retainer fee, and opening bank accounts were steps down the new road of her future. The prospect of life without bosses or interoffice politics was becoming as appealing as an unclouded sunrise over the marsh. Soon, she'd be able to invite Gwen to join her.

The following morning, Alex called Gwen at the office and told her about the house on King Street.

"That's great," Gwen said. "Just a minute. I need to do something."

Alex listened to a few seconds of silence.

"Okay. I've put back all the stuff I had in my purse that I've stolen from Leggitt & Freeman. I'm ready to move on to my new job."

Alex laughed. "You'll have time to borrow a few more ink pens before I ask for your résumé."

"I'm sitting on ready. You'll be a big success."

"I've talked to most of my clients, and they want me to continue representation. I have a list of files to pick up from the office."

"Uh, they're not here," Gwen said slowly.

"What!"

"Ralph Leggitt sent his snippy paralegal and the maintenance man to box them up. The last time I saw the files they were on hand trucks going down the hall. I asked Vicky where they were taking them. She wouldn't tell me anything except that she was following Mr. Leggitt's instructions."

"That's ridiculous! The ethical rules are clear. If the client wants me to continue representation, the case goes with me. The firm doesn't own them or me. All Leggitt & Freeman has a right to are the unpaid billings generated while I was still working there."

"Don't argue with me. I'm on your side. I tried to find out what was going on."

"Sorry. It's so pointless."

"What are you going to do?"

"I was going to come by and pick up the files this morning, but I'd better get written authorization from each client. I'll have to make house calls all over Santee. Can you find out when Mr. Leggitt is going to be there in case I need to confront him later today?"

"Yes. I'll call you back later."

Alex was fuming when she hung up the phone. There was an easy way and a hard way to accomplish most things in the law, and Ralph Leggitt could insist on written notice from Alex's clients before releasing their information. She would get it, but if he stepped one inch over the line and balked at turning over records, she would file so many complaints with the state bar association that his desk would be covered with grievance forms. Alex turned on her computer and created a form for her clients to sign instructing Leggitt & Freeman to deliver their case files to Alex. She added a final line for Ralph Leggitt to sign giving his consent to release the information. If he made her obtain written authorization, she would rub his nose in it as many times as possible.

Several hours later, Alex was in her car leaving Eleanor Vox's house when Gwen called her cell phone.

"How is it going?" the secretary asked.

"I've met with five of the clients who have the most urgent cases. I spent half an hour with Eleanor Vox and feel better after nibbling the pastries she'd made. Where's Leggitt?"

"He came in a few minutes ago and will be leaving for the rest of the day after lunch. Do you want me to transfer the call to his office?"

Alex hesitated. "No. If I tell him I'm coming, he may bolt out the door to frustrate me. I think it would be better to show up and demand the files."

"I did some snooping since we talked this morning. The boxes are in a closet in Vicky's office."

"How did you get in there without her knowing it?"

"I paged her from another extension, put a handkerchief over the phone receiver, and told her a Mary Kay representative was here to see her."

Alex smiled. "I'll be there in five minutes."

Alex's heart began beating faster as she turned into the familiar parking lot. She picked up the release forms and noticed that her hand was slightly damp. Instead of immediately opening the door of the car, she sat still and forced herself to breathe normally. There was no reason why she should be so uptight. She'd faced the worst Ralph Leggitt had to offer when he tried to intimidate her into compromising herself in the Richardson case, and he had no right to keep her from representing her clients. However, her rationalization didn't work and her jitters didn't leave.

The familiar hallway was unchanged. As she walked toward Gwen's desk, Ken Pinchot turned a corner and suddenly faced her. He was drinking a cup of coffee. When he saw her, he stopped so suddenly that the coffee spilled onto his tie and splattered the front of his immaculate shirt.

"Look what you made me do!" he blurted out.

The idiocy of Pinchot's juvenile attack did more to calm Alex's nerves than fifteen minutes of confidence-building speeches.

"Sorry, Ken," she said. "I didn't realize you would be in the hallway drinking a cup of coffee without looking where you were going or thinking about whom you might meet."

Pinchot grunted. "I didn't know you'd be coming back. Your office is empty."

Alex held up the client release forms. "I'll be visiting on a regular basis until all my clients make a decision about future representation."

"You'll need to talk to Ralph about your cases. The files aren't in Gwen's office anymore."

"I know. I hope the stain comes out of your tie and shirt."

Alex continued to Gwen's work area. The secretary was shaking her head.

"Don't tell me. I heard," Gwen said. "The Prince has been in a foul mood all week. The other partners are giving him grief about his accounts receivable. He's owed over $100,000, and some of the bills are over nine months old. I heard Mr. Leggitt tell him yesterday that you never let your receivables get out of hand."

"Maybe in a year they'll nominate me for sainthood. Wish me luck. I'm off to force my way into Leggitt's office."

"If it gets ugly, scream at the top of your lungs, and I'll call 911."

Alex walked down the hall and turned the corner to the waiting area for the senior partner's office. Leggitt's secretary looked up.

"Is Mr. Leggitt busy?" Alex asked. "I need to talk to him about several clients."

The woman picked up the phone and had a brief conversation. Alex prepared her next line of argument if he refused to see her.

"Go in," the secretary said.

"Oh, thanks."

Alex opened the door. Leggitt was standing at the end of the room where the conference table was located. He turned around. Alex stepped forward with the sheets signed by her clients in her hand.

"I've come to pick up some files," she said. "I have authorization forms—"

"Just see Vicky," Leggitt interrupted. "I asked her to put your files into her office so there wouldn't be any confusion. We've hired a new lawyer who will be moving into your old office next week. He's bringing business with him, and we needed to clear out the filing space next to Leonard."

"Okay. I have the request forms from five of my clients."

"I don't need to see them," he said nonchalantly. "Make copies of the authorizations for our records, but in the future a letter from you letting us know that you are assuming representation will be enough. Of course, we'll expect you to reimburse the firm for any expenses incurred while the files were here and pay business credit on billings prior to your leaving, but there's no need to obtain written authorization from the clients. We'll trust your accounting."

Alex's mouth dropped open. "Uh, thanks. How often do you want me to file a report?"

"How about once a quarter? You stay on top of your accounts receivable so it should be cleared up within six months."

"Okay."

Ralph Leggitt motioned toward the conference table. "Have a seat. I'd like to talk to you for a few minutes."

Alex pulled back a chair. "Thanks for the cooperation. After what happened the other day, I wasn't sure what kind of reception to expect."

"I was upset with you, but the more I've thought about it, the more I believe it will work out for both the firm's good and yours as well. The new lawyer is going to be helping Bruce and me in the business transaction area, and we're getting totally out of the divorce business. If I get a call from a prospective client, I'll send them your way."

"That's great," Alex said but raised her guard in anticipation of a salvo of manipulation.

"I heard you made an offer on a house on King Street."

"Yesterday. News travels fast."

Leggitt gave her a wry smile that wasn't exactly friendly. "It's my business to know what happens in Santee. I think it's a good location. It's close to the courthouse and in an area where there are going to be more and more professional offices. If you need a good word at the bank, let me know."

"Thanks, but I've already made an application. Is that what you wanted to talk to me about?"

Leggitt rubbed his hand across the top of his head. "No. I'll get to the point and not waste your time. Are you going to represent Rena Richardson on the assault and battery charge filed after she slapped her father-in-law at the hospital?"

That's it, Alex thought. She sat up straight in preparation for Leggitt's attempt to convince her to abandon Rena. Her former boss's friendly overtures of the previous few minutes were about to prove vaporous.

"Yes," she said.

"Good," Leggitt responded matter-of-factly. "I've recommended that Ezra drop the criminal complaint before it goes to hearing before a magistrate. He and Rena may not like one another, but it will be hard for them to cooperate at any level if there are criminal charges flying about."

Alex was stunned. "Is he going to take your advice?"

"He's authorized me to contact the police officer who processed the complaint and notify the magistrate that there is no need for a hearing. I'll try to call them this afternoon and confirm everything to you in writing. Where do you want me to send a letter?"

"Uh, care of Rachel Downey's office. I'll be there for several weeks before the renovation of the house is completed."

"Very well. I'm sorry you won't be able to bill your new client very much on the case."

"That's fine. I'll be busy."

Alex got up to leave.

"Please sit down. There is one other thing," Mr. Leggitt said.

Alex resumed her seat.

"I've also recommended that Ezra correct the problem that caused Rena to become upset. As I'm sure you know, he transferred money from

Baxter and Rena's checking account and put it in a separate account for Baxter's benefit. He will put all the money back into the joint account within a couple of days. Rena should call the bank on Friday and make sure it's been properly credited."

"Why did he change his mind?" Alex asked suspiciously.

"Calmer heads prevailed. This has been a very stressful time for the whole Richardson family. They've all made mistakes."

Alex was having trouble believing that such a total change of heart had occurred. She tested the waters.

"Has Mr. Richardson used the power of attorney to make other transfers from Baxter's name? Rena doesn't know the details of the family businesses. She needs to be reassured that Baxter's estate will be intact if he dies and his ownership interests preserved in case he doesn't."

Leggitt met Alex's look and blinked a couple of times. "Ezra thought about safeguarding everything Baxter owns and asked me to prepare the documents to set up a trust but didn't go through with it."

Alex wanted to probe further but couldn't think of a way to do so without implying that Ralph Leggitt was lying to her.

"I see. If I have specific questions, will you be willing to provide additional information?"

"Within reason and the bounds of the law. Baxter is a minority shareholder and has the rights granted by the Corporations Act. If Rena assumes his ownership interest, she'll be on the same footing."

"But what does that mean in terms of access to business records? The only way to know what Mr. Richardson is doing will be through disclosure."

"We'll consider it on a case by case basis. Ezra is holding out an olive branch," Leggitt said with an edge in his voice. "He doesn't have to become adversarial."

Alex didn't back down. "And I'm willing to cooperate, but after what has happened to the checking account, Rena will have trouble trusting her father-in-law. It will take time to prove that she is going to be treated fairly."

Leggitt's tone relaxed. "I totally agree. Dropping the criminal charge is the first step. Our conversation is the second. Transferring the money back into the checking account is the third. Ezra realizes it will be a gradual process. A key aspect will be our communication."

Alex tapped her fingers on the arm of the chair. In the pit of her stomach she felt she was being led astray but couldn't see how or for what motive.

"Does this mean Ezra is waiving any objection to my representation of Rena?" she asked.

"Yes. He has agreed to sign a waiver. What is Rena's position?"

"The same."

"Good. Nobody loses." Ralph Leggitt stood to his feet. "Call me if you have any questions. You know the number."

28

Believe one who has proved it. Believe an expert.
Virgil

Alex stopped by Vicky's office and found the paralegal cheerful and willing to help. The firm had a small cart for moving heavy items around the office, and Alex loaded up as many boxes of files as she could put in the trunk of her car. While pushing them down the hall toward the exit, she passed Gwen's desk.

"I'll talk to you before I leave," Alex whispered.

Alex returned the empty cart and made arrangements with Vicky to retrieve the remaining boxes. Then she stopped by to see Gwen.

"Where's Leonard?" Alex asked.

"Out of the office. Maybe the Prince sent him to the cleaners."

Alex chuckled. "Do you still have my résumé stored in your computer?" she asked. "I'm thinking about reapplying for a job with the firm."

"What's going on?" Gwen responded dubiously.

"Mr. Leggitt was like sugar on strawberries. He's going to refer divorce cases to me and let me take all my files without a whimper or a fight."

"You're kidding?"

"You saw me hauling out the boxes. Vicky even offered to help carry them to the car. I'm not sure it's on the level."

Gwen narrowed her eyes. "If Ralph Leggitt is giving something with one hand, it's because he's taking four times as much with the other. You know better than to be duped."

"You're wrong," Alex corrected. "He'd heard about the house I'm going to buy on King Street and offered to help me get a loan. Deep down, he's a generous, kindhearted man."

"Stop it, Alex. If you keep this up, my blood pressure is going into the red zone, and I'm going to have to slap you back into reality."

Alex smiled. "Yes, ma'am. I don't want a spanking, but until any ulterior motives are exposed, I'm going to take advantage of the opportunity to build my practice."

"I can't blame you for that."

"Oh," Alex lowered her voice. "Do you know about the new lawyer who is going to be moving into my office?"

Gwen shook her head. "No, what did he tell you?"

"He's going to do the same kind of work as Mr. Leggitt and Bruce."

"Boring," Gwen responded. "Forms, forms, forms."

"Perhaps the end is in sight. When the contractor doing the renovation of my new office gets to your space, I'll let you know so you can help decorate it."

Gwen smiled and patted Alex's hand. "That will be fun."

Alex phoned Rena and left a brief message on her answering machine. Then she drove to Rachel Downey's office. The real-estate company where Rachel worked occupied a commercial building that had previously been an accounting office. The reception area was nicely furnished, and there were two conference rooms.

"The office is not what you're used to," the realtor said, "but it will work as temporary quarters."

She led Alex past the kitchen area and down a long hall until they reached a dead end at a door with a red exit sign over the top.

"It's on the left," Rachel said.

They went into a room that was bigger than Alex's office at Leggitt & Freeman but without any style. The walls were covered with thin paneling that had begun to buckle slightly along the joints. There was a thin carpet on the floor and a plain wooden desk in the middle of the room with a worn-looking leather chair behind it. A single window offered a view of the parking lot at the back of the building. A beige phone was on a small stand that looked like it would buckle under the weight of anything heavier. It was worse than Alex had expected. Rachel saw the disappointment on Alex's face before she could hide it.

"I wouldn't expect you to bring clients back here," the realtor said. "You can meet with them in one of the conference rooms. Just make sure we haven't scheduled a closing or another meeting. The receptionist has a sign-up sheet that will let you know what's going on. She knows to forward your calls to this office. Your extension number is twenty-four."

"This will work fine," Alex said, regaining her footing. "I just need a place so I won't be trying to practice law from my kitchen table. I have boxes of files in the car. I'll bring them in here and line them up along the wall."

"Did you apply for a loan to buy the house?"

"Yes. I'm delivering my tax returns and bank statements later today."

"Good. Let me know if you need anything."

Alex moved her car to the back of the building. It was just a few steps from the rear parking lot to her office. She was bringing in the final box when her cell phone rang. It was Rena. Alex sat behind her desk and summarized her conversation with Ralph Leggitt. Rena was openly skeptical.

"This is confusing," she said. "I'm relieved about the criminal case going away and glad you can help me, but I'm surprised about the money. It's not like Baxter's father to let go of control. I'll believe it when I see the money back in my checking account."

"You're right. The proof will be in the practical steps they take. I'll verify with the police in Greenville that the assault and battery charges have been dropped. As soon as the money shows up in your bank account, take most of it out and deposit it in an account that is solely in your name. We also need to find out if Leggitt was telling the truth about Baxter's ownership interests in the family businesses. Do you think your source can help?"

"I'll ask him."

"Good. I'm going to call Dr. Draughton's office in a few minutes. Ralph Leggitt didn't ask me about Baxter, and I doubt they suspect what we're planning to do. Does your source know about it?"

"Uh, why would that matter?"

"I'd like to know who is in the loop of our discussions."

"I haven't talked to him since you and I met at the deli."

Alex tapped her fingers on the top of her desk. "Things are much different now than when we talked. Are you sure you want to file the petition to terminate life support at this time? Once it's filed, any cooperation with your father-in-law may go out the window. It might make sense to wait and find out more about Ezra's intentions."

"No," Rena said emphatically. "Do it as soon as possible."

Alex heard the tone of Rena's voice but didn't cave in. "At least let me delay until next week. That way there will be time for the money to be redeposited to your checking account."

There was silence for several seconds. "After you file the papers, how long will it take for the judge to decide?"

"A hearing will have to be set and subpoenas issued to the witnesses. If one of the doctors can't come in person, we will have to take his deposition. Under normal circumstances it could take several months to work through the process—"

"Months!" Rena blurted out.

"But this is an extraordinary proceeding. Realistically, it will take at least seven to ten days to schedule a hearing. The judge will set it based on his or her court calendar; however, it will be a quick ruling."

"That's what I want. As quick as possible. A few thousand dollars in a checking account is not as important to me as Baxter. No matter what happens, I think we'll end up in a fight with my father-in-law."

"Before you make up your mind, let me talk to Dr. Draughton. The strength of his opinion may help us decide."

Rena spoke slowly. "Okay, if that's what you recommend. Call me back as soon as you talk to him."

Alex put the phone down on the scratched surface of the desk and stared at the wall for a few seconds. Her conversation with her new client made one thing crystal clear. Rena Richardson might have forgiven Baxter, but she didn't want him to live.

—

Ted Morgan was on a ladder at the highest corner of Marylou Hobart's rickety house. He hummed the opening measures of the *Sonata in B Minor* by Franz Liszt as he probed the soffit for rotten wood. The old woman was leaning on her cane near the bottom of the ladder and peering up at him through thick glasses. Mrs. Hobart was a nonpaying customer. She wasn't

even a member of the Sandy Flats congregation. But the need for a carpenter, painter, and handyman is universal, and Ted occasionally performed volunteer work for people in the community. A church member
mentioned Mrs. Hobart to Ted as a person who needed help, and since
then Ted had made many trips to the elderly woman's home.

Mrs. Hobart lived in the same house where she had been born. She'd
married and moved away to Alabama, but when her husband had died,
she had returned to Santee and the place where her life had begun. The
frame house had weathered two hurricanes, but the cumulative effects of
the coastal weather had taken their toll. Ted was frustrated that every
repair revealed two more problems, but his affection for Mrs. Hobart
overcame any resentment. The old woman was so deaf that she could
barely hear Ted hammering a nail in the next room, and their conversations were like separate speeches that would tangentially intersect.

When he asked her how old she was, Mrs. Hobart replied in a
crackly voice, "1742 Franklin Road. Years ago it used to be 1246, but
they built more houses and changed the numbers. Don't ask me how
they figure it."

"I'm forty-five!" Ted yelled.

Mrs. Hobart squinted at him. "I'd say that's about right. By the time
my husband, Harry, was your age, he was bald as an egg. He only had a
little fringe over his ears that was more trouble than it was worth. He
should have changed his name. You have such nice, thick hair."

"Thank you."

"Don't thank me. I should thank you for all you're doing around this
place. Did you know we didn't have running water in the house until
Dwight Truman was president?"

"That's Harry Truman," Ted shouted.

"Not my husband," Mrs. Hobart replied in exasperation. "The president of this here country. Are you married? I don't see no wedding ring
on your finger."

"No, ma'am."

"Why not? You have a fine head of hair and are handy around the
house."

"I'm divorced."

"Delores? I don't know who you're talking about. I don't get out much no more. But I'd like to meet her. What does she like to eat?"

At that moment Alexia Lindale flashed across Ted's thoughts, and he asked himself the same question. He'd offered her steak without trying to find out what she liked to eat. Her food preferences were unknown territory.

"I don't know!"

"You're not skinny. You must be a good cook. Ask her over to your house and feed her yourself." Mrs. Hobart wagged a wrinkled finger. "And she'll ask you back if'n she has any manners at all."

And so, in a roundabout way, Mrs. Hobart confirmed Ted's decision to act on his tentative interest in Alexia Lindale.

———

Alex phoned Dr. Draughton's office. She'd researched brain injuries on the Internet and prepared a series of questions that would connect the practical effects of a severe head trauma to the legal guidelines for termination of life support. There was no answer on the physician's private number, so she waded through three levels of prerecorded voice prompts before reaching a live person who paged the doctor's nurse. The nurse came on the line, and after Alex explained her mission, the nurse put her on hold while she talked to the doctor. Ten minutes later Alex was still waiting. As time passed, Alex discovered that someone had carved his or her initials on the lip of the desk in her office. She then completed a series of complicated doodles across the top of her legal pad.

Finally, the doctor picked up the phone. Within a few minutes, Alex concluded that if the physician's demeanor on the witness stand was as effective as his telephone voice, he would make an excellent witness.

"What was your initial assessment of Baxter's condition?"

"It was obvious from external trauma that the patient had received a severe blow to the head. He had a stellate skull fracture with multiple linear fracture lines diverging from a central point of impact. By history, I knew that he had fallen from a cliff and struck his head on a large rock. This was consistent with the trauma observed by examination and plain x-ray films."

"What effect did this blow have on his brain?"

"He had severe localized swelling in the area of the fracture, and a significant subdural hemorrhage that increased in size during the forty-eight hours after his injury. All of this is documented on successive MRI scans and the readings from an intracranial pressure monitor."

"Do you have copies of the scans in your office?"

"Yes."

Alex made a note in the margin of her legal pad. "Could you make them available to a medical illustrator and then review the drawings prepared for accuracy?"

"Certainly."

"Did you assess the severity of his coma?"

"Yes."

The doctor then explained the Glasgow Coma Scale and the profile developed by the Institutes for the Achievement of Human Potential that assessed sensory and motor functions.

The more Alex heard, the more confident she became.

"Have you continued to monitor Mr. Richardson's condition?"

"Yes."

"Have you performed any other type of testing?"

"Yes, both electroencephalogram and evoked potential tests."

"I've read about those procedures but wasn't sure exactly what they measured."

By the time the doctor finished his explanation, Alex understood the purpose of the testing and had reached a legal conclusion: The neurologist could provide the medical expertise needed to support an order terminating Baxter Richardson's life support.

Some chord in unison with what we hear is
touched within us, and the heart replies.
WILLIAM COWPER

RENA PHONED JEFFREY at his office. Before reaching her brother-in-law she had to listen to expressions of concern and self-centered sympathy from Jeffrey's secretary, a brunette woman about the same age as Rena.

"I'm so sorry to hear about Baxter," the young woman said in a deep drawl. "I guess you're devastated."

Rena flipped on her story switch. "Yes, it was a terrible accident."

"If something like that happened to my Rick, I think I would have jumped over the cliff after him. You know, we were married a couple of months before you and Baxter. Nothing nearly as fancy as y'all, but it was nice, and we had a reception at—"

"Could I speak to Jeffrey?" Rena interrupted. "It's important."

"Just a minute," the woman snipped.

Rena didn't care if she made the secretary mad. Baxter had mentioned that Jeffrey went through clerical help almost as quickly as he did girl-friends.

"What is it?" her brother-in-law asked.

"I've got to talk with you," she said. "I just—"

"Why did you call me?" Jeffrey asked in a harsh voice. "I don't have anything to say to you."

The phone clicked off. Rena stared at it in disbelief. Jeffrey had turned against her as dramatically as Ezra had turned toward her. While she was trying to sort out what to do, her cell phone rang. She retrieved it from her purse and looked at the number. It was someone from

Richardson and Company. Not sure which Richardson was calling, Rena thought about letting her voice mail take a message, but on the third ring she pressed the talk button.

"Hello," she said in a tentative voice.

"It's me," Jeffrey said.

"Why are you calling? You hung up on me."

"Sorry about that. My father doesn't know we're communicating, and I don't want him to suspect any cooperation. He may be recording my telephone conversations from the office phone."

"Why would he do that?"

"For the same reason I have a tap on his phone."

"You record your father's phone calls?"

"Not all of them. It's set up to catch specific numbers as a way of keeping track of what he's telling certain people."

Rena had no aversion to lying, but she was used to deception of her own making.

"Did you tap Baxter's phone?" she asked.

Jeffrey didn't directly answer. "Just relax. Nothing bad has happened to you since we talked, has it?"

"No, but it makes me nervous that someone could be watching me."

"Pretend it's like the Secret Service. They don't do anything unless there is danger."

Rena walked to a window and looked outside. The large, flat lawn in front of the old house was empty, and the only cars in the semicircular drive were Baxter's SUV and her own red convertible.

"Is someone watching me now?"

"Probably not, but I know you had lunch yesterday with Ms. Lindale at Katz's Deli. What did you talk about?"

"You tell me," Rena shot back. "Your friends probably had one of those listening devices in a van outside the restaurant."

"I told you to relax. I'm glad you met with her. Is she going to help us?"

Rena summarized her discussion with Alex at the deli. She didn't add the postscript about their subsequent phone conversation and Ezra's apparent change of heart.

"I disagree," Jeffrey said. "She needs to file the case against my father as soon as possible. Baxter isn't going anywhere, but every day the power of attorney remains alive can complicate the business side of things. You've paid the lawyer a good retainer. Tell her to seek a temporary restraining order that will stop my father. That should do the trick without having to go any further."

Jeffrey's comments reassured Rena that her own phone wasn't tapped. He didn't know what Alex had told her, but his lack of knowledge about Ezra was disturbing. Jeffrey's supposedly sophisticated spy network hadn't picked up the information about his father's change of mind about the power of attorney.

"Do you have specific information I can give Alex about the way your father is using the power of attorney to transfer property out of Baxter's name?" Rena asked.

"Besides the checking account?"

"Yes."

There was a brief pause on the other end. Rena could hear Jeffrey talking to someone while covering the phone with his hand.

"Rena, I have to go to a meeting. I have plenty of documentation to give your lawyer at the right time, but I have to be very careful or I'll run the risk of destroying everything we've built. My goal is to influence the direction of the business and who receives the benefits of it. You stand more to gain in this than anyone else. You'll have to trust me on when to release information." He spoke rapidly. "I have another ten thousand dollars for you. Where do you want it delivered?"

"Uh, put it in the passenger seat of my car by eight o'clock in the morning. I'll leave it unlocked."

"Okay. I'll send a courier."

Rena put the phone back in her purse. She doubted Jeffrey's delivery-man would be wearing a FedEx or UPS uniform.

———

The following day, Alex arrived early at her temporary office with her first priority contacting the remainder of her clients. Over the next three hours she made almost as many phone calls as a telemarketer. All but ten of her clients wanted her to continue representing them, and those who opted out had connections with Leggitt & Freeman that predated Alex's representation. One of the calls she dreaded the most was to a woman named Mona Jones, a perpetual complainer who was impossible to please.

"What in the world would cause you to leave Ralph Leggitt?" Mona asked. "He's the most respected lawyer in Santee."

"It was a decision that had to be made," Alex replied. "It was time for me to move on."

"Well, before I let you continue to handle my case, I want to talk to Ralph about it."

"Go ahead, that's your right."

Mrs. Jones grew more indignant. "I wasn't sure I should let someone so young handle my case, but Ralph reassured me that you knew what you were doing. Now I find out that you're going out like a vagabond on your own."

If the personal attack had been more subtle, Alex might have gotten angry. As it was, she had to stifle a laugh.

"Mrs. Jones, you're right. It would be better if you hired another lawyer, one with more experience who works at a larger firm. That way you would have more confidence about the advice you receive."

"Are you saying you're not going to represent me?" the woman asked in surprise at the turn of events. "I'm not sure that's what I want to do."

"It's what I want to do," Alex said with emphasis. "I'm going to file a motion with the court to withdraw as your attorney. There isn't much left to do in your divorce, and someone else can adequately handle the remaining matters. Your file will be available for you to pick up or I can mail it to you by certified mail."

"Well, if that's your attitude, I demand that you send everything to me immediately."

"It will go out in today's mail. Same address?"

"Of course. Unlike you, I'm not going anywhere!"

Alex hung up the phone and crossed off Mona Jones's name with relief. After several more calls, she took a break and drove to Leggitt & Freeman to pick up more boxes of files.

Gwen was too busy to talk, but the third time Alex walked down the hallway the secretary motioned for her to come over to her desk. Alex wiped a few beads of perspiration from her forehead.

"How many more boxes are there?" Gwen asked.

"This is it. Mona Jones doesn't want my help anymore so I'm leaving her file and a few others. I told her if she has any questions to call here and ask for your extension."

Gwen made a face. "I learned fast to pass her on to you without wasting my time. Mona was in a class by herself."

"Actually, I fired her," Alex said. "If you have time, box up her stuff and send it to her today. There isn't much to do in her case. The final order has been signed, but it will be someone else's headache to implement it."

"Will do. Did she ask you for the name of another attorney?"

"No, and there's no one I hate enough to send her to."

Gwen lowered her voice. "What's happening with Rena Richardson? Her father-in-law and Baxter's brother, Jeffrey, spent a couple of hours with Mr. Leggitt and Bruce Fletchall yesterday."

"Are you sure it was Baxter's brother?"

"Yes. He's a good-looking guy but a bit oily around the edges. He used to date my friend Sandra's niece. Sandra can't stand him. Jeffrey showered her niece with expensive gifts and then dumped her for no reason. Sandra says he should have been the one who fell off a cliff."

Alex put her finger to her lips. "Don't tell me anything else. All I can say is that I'm helping Rena, and Leggitt is representing Ezra. There have been some skirmishes, but full-scale war hasn't erupted. If it does, it wouldn't be right for me to obtain any information from you."

Gwen shrugged. "I don't know any details. What about the house you want to buy for your office?"

"The bank has everything they need from me. Once the appraiser sends in a report and the title work is complete, I want to begin the renovation as soon as possible."

"Do you have a contractor?"

"Yes. Do you remember the minister I contacted in Barbara Kensington's case?"

"Fred something at Sandy Flats Church."

"His name is Ted. I asked him to take a look at the house on King Street, and he's putting together an estimate."

"Have you seen any of his work?"

"Uh, he was painting the old parsonage one of the days when I went by the church. I think he was doing a good job."

Gwen perked up. "How many times have you been by the church to see Rev. Ted?"

Alex hesitated. "I'm not sure."

"More than two?"

"Maybe five or six. His full name is Ted Morgan."

"Do you know his middle name?"

Alex grinned. "No."

Gwen leaned forward. "What's the draw? You don't even go to church on Sunday, much less during the week."

Alex glanced over her shoulder.

"Leonard is gone for the afternoon," Gwen said. "Tell me."

Alex stepped to the side so that she wasn't visible from the hallway.

"He's a musical genius who can play the piano well enough to perform in Carnegie Hall. The first time I went to the church, I couldn't believe what I was hearing. It was incredible—like listening to someone in a recording studio. I don't know why he moved to a place like Santee. He could be in New York, Los Angeles, or at least in a big church somewhere. He's divorced and his daughter is a professional musician in New York."

"Wait," Gwen interrupted. "His daughter is an adult? Is this guy a prospect for you or for me?"

"Either, I guess," Alex responded playfully. "Do you want me to set you up?"

"No, but I don't want you running after an old man. If he's out of shape, you might catch him."

"How many men have you seen me chasing recently?" Alex asked.

"Okay," Gwen admitted. "But are you interested in dating him?"

"I don't know. He's asked me over to his house tomorrow night for dinner, and I accepted. He's cooking steaks, and we'll probably drink fresh-squeezed lemonade. The invitation was a surprise to me. I thought he was spending time talking with me because he wanted to convert me, but he admitted that he's been interested in me ever since we met."

"Of course. You're gorgeous, smart, and love classical piano music."

Alex remembered the list she'd given Ted for the ideal woman. "Thanks, but even if that's true it's not enough for this guy. He wants a spiritual relationship."

"A what?" Gwen asked.

"A soul mate thing with God in the middle of it. It was beautiful the way he described his relationship with his ex-wife. Their unity, etc."

"That's a new angle. Where is the ex-wife now?"

"I think in California. She's remarried and not in the picture."

Gwen sat back in her seat. "I miss you being here. And this minister pursuing you is too juicy not to get up-to-the-minute news reports. I hope he's not like some of those preachers on TV."

Alex shook her head. "He's not, except he wears a silver jacket that sparkles like a thousand diamonds when the light hits it right. It's beautiful when he walks across the room toward me. It sends shivers down my spine."

Gwen threw a paper clip at her. "Enough. I only want the facts."

"There's not much else to tell. He's forty-five, has curly brown hair, and wrinkles his forehead when he's thinking."

Gwen quickly did her own math. "That's pushing it for both of us, but it could work. If you decide he's not your type, I'll put on a nice dress and sign up for the choir."

———

Detective Giles Porter had huffed and puffed along the trail to Double-Barrel Falls. He knew going back up to his car would be twice as hard. The detective had lived in Mitchell County all his life but never went hiking or camping. His father, who worked twelve-hour shifts at a local textile mill, didn't want to spend his free time wandering through the woods, so camping for pleasure had not been part of Porter's childhood. During his years in law enforcement, the detective had once spent all night in the woods waiting for a suspect to come out of a house and on several occasions trudged through vines and underbrush following the bloodhounds used to track fugitives. Those experiences squelched any idyllic sentiments about nature that might have lingered within him.

He watched the water rush together in a narrow funnel, accelerate, and then split on opposite sides of a boulder that sat securely lodged in the center of the stream. In a thousand years, the boulder might be worn away enough for the flow of water to catapult in unity over the edge of the cliff. But for now it remained as separated as Porter's efforts to connect his guesses and suspicions about what had really happened between Baxter and Rena Richardson at the waterfall. Porter didn't have a firm theory implicating Rena in Baxter's accident, but the idea of visiting the site to see if it helped his thought process had nagged him off and on until he gave in.

The detective inched to the edge of the falls and looked down. It amazed him that anyone could survive a fall to the rocks that waited unsympathetically below. However, it wasn't Giles Porter's job to understand why Baxter was alive. His task was to discover whether the young man's wife had pushed him to the brink of death. All the detective knew for certain was that Rena had lied to him. Either she didn't attempt CPR to revive her husband, or she thought he was dead and told the detective Baxter's body was cold by the time she reached the bottom of the waterfall. The former lie could be the product of someone who wanted to look like a heroine but wasn't. The latter was the type of mistake made by an overconfident criminal.

Rena's other reactions were equally ambiguous: her reaction to the news of her husband's survival, inappropriately wanting to avoid the detective's questions, and hiding behind the female lawyer who conveniently showed up at the hospital right before the detective was going to turn up the pressure. Porter couldn't read another person's mind but had a skill almost as valuable—the ability to make people think that he could. He sensed Rena's fear, and it attracted him like a shark to a widening pool of blood in the ocean.

He knelt down and let the water rush over his fingers. It was cold. More leaves had fallen from the trees since Rena and Baxter had been here. He closely inspected the ground, not sure what he might find, but checking out of habit. Amidst the pebbles he found a piece of cork that could have come from the bottle of wine the Richardsons drank. He picked it up and put it in a Ziploc bag.

Expanding his search, he carefully inspected the ground around the nearby boulders. Nothing caught his eye, and he returned to the overlook. Near the place where the open area gave way to scraggly trees he saw a piece of wood lying on the ground. It was too straight and thick to have fallen from one of the nearby trees. He picked it up. It was a rough walking stick that a hiker had brought to the waterfall and then abandoned or misplaced. On closer inspection, he saw that a few bits of bark had peeled from one end, and the other was dirty and slightly splintered from contact with the ground.

A hiking stick would be useful on the way back to the parking lot. In their brief conversations, Rena hadn't mentioned anything about sticks amid the stones of the overlook. It would be a topic he'd like to bring up the next time they talked.

30

Ill weed groweth fast.
JOHN HEYWOOD

ALEX LUGGED THE last box into her new office and dropped it on the floor. She was tired. Boris could forget swimming in the ocean this evening. The receptionist for the real-estate office buzzed her, and Alex picked up the phone.

"Yes?"

"Uh, Ms. Lindale, someone is calling for Alex Lindale."

"That's me. I should have told you. Who is it?"

"Rena Richardson."

Alex found the notes she'd taken during her conversation with Dr. Draughton.

"I'll take it."

Rena spoke first. "I've been trying to reach you, but I didn't want to leave a message. Did you talk to the doctor?"

"Sorry, I've been moving my files and touching base with my other clients. Yes, I had a very productive talk with Dr. Draughton. He knows a lot about head injuries and has the expertise to offer an opinion about Baxter."

"Will he help us?"

"Definitely. And if a judge wants to believe his testimony, he will support an order terminating life support."

"That's great, uh, good."

"Of course, there will be other opinions from other doctors."

"I know, but now you have enough to file the petition."

"Yes, I'll work on it tomorrow. When are you going back to Greenville?"

"I'm not sure. I called the hospital today and spoke to one of the nurses in ICU. She pulled Baxter's chart and told me there was no change in his condition."

"Has your father-in-law returned the money to your bank account?"

"Not yet, but tomorrow is the day he promised it would redeposited."

Alex twisted the phone cord in her hand. "I found out that Ezra and Jeffrey were at Leggitt & Freeman yesterday. They spent a couple of hours with Ralph Leggitt, but I don't know what they talked about or did."

"Jeffrey said he had to go to a meeting."

Alex couldn't resist a gentle probe. "Have you been talking with Jeffrey?"

"Yeah, a little bit. He's been very nice."

"Have you asked his opinion about terminating Baxter's life support? He could be a witness for us."

Rena didn't immediately answer. "Would it matter what he thought? His father and I are the ones who disagree."

"Maybe. Jeffrey is Baxter's brother, so he has a right to express an opinion. His viewpoint would be thrown into the mix of things the judge would consider, but it wouldn't be given as much weight as your wishes."

"I could ask him, but right now I don't think he wants to get directly involved in the dispute over Baxter's care. He's more concerned with his father's use of the power of attorney to take all my property. He thinks I should file something on that first."

"It's not necessary to file anything if Ezra puts back the money and hasn't done anything else."

"But we don't know what else he's done."

Alex paused. "That's why we need the information from your source."

"Okay. I'll work on it and find out what I can."

"Good. When I finish the petition, I'll need you to sign a verification that everything in it is true. Do you know where Rachel Downey's office is located?"

"No."

Alex gave her directions. "I'll call you as soon as it's ready tomorrow."

By noon of the following day, Alex had turned her makeshift office into a temporary command center. She bought a powerful computer, a new printer, and a fax machine. The equipment sat on a swirled cherry stand that matched the executive desk she'd selected and placed on hold for delivery to her new office. The expensive desk and computer stand had been gathering dust at the local office supply store for several months, and the owner was more than willing to let Alex make interest-free payments. She didn't pick out a secretarial desk and chair. That privilege would fall to Gwen so she could express her own taste in the furniture that would occupy her home away from home.

A large desk blotter covered the scratched surface of Alex's temporary desk, but she'd brightened up the room with an arrangement of fresh-cut flowers in a vase that she put on the left front corner. Before her was the promised letter from Ralph Leggitt confirming the dismissal of the criminal charges against Rena. Rachel Downey knocked and poked her head in the door.

"Hey," she said. "You work fast. This room hasn't looked this nice since forever. The last tenant in here was a man who bought and sold soybeans."

Alex looked up. She'd been typing the first draft of the petition to terminate Baxter Richardson's life support.

"That explains why I've found several beans on the carpet."

"Sorry. It was supposed to be vacuumed."

Alex patted her new piece of furniture. "Do you like the computer stand? I've placed a hold on a matching desk."

Rachel walked over and stroked the reddish wood. "It's classy. Feminine, yet businesslike."

"I think it will look nice in the new office."

Rachel snapped her fingers. "And I know some wallpaper that will work perfectly. I'll get you a sample. Is everything moving forward on the loan?"

"Yes."

"Good. There were two people standing behind you who wanted to buy the house. You slipped in under the wire."

Alex opened the top drawer of the desk and took out a check. "Here's five thousand dollars as earnest money on the contract. I was going to give it to you yesterday, but you were out of town. I'm meeting with my contractor this evening, and I hope he will be able to start ASAP."

Rachel took the check. "Thanks. You'll never guess who else was interested in the house."

Alex thought for a moment. "Ralph Leggitt? He knew I'd bought it and claimed it was because he kept up with everything that happened in Santee."

Rachel nodded. "Yep."

"What a snake."

"If you'd hesitated, he could have fixed it up and rented it to you."

Alex moved her chair and heard something crunch. She leaned over and picked up a smashed soybean. "I'd rather work in a soybean patch."

When Rachel left, Alex put the finishing touches on the petition and called Rena's cell phone. Rena answered on the second ring.

"The petition is ready, and I'm typing the verification," Alex said. "When can you come by to sign it?"

"I'm on my way. I want to stop by the bank first. The money is back in my account. I'm going to take it out and put it in a separate account that's only in my name."

"Was all of it returned?"

"Yes, plus several thousand extra."

"That's quite a turnaround. Did he call you?"

"No, which is a relief. Never knowing what he might say or do drives me crazy. I know he's a smart businessman, but I think he's mentally unstable."

Alex remembered the sound of Rena's distraught voice on the phone but didn't debate with her which Richardson had the more precarious emotional equilibrium. "I received written confirmation of the dismissal of the criminal charges this morning," she said. "But continue to avoid your father-in-law. It would only make him furious if you have a cordial conversation one minute and serve him with the petition to terminate Baxter's life support the next."

"Yeah, I really don't want to talk to him."

Thirty minutes later, Alex and Rena were sitting side by side in one of Rachel Downey's conference rooms. Rena was reading the petition.

"Why doesn't it mention Dr. Draughton?" she asked as she turned over the first page.

"We don't have to identify our expert witnesses in the pleadings." Alex reached across the table and pointed to the top lines of the second sheet. "It's covered in the paragraph that states: '*The greater weight of competent medical evidence supports a determination that Baxter Richardson is in a persistent vegetative state or other condition of permanent unconsciousness which renders continuation of extraordinary life sustaining measures contrary to generally accepted medical practices and the express instructions made by him in the Declaration of Desire for a Natural Death, a true and correct copy of which is attached hereto as Exhibit A.*' If the other side wants to know who is going to testify, I'll tell them. Because it's an expedited request, there won't be time for formal discovery and depositions prior to the hearing, and I don't want the judge to exclude a witness because I tried to sandbag the other side."

"Formal discovery? What's that?"

"Written questions about the case. The law gives thirty days for answers, and I want to schedule a hearing within seven to ten days. There won't be time for either side to find out much before going to court so there may be some surprises."

"What kind of surprises?"

Alex shrugged. "We suspect Dr. Berman and Dr. Kolb will not support termination of life support as strongly as Dr. Draughton, but from what you told me, they will have to admit that Dr. Draughton is an expert in the field. Otherwise, they wouldn't have called him in for a consultation. Your father-in-law can probably find another medical authority in the field of head injuries who will disagree with Dr. Draughton. Plenty of doctors are out there for hire in every specialty. It's a big business."

Rena read to the end of the petition. Alex watched her face, looking for an emotional reaction to the implications of the petition for Baxter. She saw nothing. Rena was more businesslike than in any of their previous meetings and showed no hint of either revenge or sorrow.

"I want to make sure I understand this last part," Rena said.

Alex looked at the place where Rena had placed her finger. "That's the prayer for relief. We're asking the judge to enter an order taking Baxter off the ventilator and terminating the feeding tube and hydration via an IV."

"Okay," Rena said. "That's what I want to do."

Alex flipped over the next sheet. "Then sign here. This means everything in the petition is true, and you want the judge to grant the relief we've requested."

Rena signed the verification without hesitation. Her signature flowed steadily across the page.

"I'll call the court administrator this afternoon and get a date for the hearing," Alex said. "Because time is so important, I'll ask Ralph Leggitt if he is willing to acknowledge service on behalf of Ezra. That will save the step of mailing the petition to your father-in-law or sending a deputy sheriff out to serve him personally."

"Will he agree?"

"Oh, yes," Alex responded with a slight smile. "If he has the petition then Leggitt & Freeman will be automatically retained to handle the case. An attorney named Ken Pinchot will probably get involved."

"Is he good?"

"Yes, one of the best trial lawyers in this part of the state. He will do everything he can to keep us from getting what we want. It will be a fight."

"I can't lose this," Rena said anxiously.

"I don't intend to lose," Alex responded, "but there aren't any guarantees. No lawyer can predict exactly what will happen in a case like this one. It's not a cut-and-dried situation. There will be evidence supporting both sides."

Rena looked directly into Alex's eyes. "Do whatever it takes."

"Then contact your information source. I need to know if your father-in-law made any transfers of assets or ownership interests out of Baxter's name. The extra money in the checking account doesn't convince me that everything is on the level. If he's lying to us, we can still make him look bad in front of the judge and argue that he only wants to keep Baxter alive so he can pillage his property."

"And if nothing has happened?"

"Then we rely on Dr. Draughton, the declaration of desire for a natural death signed by Baxter, and the sincerity of your face."

After Rena left, Alex phoned the court in Greenville and was able to schedule the hearing for the following Friday. The court administrator blocked out the whole afternoon. After filling in the date and time on the notice of hearing, she drove to Leggitt & Freeman. This meeting with Ralph Leggitt might not be as congenial as the last one.

———

Rena returned home. Inside the front door of the rambling white house, she entered a large foyer with a wooden floor covered by an expensive Persian rug. To the left was the living room with a row of windows that overlooked the front lawn and to the right a formal dining room that featured a large chandelier and a table with chairs for twelve. The furniture in the downstairs rooms was a mixture of antiques and more contemporary pieces. Rena had furnished the house based on her affinity for individual items rather than an identifiable theme or emphasis on a particular time period. She had refused the services of an interior designer, and Ezra had grumbled that the result resembled a furniture showroom more than a well-decorated home.

During the drive home from her meeting with Alex, Rena glanced in the rearview mirror and saw a dark blue car with heavily tinted windows behind her. A similar car had parked near her when she went into the grocery store the previous day. Santee was small enough that it wasn't unusual to see the same vehicle several times a week, but Rena suspected the car contained the person or persons Jeffrey had dispatched to keep an eye on her. She reached a traffic light as it turned red and sped through it. The car stopped, and by the time the light changed, Rena had made the turn onto the street that ran in front of her house. She stopped in the middle of the driveway and waited to see if the car appeared. Seeing nothing, she drove slowly into a garage that stood to the left of the house and was connected to it by a short covered walkway. Behind the garage was the cozy, one-bedroom guesthouse where Rena and Baxter had lived for a few weeks while waiting for the renovations on the main house to be completed.

Instead of entering through the side door, Rena walked around to pick up a newspaper that lay on the brick steps in front of the house. When she leaned over, she saw the blue car pass by the driveway. It didn't stop but appeared to be moving slower than normal. She hurriedly unlocked the door and went inside. She called Jeffrey's cell phone.

"Can you talk?" she asked.

He answered in a muffled voice. "Just a minute. I'm going to walk into another room."

While she waited, Rena looked at her face in a gold-framed mirror that hung on the wall of the foyer. The stress of the recent days had taken its toll. The cuts on her face had healed nicely, but there were gray circles under her eyes. She determined to take an afternoon nap.

"Okay," Jeffrey said.

"Do the people who are watching me drive a dark blue car?" she asked.

"I told you not to worry about it. What do you want?"

"Tell me. It will make me feel better."

After a few seconds of silence, Jeffrey said, "No."

Disappointed, Rena asked, "What kind of car do they drive?"

"Different ones. You're wasting my time. Why did you call?"

"Your father has put all the money back in my checking account."

"That doesn't surprise me. He doesn't want you to file the action against him for using the power of attorney. If he hadn't put back the money, it would have forced you to do something. Nothing has changed. Tell your lawyer to file a complaint attacking the power of attorney."

"How can I do that if he's put back the money?" Rena asked in a slightly louder voice.

"How do you know that he hasn't done something else?"

"I don't!" Rena retorted. "And unless you help me, there is no way I will be able to find out. I can't ask Alex to file a lawsuit without knowing what has happened."

There was a brief silence on the other end of the phone. "Okay, I can give you something on Monday. My father is going to Greenville this afternoon to spend the weekend visiting Baxter. While he's gone, I'll have access to the files I need. I'll have to give you a little bit of information at a time. Otherwise, he'll know what I'm doing."

"Can you tell me anything now?"

"No. And don't ask."

Rena started to raise her voice and issue another demand but stopped. There was no point in trying to force Jeffrey to reveal information. She'd pushed as hard as she could.

"Okay, I'll be here on Monday," she said. "I won't be going back to Greenville if your father will be there this weekend."

Before Rena could hang up, Jeffrey asked, "When are you going to try to cut off Baxter's life support?"

Caught off guard by the sudden shift in the conversation, Rena cleared her throat before answering.

"Uh, Alex and I talked about it today."

"I'll need some time before you do it."

Rena had a sinking feeling in the pit of her stomach. She'd pushed Alex without thinking about Jeffrey's opinion.

"Uh, whenever we do it, I won't make you testify even though you promised you would," she said. "The decision to terminate life support depends on what the doctors think."

Jeffrey wasn't diverted. "I hope your lawyer isn't about to file something in court," he said firmly.

Rena didn't know what to say. Jeffrey would know sooner or later about the petition. She wasn't about to call Alex and stop her. She tried to sound as casual as possible.

"It's too late. Alex is going to schedule a hearing as soon as possible."

"What! That's not what I told you to do!"

Rena bit her lip. "I'm sorry, I should have let you know."

"Well, you're right about one thing. You're on your own with it. I can't help."

Rena tried to salvage something. "Will you still call on Monday and let me know what you find out?"

"Maybe. Bye."

The phone clicked off.

After she said good-bye, Rena stared out the front windows for several seconds. She hated having to rely on Jeffrey. She set her jaw. For now, she was trapped and had to rely on her brother-in-law, but when the opportunity came, she would grab her freedom and not let go. Neither Jeffrey nor any other man would stop her. She turned away from the window just before a dark blue car drove past the end of the driveway.

Rena put her cell phone on the kitchen counter and trudged upstairs to attempt a nap. She'd been sleeping with the bedroom door locked and a chair in front of the door to Baxter's closet. The sight of her husband's shirts, belts, shoes, and other personal belongings was troubling, and she'd considered moving into one of the guest bedrooms. Kicking off her shoes, she lay down on top of the bedspread, closed her eyes, and fell into an uneasy sleep. A half-hour later, she rolled over to change position and barely opened her eyes.

Baxter was lying beside her.

His back was to her, and he was wearing his favorite brown-and-green shirt with khaki slacks. Stifling a scream, she stared at his sleeping form. His head was turned away from her so that she could just see the top of his brown hair. His side was moving up and down in regular rhythm. With her heart pounding loudly in her ears, Rena moved her hand slowly toward his body. If she could thrust her hand through him, it would confirm to her senses that he wasn't any more real than an image on a TV screen. Just as her hand came within an inch of his back, she blinked, and he disappeared.

Rena stared intently for several seconds at the now smooth place on the covers. Then she rolled onto her back and stared at the ceiling. In a few moments her heart rate slowed. She glanced apprehensively to the side, but the bed remained empty. The fact that she had been able to maintain her composure during the encounter was a major triumph. Baxter was an illusion, and the fact that she could exert her will in the midst of the experience was encouraging. Of course, she didn't want to see him, but if it was an unavoidable part of her future, the ability to respond in a way that maintained her sanity was a huge step forward.

She closed her eyes again to sleep with less fear of who might appear when she awoke.

31

You are the light of the world. A city
that is set on a hill cannot be hidden.
MATTHEW 5:14 (NKJV)

HOLDING THE SERVICE copy of the petition in an unsealed envelope, Alex debated whether to go through the main entrance to Leggitt & Freeman or use the familiar side entrance that bypassed the gatekeeper in the reception area. Sooner or later Alex would have to discard any remaining vestiges of her employment with the firm, but today she rationalized use of the side entrance by the fact that she needed to drop a list of files she'd taken to her new office by Vicky's desk. Gwen wasn't in sight, and Alex went directly to Leggitt's secretary. If the senior partner wasn't in his office, she could leave the petition with the secretary and address the fallout over the telephone. Vicky was coming out of Ralph Leggitt's office when Alex walked up.

"Here is the list of files I've taken," Alex said as she handed the sheets to Vicky. "Is he busy?"

"Not really. I'll let him know you're here."

Vicky went back into the office and returned in a few seconds. "He'll be with you shortly. He needs to make a quick phone call."

Alex sat in one of two leather chairs that served as a secondary reception area for those waiting to enter the office. Leggitt's secretary was typing dictation and ignored her. The phone call stretched to several minutes, and Alex began to fidget. She loved to relax at home, but inactivity during the workday was a pet peeve. Waiting was an unavoidable part of law practice, but it was impossible to avoid a feeling of frustrated tension when she was forced to delay. It was hardest when she was waiting for a trial to start and had to sit quietly across a courtroom from her opponent like a prizefighter waiting for the opening bell. The phone on the secretary's desk buzzed. She picked up the receiver and turned to Alex.

"You can go in."

Dressed casually for Friday afternoon, Ralph Leggitt was sitting behind his desk. He stood up when Alex entered.

"Have a seat," he said. "I was talking to Ezra Richardson. He made a deposit to Rena's checking account yesterday afternoon."

Alex sat down. "She confirmed it with me this morning."

"Did you receive my letter about dismissal of the criminal charges?"

"Yes, thanks."

"Good. What's on your mind?"

Alex held the envelope lightly in her hand. "Baxter's doctors requested a consultation with a neurologist who specializes in traumatic head injuries. He has evaluated Baxter and believes it would be appropriate to terminate life support."

Leggitt took out a pen. "What's his name?"

"Dr. Vince Draughton," Alex replied, spelling the doctor's last name.

"Do you have a report?"

"I've talked to him but don't have anything in writing. When I was in Greenville, it was obvious that Ezra and Rena had different opinions about maintaining life support, but Rena was willing to hope for the best. Over the past few days Baxter has not made any progress, and according to Dr. Draughton, there is no medical reason to keep him going."

Mr. Leggitt tapped his fingers on the surface of his desk. "Ezra was on his way to Greenville when I called him. He didn't mention anything about deterioration of Baxter's condition. In fact, one of the neuro-surgeons told him this morning that Baxter was stable."

"I realize there may be different opinions from the doctors, but Rena believes Baxter would not want to be kept alive hooked up to feeding tubes and dependent on a ventilator. You and I know the law gives Ezra priority in directing Baxter's medical care unless his condition meets the criteria for the declaration of desire for a natural death."

Alex paused, but Ralph Leggitt didn't respond. She knew he was waiting for her to reveal her plan. She kept her tone of voice matter-of-fact.

"Rena instructed me to prepare a petition to terminate Baxter's life support. A hearing is set in front of a judge in Greenville for next Friday afternoon beginning at one o'clock." Alex put the envelope on the edge of Mr. Leggitt's desk. "Here are the papers. It should be filed in Greenville on Monday. There is also an acknowledgment of service for you to sign as Ezra's attorney."

Ralph Leggitt didn't pick up the envelope. His eyes narrowed. "Are you sure this is what you want to do?"

Alex remained steady. "It's what my client wants to do, and there is medical justification for her request."

"Did you tell her how this might affect the cooperation she's received from her father-in-law?"

"Yes."

His face grim, Leggitt put his pen down on his desk. "After our conversation the other day, I thought we were moving toward family harmony, not conflict. Ezra is going to be very upset when he finds out about this, and it makes my advice that he be generous toward Rena look foolish."

"You told Ezra to do the right thing, and even though he had no business taking the money out of Rena's checking account and filing criminal charges against her, his change of heart didn't go unappreciated. Rena thought about calling him, but I suggested she wait because of their differences about maintaining Baxter's life support. Even now, we're willing to discuss the situation with him and try to come to an agreement."

Leggitt snorted. "Do you expect Ezra Richardson to speed up his son's death when the doctors still hold out hope of a recovery?"

"We could arrange a conference call or meeting with Dr. Draughton. I've talked to him, and he can explain the situation in a way that's easy to understand."

The cloud over Ralph Leggitt darkened. "Don't patronize me or my client, Alex. You sandbagged me, and now I'm going to look like an idiot."

Alex flushed slightly. "Uh, I didn't mislead you. We didn't talk about—"

The older lawyer interrupted. "You knew all along that Rena wanted to pull the plug on Baxter, but you waited until you got what you wanted before filing the petition. I told Ezra I could trust you to be honest with me. I was wrong."

Mr. Leggitt stood up. "I won't make the same mistake again."

Alex remained seated. "If I were in your place, I'd be mad, too. But there is medical support for Rena's request, and it deserves a hearing in front of a judge."

"Save your arguments. I know what's going on."

"What do you mean?"

Leggitt didn't answer. "We'll acknowledge service for Mr. Richardson."

Alex stood. Leggitt didn't make a move to escort her out of his office.

He spoke in a low voice. "Your client has chosen the hard way, and I'll do everything I can to make sure she regrets it," he said.

Alex didn't respond. She had a policy not to engage in verbal threats before going to court. It sapped her energy.

"Thanks for seeing me," she said as she walked from the office.

In the hallway outside, Alex took a deep breath and exhaled. In some ways she preferred Ralph Leggitt as an adversary rather than an ally. As an enemy, his actions were unerringly predictable—whatever served his self-interest was the unfailing principle.

———

Ted Morgan had returned to work at Marylou Hobart's house Friday afternoon. In the heat of the summer she relied on two single-room air conditioners to stay comfortable, but it wouldn't be hot again for many months, and the old woman wanted to put screens in her windows so she could enjoy the fall breeze. Ted found the screens in a shed behind the house and cleaned them with a hose and soapy water. He didn't think it would be a difficult job, but when he attempted to install the first screen, it didn't fit.

"There's a problem," he told Mrs. Hobart, who was standing inside the house on the opposite side of the open window and peering out at him.

"I'm not upset," she answered. "I know you came as soon as you could."

Ted pushed on the screen, but it was a half-inch too long. Mrs. Hobart tapped the window sill.

"Oh, that one must go somewheres else," she said. "Each one is different. They're customer made."

Ted nodded. The house was so old and the windows so irregular that Mrs. Hobart's mother must have ordered custom-made screens. None of the screens or windows had been labeled by the last person who had removed them. The result was a giant jigsaw puzzle. Ted took all the screens to the first window and tried each one until he found the matching piece. He repeated the process as he moved from window to window until he finished the downstairs.

The second story of the house had six windows. Ted was used to scrambling up and down ladders, but the prospect of doing so repeatedly on Mrs. Hobart's rickety ladder with an armload of screens was not a pleasant prospect.

"You don't use the upstairs, do you?" he called to Mrs. Hobart, who was sitting in a rocking chair on her back porch.

"I haven't been staring at you. I trust you to do a good job."

Ted came closer and repeated his question. The old woman smiled.

"I'm sorry. I haven't been up the steps in ages. No need to risk breaking your neck on the ladder. What you've done is just fine. Come inside and have a glass of tea. It'll perk you up."

Mrs. Hobart's tea was so sweet it could have been used for pancake syrup. Ted liked sweet drinks, but he filled his tea glass to the top and added extra water as soon as the old woman's back was turned. Even then, it was not a drink for those on a low carbohydrate diet. Ted took a tentative sip. It tasted great. Mrs. Hobart must have forgotten and cut the amount of sugar in half.

"This is good," he said, holding up his glass.

She smiled at the compliment. "It could be sweeter."

"Do you remember talking about the woman I wanted to invite over to my house for supper?" Ted called out.

"Delores?" the old woman replied.

"No. Her name is Alex."

As soon as he said it, Ted realized his mistake. Mrs. Hobart gave him a strange look that let him know she'd heard him clearly. She shook her head.

"I don't agree with the women who are trying to be men. I never told anyone to call me Lou. My name has always been Marylou."

"Alex is her nickname," Ted responded in a loud voice. "Her real name is Alexia. Her mother is Russian."

Mrs. Hobart's frown deepened. "Can you understand her when she talks to you?"

"Yes, ma'am. She's lived in the United States all her life."

Mrs. Hobart sighed. "I know you're a preacher, but I'm going to pray for you myself. Most men don't understand the first thing about women. It took me years to get Harry straightened out. You're too good a man to get trapped by the wrong person."

Ted had an old-fashioned charcoal grill. He preferred genuine smoked flavor in the food he cooked for the same reasons he appreciated the nuances produced by his Steinway over the sounds generated by a mass-produced piano. He set up the grill in a shaded grassy area behind the house. Several older trees kept most of the yard in perpetual shadow, and sometimes Ted would sit in a lounge chair in the backyard and read. It was a peaceful place. The residents of the nearby cemetery were quiet neighbors, and the nearest houses to the church were several hundred yards away.

The charcoal briquettes were beginning to turn gray around the edges when he heard the wheels of a car crackle across the seashell-covered driveway in front of the parsonage. He walked around the corner as Alex got out of her BMW. She'd gone home after work to take care of her pets and changed into tan slacks with a white top. Plain clothes always brought out the color of her green eyes.

"Welcome," he said.

Alex gave him a smile. "Thanks. It's going to be a beautiful evening. I live on the marsh and can usually tell when it's going to be nice weather by the color and type of the clouds at sunrise and sunset."

"You live on the marsh? Tell me about your house."

Alex had brought half a cheesecake she'd bought from Edith Katz. She retrieved it from the passenger seat, and they walked together toward the front door.

"It's off Pelican Point Drive. I have a view of an uninhabited barrier island."

Telling him about her pets and her little boat, she followed him into the house. It was obvious he'd spent time making it clean and neat. He'd put a white tablecloth on the kitchen table where they'd sipped lemonade. The steaks were in a plastic bag, soaking in a dark-colored sauce.

"What's in the marinade?" Alex asked.

"Wine, garlic, olive oil, and a few pinches of other stuff. How do you like your meat cooked?"

"Medium rare. I like it rare, but if I eat too much raw meat, it makes me mean."

Ted laughed. "I'll be careful to cook it enough to avoid problems."

Ted had put two chairs in the backyard. Since it was past the season for insects, they went outside and sat while they waited for the briquettes to thoroughly ash.

"This reminds me of my grandmother's house and backyard," Alex said. "Very relaxing and peaceful."

"In Russia?"

"No. My father is from central Ohio. He grew up on a farm surrounded by corn and soybean fields. When we visited my grandmother, it was an excuse for other relatives to come to the house for a big meal. After we ate, my grandmother liked to sit outside in the evenings and talk until the stars came out."

"What did she talk about?"

"People I didn't know anything about. My family had lived in the same house for three generations, and she knew everybody for miles around." Alex paused. "Sometimes she talked about her faith, and when I was small, I thought she'd memorized the entire Bible. Whenever a problem came up, she often quoted a verse that was supposed to be the answer."

"She sounds like my Uncle Frank. He was the bass singer in a gospel quartet and really knew the Bible. I think it was the only book he ever read. Do you remember any of the verses your grandmother quoted?"

"Let me think. She died when I was twelve." Alex looked up at the darkening sky and tried to retrieve a memory. "Here's one. *You are the light of the world. A city that is set on a hill cannot be hidden.* I used to think it was funny because there wasn't a hill for miles and miles until you reached Cincinnati."

"That's Matthew 5:14. It's from the Sermon on the Mount. Why would she quote that verse?"

"Actually, she said it to me several times. Even when I was a little girl, I had a strong desire for justice, you know, to see the right thing happen. I guess she picked up on it and thought the verse applied to me. She even wrote it on a piece of paper for my birthday one year and gave it to me inside a card. I have it somewhere at my house."

"Are you letting your light shine?"

Alex nodded. "I'd say so. My clients aren't always in the right on all issues, but I do my best to expose the darkness and bring in the light."

Ted walked over to the grill.

"The coals will be ready in a few more minutes," he said. "Is everything in your life related to being a lawyer?"

Alex opened her mouth and then quickly closed it. She wasn't sure she wanted to hear her answer. The minister's casual question came at a vulnerable moment and exposed the narrow focus of her existence. She enjoyed her private world of grand seclusion on the marsh, but all her true energy was directed toward her clients and her work. Except for Gwen, she didn't have any close friends.

"Why did you ask me that question?" she asked slowly.

Ted leaned over and pulled up one of the last dandelions of the season. He blew it and watched the feathery seeds cascade away in the early evening air.

"It's easy for a person who passionately cares about what they do to get so involved with work that it consumes them. I know it's necessary for you to represent your clients zealously, but I think the verse you mentioned has a broader application than what you do in your job."

Alex tried to regain her footing. "You're preaching again, aren't you?"

Ted glanced toward her with kind eyes before answering.

"I'm filling in for your grandmother. If she were here, I bet she'd ask you the same thing."

And the Holy Spirit moved across Alex Lindale's heart. It was a divine moment—a delayed response to the faith-filled prayers of an Ohio farm wife who had quietly walked into the upstairs bedroom where her dark-haired granddaughter slept and asked that the child's life might one day shine with the light of Jesus Christ. The passage of a quarter of a century is less than the width of an eyelash in the perspective of eternity. All God-inspired prayers are answered in the fullness of time.

First in a rural church in Santee and later on the shores of southern France, the door of Alex's heart had been slowly opening in response to the knock of heaven. Her chest felt heavy. Moisture collected in the corners of her eyes. She rubbed away the tears with her palms, but fresh pools immediately formed. Ted didn't speak. Alex stared at the ground, but the blades of grass blurred through the prism of her tears. She looked up through bleary eyes at the cemetery, irrefutable evidence of the transitory nature of life on earth. A divine stillness settled upon the peaceful yard.

You are the light of the world.

Ted went into the house. He returned with the steaks and a few tissues that he gently placed in Alex's hands. She was aware of Ted, but his activity didn't recall her from the realm where her thoughts and feelings took her. With yearning beyond words, she wanted the kind of light her grandmother talked about to shine through every pore of her being. Bowing her head, she sent her request to the only One who could give it to her, and in an instant, the flame of eternal life was kindled in her heart.

A city that is set on a hill cannot be hidden.

And Alex caught a glimpse of life lived outside the bounds she'd set for herself—an existence beyond the controlled world where she lived in self-protected isolation, occasionally riding forth to right a wrong and then retreating to the refuge of her home and the walls of her mind. There was something more, a broader sphere of influence, a chance to effect change on a deeper level, a greater risk, a greater reward. She wasn't sure what it looked like, but the new light within her birthed an ache to know.

God answered her grandmother's prayers.

The policeman's lot is not a happy one.
SIR WILLIAM GILBERT

TED AND ALEX had a quiet dinner. Normal conversation was difficult because every time Alex began to speak she quickly progressed to tears.

"This isn't like me," she insisted. "I'm not a weepy woman, but both times I've come to your house I've ended up crying."

"Don't worry about it," Ted reassured her. "They're good tears."

"I know," Alex sniffled. "But you talk, I'll listen."

"What about all the questions you were going to ask me?"

Alex shook her head. "That's not on the menu."

Ted smiled. "Okay. Let's talk about you. Some people let their emotions dribble out a little bit at a time. Others store their feelings in great cisterns that only crack open when there is an earthquake."

Alex's eyes glistened. "That's me, and my world has been shaken tonight."

Ted continued. "When God touches a person, it's also like a great symphony—simple yet complex. There are common themes of love, forgiveness, repentance, and faith that are not complicated, but the way they play out in each individual's experience is unique and special."

"That's true. I felt so special. It was the way my grandmother made me feel only greater. I wanted the words she'd spoken to me to come true."

"And you're sure it happened?"

Alex put her hand over her heart. "Yes. It wasn't just a thought. There was substance to it like waves washing over me when I'm at the beach. It was unlike anything I've ever imagined about God. He wasn't far away; he was with me under the trees. It was amazing."

"That's why they call it amazing grace."

They finished the meal by each eating a generous piece of cheesecake.

As they cleared the table together, Ted asked, "Would you like to go to the church for a few minutes?"

Alex nodded.

It was the trailing edge of dusk as they walked across the parking lot to the church. Several stars were already in view. Ted unlocked the door, and they entered the sanctuary. It was dark inside, and Ted turned on the lights in the narthex.

"Do you want me to play the piano?" he asked.

"Yes," Alex said simply.

"I don't need the lights in the sanctuary," he said as they walked to the front. "These will be enough. Often, I play when it's totally dark."

Alex nestled on a pew near the piano with her legs curled up beneath her.

"Any requests? Beethoven, Liszt, Ravel?" Ted asked. "I forgot to bring a glass for tips."

Alex shook her head. "Not them. I want something by Ted Morgan. A new composition." She paused. "I'd like you to play what God has done in my life tonight."

Ted exhaled slowly. "Whew. You've asked a hard thing. I'm not sure I fully understand, myself."

"I trust you."

Ted turned toward the keyboard, bowed his head, and put his hands on the keys. Over a minute passed before he began to play. Alex waited. He began. The notes were tentative at first and doubts rose in Ted's mind that challenged his ability to duplicate in music the work of the Holy Spirit. But as he persevered, he realized that hesitancy was part of the story. It reflected the condition of Alex's heart as she drove up to the parsonage and got out of her car.

With growing confidence, he played the prayers of Alex's grandmother and brought forth the magnificence of Matthew 5:14. *You are the light of the world. A city that is set on a hill cannot be hidden.* It was a scripture both intensely personal and profoundly universal. Chords built to crescendos that called out to the nations to come into the light. Nuances of healing, forgiveness, deliverance, and submission followed. He was in the midst of a strong progression that proclaimed the dawning of a new day of influence when suddenly, he stopped.

Alex, who was sitting with her eyes closed, opened them.

"Why did you stop?" she asked. "It was glorious. I could see glimpses of myself and what I felt in the music."

Ted turned sideways on the piano bench. Alex's face was hidden in the shadows cast by the diffused light from the narthex behind her.

"That's where you are," he answered. "In the middle of the beginning. The rest will depend on what you do from this night forward."

After Alex left, Ted stayed in the sanctuary. His plans for a romantic evening had been totally eclipsed by the intervention of God in Alex's life. He began to play quietly. Whether there would be any type of relationship between himself and Alex Lindale beyond being members of God's family was less clear now than when the evening began. One thing Ted had learned better than most people was patience. He would rather wait for God than rush ahead into something that fell flat when human energy waned. Tonight, all that mattered was the wooing of a new soul into the kingdom of God. He transitioned into a piece by Bach that expressed the joy of salvation.

———

When Alex awoke the following morning, she lay quietly in bed for several minutes. The supercharged emotions of the previous evening were gone; however, a sense of peace remained. She didn't have to get out of bed to prove anything to herself or anyone else. She pulled the covers up to her chin and closed her eyes for a Saturday morning nap, but a loud bark from Boris reminded her of practical responsibilities. She went downstairs to let her pets outside and fixed a cup of coffee.

A typical fall mist rose over the marsh, and there was a snap of coolness in the air as she sat on the screened porch. Before going to sleep, Alex had found the box of childhood mementos containing the paper on which her grandmother had written Matthew 5:14. The small square piece of paper was protruding from a pocket-size New Testament Alex had forgotten about. Her grandmother had written Alex's name and the date in the front of the New Testament and given it to her at the same time she wrote out the verse. When she saw her grandmother's spindly handwriting, Alex bit her lip to hold back more tears.

Alex had always focused on her romantic Russian heritage and ignored her plain roots in the black soil of central Ohio. Her mother's courage and the majesty of St. Petersburg were undeniable, but Alex now realized that there was also treasure in a lineage of simple faith. Opening the New Testament, she began to read. Within minutes she was caught up in Matthew's narrative and didn't stop until she reached the end of the book. When she finished, she stood and stretched, amazed that she had enjoyed reading the Bible, a book she had always considered dull and disjointed. It was her first interested look at an overview of Jesus' life and ministry and further internal proof of a change in her heart.

Boris interrupted her thoughts with a different kind of bark. She went inside and found him standing at the back door with a deep growl rumbling in his throat.

"What is it?" Alex asked him.

Boris lifted his paw and scratched the base of the door.

Alex opened the door, and the dog quickly skidded across the deck and down the steps. Alex stepped outside and watched him run around the side of the house and down the unpaved road toward Pelican Point. Glancing up, she saw two men about a hundred yards away step from the scrubby trees and get into a tan van. Before Boris reached the vehicle, they backed up and turned around. From the distance, Alex couldn't read the license plate, but she could tell it wasn't from South Carolina. Boris chased the vehicle for a few seconds and then stopped.

It was unusual for someone to drive toward Alex's house. All the best places for fishing in the marsh were in the opposite direction. And Alex hadn't seen any fishing poles in the men's hands.

She went inside and checked the front door to make sure it was locked.

———

Rena had avoided contact with her acquaintances in Santee. Normally, her social life revolved around a few tennis buddies, but she hadn't wanted to talk to anyone since returning from Greenville. That way she avoided endless explanations. The phone at her home started ringing as word spread through the community that she had returned, but she let the answering machine respond with a message that she was resting and unavailable. However, by Saturday afternoon, sitting alone watching TV for hours at a time had began to take its toll. It was almost as bad as the interminable hours with nothing to do at the hospital.

On the spur of the moment, she decided to take a ride to Charleston and do some shopping. Spending money was a trustworthy way to lift her out of the doldrums. As she walked outside to the garage, she glanced down the driveway. No cars were in sight. It was a nice afternoon, and she decided to drive her convertible. She drove down the driveway and turned left. After three quick turns, she slowed down and checked her rearview mirror. No dark blue cars in sight. If her keepers were on duty, she had caught them napping. To avoid attracting attention, she kept the top up until she reached the edge of town and then lowered it.

Driving rapidly, she took the shortest route that intersected with the coastal highway and drove toward Charleston with the wind rushing through her hair. There was a new jewelry store in the downtown area that specialized in unusual items from estates, and she wanted to check it out. It was exhilarating, and Rena felt the oppression that had stalked her since the failed attempt at the waterfall sweep out the back of the car. She drove faster in response to the rush of adrenaline. It was a glorious day. Exactly suited for a ride in a convertible.

She took several deep breaths. It was easier to think in the open air. Events and circumstances outside her control had been frustrating Rena since she received the news from Detective Porter that Baxter was alive. Now, with the money from Ezra safely in her hands, she didn't have to totally rely on Jeffrey and could maintain a level of contact with him that allowed her to use him for her purposes without becoming his pawn. With the money in her individual account she could survive several months without any outside financial help—plenty of time for Alex to take care of the attacks that threatened her.

Several miles from the outskirts of Charleston, she flashed by a Charleston County police car waiting in the shadow of an old billboard advertising a local seafood restaurant. It took the police cruiser almost three minutes to catch her and turn on his blue light. Rena looked in the rearview mirror and turned pale. She had been driving at least twenty-five miles over the speed limit. She turned into a deserted side road, pulled onto the grassy shoulder, and leaned her head against the steering wheel.

The officer parked and strolled up to her. He was an older man with closely cropped gray hair and a large stomach that spilled over a broad, black belt around his waist. Countless late-night snacks of French fries and onion rings had come to rest around his midsection. He hitched up his pants as he reached the car.

"I'm Officer Claude Dixon. Do you know the speed limit on this road?" he asked with a deep drawl.

"Uh, I think it's fifty-five. I'm sorry if I was going too fast."

"May I see your driver's license?"

Rena reached for her purse and looked for her wallet, but it wasn't there. She frantically rummaged through the small handbag for several seconds. Officer Dixon rested his stomach on top of the car door and leaned over her shoulder.

"It's not that big a purse. Did you forget your driver's license?"

"I'm afraid I left it in another wallet. I think it's on the kitchen counter at my home in Santee."

The officer flipped open a small notebook and took a thick pen from his front pocket. "What's your name?" he asked.

"Rena Richardson."

"Have you drunk any alcohol or taken any drugs in the past twelve hours?"

"No."

The officer asked a standard litany of questions. Rena answered in a timid voice.

"Do you have the vehicle registration and proof of insurance for this car?"

Rena remembered that Baxter kept it in the glove compartment of the SUV and hoped it would be in the same place in this vehicle. She found the owner's manual and service papers but nothing else.

"No. I'm sorry. I don't know where my husband put it. He's in the hospital in intensive care, so I can't call him."

Officer Dixon closed his notebook. Hope rose in Rena that he was going to let her off the hook.

"Have you ever been arrested?" he asked.

Rena shifted nervously. She wasn't sure how to answer. Alex had told her the assault and battery charges had been dismissed, but she couldn't undo the arrest.

"Uh, no," she said.

"Well, there is a first time for everything. There are too many violations for me to simply give you a ticket and send you down the road. Please get out and come back to the patrol car."

Rena dissolved in tears. She made no effort to open the door.

"Please, don't do this!" she wailed. "Give me as many tickets as you want!"

Claude Dixon had seen distraught women before and didn't respond. He waited until Rena came up for air before he spoke.

"Ma'am, as soon as you calm down, please get out of the car."

Rena continued sniffling. "Why can't you give me tickets for speeding and not having my driver's license?"

"You were going over eighty in a fifty-five mile an hour zone. I also want you to undergo a blood test to determine if there is any alcohol or drugs in your system."

Rena looked up at him in shock. "But I told you I hadn't had anything to drink!"

"I've heard that before."

"No!" Rena raised her voice and banged her fists against the steering wheel. "This is not fair!"

The officer's eyes grew larger, and he touched the handcuffs attached to his belt.

"Mrs. Richardson, it will be better if you cooperate, so I don't have to use restraints. Please get out of the car."

Rena jerked open the door, and the officer backed up. When he did, he stepped in a small hole, lost his footing, and fell backward. His head slammed against the edge of the pavement with a loud snap. He groaned once and then lay still.

Rena gasped and stared at the lawman's motionless form. She looked over her shoulder. Cars were whizzing by on the nearby highway, but unless someone looked directly down the side road they would not see the officer's body. Rena stared at his face. A fly landed on the policeman's large nose and walked around it several times before buzzing off. The officer's mouth was opened wide, and Rena could see several gold crowns on his upper molars. She shuddered. She did not want to touch another body that looked dead.

She crept from the car and knelt down beside the body. Leaning over, she put her ear as close to Dixon's gaping mouth as possible. There was no sound of air coming in or going out. She listened for several seconds but couldn't detect the whisper of a wheeze or rasp. The deputy's chest was motionless, and there was no sign of a heartbeat in the large arteries that ran up the side of the neck. The notebook containing the written record of their conversation lay several inches from his left hand. Gingerly picking up the notebook, she got back into her car and tried to think through her options.

She could start the car's engine and be gone in fifteen seconds; however, she had to assume the officer had reported her license plate number when he stopped the car. There was no chance for anonymity if she fled. The police would be in her driveway before nightfall and drag her to jail for a crime she didn't commit.

But how to explain what had happened if she stayed and phoned 911 created an equally troubling dilemma. She'd done nothing wrong except violate a few minor traffic laws that the fat deputy blew out of proportion. The body lying on the side of the road was not her fault.

It was a tragic accident.

33

He who permits himself to tell a lie once, finds it much easier to do it a second and third time, till at length it becomes habitual.
THOMAS JEFFERSON

ALEX'S NERVOUSNESS about the unknown intruders quickly subsided, and in the afternoon she went out for a swim. It might have been her imagination, but her appreciation for the beauty of the marsh and the barrier island was heightened by the new vision that had come to her spirit. The texture of the marsh grass, the purity of the sand dunes, and the majesty of the ocean had never been more vivid. Even Boris seemed more alive as he stood proudly in the bow of the little boat and later ran wildly down the beach.

The phone rang in the kitchen. Still rubbing her hair with a towel, Alex picked up the phone. It was Rena Richardson. She spoke rapidly in a breathless voice.

"Alex. It's Rena. My car was stolen this afternoon."

"What?"

"My red convertible. I'd left it in front of the house with the keys in it, and someone must have taken it for a joy ride. They drove toward Charleston and were stopped for speeding by the police."

"Where is it now?"

"In Charleston. But it's more serious than a carjacking. The officer who stopped the thief was killed. Whoever took the car knocked him down and broke his neck. A detective from Charleston is on his way to Santee and wants to interview me. I need you with me."

Alex looked at the clock. "I'll be there as soon as I can."

"What should I do if the detective gets here before you?"

"Be polite, but ask him to wait until I arrive. You've not done anything wrong, so it won't be a problem. He should know the rules."

———

Peering around the curtains in the living room, Rena saw a gray sedan drive slowly up the driveway. Only an unmarked police vehicle could be so nondescript. She stepped back and leaned against the wall. The detective from Charleston couldn't be as bad as the disfigured Giles Porter. She'd survived the Mitchell County officer's inquisition and should be able to weather another one, especially with Alex at her side from the beginning.

The doorbell rang, and although Rena was only a few steps away, she slowly counted to twenty-five before answering it. A tall, thin man with round glasses and a thin mustache, wearing an open-collared shirt and olive pants, stood on the landing. He looked more like an accountant than a homicide detective. His normal appearance immediately set Rena at ease.

"I'm Detective Byron Devereaux with the Charleston County Sheriff's Department," he said in a friendly yet serious voice. "Are you Mrs. Richardson?"

Rena nodded. "Yes, please come in. I thought we could talk in the study."

She led the detective through the living room into a smaller rectangular room that was filled with leather furniture. Along the walls were wooden bookcases of three different heights. Neither Rena nor Baxter were avid readers, and the bookcases contained few books. A large oriental rug covered the center of the floor.

"Have a seat," she said. "Would you like a cup of coffee?"

"Yes, black would be fine."

Rena left the room, satisfied that she was performing perfectly as a southern hostess. When the coffee was ready, she lingered in the kitchen, hoping Alex would arrive before she had to return and face the detective. The doorbell sounded again, and Rena rushed to answer it. It was Alex.

"Come in. He's already here," Rena whispered. "But we haven't talked at all. I was getting him a cup of coffee."

Rena led Alex to the kitchen.

"Is there anything I shouldn't say?" Rena asked in a low voice as they put a silver coffeepot and three white cups on a silver tray.

"About what?" Alex responded. "Just tell him the car was stolen. He'll want to know when you noticed that it was missing and whether you've seen any suspicious people in the area. It should be routine. Do you have any idea who stole it?"

"No, but after what's happened to me recently, I'm terrified of the police."

"I'll try to take care of as much as I can," Alex reassured her.

They went into the study. The detective was standing in front of one of the bookcases. Alex introduced herself.

"I asked Ms. Lindale to come over in case you have questions that I can't answer," Rena said. "She handles everything for me and my family"—she paused and glanced at Alex—"I mean for me."

Rena sat down on a love seat beside the sofa and poured a cup of coffee for Alex, who sat across from the detective. Rena's hand trembled slightly when she tipped up the coffeepot. She glanced at the detective, who was closely watching her.

"I'm sorry," she said. "This whole thing has really upset me."

"It's normal that you'd be nervous. I'll try to be as quick as possible. We're just beginning our investigation."

He took out a small notebook identical to the one used by the officer who had stopped Rena and began with several background questions. When he asked whether she was married, Rena picked up a tissue and looked away.

"Ms. Richardson's husband is on life support in a hospital in Greenville," Alex quickly interjected. "He fell from a cliff while they were hiking a few weeks ago and has never regained consciousness."

"I'm sorry," the detective replied. "Do you need to take a short break?"

"Go ahead," Rena sniffed. "I want to help you."

"Okay. When did you first notice that your car was missing?"

"It was in front of the house in the same area where you parked. I'd gone out for a long walk, and when I got back, it was gone."

"You mentioned on the phone that you'd left the keys in it. Why did you do that?"

"I grew up in the country where we didn't worry about car thieves. I drove the car early this morning and didn't bother to take out the keys.

My husband has told me not to leave the keys in it"—Rena touched her right eye again with the tissue—"but I guess I forgot. I never suspected anyone would steal the car from our driveway, and the thought that they could have come into the house terrifies me."

The officer looked down at his notebook. "What did you do when you saw it was gone?"

"At first I thought someone was playing a joke on me. You know how things go through your mind when you're caught by surprise. I checked in the garage and walked back to the street to see if someone had driven it around the corner. When I realized it was really gone, I called 911 and reported it missing."

"What time did you call 911?"

"I don't remember exactly. I think they keep a record of that, don't they?"

"Yes. I'm just trying to see what you remember."

Rena's heart sped up. The detective was trying to trap her. She spoke slowly.

"It was about an hour before you phoned from Charleston."

The detective tapped the notebook with his pen. "What did you tell the 911 operator about the theft?"

Rena froze. She couldn't remember what she'd told the 911 operator. The events she'd manufactured in her mind during the taxi ride from Charleston grew fuzzy.

"Uh, what I'm telling you. If I told the 911 operator anything else, I can't remember it now. Have you listened to the tape of the call?"

"No," the detective answered casually. "It might be helpful for you to hear it and see if it jogs your memory."

"There's not much to remember," Rena replied. "The car was here. Then it was gone."

"What time did you drive the car this morning?"

"Very early. Before seven o'clock. I couldn't sleep and went out to get a bagel and cup of coffee."

"Where did you go?"

"Just to a convenience store."

"Which one?"

Rena turned toward Alex. "It's near the courthouse. What's the name of the one on the corner?"

"Franklin's Quick Stop. It's an independent store on the corner of King Street and Burns Avenue," Alex said.

"That's it," Rena said.

"Did you see anybody you know there?" he asked.

"No. I've lived here less than a year, so I don't know a lot of people."

The detective made notes. "Okay. What time did you leave to go on your walk?"

"Around noon."

"Where did you go?"

"I walked all the way to Freedom Park. I had a lot to think about with everything that has happened with my husband and needed some fresh air to clear my head. I sat on a bench for a while and read."

"What did you read?"

"A woman's magazine."

"Did you see anybody you knew at the park?"

"No. There weren't many people there."

The detective backtracked in time. "Did you notice anyone unusual in the area when you left the house?"

"No. It's a quiet street. Most of the homes are older, and we haven't had any problems with crime as long as I've been here. I know the police send a car through the neighborhood several times a day."

"Is there anyone who knows you leave your keys in the car?"

"No one except Baxter."

"Who is Baxter?"

"My husband."

The detective made another note. "Sorry. What about any yard workers, maids, friends?"

Rena shook her head. "I have a maid who cleans twice a week, but she barely speaks English, and I don't think she drives. There is a company that does all the landscaping and work on the lawn, but I don't know any of them personally. None of my friends know about the car keys except one woman I play tennis with."

"What's your friend's name and where does she live?"

"Jeannie Coulter. She lives in Vanguard Point."

"It's a golf course neighborhood about a mile from town," Alex said.

"And she has a new Mercedes convertible," Rena added. "Please don't contact Jeannie and say that I thought she stole my car."

"I wouldn't do that," the detective replied. "And the maid's name?"

Rena blushed. "I think it's Marie. I don't know her last name. She didn't come today."

"Where does she live?"

Rena turned her palms up in front of her. "I don't have any idea. She came from a housecleaning service in town called Ready Maids."

"Did the landscape company come today?"

"No."

The detective closed his notebook and took out a fingerprint card. "I apologize for asking you to do this, but I need your fingerprints."

Rena swallowed but her mouth was suddenly dry. She couldn't imagine what she'd said that proved she was lying.

The detective continued. "We want to dust the car and identify any prints that are not yours."

"That's not a problem," Alex said. "Go ahead, Rena."

Rena tried to dispel the sudden surge of anxiety that had swept over her.

"I've never done this before," she said, nervously glancing at Alex. "I mean except for a situation that was a misunderstanding."

The detective ignored her comment, gently took her index finger, inked it, and rolled it across a small rectangular box on the card.

"Did your husband ever drive the car?" he asked.

"A few times."

"We'll need to contact the hospital and get a set of prints from him, too. Whoever took the car wiped the steering wheel and shift lever with a cloth before abandoning it. There are plenty of fingerprints on the seats, door handles, glove compartment, and other places. We can only hope a stray print survived that will match something in the national data bank."

"Where did you find the car?" Alex asked.

"In a Wal-Mart parking lot on the north side of Charleston County."

"Is it okay?" Rena asked.

"Yeah. But we need to check it out completely before you pick it up. Anytime an officer is killed in the line of duty we turn over every stone."

"What happened to the patrolman?" Alex asked.

The detective snapped shut the ink pad. "Broken neck. He died instantly. He sent a radio message that he'd stopped a red convertible with a single occupant for speeding. The radio transmission wasn't clear, and the dispatcher didn't write down the complete license number. We weren't able to identify Mrs. Richardson as the owner of the car until she notified the police that the vehicle had been stolen. As soon as the description came across the system, we suspected it would match. An officer spotted the car in the parking lot thirty minutes later."

"Did the deputy who died describe the driver?" Alex asked.

Rena's eyes grew wide, and she held her breath.

"We're not sure. We're going to send out the tape of the radio transmission for deciphering, but I didn't hear anything when I listened to it. There was no sign of a struggle. Apparently, the thief pushed the deputy down, and he hit his head on the edge of the pavement. If the carjacker was a kid, he probably panicked and took off. We'll find him. Someone who saw something will come forward after they watch the reports on the evening news. We'll keep you informed. Thanks for your help."

After the detective left, Rena said to Alex, "Come out to the kitchen while I wash my hands."

When she finished cleaning up, Rena poured each of them another cup of coffee. The two women stood on opposite sides of a large island in the center of the kitchen. Overhead, an expensive set of pots and pans hung down from a rack suspended from the ceiling. The island was covered with hand-painted, imported tiles.

"Do you think the detective was trying to blame me for what happened?" Rena asked anxiously.

"What made you think that?" Alex asked with surprise. "You're a victim, too."

Rena sighed. "I know, but I can't shake the horrible feeling that the police are after me. Why did he ask me all those questions?"

"He's trying to find out who stole the car. You don't have anything to worry about."

"I hope you're right."

Rena put a little more sugar in her coffee. "I forgot to ask him when I could pick up the car."

"I'll call him on Monday," Alex said.

After Alex left, Rena went upstairs and retrieved the notebook she'd taken from the dead sheriff's deputy. She started a small fire in the living room fireplace and burned it. The taxi driver who drove her from Charleston had let her out of his car four blocks away, and there hadn't been a public trash receptacle where she could throw it away before arriving home.

She anxiously watched the evening news from Charleston. The report on the death of Officer Dixon was the primary news item for the show. It included a file photo of a slightly slimmer policeman taken several years before. He was a Marine Corp veteran who had served on the local police forces for thirty-one years. Following the picture of the officer was a photo of Rena's car and a description of what the police believed might have happened. The segment concluded with an interview of Detective Devereaux in which he asked anyone with information about the case to contact the sheriff's department. Rena was nervously playing with a heavy glass ashtray and wanted to throw it at the screen to get him to shut up.

A few minutes after the show ended Rena's cell phone rang. She jumped at the sound and looked at the caller identification. It was Jeffrey.

"I guess you saw the news," she said.

"Yeah. Are you okay?"

"No, I'm a nervous wreck."

"When was the car stolen?"

Rena told him, and Jeffrey began an interrogation not unlike the one conducted by Officer Devereaux. Rena answered a few questions about the car but then began to wonder what the guardians sent by Jeffrey had told him about her activities. They might know whether or not she'd walked to town, and she didn't want to get caught in a lie.

"Why are you asking me questions?" she responded when Jeffrey asked what she had been doing all day. "Get a report from the people who are watching me all the time. Maybe they know who stole the car."

"Okay, relax. I'm sorry."

"Do you have any information for my lawyer?" Rena asked.

"Not yet. I've been on the golf course all day, and I have a date tonight with someone I met in California. I'm driving to the airport to pick her up in a few minutes."

Rena grunted. Jeffrey had exhausted the local stock and was importing a new girlfriend. She couldn't believe she'd actually considered him as a suitor when they went to dinner in Greenville.

"Will you be coming to the hearing in Greenville on Friday?" Rena asked.

"No. I've not changed my mind. You and your lawyer are doing everything backwards. Baxter isn't a threat to anyone. The power of attorney is your enemy. You need to convince Lindale that the best way to help you is to go after my father."

"I just don't want Baxter to suffer," Rena said. "It's not right."

"I've got to go," Jeffrey responded.

After she clicked off the phone, Rena went to the medicine cabinet and took out a bottle of prescription sleeping pills. She didn't want to stay awake and continue to worry. Shaking a couple of pills in her hand, she swallowed them with a gulp of water and went to bed.

34

*Have nothing to do with the fruitless deeds of
darkness, but rather expose them. For it is shameful
even to mention what the disobedient do in secret.*

EPHESIANS 5:11–12

TED ALWAYS SAT on the piano bench until it was time for the sermon.
The order of worship at Sandy Flats Church was the product of a committee, and Ted had specific, nonnegotiable duties. To do something
other than what was printed in the Sunday morning bulletin would be
tantamount to editing the Ten Commandments. Ted provided as much
spiritual vitality as possible within the rigid guidelines, but it has always
been difficult trying to breathe life into dry bones.

During the first hymn, he looked out at the congregation and saw
Marylou Hobart. She was wearing a yellow-and-green dress, and her hair
was wound in a tight, gray bun. She was holding a hymnbook and her
lips were moving. Mrs. Hobart wouldn't be able to hear the piano well
enough to keep pace with the melody and the rhythm, and Ted could
only imagine the sounds that were coming from her lips. He inwardly
chuckled at the thought of her making a joyful noise to God. During the
third verse, he glanced toward another part of the sanctuary and saw
Alex. She was dressed in an elegant, dark green dress, more feminine than
the clothes she'd worn during their previous meetings.

The service followed a course as steady and predictable as a river
winding its way through an old valley. The layman assisting in the pulpit read a list of announcements, and John Heathcliff led the congregation in the Lord's Prayer. The prayer was followed by the offertory. While
he played, Ted saw the shiny brass plate pass in front of Marylou Hobart,
who deposited several wrinkled bills. She looked up, saw Ted, and
rewarded him with a gap-toothed smile.

Ted played the piano during the anthem and simultaneously directed the choir. When he needed to emphasize a choral transition, he maintained the flow of the melody with his right hand and signaled entrances and cutoffs with the left. The last note by all the voices was crisply stopped with a flick of Ted's hand.

Rev. Heathcliff spoke on the parable of the talents. After listening for ten minutes, Ted set his jaw firmly to stifle the yawns that threatened to pry open his mouth. John Heathcliff wasn't a bad minister, but his skills at maneuvering his way through church politics were more highly developed than his ability to preach the truths of Scripture. Precisely at 11:55 A.M., Rev. Heathcliff finished the sermon, and Ted resumed his seat at the piano for the closing hymn. If the song had four verses, the insistent call of Sunday dinner usually required that the third verse be omitted. Sandy Flats Church was not located near the main restaurants in the area, and most members of the congregation didn't want to be penalized in their race to the buffet line by a long closing hymn. Ted timed the final note perfectly as watches beeped the top of the hour all over the sanctuary.

He was playing the postlude when Alex and Mrs. Hobart converged across the altar rail from the piano.

"Hello!" he shouted at Mrs. Hobart.

At the sound of his voice, Alex stopped and took a step backward.

"You don't have to yell," she said.

"I'm talking to her," Ted replied, taking his left hand off the keyboard to gesture toward Mrs. Hobart. "I'll be finished in a minute!" he shouted.

Mrs. Hobart gave him a wrinkled smile. "I'd like to go out to eat. I haven't had any fish to eat in ages. Could we go together?"

Ted nodded. "Yes!"

"I'll tell the woman who brought me to church to go on home."

The old woman turned and walked toward the back of the sanctuary. Ted finished playing the piano with a run from the bottom to the top of the keyboard and then swiveled on the bench toward Alex.

"Mrs. Hobart is mostly deaf," Ted said. "Would you like to join us for lunch? I think we're going to eat fish."

Alex laughed, and Ted could see joy shining from her eyes.

"Yes. Fish sounds great."

They walked together down the aisle to the narthex. Marylou Hobart was shaking John Heathcliff's hand and talking to him. The minister had a puzzled look on his face. Ted introduced him to Alex, and he perked up.

"I hope you'll come back."

"I'm sure I will," she said.

Ted, Alex, and Mrs. Hobart walked down the steps together.

"Can we take your car?" Ted asked Alex. "I'd rather not cram three people into my truck."

"Sure."

The older woman eyed Alex as they walked across the parking lot.

"You're a pretty young thing," she said. "What's your name?"

Alex felt thirteen instead of thirty-two. "Alexia Lindale."

"Alicia? That's a pretty name." Mrs. Hobart looked at Ted. "It's a good name for a woman. No one will think you're a man!"

Ted rolled his eyes at Alex.

"Should you avoid calling me Alex while we're with her?" Alex asked.

"No. Now that she thinks you're Alicia that's all she will hear."

Mrs. Hobart sat in the backseat of Alex's BMW and stroked the smooth, gray leather. "This is nice vinyl on your seats."

"Thank you!" Alex answered. Turning to Ted, she asked, "Where should we go?"

"Someplace where the fish is soft and easy to chew," he answered. "How about Martin's Fish Camp?"

"Okay. I haven't eaten there in ages."

The restaurant was famous for fried seafood, but unless the cooking oil was fresh, everything tasted similar.

"It was good to see you this morning," Ted said. "You look very nice. The green dress makes your eyes shine."

Alex smiled at the compliment. "Thanks."

"Did you enjoy the service?"

"Yes. Especially the sermon."

"Really? Why?"

"He raised some questions that I need to answer. The idea of dedicating my talents and ability to God is very relevant to me right now. It's going to take time for me to sort it out."

Ted nodded without comment, but it made sense that Alex would have to deal with issues he'd faced twenty years before. The road of discipleship passes common landmarks.

Martin's Fish Camp was a rambling wooden building painted gray to give the boards a weathered look. It featured several open dining rooms. Patrons sat at simple long wooden tables with ladder back chairs. There was a large hole in the middle of each table and a trash can beneath it for debris. The setup was especially suited for oyster roasts. Iced tea was served in giant, clear plastic glasses. A teenage hostess led them to a table in the corner and handed them menus. Mrs. Hobart didn't open hers.

Ted leaned toward her better ear. "What do you want to eat?"

"I don't need to look at the menu. I want fried fish with hush puppies and slaw."

"Do you want flounder?" Ted asked loudly.

Mrs. Hobart smiled. "Yes, I'm glad you found her!" Then, turning to Alex, she said, "I've been tellin' him he needed to meet a nice girl. He's a good man. Very handy around the house. Did you know he fixed the leaks in my roof and stopped the toilet in my downstairs bath from runnin' all the time?"

Alex looked at Ted. "I'm impressed."

Ted ordered the flounder for Mrs. Hobart and scallops for himself. Alex chose a salad served with broiled seafood on top.

A waitress brought them tea. Alex watched Mrs. Hobart deposit an extra bag of sugar in her glass.

"Does she know it's already sweetened?" she asked Ted.

"Yes, but not sweet enough. It's the secret of her longevity."

"How old is she?"

"I've never been able to get a straight answer." Ted leaned toward Mrs. Hobart. "How old are you?"

The old woman put down her glass of tea and gave Ted a strange look. "Don't you know? You're gettin' mighty forgetful. I'll be eighty-four next month. Harry and I were married fifty-four years before he died."

Mrs. Hobart was sitting so she could see the main dining room of the restaurant.

"I enjoy watching the people," she said. "You two go ahead and talk. If you want to tell me something, tap me on the arm, and I'll give heed."

"Won't she be offended if we don't try to talk to her?" Alex asked.

"No. She's been in her own world for so long that she's used to it. She knows I like being with her. That's all that matters. Sometimes when I visit her, we will sit and sip tea for fifteen minutes without saying a word."

The waitress brought their food, and Ted prayed a blessing. He opened his eyes when he finished and glanced at Mrs. Hobart. She hadn't heard him say "Amen" and was sitting peacefully with her head bowed and her wrinkled hands folded in front of her. Both Ted and Alex watched her for several seconds until Ted leaned forward and in a louder voice said, "Amen!" Mrs. Hobart jerked up her head.

"That sure was a long prayer," she said. "Let's eat!"

Mrs. Hobart took a tiny bite of fish, chewed it for a few seconds, and gave a satisfied sigh. Ted smiled at her and then turned toward Alex.

"What's been happening in your life since Friday night?" he asked.

Alex told him about her experience reading the Bible on Saturday morning. "I've never been interested in reading it before, not even for cultural reasons. It was surprising to me how much I enjoyed it."

"That happens to a lot of people. You're tuned in to a new station, and after what happened at my house, you have the ability to hear it."

They sat in silence for a few moments. Mrs. Hobart was not a rapid eater. She savored every bite as if it were her first.

Ted spoke again. "You know, it's a good thing you left your law firm."

"Why do you say that?"

"While we've been eating, a Bible verse came to mind that fits the situation. It's in Ephesians and says, *Therefore do not be partners with them.*"

Alex smiled. "Is this a joke?"

"No, I'm serious."

"That's a statement without context. I mean, it sounds like the punch line for something else."

Ted nodded. "You're right. I should read the surrounding passage."

He took a small New Testament from the pocket of his shirt and opened it. Mrs. Hobart saw him.

"Are you going to stand on your chair and preach?" she asked with a twinkle in her eye. "Speak up loud and clear. I couldn't hear much of the sermon this morning."

Ted pointed to Alex. "I'm preaching to her."

Mrs. Hobart reached out and patted Alex's hand. "Listen to him. He's smart, and you can trust him."

Alex answered but looked into Ted's eyes. "I think you're right."

Ted gave her an appreciative look and then said, "Here is the section that contains the sentence I quoted. *Let no one deceive you with empty words, for because of such things God's wrath comes on those who are disobedient. Therefore do not be partners with them. For you were once darkness, but now you are light in the Lord. Live as children of light (for the fruit of the light consists in all goodness, righteousness and truth) and find out what pleases the Lord. Have nothing to do with the fruitless deeds of darkness, but rather expose them. For it is shameful even to mention what the disobedient do in secret.*"

The minister stopped and glanced up. "What do you think?"

The words described everything that had happened to Alex personally, the law firm, and the Richardson family during the past few weeks.

"That's in the Bible?" she asked.

Ted handed it to her with his thumb on the place where he'd started reading. "See for yourself."

Alex read the passage again while Ted finished the last few bites of his meal.

"I want to be a child of the light," she said. "And in my work, I'm often trying to uncover what happens in secret so I can help my clients."

"I bet you're good at it, aren't you?" Ted asked.

Alex nodded. "Yes. It's one of my talents."

Ted took a last sip of tea. "Then imagine how good you will become at exposing the deeds of darkness if you dedicate your talent to God."

Mrs. Hobart wanted a piece of key lime pie for dessert, so Ted ordered one for her and himself.

"How about you?" he asked Alex.

"No thanks," she said.

When the waitress brought the pie, there were two forks on the piece she set in front of Ted. He handed one to Alex.

"Eat a bite. It's your destiny."

Alex cut through the meringue, the filling, and the graham cracker crust. It was sweet with a touch of tartness.

"Yum," she said.

Ted followed after her and ate two quick bites. Before he ate another, Alex reached across and sliced off a large chunk. She slightly lifted it from the plate and then looked at Ted with a question in her eyes.

"Are you sure you don't want me to order a piece for you?" he asked.

"I'd rather share," she said looking into Ted's eyes.

Mrs. Hobart spoke, "Are y'all talking about the stock market? I've never been much on stocks. It seemed like gamblin' for rich folks. 'Course, I've never had no extra money anyway."

Ted laughed. "How's your pie, Mrs. Hobart?"

"Good, but it could be a little sweeter."

When they finished their pie, Ted paid for the meal, and they drove from the restaurant to Mrs. Hobart's house.

"I'll be taking a nap today," she said as Alex stopped the car. "And dreaming of fish and hush puppies. Thanks for dinner."

"You're welcome!" Ted responded.

Mrs. Hobart patted Alex on the arm. "You have a sweet face and happy eyes. Do you have a job?"

"Yes, ma'am. I'm a lawyer."

Mrs. Hobart opened her eyes in surprise, and Alex braced herself for a negative comment on women in the law.

"That's fine as long as you're careful."

It was Alex's turn to look puzzled.

"Yes, I'll be careful."

Mrs. Hobart got out of the car and walked slowly to her front door.

As they drove away, Alex glanced at Ted, "Why did she tell me to be careful? Did she hear me when I told her I was a lawyer?"

Ted shrugged. "I don't know. I usually go with the flow of whatever she says. It's more fun that way, and she seems to enjoy it, but sometimes it doesn't make a lot of sense."

While they drove back to the church, Ted glanced sideways at Alex. Now that they were alone, he was acutely aware of her femininity. Mrs. Hobart was right about the young lawyer—she had a sweet face and happy eyes. And now she had a glow about her countenance that Ted attributed to her recent encounter with the Lord.

The combined effect was an attraction that touched him at an even deeper level than the interest sparked by her previous appreciation for music. He struggled with how to respond. He wanted to take a step toward her but didn't want to tread heavily on the new spiritual growth springing up inside her. The minister and the man were in conflict as they turned onto McBee Road and approached the church. When they reached the old parsonage, Alex stopped the car, and Ted started to get out in a condition of stalemate.

"Could I stay a minute?" Alex asked. "I'd like to go to the backyard."

"Uh, okay."

An afternoon breeze eased in from the ocean that made it cooler than when the church service had ended at noon. They walked around the corner of the house. It was as quiet as only a Sunday afternoon can be. Alex went to the place where she'd stepped into the light. Ted held back, not sure what she wanted to do. She looked at him over her shoulder.

"No, please come here," she said. "I want you with me."

Ted joined her as she gazed across the yard. Neither spoke. Alex reached across and took his hand. It was a simple gesture, but Ted swallowed at the intensity of what he felt. They continued looking forward, but Ted saw nothing. Every sense in his being was focused on his contact with Alex. He wanted to soak in the moment so completely that it would remain as a memory with power. Then she turned toward him, took his other hand, and looked up into his face.

"Thank you," she said.

Ted looked puzzled. "For what?"

Alex smiled slightly. "For more than you can imagine."

She raised each of his hands in turn and lightly kissed them.

35

Someone had better be prepared for rage.
ROBERT FROST

ON WEDNESDAY MORNING, Alex was sitting at her desk when Byron Devereaux phoned and told her Rena's car was ready to be released.

"Has anything else developed on the case?" Alex asked.

"We have several leads but nothing definite. Most investigations like this break quickly, but it hasn't happened in this one."

"I saw the clip on the news the other night about the officer's funeral."

"Yeah. We received more calls after the show, and I'm sifting through them."

"What about the fingerprints?"

"Of course, your client's prints are everywhere. The hospital in Greenville sent prints from Mr. Richardson by overnight courier. They matched several spots in the car, and there are other unidentified prints on the passenger door handle. They were fairly clear, so we lifted them and sent them to the FBI lab in Washington. We don't think the car holds any more clues."

"Is there anything else Mrs. Richardson can do to help?"

"Just keep her eyes open for anything suspicious around her house and let us know if she remembers anything else. We've requested help from the Santee police since the murderer may be from that area. Most professional car thieves don't prowl small towns looking for vehicles. They stick to metropolitan areas. I think this was a joyride that went bad and doubt that the person who did it lives in Charleston."

Alex called Rena with the news and gave her the address where the car was being stored.

"Do they have any suspects?" Rena asked.

"Not yet."

"I don't want the car back," Rena said. "The thought of driving it after what happened makes me sick to my stomach. I'd rather trade it in on something else."

"What do you want to do about picking it up?"

There was a moment of silence on the other end of the line. "Could you get it? I don't want to have anything to do with it."

Alex jerked back her head. "That's not my job. Call a wrecker and tell them to tow it to a dealer who can sell it."

Rena continued whining. "Would you set it up with the police? I don't like talking to them."

Alex sighed. "Okay. Where do you want the car towed?"

Rena named a car dealership south of Santee as the destination.

"I'll notify Detective Devereaux and let him know," Alex said. "Is Jeffrey going to attend the hearing on Friday?"

"No, I talked to him after the theft of the car and brought it up again. He'd promised to help, but he backed out on me."

"Does that mean he's not going to give us any other information about your father-in-law?"

It was a slip, and as soon as she spoke, Alex wanted to reel the words back into her mouth. Rena hadn't specifically identified Jeffrey as her friendly mole.

"I hope not," Rena responded without indicating she'd realized the implication of Alex's question.

Alex quickly continued. "Do you think it would help if I contacted him? I've never met him, but I could explain the process and try to persuade him."

"Who knows? He only cares about himself. Don't bother."

"Whether he testifies is not that important," Alex said. "The doctors will be the key witnesses. Dr. Draughton has confirmed that he will be there, and I sent a subpoena to make sure Ken Pinchot, the lawyer from my old firm who will be representing your father-in-law, has subpoenaed Dr. Berman and Dr. Kolb. I've tried to reach them by phone but haven't gotten through. It would be good to have an idea about their testimony before we go to court, so I'm going to Greenville on Thursday morning and try to interview them. They might even try to avoid coming to the hearing."

"I thought they would have to come if they are subpoenaed."

"Yes, but neurosurgeons can come up with great excuses such as they can't leave a patient on the operating table to run down to the courthouse and talk to a judge. I won't be surprised if their lawyer files a motion to quash the subpoena."

"It would be good for us if they didn't come, wouldn't it?" Rena asked.

"Yes. If Dr. Draughton is the only doctor who shows up, it could be a quick hearing."

"How soon would they turn off Baxter's life support?"

"I will have a proposed order with me at the hearing. It's nothing fancy, but it contains the proper legal language with the date left blank for the judge to fill in. If we win, I'll ask the judge to make it effective immediately."

"It's hard to believe something is finally going to be done," Rena said. "I thought this nightmare would never end."

"There's no guarantee—"

"I know, I know," Rena interrupted. "But it's a step in the right direction."

"Have you called the hospital to check on Baxter?" Alex asked.

"I contact the nurses' station every day, and they always say the same thing. He's in critical condition but stable."

"Okay. Can we meet at the hospital at three o'clock on Thursday afternoon? It might help me reach the doctors if you are with me."

"I'll be there. What should I do if Ezra shows up before you do?"

"Leave until I arrive. Go to the room where we met with the doctors and wait for me there."

Alex hadn't called Ken Pinchot to talk about the case. She'd received a faxed copy of the response he filed with the court in Greenville. It was a brief denial of the relief sought by Rena with a conclusion that the medical evidence did not support a finding that Baxter's condition was sufficiently serious to warrant termination of life-sustaining measures.

Later, she received a phone call that the bank had approved her loan to purchase the house on King Street. She walked down the hall and shared the good news with Rachel Downey, who promised to arrange the closing as soon as possible. The sellers weren't planning on coming to Santee.

"They're going to give power of attorney," Rachel said. "I think they're naming a relative who lives in the area so she can sign the deed on their behalf and receive the settlement proceeds."

Alex held up her hand. "Please, I don't want to hear the words 'power of attorney.' I'm in the midst of a case that raises every issue you can imagine about them."

Rachel patted her on the shoulder. "This one will be routine. I promise."

Alex spent the rest of the day preparing to be out of town for the remainder of the week. With no backup, she had to give her cell phone number to an increasingly larger circle of people. She put everything she'd accumulated regarding the Richardson situation in a large briefcase. The hearing was going to be more of a trial by ambush than usual, and she didn't want to be caught without a stray bit of information at her fingertips. She missed Gwen's practical help and camaraderie. Taking a break, she called Leggitt & Freeman. There was a new receptionist who didn't know Alex and asked her name before transferring her to Gwen's desk.

"Who's the new voice on the telephone?" Alex asked.

"Don't know her history," Gwen replied. "She hasn't stopped by my desk to share her life story. What's up?"

"I'm missing you," Alex responded. "You always helped me through the day."

Gwen's voice softened. "You're a sweetie, Alex. Once you get your new office situated, we'll start having fun again."

"The loan has been approved, so everything will move forward quickly."

"Is your preacher friend going to do the work?"

"I hope so. We haven't signed a contract, but he inspected the house for me and told me he was interested in helping me."

"Are you going to do a prenuptial agreement with him at the same time? It would be the efficient way to go."

Alex laughed. "No, but I went to church on Sunday."

"I figured that when you didn't call me. I put my red dress and white shoes back in the closet and stayed home. I don't want to distract him if he's interested in you."

"A lot has been happening."

Gwen's voice turned serious. "Tell me."

"Can you talk? I don't want you to get in trouble."

"Don't worry. I've got Leonard shipshape, and Bennie, the new lawyer, doesn't seem to be doing very much."

"Okay, but it's not just about Ted Morgan."

"I'm listening."

Alex told Gwen about the night at Ted's house. At first, Gwen interrupted with questions, but she grew quiet when Alex described what she felt when Ted mentioned her grandmother. A hint of a tear returned to Alex's right eye, and her voice cracked.

"Then we went to the church, and Ted played the piano for me. The lights were off in the sanctuary, and he played something he made up on the spot. It was his way of describing what had happened to me through music. It was beautiful."

"Wow, if I didn't know you were a levelheaded woman, I'd say you were telling me a dream."

"I know. It was the most real, yet unreal, thing I've ever experienced."

"What about the minister? Is he part of the picture, too?"

Alex paused. "Yes. He has helped me in a very gentle way through what has happened, and we've spent a lot of time together. He's a good man. I can trust him."

"That's saying a lot."

"I know. After what happened with Jason, I needed to meet a decent person. But I don't know that much about Ted. The focus has been on me, not him. He's a mix of minister, pianist, and house painter, but I'm not sure how he fits together."

"This is so cool," Gwen answered. "I'm not sure about the religious stuff, but if this guy is the way you describe him, he's worth taking for a spin around the block."

"Yes, I think so, too."

Alex was about to tell Gwen about her brief physical contact with Ted in the backyard on Sunday when the secretary said, "Gotta go. Here comes Leonard with a big stack of stuff."

The following day, Alex left for Greenville in the early afternoon. She enjoyed trips because it gave her the opportunity to turn her car into a symphony hall on wheels. As she listened to the music, she decided that when she had a lot of money she would finance production of a compact disk for Ted Morgan. The minister's talent shouldn't languish in obscurity; he deserved a wider audience than the stained-glass windows at Sandy Flats Church. It was a pleasant fantasy that kept her mind occupied for much of the trip. As she approached Greenville, she turned off the music and returned to the immediate challenges of the upcoming hearing. She arrived a few minutes early at the hospital.

She pushed the button to receive a ticket for the parking deck. Baxter's condition might not have changed much since the last time she'd walked through the main entrance to the hospital. Her own life, however, had never taken several dramatic turns in such a short period of time.

Rena wasn't in the ICU. The only familiar face in the room belonged to Ezra Richardson. When he saw Alex, the older man's face clouded over, and she saw his right cheek twitch with tension. Instinctively, she backed away.

"Ms. Lindale!" Ezra called out. "I have something to say to you."

Alex stopped and met the fire that sprang to life in the older man's eyes. She always faced anyone who attacked her. Dominant personalities weren't used to people who didn't cower before them, and her response either provoked the other person to embarrassing anger or caused them to disintegrate into a harmless bluster. Anger always produced mistakes; bluster revealed weaknesses.

"Yes?" Alex asked.

Ezra approached, and she could see that the veins in his neck were distended. Several people in the ICU waiting area stopped their conversations and looked in their direction. Ezra glanced sideways and saw that he was being watched. He lowered his voice and almost spit the words out of his mouth.

"I demand that you let me talk to Rena. I don't know what you've told her, but the two of you are not going to kill my son."

"I'm not trying to kill anyone."

"Then what do you call it?" Ezra's face was flushed a deep red.

Alex didn't answer, and the older man took a step closer.

"Answer me!"

Alex held her ground. "You're represented by an attorney, Mr. Richardson. If your lawyer wants to set up a meeting, he can call me."

Ezra lowered his voice but maintained the same level of intensity. "I want to talk to Rena. You can be there, but this can't wait."

"Where is Ken Pinchot?"

"I don't need him."

Alex didn't budge. "Without Mr. Pinchot's permission, I will not talk to you about the petition or allow you to meet with Rena."

The color returned to Ezra's cheeks. "If you don't stop this, you and Rena will both regret it."

Mr. Richardson was close to the edge of legality. Alex wished she had a tape recorder. Any form of overt threat would be a potent weapon for future use.

"What do you mean?" she asked.

Ezra glared at her. He opened his mouth and then snapped it shut. "That's all I'm going to say."

He turned and walked out of the ICU. Alex's heart was pounding. She waited a few seconds and then went to the door and looked down the hall in the direction of the elevators. Rena didn't need to encounter Ezra in the hallway. He was gone, and Rena was nowhere in sight. Not satisfied, Alex decided to retrace her steps to the parking deck in hope she could head off a random meeting between father-in-law and daughter-in-law. As she waited for the elevator, the door opened, and Rena stepped out. She was alone.

"You didn't see your father-in-law, did you?" Alex asked quickly.

Rena shook her head. "No. What happened?"

Alex related the brief encounter in the ICU.

"Now you know what I've been up against in my marriage," Rena said. "Baxter never crossed him. His father's word was the law."

"It won't be the law in court on Friday. Until then, don't come to the hospital unless I'm going to be here, too. I don't want him trying to intimidate you."

"What did he mean by his threats?" Rena asked.

"I don't know unless it has to do with your money. That's the only thing he can try to control. Did you follow my instructions about the checking account?"

Rena nodded. "Yes. The joint account has less than a hundred dollars in it."

"Then it may have to do with the businesses."

"Jeffrey promised—" Rena stopped.

Alex shrugged. "Go ahead. I knew your source had to be a family member, and Jeffrey is the most likely one with the kind of access you mentioned."

Rena looked over her shoulder. "I don't guess it matters. I'm not even sure why he made me promise not to tell you. So far, he hasn't done anything except give me the money to pay your fee. He claims his father is using the power of attorney against me but hasn't shown me any proof. It's been frustrating."

Alex looked in Rena's face. "What are you leaving out?" she asked.

"Nothing."

Alex persisted. "Why is Jeffrey turning against his father?"

"Because he's like him. He wants to control everything."

"Does he know what really happened at the waterfall?"

"No. I swear that you're the only person on earth who knows the truth. Jeffrey wants to be in charge of the family businesses and offered to help me. That's all."

Alex watched Rena closely and saw something she'd seen before in the faces of women she'd represented.

"Are you afraid of him?" Alex asked.

Rena blushed. "Jeffrey? Of course not. He's my brother-in-law."

It was all Alex needed to see. Rena wasn't telling the truth. For some selfish reason, Jeffrey was seeking to manipulate Rena, and she was scared.

"Do you want to talk about it?" Alex asked.

Rena answered with an edge in her voice. "There's nothing to talk about. And keep this confidential."

"That's always true," Alex reassured her and backed off. "And if you change your mind later and want to talk, I'm here to listen."

"Okay," Rena said as she began walking down the hall to the ICU. "Let's go see Baxter."

Alex followed her. The attendant on duty recognized Rena and told them to check with the nurses inside the ICU area.

A nurse pulled Baxter's chart for Rena. Alex could see the young man's motionless legs from the counter where she waited. It was sad to think that the body that had been so active a few weeks before was simply waiting to die.

"His condition remains the same, Mrs. Richardson," a young nurse said. "Dr. Berman saw him this morning and requested an update from Dr. Jackson, the pulmonologist."

"Do you know who will come this afternoon?" Rena asked. "I'd like to talk to one of the main doctors."

"We never know, although Dr. Kolb usually handles the afternoon rounds." The nurse looked at her watch. "He could come by anytime between now and six o'clock."

Rena and Alex walked slowly into Baxter's room. The sound of the ventilator greeted them. Even to Alex's untrained eye, Baxter was beginning to deteriorate. He was pale and pallid with a pasty funeral home tint to his cheeks. Rena reached out and with trembling fingers touched the side of his face. There was no response.

Alex took in every detail. Ezra Richardson could rant and rave, but the body in the bed was not living. Any doubts Alex had about the merits of the petition she'd filed with the court evaporated when faced with the artificiality that dominated the room. The merciful, kind thing to do would be to release Baxter from his expensive prison.

"I'll leave you with him," Alex said.

"No, it's too painful for me to see him like this," Rena answered.

Alex looked for tears in her client's eyes, but they were dry.

"His father was the reason Baxter was depressed and angry," Rena continued in a quiet voice. "I wish I could turn back the clock. I would insist that we move away from Santee and make Baxter get help for his depression. We could have lived anywhere in the world, but he couldn't escape from his father's grip. It wasn't supposed to end like this."

They returned to the waiting room, but neither Dr. Kolb nor Dr. Berman appeared. Alex called the neurosurgeons' office, but the receptionist was no help. The physicians were somewhere in the hospital and wouldn't be returning to the clinic where they worked until the following day.

"I'm going to the hotel," Alex said. "I'll be working on the case tonight and in the morning. Call me if you think of anything. Where are you staying?"

"In a suite at the Weston Poinsett."

Alex wrote the name and phone number of her hotel from the confirmation sheet she'd printed from the Internet and gave it to Rena.

"When will we get together?" Rena asked.

"I'll want to meet with you in the morning about 10:30 to go over your testimony."

The two women walked out together. There was no sign of Ezra Richardson, and Ken Pinchot hadn't called Alex's cell phone. Alex wasn't surprised. Pinchot knew there was nothing to do but go to court, and Alex suspected he'd advised Ezra that a meeting was a waste of time. In the case of In Re Baxter Richardson, there was no common ground for discussion or compromise. It was truly a case of life or death.

36

Thy will be done in earth, as it is in heaven.
MATTHEW 6:10 (KJV)

EVEN THOUGH RENA would ultimately pay the bill for her expenses, Alex hadn't considered the Weston Poinsett for herself. She was working and needed a quiet place to focus, not a luxurious suite with distractions. After she unpacked at a local Hampton Inn, she kicked off her shoes and lay on the bed. The time at the hospital had emotionally drained her. Nothing had happened after Ezra left, but the inherent tension of the ICU and the uncertainty of what lay ahead had sapped her energy. She propped up a couple of pillows and mentally ran through her preparation for the hearing.

In her briefcase was a detailed outline of questions for Dr. Draughton designed to insure that the pertinent information was communicated to the judge. However, strict adherence to a script could cause Alex to overlook the potential of an unexpected answer that opened the door to valuable testimony. At the top of several pages of her questioning, she'd written "Slow Down and Listen to the Witness." Experience had taught her that direct examination needed to have a leisurely, narrative feel. She wanted to lead the judge to a conclusion, not drive her in a heavy-handed way. Even technical medical data could paint a picture, and Alex wanted Judge Holcomb to visualize Baxter's condition for herself.

The greater challenge lay in trying to anticipate the testimony of Drs. Kolb and Berman, whose specific opinions about terminating Baxter's life support were unknown. The possibility that Ken Pinchot would bring in another doctor hired to testify at the hearing created an additional challenge that Alex would have to meet on the run.

Cross-examination of Ezra would be tricky. She wasn't sure how hard to push a man whose son was dying. Yet if Ken Pinchot tried to paint Rena as an overeager widow, Alex would have no choice but to show that the elder Richardson has his own motivation to keep his son alive and the power of attorney intact. After their sparring match at the hospital, Alex had little doubt that she could provoke the elder Richardson to anger.

She skipped supper and went for a swim in the indoor pool. No one else was in the water. The controlled environment of the hotel swimming pool was a different world from the raw ocean. No hidden riptides lurked beneath the surface. The only current in the pool was the gentle swirling caused by the filtration system. Once in rhythm, Alex swam on autopilot. It was exactly twelve strokes from one end of the pool to the other. She missed Boris. An hour later, she stepped out of the water.

She returned to her room and got ready for bed. Instead of flipping through the TV channels until she became sleepy, she took out the Bible that she'd packed in her suitcase. Drawing up the covers to a cozy level, she opened the book and resumed reading in the New Testament. The words continued to speak to her on a level she'd never known with anything else she'd studied. It wasn't a matter of intelligence; it was the result of a new capacity to understand spiritual truth. She was alive to what God had to say. Pausing, her thoughts returned to the Richardson hearing, and for the first time, Alex, the zealous advocate, prayed about the outcome of a case.

"God, let me win this hearing," she began. "It's not right for Baxter Richardson to lie unconscious in a hospital room being kept alive by a bunch of machines. Don't let the judge be fooled by what the other doctors say."

Something felt awkward, and she stopped. She didn't have the confidence that what she prayed was convincing the Almighty of the justice of her cause.

"What's wrong?" she asked the empty room.

No answer came from the beige-colored walls. On a slip of paper in her Bible she'd written Ted Morgan's phone number. Picking up her cell phone, she punched in the number but didn't press send. The minister wasn't a lawyer, and she wasn't sure exactly what to ask him. She held the phone lightly in her hand for a few more seconds and then pressed send. The minister answered on the third ring.

"This is Alex," she said. "I hope it's not too late to call."

"No. It's odd, but I was working on the estimate for the renovation on your office. I should have it ready tomorrow if you want to go over it."

"Thanks, but I'm in Greenville and won't be back in Santee until the weekend. I need some advice about a case."

"What kind of advice?"

Alex couldn't believe what she was doing, but plowed ahead. "I'm in my hotel room and wanted to pray about a court hearing, but I'm having problems. I've never asked God to be involved in one of my cases, and it didn't seem right when my prayer sounded like the opening statement I've prepared for the judge."

Ted laughed. "That's a good start. Most people are so busy praying their own desires that they never ask God what he thinks."

"I don't know what he thinks."

"Ask him."

"I'm not sure I can hear him, and I thought you might tell me."

There was a brief pause. "What kind of case is it?"

There was no ethical reason that prohibited Alex from telling Ted the basic issue in the Richardson case. She took a deep breath.

"It's about Baxter Richardson."

Ted's voice was immediately more serious. "How is he?"

"Not well. We have a hearing tomorrow to determine whether his life support should be terminated."

"A court hearing?"

"Yes."

"I thought those type of decisions were up to the doctors and his family?"

"They don't agree, and I'm representing his wife. She wants to terminate his life support and let him go. His father doesn't agree. The doctors are split."

Ted was silent for a few seconds. "So, if the judge rules in your favor, Baxter will die."

"Yes, they will stop hydration and artificial feeding. The most well-respected physician in the case thinks nothing else can be done, and there is no realistic chance for recovery."

"And you don't feel right asking God to make the judge rule in your favor?"

"Oh, I believe I'm right, but I'm not sure what to pray."

"Have you been reading your Bible?" Ted asked.

"Yes. That's what I was doing before I called. It's neat how it makes sense, but there wasn't anything that seemed to fit the situation."

"Then if the Lord doesn't give you direction, simply pray that God's will be done. It's not a cop-out; it's in the Lord's Prayer. *Thy will be done in earth, as it is in heaven.*"

The image of healing at the pool of Bethesda in the stained-glass window at Sandy Flats Church suddenly flashed through Alex's mind. She shook her head slightly and dispelled it.

"Where is that verse from the Lord's Prayer in the New Testament?" she asked. "I read it the other day but don't remember."

"It's in Matthew 6. I'm not sure about the exact spot. Pray the verses and keep asking the Lord for something specific. I'll be praying about it myself."

"What are you going to pray?"

"I'm not sure, but it seems a shame to give up if there is any realistic hope of recovery."

"I agree, but there isn't. I've seen Baxter for myself. It's incredibly sad and hopeless."

"When is the hearing?"

"Tomorrow at one o'clock."

"Okay. And don't feel awkward about calling," Ted said.

Once again the minister demonstrated his uncanny ability to read her mood.

"Thanks," she said.

After she hung up the phone, Alex turned to Matthew 6 and read the pattern prayer. The words fell flat. She was not at peace, and the thought of Ted Morgan possibly praying that she lose the case didn't help.

She awoke the following morning and contrary to her usual routine ate a hearty breakfast. The hearing would begin immediately after lunchtime, and she wouldn't have anything other than a quick snack until the end of the day. As soon as the clerk of court's office was opened, she called to find out if any of the physicians subpoenaed for the hearing had filed motions to avoid appearing in court.

"No," the clerk said after Alex had waited on the line for more than five minutes. "The only papers in the file are the petition, answer, and notice of hearing."

"Is it still scheduled in front of Judge Holcomb?"

"At one o'clock this afternoon."

After she confirmed with Dr. Draughton's office that he would be present, Alex spread everything out on the bed in her room. She walked back and forth in a sweat suit, visualizing the scene in the courtroom and practicing her opening remarks to the judge. At 10:45 A.M. there was a knock on the door. It was Rena.

She was dressed in a conservative dark gray dress that made her look older but still feminine and vulnerable. Her face showed the strain of the past twenty-four hours.

"I didn't sleep more than an hour last night," Rena said. She brushed past Alex and sat down in the only comfortable chair in the room. "It's going to be hard for me to make it through this. Are you sure I have to say something? Won't Dr. Draughton be enough?"

Many of Alex's clients talked confidently in the office about their testimony, but it didn't always carry over to the courtroom. Rena had always been fragile. Alex moved immediately to shore her up.

"You hold the health care power of attorney and have to let the judge know what you want to do," Alex said matter-of-factly. "The other side will be waiving Ezra's durable power of attorney all over the courtroom, and even though it has legal priority, the judge will consider what you think. Besides, you're his wife—the person he chose and trusted."

Rena put her head in her hands. "I just wish he would go ahead and die!"

Alex kept her voice calm even though she was alarmed by the intensity of her client's reaction. "You have every reason to be upset, but you need to channel your emotion in the right way. The judge won't expect you to sit like a statue on the witness stand, and she obviously can't know the whole story about what happened at the waterfall. You said you'd forgiven Baxter, but it's impossible not to have mixed feelings. Put that behind you for the next few hours. The important thing is that you focus on why you want his life support stopped." Alex spoke slowly. "Let's practice. Mrs. Richardson, why do you want to terminate life support for your husband?"

Rena sighed. "It's the merciful thing to stop his suffering, and it's what Baxter would want if he could tell us."

"Good words, but it sounds flat. Say it like you believe it."

Rena repeated the sentence.

"That's better. Let's back up to the beginning so you can build up to it. I've also thought of a few more questions Ken Pinchot may ask you."

An hour passed quickly. Alex looked at her watch.

"We need to leave in a few minutes, and I have to change clothes."

Alex put on a traditional black business suit. She didn't know anything about Judge Holcomb, and it was always better to err on the side of conservative clothes when going to court. With Alex carrying her largest briefcase and a large portfolio containing medical illustrations and charts, the two women left the hotel. It was a fifteen-minute drive to the courthouse. They rode in silence from the hotel. Alex's mind was churning, and Rena wasn't in the mood for chatter. Turning into the parking lot, Alex looked for Ken Pinchot's silver Mercedes but didn't see it.

Once they passed the security checkpoint, the shiny hallway on the main floor of the building was deserted. It was Friday afternoon, and most of the business of the week had been concluded. The courtroom was on the third floor, and they stepped from the elevator into a narrow hall lined with dark wooden doors differentiated by numbers on brass plates. They located Courtroom 302 and pushed open the door.

Ezra Richardson was already seated at one of the counsel tables. He glanced over his shoulder at the sound of the door opening. Alex looked for Ken Pinchot and saw him huddled in the back corner of the room with Drs. Berman and Kolb. Dr. Draughton was not in sight. Alex led the way to the other counsel table, positioned Rena at the opposite end from Ezra, and began unpacking her briefcase.

A large clock hung on the back wall of the courtroom. It was 12:50 P.M. Alex wanted to grab a few minutes with Berman and Kolb, who were in the back talking to Pinchot. The lawyer didn't seem like he was in a hurry. She suspected he intended to keep them occupied until the judge entered the courtroom. She leaned over to Rena.

"I'm going to break up the conversation in the rear of the room."

She walked up to the three men.

Before she could speak, Pinchot said, "Just a minute, Alex, I'm not quite finished."

"The judge will be coming out in a minute," she responded. "I need to speak to the doctors before the hearing."

Pinchot gave her an ingratiating smile. "Of course. I'll try to hurry."

Alex had no choice but to retreat. She returned to her counsel table but kept one eye on Ken and the other on the rear door of the courtroom. The absence of Dr. Draughton was beginning to be a matter of concern. Ken prolonged his discussion until the judge walked into the courtroom through a side door behind the bench.

"All rise!" the deputy on duty commanded.

Judge Holcomb was a tall, slender woman with magnificent white hair. She was wearing black judicial robes with reading glasses suspended from her neck by a silver chain. Women who had spent more than forty years in the law were uncommon, and for a southern woman to attend law school in South Carolina in the late 1950s was almost as radical as the notion of a female cadet at the Citadel. She glanced imperiously around the courtroom.

"Be seated and come to order. Proceed for the petitioner."

The judge's voice was clear and strong. She spoke with a distinctly southern accent more commonly heard in Charleston than the mountains of the Piedmont. It was clear who would be in charge of the hearing. Outside the courtroom, the judge might be a doting grandmother, but behind the bench she was robed in black steel.

Alex stood and introduced herself. "May I offer an opening statement?"

"That won't be necessary," the judge said curtly. "I've read the pleadings and know the issues. Put on your proof."

Alex quickly glanced over her shoulder. Dr. Draughton was not in sight.

"Your Honor, I intend to present medical testimony from Dr. Vince

Draughton, a neurologist who has evaluated Mr. Richardson; however, the doctor has not yet arrived."

"Is he under subpoena?" the judge asked.

"Yes, ma'am. I spoke with a nurse at his office this morning, and she informed me he would be here at one o'clock. Could we delay the start of the hearing for a few minutes while I try to locate him? It's possible he's in the building."

"Anything is possible, counsel," the judge responded. "We could wait here all afternoon for a doctor to arrive. Do you have other witnesses?"

"Yes."

"Then let's hear from them. The order in which the witnesses testify is not going to influence my decision."

Normally poised, Alex felt a momentary wave of fear. "But if something prevents Dr. Draughton from appearing, I will not be able to complete my case."

Before the judge responded, Ken Pinchot stood to his feet and introduced himself. "Your Honor, the respondent would not object to taking Dr. Draughton's testimony by deposition and submitting it to the court after today's hearing."

Alex wanted the judge to see her witness, not read a dry transcript. If all the medical evidence presented in person at the hearing went against Alex and Rena, it would be almost impossible to convince the judge to grant the petition based on a deposition. Rena touched Alex's arm, and the lawyer leaned over.

"They've gotten to Dr. Draughton and paid him off!" she whispered fiercely.

"Ms. Lindale?" the judge asked. "You can either proceed or withdraw your petition."

"May I consult with my client?" Alex asked.

The judge stared hard at Alex, who felt herself beginning to wilt under the glare. "Very well. The court will be in recess for five minutes."

Judge Holcomb left the courtroom. Alex sat down beside Rena.

"We should have paid him more money!" Rena continued. "You told me the doctors could be bought and sold to the highest bidder."

"Wait," Alex said, trying to regain control. "I never said that and there's got to be another reason why he's not here. Maybe he had an emergency or an auto accident. Whatever happened we have to decide what to do. If Dr. Draughton doesn't come, we can offer your testimony, cross-examine their witnesses, and take the doctor's testimony in the next few days and send it to the judge. Our other alternative is to dismiss the petition, refile it next week, and schedule another hearing."

"Never!" Rena blurted out so loudly that Alex saw Pinchot glance in their direction.

Alex leaned over. "Quiet! We may not have a choice, and it's not such a bad option. A delay would give me the chance to talk to the other doctors about their opinion and perhaps convince Dr. Draughton to sway them with his assessment. One doctor talking to another doctor can be much more effective than a lawyer trying to persuade them."

Rena's face was red. "I don't want to keep waiting!"

Before Alex answered, the door at the rear of the courtroom opened. Everyone turned in their chairs. In walked a short, bald man wearing a white shirt with the top button undone and navy pants.

"Dr. Draughton?" Alex called out.

"Yes," the man replied.

Alex hurried back to the door and greeted him.

"Sorry, I'm late," he said. "It was on my calendar to be here at two o'clock. When my nurse told me the correct time, I left in such a hurry that I forgot my tie and jacket."

Alex would have been glad to see him even if he'd worn shorts and sandals.

"It shouldn't be a problem," she said.

The doctor nodded in greeting to Drs. Kolb and Berman, who were sitting on one of the benches behind Ken Pinchot and Ezra.

Alex saw the gesture and asked, "Have you had a chance to talk to them recently about Baxter's condition?"

"Yes. We were all in the ICU this morning and reviewed his status."

Alex's mouth was suddenly dry. "Are you in agreement?"

"On some matters; however, Dr. Kolb believes—"

The judge's reentry into the courtroom stifled further conversation. Alex walked back to the table with the doctor.

"There's no time now to tell me," Alex said. "Can you address it in your testimony?"

"Yes."

"Then do it whenever it makes the most sense."

The judge took her seat and looked expectantly at Alex.

"Your Honor, Dr. Draughton has arrived, so we are ready to proceed with the case."

"Call your first witness."

Alex asked Dr. Draughton to take the witness stand. The judge administered the oath, and the physician took his seat in the witness chair. He smiled at Alex and the judge. It was Alex's first real chance to evaluate his appearance. Dr. Draughton was pleasant and friendly.

"Dr. Draughton, please tell the court your educational and professional qualifications."

"I received my undergraduate degree summa cum laude from Georgetown University. Then I attended medical school at Johns Hopkins in Baltimore where I completed a residency in neurology. I moved to Greenville nineteen years ago and established my own practice."

"Why did you choose Greenville?"

"I was recruited by Greenville Memorial Hospital. There was a need for someone with my background in this part of the southeast." The doctor paused. "Dr. Kolb was on the committee that met with me and asked me to consider moving here."

"Is Dr. Kolb in—"

"I know Dr. Kolb," Judge Holcomb interrupted. "And his partner, Dr. Berman. They are neurosurgeons; Dr. Draughton is a neurologist. Move on to the substantive testimony as quickly as possible."

Alex wanted to provide more background information and risked the judge's ire by not abandoning her script.

"Yes, ma'am. Dr. Draughton, are you a board-certified neurologist?"

"Yes, since my first year of eligibility up through the present time."

"Do you have any particular areas of interest and expertise within the field of neurology?"

"Traumatic head injuries and reflex sympathetic dystrophy."

"Which condition affects Baxter Richardson?"

"He has a serious, traumatic head injury."

Alex turned over the page on her legal pad.

"Dr. Draughton, what are the similarities between a neurologist and a neurosurgeon?"

The doctor relaxed in the witness chair. "Of course, both are physicians. A neurologist completes medical school, a one-year internship, and three years of specialized training. I followed my three-year training program with a two-year fellowship in treatment of patients with severe head trauma at Johns Hopkins. A neurosurgeon completes a one-year internship followed by a neurosurgical residency program of five to seven years. There is overlap in evaluation and treatment of serious head injuries."

"What are the major differences between the two specialties?"

"A common comparison is that a neurologist is to a neurosurgeon what a cardiologist is to a cardiac surgeon. A neurosurgeon is trained to perform surgery affecting the brain, spinal cord, and peripheral nerves. A neurologist does not perform surgery, but often has greater expertise in diagnostic testing that identifies the nature of problems in the central nervous system."

"Ms. Lindale," the judge said dryly. "I have no intention of becoming either a neurologist or a neurosurgeon. I told you to move to the substantive issues. Do you know what that means?"

Alex remained poised. "Yes, Your Honor. We offer Dr. Vince Draughton as an expert witness in the field of neurology."

Ken Pinchot stood up. "No objection."

Alex moved from the academic to the specific.

"Dr. Draughton, have you had an occasion to examine Baxter Richardson, a young man who is a patient at Greenville Memorial Hospital?"

"Yes."

"Who requested that you evaluate Mr. Richardson?"

"Dr. Kolb tried to contact me on the evening that the patient was admitted to the hospital; however, another neurologist from my office was on call, and I was not available during the first twenty-four hours of Mr. Richardson's care. Thereafter, because of the seriousness of the patient's condition, I assumed primary responsibility for neurological evaluation. I've seen him alone and in consultation with Drs. Kolb and Berman."

"Would it be accurate to say that although Mr. Richardson has a serious head injury there has not been much a neurosurgeon could do to help him?"

Ken Pinchot stood up. "Objection to leading the witness."

"Sustained," the judge replied.

Alex moved on to make her point directly. "What brain surgery has been performed in this case?"

"None, other than the insertion of an intracranial pressure monitor, a device placed inside the brain through a tiny hole in the skull that lets us know about changes caused by swelling in the patient's cranium. It's diagnostic, not corrective."

"Who recommended the use of the monitor and why?"

"I suggested it to Dr. Kolb because of the seriousness of cerebral edema in the patient's brain, and he concurred. I was present when he performed the procedure, which took less than an hour. Thereafter, our focus has been on stabilizing Mr. Richardson's condition in hope that he would improve. No additional surgery has been suggested or performed."

"What can you tell the court about the nature and location of the swelling in Mr. Richardson's brain?"

"It was obvious from external trauma that the patient had received a severe blow to the head. He had a stellate skull fracture with multiple linear fracture lines diverging from a central point of impact. By history, we understood that he fell from a cliff and struck his head on a large rock. This was consistent with the trauma observed by examination and plain x-ray films."

"What effect did this blow have on Mr. Richardson's brain?"

"He had severe localized swelling in the area of the fracture, and a significant subdural hemorrhage that increased in size during the forty-eight hours after his injury. All of this is documented on successive MRI scans and the readings from the monitor I mentioned."

Alex had copies of the scans enhanced by a medical illustrator so that the swelling could be understood by an untrained observer. She took them from her portfolio and handed them to the witness.

Pointing to the pictures, the doctor continued, "Even differences in millimeters can have profound impact on the resulting areas of the brain. The scans taken over the first forty-eight hours show the scope of increased swelling."

"What was Mr. Richardson's level of consciousness at the time of his admission?"

"He was comatose—unresponsive to external stimuli."

"Are there different types and levels of coma?"

"Yes."

The doctor then explained the Glasgow Coma Scale and the profile developed by the Institutes for the Achievement of Human Potential that assess sensory and motor functions through a forty-two-box grid of brain function.

"What was Mr. Richardson's reading on the Glasgow Scale?"

"Dr. Kolb assigned an eight, and after examining the patient, I concurred. This reading indicates severe compromise of all three functions evaluated."

"Has there been any subsequent improvement?"

"No, but not a precipitous drop either."

Alex winced slightly at the gratuitous additional comment that didn't help her case. Sometimes in an effort to appear unbiased, expert witnesses unnecessarily lessened the impact of their testimony. Fortunately, Alex had saved her best evidence for last.

"What recent tests have you performed to determine Mr. Richardson's brain activity?"

"Electroencephalogram and evoked potential tests. The EEG is a recording of the electrical activity of the brain similar to an EKG test of the heart. There are three types of evoked potential tests that use computerized EEG analysis of brain recordings of different sensory stimuli, such as visual, auditory, or peripheral sensory stimuli, to provide information about remaining functioning."

"Who supervised these tests?"

"I did."

"What was the purpose for the tests?"

"To quantify the reason for lack of improvement in the Glasgow Coma Score ratings."

Alex had prepared two charts to illustrate the results of the EEG and evoked potential testing. The raw numbers held no significance without the doctor's analysis, and she guided him through the data as quickly as possible. Alex put the charts on an easel, and the doctor used a laser pointer to assist his explanation.

"This row of numbers relates to visual response, the second is auditory, and the third is peripheral. The numbers provide a uniform picture of the patient's cerebral function. Each test was administered on three separate occasions. As you can see, the findings from the three times the tests were given are very consistent. This is necessary to avoid an aberrant response that would call into question the reliability of the data. Compared to the norms I've listed at the top of chart number one, you can see the severe decrease in brain activity for Mr. Richardson."

"How would you compare the accuracy of the testing performed on Baxter Richardson with other patients?" Alex asked.

Dr. Draughton clicked off his pointer. "The results in this case are as accurate as any I've performed."

Carefully laying the charts against the table so that the judge could still see them, Alex put down her notes. She had memorized the last question for the doctor and didn't want anything to hinder the impact of his response. She spoke in a louder tone of voice.

"Dr. Draughton, based upon the level of response revealed by the EEG and evoked potential testing, do you have an opinion about Baxter Richardson's current mental status and the potential for improvement in the future?"

The doctor looked up at the judge.

"I regret to say that the initial test results, which have been verified on two subsequent occasions, show that Baxter Richardson is in a persistent vegetative state from which there is no reasonable likelihood of recovery."

37

A thousand fantasies begin to throng into my memory,
of calling shapes, and beck'ning shadows dire.
JOHN MILTON

ALEX SAT DOWN, and Ken Pinchot stood to his feet. Even though the scheduling of the hearing had been quick, Alex knew the older lawyer would have a well-organized line of attack.

"Dr. Draughton, even though an EEG of the brain is similar to an EKG of the heart, are there differences between the accuracy and precision of the two tests?"

"Yes."

"Could you explain your answer for the court?"

"An EKG tests the electrical activity of the heart with very little interference. The results of an EEG can be affected by the thickness of the skull. The measurements are made in microvolts and in some places the skull may reach one-half inch in thickness. This requires a higher degree of interpretation to reach a conclusion."

Pinchot held several sheets of paper in his hand. Alex could see from the title page that it was a medical journal article and suspected it documented the potential deficiencies of EEG testing. However, instead of attacking Dr. Draughton with the opinions of the physicians who wrote the article, Pinchot wisely gave the doctor the responsibility of independently admitting the limitations in EEG and evoked potential testing. If he didn't give a complete list of problems, the article was there for backup proof that the neurologist didn't have a comprehensive grasp of the subject.

"Would you agree that, in common medical understanding, an EKG test is more accurate in evaluating the heart than an EEG of the brain?"

"As a general principle, I agree; however, the medical community accepts the efficacy of the evoked potential and EEG tests as diagnostically sound."

Pinchot continued to press forward. "Is there a subjective component to your interpretation of these types of tests?"

Alex squirmed in her seat. She suspected where Pinchot was going but wasn't sure. She wished she'd traveled this road with the doctor beforehand.

"What do you mean? The numbers are absolute."

"By subjective, I simply mean the interpretation of the data is an opinion, an educated guess if you will, taking into consideration your years of training and experience."

"An opinion, not a guess."

"But it's not based upon totally objective data such as an x-ray of a broken bone."

The doctor's face became puzzled. "It requires more training and expertise to interpret the tests we're discussing than to diagnose a severely fractured leg on a plain x-ray."

"And with these more sophisticated tests could other neurologists reach different conclusions when presented with the same data?"

"It's possible." The doctor opened his mouth and then shut it.

Pinchot waited a second before continuing. "Did anyone else interpret the test results?"

"Not at the time."

"How many other neurologists have subsequently reviewed the test results?"

Dr. Draughton glanced at Alex. She could tell he was troubled by the line of questioning but couldn't guess why.

The doctor spoke. "An associate in my office, Dr. Weatherman, provided the initial care for the patient at the hospital. He saw my findings and prepared a memo, which we discussed during an intraoffice staffing review."

"Do you have that memo with you?"

"No."

Alex leaned over to Rena.

"Do you know Dr. Weatherman?"

Rena shook her head. "No, I never met him. Ezra is giving me so many dirty looks that I can't follow the testimony. Can you ask the judge to tell him to keep his eyes to himself?"

Alex wouldn't be drawn into a petty battle on the sidelines. "No. Just don't look over at him," she whispered.

"Did Dr. Weatherman concur with your interpretation of the test data you've discussed today?" Pinchot asked.

"Not completely, but he has not spent as much time working in this area as I have."

"But didn't you state earlier that the numbers were absolute?"

"Yes."

"So can different neurologists reach different conclusions using the same data?"

"To a certain degree, but usually not in a significant way."

"Did Dr. Weatherman conclude that Baxter Richardson is in a persistent vegetative state?"

Alex held her breath. Unless he had a copy of the memo, Pinchot was on thin ice.

"Not initially," the doctor admitted. "But later he modified his position. We often challenge one another during staffing meetings. It's a valuable way to make sure that we're not overlooking something."

Pinchot picked up a sheet of paper from his table. Alex was sure it had to be the memo.

"Did Dr. Weatherman prepare a subsequent memo changing his opinion?"

"If he did, I haven't seen it."

Pinchot dropped the sheet back onto the table and looked at the judge.

"That's all from this witness."

Pleased that she didn't have to do any damage control, Alex quickly moved to close the door for further questions.

"Your Honor," she said, "to avoid being redundant, we have nothing to add to the testimony offered by Dr. Draughton on direct examination."

"Very well. Call your next witness."

Alex touched Rena on the arm.

"Rena Richardson."

Alex had seen Rena exhibit a broad range of moods, and as her client walked to the witness stand, she wondered which Rena Richardson would testify. Seated close to Judge Holcomb, her client looked young and vulnerable.

"Please state your name," Alex said.

"Rena Richardson," she said in a steady voice.

Alex didn't jump directly to the accident at the waterfall. She spent time painting a picture of Rena and Baxter's short life together. She paused at their meeting with the former Leggitt & Freeman lawyer whose failure to cancel Ezra's power of attorney had created the mess that brought them to the courtroom.

"How many meetings did you have with Mr. Lipscomb?"

"Two."

"What did you discuss at each one?"

"First, we talked about our wills. That took up most of the time. Then he told us we needed to consider signing papers that gave instructions about our medical care in case we were in an accident or had a serious illness. He gave us forms to take home and read."

"Did both of you read them?"

"Yes."

"Did you and your husband discuss the documents Mr. Lipscomb prepared?"

Pinchot stood up. "Objection as hearsay, Your Honor."

Alex stepped forward to respond. "Mr. Baxter is unable to testify because he is in a coma. We have the documents signed by Mr. and Mrs. Richardson to tender into evidence as proof of their decision. This testimony is offered as proof that they were signed voluntarily by Mr. Richardson with full understanding of their contents."

"What are the documents?" the judge asked.

"A declaration of desire for a natural death and a health care power of attorney granting authority to Mrs. Richardson."

The judge looked at Pinchot. "Have you seen the forms she mentioned?"

"Yes, but the health care power of attorney is subordinate to the durable power of attorney held by my client."

"I'm aware of the issue. At this time, all I want to know is whether there is going to be any objection to admitting the documents mentioned by Ms. Lindale into evidence?"

"I would like to reserve my objections until after I conduct my cross-examination."

"Then I'll let the witness answer the question and give it the weight I deem appropriate. Proceed."

Alex looked at Rena. "Go ahead," she said.

"I forgot the question," Rena said meekly.

It was a nice touch and added to Rena's air of innocence. Alex repeated the question, and Rena sat up straighter in the witness chair.

"Yes, we talked about the different places to check on the forms and what it meant. We decided that we didn't want to be kept alive with machines and tubes. Both of us believed the same way."

Rena stopped and touched her right eye with a tissue she'd wadded up in her hand. "Of course," she continued, "we had no idea what would happen a few months later."

"I know it is difficult, but please tell the judge how Baxter was injured."

Alex and Rena had discussed how to handle the sensitive issue of the events at Double-Barrel Falls without revealing Baxter's conduct. Alex told her client to keep it simple and avoid details other than the facts surrounding the hike and that Baxter fell to the rocks below.

Rena paused again before answering. As she did, the back door of the courtroom opened. Alex didn't turn around until she saw the look on Rena's face. All the color drained from her client's cheeks. Glancing over her shoulder, Alex saw the scarred visage of Detective Giles Porter. The detective sat down on the back row and folded his arms across his chest.

Rena held out her hand and pointed. "Get him out of here!" she cried out.

Startled, the judge looked toward the back of the room. "Sir, who are you and what is your business here?"

The detective rose to his feet and introduced himself. "I have an interest in this matter since I was the one who found Mrs. Richardson and told her that her husband was alive. It was my understanding that this was an open hearing."

Alex spoke. "Your Honor, there has been a history of intimidation of my client by Detective Porter, and I ask that he be banned from the courtroom during her testimony."

The judge looked skeptically at Alex. "Intimidation? Are there any criminal charges pending against your client?"

"No. But there was a confrontation at the ICU waiting room at the hospital, and I told Detective Porter that any further contact with my client would have to go through me."

Ken Pinchot stood up. "The respondent has no objection to the detective remaining in the courtroom."

"But there is no reason for him to be here," Alex insisted. "He is not going to be a witness for either side."

The judge gave Alex a hard look. "And I haven't heard a legitimate reason to exclude him. Continue with the testimony."

There was a wild look in Rena's eyes, and Alex made a quick decision. She deleted every question related to what happened at the waterfall. Picking up the declaration of desire for a natural death and health care power of attorney, she approached the witness.

"Are these the documents your husband signed during your second visit to the lawyer's office?"

Rena looked down at the signatures.

"Yes."

Alex stayed right in front of her so that Porter was shielded from Rena's view.

"As the holder of the health care power of attorney, what would you like the judge to do?"

Rena answered in such a low voice that even Alex couldn't clearly understand her.

"Speak louder," the judge commanded.

Rena kept her head down. "I think he wants to die."

It was a terrible, ineffective answer. Alex felt a rush of anger and adrenaline. Quickly, she regrouped and offered Rena a chance to rehabilitate her answer by giving the correct response in a follow-up question.

"Why do you think your husband would want to be freed from the machines that are artificially keeping him alive?"

Rena looked up at Alex without answering. The silence lasted for several awkward seconds.

"Because it's wrong to make him keep on suffering."

Alex wanted to keep going but didn't have the confidence Rena would go with her. Wary of what might happen next, she retreated.

"Your witness," she said.

Ken Pinchot sprang up like a leopard that had its prey cornered in a hopeless situation. Alex saw the fire flash across Ken's eyes and, for the first time in her career, prayed for a witness.

"Ms. Richardson, before Detective Porter came into the courtroom, were you about to tell us what caused the injuries to your husband?"

Alex stood. "Objection, Your Honor. The issue is not how Mr. Richardson was injured but whether it is appropriate to continue extraordinary life-sustaining measures."

The judge held up her hand and stared hard at both lawyers before answering.

"Counsel will note that there aren't any jurors in this courtroom, and I am not interested in listening to you joust and spar this afternoon. My responsibility is to make a very serious, life-and-death decision because the family of this unfortunate young man has been unable to do so. From this point forward, I only want to hear testimony directly related to the issue I have to decide. If the testimony wavers from that goal, it will not be tolerated. Is that clear?"

Pinchot didn't back down.

"But the motivation of Mrs. Richardson in wanting to terminate her husband's life support would have a bearing on whether—"

"No, it won't!" the judge interrupted. "My only interest is the medical question and the legal documents related to it."

"May I make an offer of proof for the record?" Pinchot asked.

"Yes, if you keep it brief."

Pinchot then told in his own words what he believed his cross-examination of Rena would have revealed if the judge had allowed him to ask his questions. It was a way of preserving the record in case there was an appeal to determine whether Judge Holcomb incorrectly limited the testimony.

"We believe Mrs. Richardson wants to use the medical power of attorney to terminate her husband's life so that she can collect the inheritance provided in her husband's last will and testament. Finally, the court observed the effect upon Mrs. Richardson of Detective Porter's entrance into the courtroom. There are serious questions about the petitioner's potential culpability in the injuries suffered by her husband."

Alex kept her eyes glued to Rena while Pinchot talked. Her client's face changed shades from rage red to ghostly white. Alex felt the urge to reel her in.

When Pinchot paused, Alex stood. "Your Honor, if there are not going to be any questions for my client, may she come down from the witness stand?"

"Mr. Pinchot, are you going to have any cross-examination of the witness within the guidelines I've set?" the judge asked.

Pinchot glared at Rena for several seconds. Alex held her breath. Based on Rena's outbursts in the ICU, there was no predicting her client's response to the pressure of the moment. As Alex watched, it appeared that Rena was looking strangely past Pinchot and focusing on someone else in the room. Suspecting Detective Porter had moved to a different seat, Alex turned slightly, but there was no one in the area where Rena was staring.

"Not if you allow me the right to recall her as an adverse witness during the presentation of my case," Pinchot said.

Judge Holcomb didn't hide her exasperation. Pinchot was clearly trying to bait the judge into making errors that he could argue to a higher court.

"Ask your questions now," the judge replied in a steely voice that hardened the lilt of her southern accent.

Pinchot bowed slightly. "No questions."

Rena came down from the witness stand and joined Alex. The lawyer could see beads of perspiration on her client's upper lip. There was still a glazed look in Rena's eyes. Alex leaned forward and picked up the documents to tender into evidence.

"He was here," Rena whispered.

"I know," Alex said, thinking she was referring to Detective Porter. "He's at the back of the courtroom."

Rena shook her head, "No, Baxter."

"What?" Alex asked.

"He was standing behind the other lawyer."

The pressure of the courtroom affected people differently, but a visual hallucination was a new manifestation to Alex. She stared incredulously at Rena and groped for a response.

"Uh, close your eyes," she said. "Maybe he'll go away."

"Oh, he's gone. It's okay. I'm fine now."

The judge spoke out, "Proceed, Ms. Lindale."

Alex abandoned her surreal conversation with Rena. "Your Honor, I resubmit petitioner's exhibits one and two—the declaration of desire for a natural death and the health care power of attorney."

"Subject to my offer of proof, respondent has no objection," Pinchot replied.

"Admitted," the judge said. "Call your next witness."

"That's all for the petitioner," Alex said.

"Very well. Court will be in recess for ten minutes before the respondent presents his case."

———

Ted Morgan had spent a busy morning building a deck onto the back of a house not far from the church. The hammering and sawing had occupied his attention, and he didn't think about Alex's hearing until he stopped for lunch shortly before one o'clock. While munching an apple and standing at his kitchen window, he let his mind return to their phone conversation the previous evening. A sense of heaviness settled on him.

Ted had been with people who made the difficult decision to terminate life support. He agreed with the writer of Ecclesiastes that there was a time to die. In some instances, the continuation of extraordinary means of life support prolonged the suffering of both the dying and the living. But there was no cookie-cutter answer. Each situation carried the responsibility of seeking God's heart and mind.

The heaviness Ted felt when thinking about Alex and Baxter Richardson lingered while he finished his apple. He considered going to the church to play the piano, but the idea didn't fit his mood. He spoke a short prayer for direction. Nothing came, and he decided to go for a walk through the cemetery. He stepped outside into the backyard. Several ocean-born clouds drifted across the sky and cast shadows like great ships as they passed overhead.

The graveyard was not a morbid place for Ted. The epitaphs chiseled on some of the gravestones were words of triumph and hope that brought encouragement from the past to the present. Walking slowly along the rows of ancient and modern markers brought order to his thoughts. He occasionally turned in the direction of the cemetery as a place of revelation.

The oldest graves were near the church, and only a few remained visible. In most areas it took no more than ten or fifteen steps to leave one century and enter another. Most of the earliest tombstones, from as far back as the 1700s, were broken pieces of nameless marble with the identity of those memorialized lost to anonymity. But some markers remained, and Ted stopped at the grave of a man named Archibald Murphy who lived from 1726 until 1798. His life spanned the birth of a nation, and the inscription on the narrow gravestone proclaimed, *He believed God, and it was accounted to him for righteousness.*

Ted prayed, "Lord, I believe you will intervene in this situation and ask for your righteousness to be revealed."

He walked on. The 1800s covered a broader and more ragged expanse of territory. Several people who died before the Civil War had been buried so far from the church that their plots weren't encompassed within the bounds of the rest of the cemetery until the late 1900s. It puzzled Ted why the distant grave sites were chosen. Perhaps even in death, the deceased refused to be reconciled with their neighbors. Whatever the reason, the unwritten stories of a single graveyard could fill a thousand books.

He stopped before a small tombstone topped with a tiny lamb. It marked the grave of an infant girl named Maybeth Wells who had died two days after her birth in January 1851. The inscription on the marker read: *A rose taken to heaven before she bloomed on earth.* There was no obvious connection between Maybeth Wells and Baxter Richardson, but when he saw the inscription, Ted knew how to pray.

38

Still achieving, still pursuing,
Learn to labour and to wait.
HENRY WADSWORTH LONGFELLOW

RENA HESITANTLY GLANCED over her shoulder. Giles Porter was no longer in the courtroom. She turned to Alex who was rearranging papers on the table.

"I'm going to splash some water on my face," she said.

"That's a good idea," Alex replied without looking up from her notes. "You need to clear your mind. I'm going to try to ask Drs. Kolb and Berman a few questions before the judge returns."

Rena saw that her father-in-law was in a huddle with Ken Pinchot and Dr. Kolb. The other two doctors were casually sitting next to one another talking. No one paid any attention to her as she walked down the aisle and pushed open the large wooden door at the rear of the courtroom.

The hallway was empty, and Rena was able to breathe. Her chest hurt, and she could feel a tension headache beginning to form at the base of her skull. The ordeal on the witness stand had been worse than she imagined. Twice a scream had clawed its way up her throat and demanded to be released through her lips. Once when Detective Porter appeared at the back of the courtroom and again when Pinchot blamed her for Baxter's accident. Each time Rena grimly clamped her teeth shut and kept the outburst imprisoned. But it had not been easy, and she was exhausted. One slip and she would be destroyed.

The sudden appearance of Baxter standing on the other side of the courtroom had not triggered the overwhelming fear of her husband's first few manifestations. Baxter was detached, casually watching the events unfold that would determine whether he lived or died. He didn't seem to care. Forcing herself to look in his eyes, Rena saw that the malevolent glare from the backseat of the SUV had been replaced by a hint of pity. He left quietly when she glanced at Alex.

Inside the restroom, she cupped her hands and filled them with water. She dried her face with a rough paper towel and studied her reflection in the mirror. The depths of her eyes contained a reservoir of pent-up sorrow. She stared at herself, and whether from a moment of genuine self-reflection or as a result of the enormous emotional pressures in the courtroom, honest tears burned hot in her eyes. Immediately, she fought to suppress them and pressed the damp paper towel tightly against her closed eyelids. In a moment she felt the warmth of her tears through the paper towel and against her fingertips.

She took two deep breaths. Rena had to win this battle. Loss of control would mean loss of her life. She pressed harder against her eyes until they hurt. The pain helped stem the flood of self-pity, and she calmed down. After correcting the flaws in her makeup, she returned to the courtroom.

————

Alex walked over to Dr. Berman and interrupted his conversation with Dr. Draughton.

"Dr. Berman, could I speak with you for a few minutes before the judge returns?"

"Are you wondering whether I disagree with Dr. Draughton about maintaining life support for Mr. Richardson?"

Startled by the physician's directness, Alex said, "Well, I had a few other questions, but that's the most important one."

"You are about to find out that there are three opinions in the courtroom," Dr. Berman said as he patted Dr. Draughton on the shoulder. "His, mine, and Dr. Kolb's. In this case, I think there are many factors favoring termination of life support, but there are not enough present for me to recommend it as the next step."

Alex glanced over her shoulder at Dr. Kolb, who was still talking to Ken Pinchot. "What does Dr. Kolb think?"

Dr. Berman looked at Dr. Draughton. "How would you describe his position?"

"As wrong. He can't be so confident that the patient doesn't have significant damage due to hypoxia. The readings are clear—"

"Not the ones taken last week," Dr. Berman interrupted.

"You heard my testimony," Dr. Draughton retorted. "Those were the least accurate in the entire series. I had a virtually identical situation with an eighteen-year-old woman in Washington, D.C. The neurosurgeon refused to face the facts, and three weeks later the girl died anyway."

The doctors' debate wasn't getting her anywhere, and every minute was precious. Alex felt her stomach churning. She interrupted.

"What factors do all of you agree support termination of life support?" she asked.

Dr. Draughton answered. "The readings from the left side of the brain, where he suffered the primary trauma to the skull, have been uniformly abysmal. Even Dr. Kolb has to admit it."

Dr. Berman shrugged. "That's a factor; however, it's not right to pull it out of context. You're doing the same thing you accused me of doing. We don't know what effect—"

The judge returned, and the sound of the bailiff calling the court to order ended further debate. Alex gave up and returned to her table. Rena joined her seconds later.

"What did Dr. Berman say?" Rena whispered.

"Not much. Apparently, none of the doctors agree. We'll find out in a few minutes."

"Proceed, Mr. Pinchot," the judge said.

Ken stood. "I call Ezra Richardson."

Because the judge was already familiar with Baxter's condition, Pinchot could take the opposite tack from Alex. His client would testify first with the medical evidence to follow. Alex suspected that Pinchot considered Dr. Kolb his strongest weapon and wanted to end on a convincing note.

As Ezra Richardson solemnly took his place in the witness chair, Alex replayed her confrontation with him in the ICU waiting room. Her cross-examination questions were designed to uncork Ezra's rage and create suspicion in the judge's mind about his true motivation for keeping Baxter alive. However, after Judge Holcomb summarily shut down

Pinchot's attempt to portray Rena as a gold digger, Alex wasn't sure the judge would let her implement her plan.

Pinchot began by asking Ezra questions about his background and business activities.

"Mr. Richardson, how long have you lived in the Santee area?"

"All my life. My parents and grandparents on both sides of my family lived in Santee."

"Is your wife still living?"

"No. She passed away several years ago. I have many cousins and relatives, but the only immediate family I have are my two sons, Jeffrey and Baxter." Ezra looked at the judge. "And I love both of them very much."

Pinchot let Ezra's statement linger for a second before continuing.

"Mr. Richardson, how are you employed?"

"I am the CEO of Richardson and Company, a real-estate development and holding firm started by my father. I also own a small company that manufactures golf equipment."

"What is the name of the company that manufactures golf equipment?"

"Flight Right. We make golf balls and a line of specialized putters."

"What role do your sons take in the business?"

"They own a minority interest, and my intent was to groom the boys to take over the business within the next few years so that I could retire."

Before Pinchot could ask another question, Judge Holcomb spoke up.

"Move on, counselor," she said. "I accept the fact that Mr. Richardson is a businessman who has two sons. I don't need to hear a lot of detail unless it's relevant to establishing the witness as an expert on the issue to be decided."

Ken cleared his throat. "My purpose is to show that Mr. Richardson is the type of person who should be allowed to exercise the powers granted to him by the durable power of attorney."

Judge Holcomb hesitated and then said, "Proceed, but make it succinct."

Buoyed by his modest victory, Ken pressed on.

"Please tell the judge about your involvement in the Santee community."

Ezra sat up straighter in his chair. "I'm on the board of directors for our oldest, locally owned bank, and over the years I've been the chairperson for various fund-raising committees. I was recognized as Santee citizen of the year by the chamber of commerce about ten years ago."

Pinchot showed the durable power of attorney to Ezra, who identified it.

Holding the document in his hand, Pinchot asked, "Why did you ask Baxter to sign this power of attorney?"

"It was something I did for both of my boys," Ezra answered. "Baxter had turned eighteen, and it was a safety net for his protection while I brought him into the family businesses."

"Did Baxter receive an ownership interest in any of your companies at that time?"

"Yes, even while he was in college. It was my way of training him by slowly giving him more responsibility."

Rena whispered to Alex. "Baxter said it was all for tax reasons. He didn't do much at the office, even after he graduated from college and we were married."

"Have you read the power of attorney?" Pinchot asked Ezra.

"Not until this came up. I told the lawyers to prepare the papers, and Baxter went by and signed it."

"When did you become aware of the provisions in the power of attorney regarding your son's medical care?"

"After Baxter was injured, I spoke with Ralph Leggitt in your office, and he informed me of the medical care aspects of the power of attorney."

"As the person designated by your son to exercise control regarding health care, why are you opposing your daughter-in-law's request to terminate life support?"

Ezra turned toward the judge. "Because I love my son and don't want to give up trying to help him until everything has been done to save him. There is disagreement among the doctors, and it wouldn't be right to deny Baxter the chance to wake up. I'm not a medical expert, but if competent physicians believe there is even a slim possibility for recovery, I want to hold on to that hope."

Mr. Richardson had answered with the level of sincerity Alex had

hoped to coax from Rena. Alex watched Judge Holcomb's face for a reaction but couldn't discern any response. Pinchot sat down. It was Alex's
turn. She stood up.

"Mr. Richardson, did I understand your testimony correctly that you
weren't present when your son Baxter signed the power of attorney?"

"That's right. He met with the lawyer himself."

"Do you know whether Baxter read the document before he signed
it?"

"No."

"Did you ever discuss it with him later?"

"Not that I recall. He never had a question about it."

"Where was the power of attorney kept?"

"At the lawyer's office. I don't know whether Baxter had a copy or
not."

"Did you discuss it with your son after he graduated from college and
returned to Santee to work in the family business?"

"No."

"What about at the time of his marriage to my client?"

"No."

Alex knit her eyebrows together. "How many times did you use the
power of attorney while Baxter was in college?"

"None. Nothing came up that required it."

"What about after his return to Santee to work with you and your
other son, Jeffrey?"

"No."

"Does that mean that Baxter never gave you any reason to believe he
was irresponsible in the way he conducted his business affairs?"

"He was a good son."

"Were you in favor of his marriage to my client?"

"Objection," Ken interrupted. "That's irrelevant."

"Sustained."

Alex returned to the previous line of questioning.

"So, was there ever a need to use the power of attorney for the reason
you originally asked him to sign it?"

"No."

"If Baxter had asked you to tear it up the day before he went on the hike with Rena, would you have done so?"

For the first time, Ezra hesitated. "Because of what has happened, I'm glad we didn't talk about it."

"It might have lessened your ability to control your son's life, wouldn't it?"

"I'm not trying to control his life."

Alex moved closer to the witness. "Isn't that what you're asking the court to do today? To let you, rather than the woman Baxter chose as his wife, decide whether he continues to lie paralyzed in a coma, artificially kept alive by machines?"

It was a potent question, but Ezra didn't flinch.

"Because of the disagreement among the doctors, I don't believe it is a decision either Rena or I have the right to make. If all the doctors told me there wasn't any hope, I'd tell Baxter good-bye and let him go. That hasn't happened, and I'm not changing my mind."

Alex turned quickly in another direction. It was time to pin Ezra to the wall.

"How many times have you used the power of attorney since Baxter and Rena were married?" she asked.

Ken was on his feet. "Objection, Your Honor. The only issues in this hearing for this witness are whether Baxter Richardson signed the power of attorney freely and voluntarily and my client's right to exercise the medical care provisions. During the testimony of the petitioner, you ruled that any other motivations are irrelevant."

Alex responded. "Your Honor, the witness testified that he asked Baxter to sign the power of attorney in order to protect his son until he could take his place as a mature adult in the family businesses. By Mr. Richardson's own admission that contingency occurred prior to Baxter's accident, and the reason for the power of attorney no longer exists. I also intend to offer evidence that Mr. Richardson has used the power of attorney for reasons other than those already stated, and his recent actions call into question his ability to exercise sound judgment."

"What type of actions?" the judge asked.

Alex looked at Ezra as she answered. "Mr. Richardson used the power of attorney to transfer money from a joint checking account in his son and daughter-in-law's name."

"Which he later returned," Pinchot added. "It was Mr. Richardson's desire to put the money in a trust for the benefit of both his son and daughter-in-law."

"We don't know that," Alex shot back. "Nothing was ever said—"

The judge banged her gavel. "I'm ruling this entire line of questioning irrelevant. Removal of the original basis for drafting a duly executed power of attorney is insufficient reason to revoke it, and any transfer of funds does not bear on the issues before me today." She looked at Alex. "Am I correct in understanding that this is a durable power of attorney without any built-in termination clause?"

Alex had no wiggle room. "Yes, ma'am."

"Then I'm going to sustain the objection and direct you, as I did Mr. Pinchot, to limit your questions to whether the power of attorney was voluntarily executed and the rationale behind Mr. Richardson's request that the court consider his wishes in ruling on the petition."

Alex didn't want to take either road offered by the judge. She had no proof of coercion when Baxter was eighteen and didn't want Ezra to repeat what he'd already said about the reason he opposed the petition.

"Your Honor, nothing further from this witness," Alex said and sat down.

Ezra left the witness stand unscarred. Alex didn't like it, but in the midst of the battle she didn't see any alternative.

"What are you doing?" Rena asked in a sharp whisper. "I thought you were going to make him look bad!"

Alex shook her head. "Not today. Not with this judge."

*When we deal with questions relating to principles
of law and their applications, we do not suddenly
rise into a stratosphere of icy certainty.*
CHARLES EVANS HUGHES

TO ALEX'S SURPRISE, Pinchot didn't call Dr. Berman. Instead, he summoned Dr. Kolb to the witness stand. The older neurosurgeon was an impressive figure with his neatly combed white hair, square jaw, and deep brown eyes that looked as alert and intelligent as if he were a recent medical school graduate. He confidently took his seat in the witness chair and answered background questions about his educational and professional qualifications.

"How many years have you practiced medicine in Greenville?" Pinchot asked.

"Thirty-eight this December," the doctor answered as he glanced up at the judge. "In fact, Judge Holcomb's husband was one of my patients prior to his death, and we have known each other socially for many years."

Alex gulped. This was going to be ugly. Everything that had happened in the courtroom up to that moment had been a colossal waste of time. No wonder the judge wanted to move the case along as quickly as possible. The only testimony that mattered would come from the distinguished doctor who had treated her dying husband and spent time chatting with her around the dining room table.

Pinchot knew he had found hidden treasure and asked Dr. Kolb to repeat much of the information about Baxter's condition. However, there was a difference between their perspectives that became more and more apparent as the doctor continued talking. Dr. Draughton spoke of Baxter as a comatose patient whose condition should be analyzed. Dr. Kolb saw him as a person with a life worth fighting to preserve. It was the difference between a scientist and a healer.

"It was almost miraculous that Baxter was alive when he arrived at the hospital," the doctor said. "Fortunately, I was already in the trauma center examining another patient and assisted the emergency personnel who brought him into the treatment area. Because I was on the scene, I was able to immediately set up the protocol. His condition was very critical, but we didn't lose him."

"Dr. Kolb, what can you tell us about the type of skull fracture suffered by Baxter?"

Once again, the evidence was repetitive, and Alex wanted to object, but the judge was listening closely and any effort to cut off the testimony would have been doomed. There was nothing Alex could do but sit back and hope for a blunder. The doctor spoke in a level voice as if mentoring a new resident.

"As Dr. Draughton indicated, it was a focal injury to the left side of the brain, not a diffuse, axonal injury that would affect the entire brain and be more likely to cause irreversible damage. With focal injuries we often see other parts of the brain begin, over time, to assume some of the functions of the damaged region. This is not an absolute remedy, but it frequently occurs and increases the level of recovery."

"What other factors point toward improvement in this case?"

"He did not suffer total loss of oxygen to the brain, a condition called anoxia. The brain can only function for a couple of minutes without oxygen. After that, the rate of deterioration is dramatic, and any chance of recovery lessens considerably. Even after suffering his injuries, Baxter was able to breathe on his own, and there is no indication of either total or partial oxygen deprivation to the brain. The damage he suffered is due to the specific trauma to a limited section of the brain. Of course, the longer he remains in a coma the greater the time period for recovery."

"What is your opinion about the EEG and evoked potential testing performed by Dr. Draughton?"

Dr. Kolb rubbed the side of his face. "I respect Dr. Draughton, and we often work together, but we have a difference of opinion about EEG and evoked potential testing. The tests measure what is taking place at the moment in time they are administered and are valuable as diagnostic tools; however, they do not have prognostic value."

"What do you mean by prognostic value?"

"They are not a valid basis for predicting the future. Only for patients with no discernable brain wave activity, commonly known as 'brain death,' are these type of procedures definitive in deciding whether to maintain life-sustaining measures. Fortunately, Baxter does not meet those criteria, and Dr. Draughton's data proves it."

"Please explain."

The doctor looked at Alex. "Could I see the chart you prepared?"

Alex reluctantly retrieved the chart and handed it to Pinchot. There were few things worse than having an adverse witness use your own exhibit to torpedo your case. Dr. Kolb proceeded to show why the numbers did not indicate an absence of brain activity sufficient to categorize Baxter's condition as "brain death."

When he finished, Pinchot asked, "Given this information, what is your opinion about Baxter's chances of recovery?"

"We can only wait and see. He could wake up tomorrow, or we might lose him. I can't predict the future, but at this time he remains in critical yet stable condition."

"What is your recommendation about continuing life-sustaining measures?"

"To maintain the current treatment regimen. It has worked thus far."

Pinchot paused. "That's all from this witness."

Alex had sparred with many types of witnesses, but the distinguished, yet kindly, doctor presented a unique challenge. The judge motioned toward her.

"Ms. Lindale, you may conduct your cross-examination."

Alex decided to start out simply.

"Dr. Kolb, do people die from focal head injuries?"

"Yes."

"How long would Baxter Richardson have lived if he hadn't been airlifted to a hospital for medical care?"

"There is no way to answer that question. It was a close call. Probably hours. Not days."

"Even after a person with a serious head injury receives medical care, is it often difficult to predict what will happen?"

"Yes. It is not an exact process. Anytime the central nervous system is affected, the outcome can vary considerably from one patient to the next."

"Has Baxter improved more or less than you originally hoped?"

"Less."

"Why?"

"Once again. It's not clear."

Alex, who had been standing in front of the counsel table, stepped forward.

"Besides his brain, what other part of Baxter's central nervous system was injured in the fall?"

"As I mentioned previously, his spinal cord was damaged in the cervical or neck area, and at present, he is paralyzed."

"Has the portion of the spinal cord that controls breathing been damaged?"

"Possibly. Baxter was breathing on his own when he came into the hospital and placed on a ventilator to help him stabilize. We don't know his current capability."

Alex saw a tiny opening and decided to peek through it.

"Have you tried to take him off the ventilator for even a few seconds to find out?"

"No."

"Why not, if he was breathing on his own when admitted to the hospital?"

"Because the family has not been in agreement about the action to take. Baxter might be able to breathe on his own; however, it could be so difficult for him to do so that it would hasten his death."

"Do you consider permanent use of a ventilator for a comatose patient medically appropriate in all cases?"

"Not permanent use. Only temporary."

"How do you define temporary?"

The doctor shifted in his seat. "It's a judgment call based on experience and evaluation of available data that can be discussed with the family. In this situation, the hospital's attorney told us the power of attorney held by Mr. Richardson gave him the authority to make medical decisions."

This was new information to Alex.

"If the hospital's attorney had told you the health care power of attorney held by Mrs. Richardson took precedence, would you have stopped the ventilator upon her request to do so?"

"Yes. But I would have suggested that it be done on a temporary basis to test Baxter's ability to breathe on his own."

Alex waited a second, debating whether to ask the question that popped into her mind. She wanted to push further and support an argument for a temporary halt to the ventilator but was afraid the doctor would drop back to his "wait and see" approach. She decided on another tack.

"Dr. Kolb, if Baxter can't breathe without the ventilator would that be a sign of deterioration in his condition since the time of his admission to the hospital?"

"Since he was breathing on his own initially, I would consider that a negative development."

Alex stopped. It was as far as she felt confident to go.

"That's all, Your Honor," she said.

Alex sat down while Pinchot asked a few follow-up questions that didn't add anything new. While Dr. Kolb was finishing his testimony, Dr. Draughton tapped Alex on the shoulder and whispered in her ear.

"Dr. Berman just told me he would recommend suspension of the ventilator. As a practical matter, if a quadriplegic patient in a coma with serious brain trauma can't breathe on his own, it's the end."

Alex turned back toward the judge. She had a strategy.

Pinchot huddled with Ezra, and Alex made a few quick notes while waiting for him to call Dr. Berman.

"Anything further from the respondent?" the judge asked Pinchot.

"Just a minute, Your Honor," he replied. "We may be finished."

Alex was caught off guard. In order to cross-examine Dr. Berman about stopping the ventilator, Pinchot needed to first call him to the witness stand.

"Has the power of attorney been admitted into evidence?" Pinchot asked the judge.

"Yes, I show it admitted," the judge replied.

"Then that's all from the respondent."

Alex stood to her feet.

"Excuse me, Your Honor, but Dr. Berman, the other neurosurgeon who has been involved with Mr. Richardson's care, is in the courtroom pursuant to subpoena. I think it would be helpful for you to hear his testimony, and if opposing counsel is not going to call him as a witness, I would like to do so."

The judge gave Alex a stern look. "Ms. Lindale, if you wanted to introduce testimony from Dr. Berman you should have done so during the presentation of your proof. The mere fact that he is in the courtroom is insufficient reason to allow you to reopen your case after you have rested."

"But Dr. Berman can provide relevant information for your consideration in reaching your decision."

"I hope it would be relevant," the judge answered wryly. "However, I have heard enough medical testimony to render a decision, and your request to call him is denied. Anything further?"

Deflated, Alex replied, "No, ma'am."

"Very well, I will give each side five minutes for a closing argument. Ms. Lindale, as petitioner you may go first."

Alex stepped back to her table and picked up the outline she had prepared in advance. It had limited usefulness. Many of the points on the sheets had never been brought out in the testimony, and Dr. Kolb's personal relationship with the judge had taken the wind from her sails. Alex had to look deep within her soul for the emotional energy to put zest into her advocacy. She began with a brief summary of Dr. Draughton's testimony and then made Rena's plea.

"A few months ago this young couple made it clear to one another the path they wanted to follow if they ever faced this type of situation. In filing the petition to terminate life support, Mrs. Richardson has acted in obedience to her husband's desire—a desire that is unequivocally revealed in the declaration of desire for a natural death. Baxter Richardson can't speak for himself, but this document speaks for him.

"Your Honor, it is unimaginably difficult for Mrs. Richardson to ask you to terminate life support. Only her love for her husband compels her to act in the face of opposition and misunderstanding, but to keep Baxter alive by attaching him to machines that artificially tie him to earth is misplaced love. There is a time to release and let go. For Baxter and Rena Richardson that time has come. Please let them say good-bye on their own terms."

Alex stepped closer to the bench. "Everyone in this courtroom would like to dream with Dr. Kolb that hope exists, but hope must be based on facts. Dr. Kolb is an experienced and compassionate physician, and my client is not asking you to ignore his opinion; however, maintaining the status quo without a reason to do so does not make sense either medically or ethically."

Alex paused. "Therefore, my client asks you to open the door to a reasonable next step that will give an unbiased assessment of Baxter's potential for recovery from his own body. We're modifying the petition to request that you order the doctors to suspend use of the ventilator on a trial basis. This will prove whether Baxter retains the ability to breathe independently. If he can breathe on his own, we can wait for further developments. If he can't, then my client would like the option of returning as soon as possible for a supplemental hearing."

Alex walked slowly back to her seat as Pinchot stood up. Rena leaned over and whispered fiercely in her ear.

"Why did you do that? We hadn't discussed it!"

Alex sighed. "If I'd asked for everything, you'd have gotten nothing. Even now, I doubt the judge will do anything except what Dr. Kolb recommends."

Rena sputtered but didn't say anything else.

Alex barely listened to Ken Pinchot. The older lawyer knew Dr. Kolb's testimony was the key to the case. He abandoned any effort to slander Rena and focused on the opinion of the neurosurgeon. He concluded by directly addressing Alex's new suggestion.

"Ms. Lindale's request to suspend use of the ventilator is not based on any testimony from the medical experts, and the court is urged not to substitute the medical judgment of opposing counsel for that of Dr. Kolb. In fact, her suggestion smacks of cruelty. Doctors need to be doctors and lawyers should remain lawyers."

Alex winced at the mention of cruelty.

Pinchot pointed toward Dr. Kolb and held the power of attorney in his hand. "The two strongest factors to guide your decision are Dr. Kolb's recommendations and my client's exercise of the durable power of attorney. One medical, one legal—these two pillars should be the basis for your ruling. Thank you very much."

The judge spoke, "Given the nature of the petition, I will announce my decision from the bench. Court will be in recess for fifteen minutes while I make some notes."

4 0

Death and life are in the power of the tongue.
PROVERBS 18:21 (NKJV)

WHILE KEN PINCHOT gave his closing remarks, Rena dug her fingernails into her palms. She needed physical pain to distract her from the mental anguish she felt at the sudden turn of events. Alex's cowardly betrayal opened wide the door for Ezra's lawyer to waltz in and ask the judge to do what he wanted and leave Rena twisting on a spit over an open fire of impending judgment. Sooner or later, the grotesque detective would drag her off for torture.

In answer to her premonition, she glanced over her shoulder and saw that Giles Porter had reentered the courtroom and taken a seat in the back row. Rena involuntarily ducked her head. When she did, Alex glanced in her direction and sternly shook her head. Rena wanted to jerk out a handful of the lawyer's hair.

And suddenly, she realized what had happened.

Alexia Lindale was secretly working for her father-in-law. Nothing had changed since the first meeting at the hospital. Alex's opening line about helping the "Richardson Family" was totally bogus. Jeffrey had been right. No one who worked for Leggitt & Freeman could be trusted, and Alex was no exception. The fake office at the real-estate company. The phone calls from the lawyer's house. The meeting at the restaurant. It was all an elaborate subterfuge. Even Jeffrey's conduct in stringing Rena along became clear. He might not have been part of the plot at their first meeting but later he directed her to Alex. Rena kicked the leg of her chair with her heel. She should have known that she wouldn't be able to find an ally in Santee. She'd been a fool. She put her head down on the table and closed her eyes. She couldn't think anymore. She couldn't feel. She simply wanted to hide.

———

Alex saw that Rena was resting her head on the table. The strain of the hearing had obviously overloaded her client's emotional circuits. She leaned over to her.

"I'm going to get a drink of water. I'll be back in a minute."

There was no response.

When she stood and turned around, Alex saw Giles Porter. She walked down the aisle and stopped beside the detective.

"Why are you here?" she asked.

The detective touched the scar on top of his head. "I'm trying to learn as much as I can about Baxter Richardson's head injury. You know how hard it is to talk to the doctors. This is the easiest way to find out about the diagnosis and treatment. Did you hear what they said about a stellate fracture?"

"Yes."

"And it's a good thing Dr. Kolb was in the trauma unit when the helicopter arrived."

Alex shrugged. "Only if Baxter recovered."

The detective motioned toward Rena. "Or if your client wanted to avoid a murder charge."

"Why don't you back off!" Alex retorted.

"Because the more I think about this case, the more convinced I am that your client is hiding something."

Alex wanted to tell him the truth but kept her mouth shut.

Porter continued, "Did your client tell you about the hiking stick?"

"Is it a crime to carry a hiking stick?"

"Perhaps if it has fragments of Baxter's skin on one end. I found it at the waterfall."

Alex couldn't remember if Rena had mentioned a hiking stick or not. Porter took an ink pen from his front pocket, jabbed it in the air in front of his chest, and then touched his neck with the end of the pen.

"It's just a thought."

Alex cut off a sarcastic reply. Porter seemed to enjoy playing petty mind games, but the true criminal was lying in a hospital bed, oblivious to the day's events in the courtroom.

"You're wasting your time," she said. "Rena Richardson has done nothing wrong."

Porter shrugged. "Ask her about the stick and let me know what she says."

Alex turned away and pushed open the door. She had no intention of being Porter's messenger girl. She walked down the hallway to a water fountain where she took a long drink of water. The cold water triggered a pang of longing for the peace of her boat gliding slowly through the marsh grass toward the barrier island. Alex was a trial lawyer because she loved the excitement of the courtroom, but her internal equilibrium required corresponding peace.

She met Ken Pinchot in the hallway as she returned to the courtroom.

"Well done, Alex," Pinchot said.

Alex couldn't tell if the words were spoken with graciousness in advance of victory or sarcasm. She suspected the latter.

"Thanks," Alex responded. "Although I didn't appreciate the reference to cruelty."

"It wasn't personal."

Pinchot continued toward the restrooms. Alex grunted as she pushed open the heavy wooden door. It was very personal and sent a message to the judge that if she agreed with Alex, she deserved the same label.

Ezra was standing in front of Alex's table talking to Rena. Alex hurried down the aisle to quickly intervene. At her appearance, Ezra slid back to his side of the courtroom. Alex sat beside Rena.

"What did he want?"

"Why don't you ask him yourself?" Rena shot back.

Startled, Alex said, "I can't talk to him. He has a lawyer."

Rena's eyes narrowed. "How many lawyers does he have?"

Before Alex could respond, Judge Holcomb reentered the courtroom with the file and a legal pad in her right hand. Ken Pinchot returned as well.

"Be seated," the judge said.

Alex moved toward the edge of her seat. The judge looked toward Ken Pinchot.

"I have reached a decision. Mr. Pinchot, I would like you to draft an order based on my ruling. I will furnish you with a copy of my notes to assist you."

Alex slumped back in her chair. Judges always assigned the task of preparing a typewritten order to the winning lawyer.

The judge continued. "I have carefully considered the testimony of the parties, Drs. Draughton and Kolb, the provisions of the health care power of attorney, the declaration of desire for a natural death, and the durable power of attorney. My decision does not require me to rule on the priority of the powers of attorney, and I specifically do not make any findings of fact on this issue. Rather, the controlling document is the declaration of desire for a natural death executed by Mr. Baxter Richardson while he was mentally competent before this unfortunate accident occurred."

Alex perked up her ears. Ezra and Rena disagreed, but Baxter's wishes were clear.

"My task is to apply the directions left by Mr. Richardson to his current medical condition as diagnosed by his physicians. It is undisputed that Mr. Richardson has suffered severe injuries to his brain and spinal cord; however, I do not accept the testimony of Dr. Draughton that Mr. Richardson is in a persistent vegetative state. On this point, the testimony of Dr. Kolb is more persuasive, and I deny the relief sought by Mrs. Richardson as set forth in the petition."

Alex heard Rena groan. The judge was picking up steam, and it wasn't hard to predict where she was going.

"Hydration and nutrition for Baxter Richardson shall be continued consistent with accepted medical protocol until further order of the court or agreement of the parties in consultation with the treating physicians."

The judge looked down at her notes before continuing. "However, I do not believe that maintaining the current level of life-sustaining measures is consistent with the expressed intent of Mr. Richardson set forth in the declaration of desire for a natural death. By its very name, this document is evidence of a desire by an individual to restrict the use of extraordinary medical measures. The cumulative effect of the injuries to Mr.

Richardson creates a sufficiently severe medical status that removal of
the ventilator is consistent with his directions in the document referred
to. My personal opinion about the best course of action might be different; however, my decision is strongly influenced by Mr. Richardson's
unequivocal intentions. Therefore, I hereby order that continuation of the
ventilator be suspended as soon as practicable. A written order shall be
prepared and exchanged between the parties prior to my signing it; however, my ruling goes into effect immediately."

Alex was shocked. The judge had adopted her recommendations verbatim. Judge Holcomb turned to her with a serious expression that
revealed nothing.

"Ms. Lindale, do you have any questions?"

"Uh, when you say as soon as practicable, what does that mean as to
specific timing?"

The judge looked toward Dr. Kolb. "When would you be able to
remove the ventilator?"

The doctor's face displayed his obvious disappointment. "It could be
done this evening if the family completes the process of preparing for the
possibility that the patient will not survive."

Pinchot stood up. "On behalf of Mr. Richardson, we request that implementation of the order be delayed at least forty-eight hours. Baxter's brother
is not in Greenville, and the entire family would like to be present."

"Where is the brother?" the judge asked.

"In Santee," Pinchot responded. "He's taking care of the family business in the absence of his father and Baxter."

"Do you have a response, Ms. Lindale?" the judge asked.

Alex leaned over to Rena. "What do you think?"

"Jeffrey could be here in a few hours."

Alex stood. "A twenty-four-hour time period should be sufficient.
Perhaps by five o'clock tomorrow afternoon."

The judge knit her eyebrows for a second. "I'm going to grant Mr.
Pinchot's request and set the time for removal of the ventilator at 5 P.M.
on Sunday afternoon. Can that be coordinated by the physicians?"

Dr. Kolb glanced over his shoulder. "I will be out of town on Sunday.
Dr. Berman will be on call for our office."

"I'm sure that will give sufficient time to communicate with the pulmonologist," Dr. Berman responded. "It can be done."

"Incorporate that into the order," the judge responded. "Any other questions?"

"None from the petitioner," Alex answered.

Pinchot didn't immediately answer. He gazed at a place on the wall behind the judge's head for several seconds.

"Your Honor, could there be additional evidence presented that would cause you to reconsider your decision?"

It was a question that could have produced a terse response. The judge responded in a more tactful tone.

"Mr. Pinchot, if you had such evidence, it should have been brought forth during the hearing. However, let me emphasize again to you and your client that I am not acting on personal belief but consistent with the parameters set by Mr. Richardson himself in the declaration of desire for a natural death. For this reason, I will not entertain a motion to reconsider if it is based on further argument or medical opinion. Only if you have evidence that the declaration was not signed freely and voluntarily by Mr. Richardson would I entertain a motion to reconsider. Does such evidence exist?"

"Not that I am aware of," Pinchot answered. "The attorney who drafted it is no longer with our firm. I intend to contact him, and if something comes up, I will file an appropriate motion."

The judge nodded. "In the meantime, draft an order consistent with my verbal ruling."

Alex was impressed. Judge Holcomb had not allowed her preferences or the opinion of a personal friend to interfere with what she understood to be her legal duty. Alex put everything neatly back into her briefcase and slipped the demonstrative exhibits back into the portfolio. Pinchot and Ezra were involved in a heated conversation and didn't glance in their direction.

"Let's go," Alex said to Rena.

They walked out of the courtroom and caught an elevator by themselves. Giles Porter was not in sight. Alex leaned against the wall as the doors slid shut. The two women stood side by side.

"That was a shock," Alex said. "I never thought the judge would refuse to follow Dr. Kolb's recommendations."

"But we still have to wait two days," Rena protested. "You shouldn't have backed down."

"Trust me," Alex said, tight lipped. "We got as much as we could from this judge."

"I wish I could," Rena replied in a snippy voice.

Alex instantly went from surprise at the judge's ruling to rage at her client. She couldn't believe Rena was questioning her fidelity to the case. If the doors of the elevator hadn't opened to a group of people waiting to get on, she would have unloaded a verbal barrage. She stormed out of the elevator and left Rena trailing behind her.

"Wait!" Rena called out. "Where are you going?"

"Home," Alex called over her shoulder. "Don't call me."

Alex reached her car and started the engine. Rena could catch a cab back to her hotel. Nothing infuriated Alex more than someone calling into question her loyalty and commitment to her clients. It hurt worst when coming from a person she'd so heavily invested in. Rena ran up to the car and banged on the window. Alex opened it a crack.

"I don't have a car," Rena said.

"Call a cab," Alex replied. "I'm off the clock. Permanently." She put the car in reverse. "I'll calculate my time and refund the balance of the retainer."

Rena ran behind the car for a moment. Then she stood still with her arms crossed. The sight in the rearview mirror was slightly silly and deflated Alex's anger. She put the car in park and got out. Rena approached her sheepishly. Alex spoke first.

Pointing her finger at Rena's face, she said, "You can question anything about my representation except my loyalty to you. If that doesn't exist, you need to get another lawyer. I've dropped everything else in my practice to help you, and I will not continue until I'm convinced we're on the same page."

"Oh, I don't know what I was thinking," Rena said hurriedly. "The hearing upset me so much, and it's all so confusing and worrying. I'm sorry."

Alex inspected her client's face, wondering if the contrition was real. It was hard enough fighting Leggitt & Freeman without having to maintain a rearguard action with her own client.

"Get in," she said.

They rode in silence until they were near the hotel.

"May I ask you a question?" Rena said in a timid voice.

"Yes."

"I didn't think waiting two extra days was a good idea because of the power of attorney. What will stop Ezra from using it against me until Baxter dies?"

Alex gripped the steering wheel tighter. Rena was right. In the swirl of the hearing, she'd forgotten to consider the possibility that keeping Baxter alive would give Ezra a renewed opportunity to use the power of attorney to plunder Rena's potential estate. It would be the most logical way to carry out the retaliation threatened during their recent confrontation in the ICU waiting room. She should have brought it up in front of the judge, but it hadn't crossed her mind. It was an embarrassing oversight and deflated what remained of her righteous indignation.

"I should have mentioned it in front of the judge," she admitted. "If Ezra does anything, we'll file the suit we discussed before he returned the money to the bank account. It won't take long to prepare the papers."

"But that will only lead to more delays and expense," Rena said. "I know you think we won, but it doesn't seem that way to me."

Alex winced. It would be a challenge to unravel any transfer of assets and convince a judge that Ezra did not have the legal authority to do what Baxter had specifically given him the power to do.

"I'm sorry I got upset," Alex said. "Although I go to court all the time, I guess I was affected by the stress as well. We'll work through this together. Forget what I said about withdrawing from your case. I'll help you if you want me to."

"I do," Rena said. "Just don't threaten me. I can't handle that very well. I like to talk things out."

They arrived at Rena's hotel. Several young men dressed in tuxedos were going into the hotel. It was either a formal college function or a wedding reception. Life goes on, Alex thought.

"Still avoid any contact with Ezra at the hospital unless other people are in the room," she said. "If an emergency comes up, give me a call on my cell phone. I'll have it with me all weekend. Of course, you can call me on Sunday after the ventilator is removed if you want to. I know it will be a hard time."

"I might not even be there," Rena said. "Is there any reason why I have to be present when they do it?"

"Technically, no."

"If he dies, I've already said good-bye. I whispered it in his ear the last time we were alone."

No life that breathes with human
breath has ever truly longed for death.
Alfred, Lord Tennyson

It was late when Alex arrived home to pick up her pets. She'd never been away from them so much as in the past two months. Misha resented going to the kennel and had started sulking for a full day before returning for regular rubs against Alex's leg. Boris reacted like a child frequently separated from his mother and was beginning to misbehave to gain her attention. Alex resolved not to leave Santee overnight for at least a month.

She spent most of Saturday at her office, reading mail and returning phone messages. Activity continued in her other cases whether she was in Greenville or Santee, and it took skill to shepherd all her responsibilities. Without Gwen to help it took Alex several hours to type answers to correspondence and draft discovery documents she could have normally dictated in one-third the time. She worked steadily until 5 P.M.

When she left the office, Alex stopped by Sandy Flats Church to tell Ted what had happened in the Richardson hearing and enjoy a musical meal. The church parking lot was deserted when she got out of her car and walked up to the sanctuary. Inside, it was dark in the narthex. No sounds of piano music flowed from the sanctuary to greet her. Disappointed, Alex turned to leave. Ted's truck was nowhere in sight. A good stereo system had satisfied her until she met a person who could produce the unhindered glory of music in her presence.

Arriving home, she responded to Boris's eager barking by putting on her swimsuit and dragging out her boat. The temperature dropped rapidly as the sun slipped toward the horizon, and by the time they reached the island, the beach grass was casting long shadows across the sand. Boris dashed ahead into the surf and then ran back to her panting with excitement.

"This will be a short swim," Alex warned. "It's almost dark."

Launching out alone into the surf was routine, but Alex drew the line at night swimming in the ocean. Gazing at the stars from the waves didn't interest her. She donned her wet suit and followed Boris into the water. Although the air was calm, the water was choppy from a storm miles out to sea. Alex spit out several salty mouthfuls as she sought a rhythm that cooperated with the waves.

She moved slowly down the beach as the sun slipped beneath the horizon. There was no moon, and it grew dark more quickly than she'd anticipated. The waters around her turned black. Boris was invisible except for the white of his eyes and an occasional glimmer of teeth. Alex kept going. The wind began to pick up slightly as the leading edge of the storm reached out toward shore.

Boris yelped, and an unexpected fear suddenly swept over her. Alex shook it off and kept swimming, but Boris abandoned her and began to paddle rapidly toward the shallow water. She hesitated, then reluctantly turned to follow. She didn't like to give in to fear. As she kicked downward, a large creature swept underneath her right leg and scraped against her exposed foot. At the unexpected contact, Alex tried to catapult herself out of the water. Frantically glancing down, she couldn't see anything. Boris was leaving her behind in his race for the shore.

Alex didn't need further prodding, yet even in her desperation the discipline of countless hours in the water kept her swimming form precise. Her legs propelled her forward, and her arms cut smoothly through the choppy water. With the force of the waves behind her, she moved rapidly for a human swimmer but not fast enough to get away from the creature tracking her. It passed beneath her again and bumped her foot, then broke the water beside her as it came to the surface.

It was a porpoise.

Alex glimpsed a happy mouth that smiled in greeting. The porpoise rolled on its side for a second and then disappeared beneath the waves. Boris reached the beach and began barking. Alex treaded water to see if the friendly mammal would return, but it was gone. A few more strokes brought her to the breaking waves, and she soon joined Boris. The dog licked her face. Alex held his head between her hands.

"You're a good watchdog," she said. "But you need to learn the difference between a shark and a porpoise. Everything that swims in the ocean isn't an enemy."

Boris pulled away from her and ran down the beach. Alex followed. The wet suit kept her from getting cool as the stiffening breeze dried her exposed skin. The encounter with the porpoise had shaken her. As she navigated her boat through the inky water of the marsh, Alex wondered if there was a lesson in the incident and decided she needed to heed the same advice she'd given Boris. There are many kinds of people in the world. Knowing the difference between a friend and a foe is not always easy. Alex didn't want to be mistaken about a friend or deceived by an enemy.

Early Sunday morning, Alex awoke and continued reading the New Testament while sitting on the porch. The twenty-four-hour period of estrangement with Misha had expired, and the cat joined her, curling up beside her in the chair. Alex occasionally stroked the cat's soft fur as she read. She finished the Gospel of John before taking a break. Taking her cup into the kitchen, she looked at the clock and was surprised at how much time had flown by. She needed to hurry to get to the morning service at Sandy Flats Church.

After arriving a couple of minutes late, she sat on one of the back pews out of Ted's line of sight. The choir was taking the Sunday off, and Ted played a piece of unfamiliar music that Alex suspected he'd written himself. It was a peaceful melody that reminded her of unhurried moments in life such as the time she spent on her porch. During the service, she found herself focusing on Ted's actions and movements. He was a graceful man. Unhurried and confident of his place.

At the conclusion of the service, she waited until Ted finished the postlude and saw her. When he did, his eyes instantly lit up. She waved, and he came over to her. They were alone as the last people streamed out of the sanctuary.

He took her hand and squeezed it gently. Alex looked up into Ted's eyes. Before, they had always been kind. Today, the gentleness was joined with masculine strength. He looked over her shoulder toward the narthex, and Alex realized that he wanted to kiss her. She stepped away from the aisle, closer to a pew. Without a word, Ted leaned over and their lips met briefly. It was more sweet than passionate, but for Alex it was a giant step in the direction of trust.

When they parted, Alex opened her eyes, looked past him, and said, "Uh-oh. Everyone isn't gone."

Ted quickly turned around. "Who's there?"

Alex pointed to the stained-glass window of the healing at the pool of Bethesda.

Ted followed her finger and smiled. "He sees everything."

"What does he think?" Alex asked.

"I have an opinion, but you'll have to ask him yourself."

"I liked it," Alex responded.

Ted's smile broadened, and he dropped her hand just as John Heathcliff returned to the sanctuary.

When he saw them, he said, "Ted, don't forget to fix the second step leading up to the pulpit. Did you hear it this morning? It creaked terribly. I'm afraid it's about to break in two."

"Sure. I'll look at it tomorrow."

Rev. Heathcliff nodded toward Alex. "It's good to have you back. Come again."

Alex returned the greeting. "I will. Don't you think Ted did a magnificent job with the music?"

"Oh, yes," the minister replied as he turned to leave. "And don't forget about the step."

After he left, Alex touched Ted on the arm. "Let's walk outside."

It was a sunny but comfortable afternoon. A few cars were still in the parking lot as people lingered in the pleasant fall air to chat.

"Does the minister not realize your talent?" Alex asked.

"No," Ted replied seriously. "I've never kissed him."

Alex laughed. "If you like, I'll tell him you have definite potential."

As they walked toward Alex's car, Ted asked, "What happened with Baxter Richardson?"

Alex crunched a seashell under her foot. "We had a hearing on Friday afternoon, and the judge took my advice." She looked at her watch. "They will remove the ventilator in about five hours."

"I'm surprised," Ted responded with a hint of regret in his voice.

"Why? Did you want me to lose?"

"Not specifically. But I'm not convinced he's a hopeless case."

"Let me tell you what happened."

Now that the hearing was over, Alex could summarize in a generic way the medical evidence. She leaned against her car as she talked. The church parking lot was deserted by the time she finished. His brow furrowed, Ted listened without comment.

"Maybe I was wrong," he shrugged.

"Given the testimony of the doctor who was a friend with the judge, it was an amazing result. I prayed that God's will would be done."

"On earth as it is in heaven," Ted completed the sentence.

Alex's cell phone began playing the introduction to Beethoven's *Ninth Symphony*. As she fumbled for it in her purse, she said, "I forgot to turn it off during the church service. I'm glad it didn't ring in the middle of a prayer."

"Beethoven would be amazed," Ted said. "Do you want me to leave?"

"No, it will just be a minute."

Alex pushed the talk button. It was Rena.

"You've got to come to the hospital," Rena began in a rush. "I don't think they're going to remove the breathing tube."

"But the judge—"

Rena interrupted. "It doesn't matter. Mr. Pinchot has talked to the hospital's attorney, and they've come up with a way to ignore the judge's order."

"What?" Alex blurted out. She looked at Ted and lowered her voice. "That doesn't make any sense. Pinchot wouldn't risk being held in contempt of court. How do you know about this?"

"I overheard two doctors talking near the nurse's station. Neither of them was at the hearing, but I think one is the pulmonary specialist. I was so shocked that I didn't know what to say."

"Where are you now? I thought you weren't going to be at the hospital."

"I changed my mind, and I'm glad I did. I'm outside the hospital on the sidewalk. They're meeting in one of the conference rooms near the ICU waiting area."

"Who?"

"Ezra's lawyer, the hospital's attorney, my father-in-law, and several doctors."

"Is Dr. Draughton there?"

"No. I don't think he was invited. Neither was I."

Alex wracked her brain for insight into Ken Pinchot's strategy. She needed more information.

"You have a right to be in that meeting."

"What can I do? That's why I need you to be here."

It would take almost four hours to drive to Greenville. Alex had to figure out a better way to intervene than a personal appearance.

"Don't hang up the phone. Go back into the hospital," Alex ordered. "Walk into the conference room and hand the phone to Pinchot so I can talk to him."

"What if he won't take it?"

Alex hesitated. "Let's give it a try."

"Okay. I'm going back inside."

Alex put her thumb across the bottom of the phone so Rena couldn't hear and spoke to Ted.

"They're trying to find a way to get around the judge's order."

"How?"

"I don't know. There is no legal reason not to do what has been ordered. Rena is taking the phone to the lawyer on the other side so I can find out what's going on."

She waited, imagining Rena taking the familiar route through the hospital corridors. Alex looked down at the phone. The connection was lost.

"She must be in an elevator. She'll call back as soon as she's on the floor."

A few seconds later, the phone rang.

"Where are you?" Alex asked.

"At the conference room. I'm opening the door."

"Just go in and hand him the phone."

Alex steeled herself for the confrontation with Pinchot. She waited. There was no sound of voices on the other end. She looked down at the phone to see if the connection had been lost, but it still showed good contact. Rena came back on the line.

"They're gone."

"Try to find him."

"Okay. I'll go into the ICU waiting area."

A few moments of silence followed until Rena said, "Not here, either."

"Are any of the doctors there? Dr. Kolb? Dr. Berman?"

"Dr. Kolb is out of town. I don't see anyone I recognize."

"Go into the ICU area to Baxter's room."

"They won't let me take the cell phone in there."

"You go and call me back. If Pinchot or Dr. Berman is there, I want to talk to one of them immediately."

Alex's level of stress was rising higher and higher. It was unusual for her to be totally blindsided during the course of litigation. Most pitfalls could be identified in advance even if the facts of the case wouldn't let her completely avoid them. In this situation, she couldn't see Ken Pinchot's angle of attack. Hospital politics or personal persuasion weren't enough to override Judge Holcomb's directive.

"I'm sorry," she said to Ted. "You can go on. I have to wait for Rena to call me."

Ted nodded. "Okay. I'll be over at the parsonage. Stop by and we'll go over my estimate for the renovation of the house on King Street."

Alex opened the door of her car and sat down. She watched Ted walk across the parking lot to his house. It should have remained a pleasant afternoon in Santee—a time for her to get to know Ted Morgan better. The phone rang.

"Yes?" she asked.

"No one is there but Baxter. He looks worse than the other day."

"Where is everybody?"

"I don't know."

"Are you sure of what you heard?"

"Of course I am!" Rena responded with obvious agitation. "Why else would I call you?"

Alex conducted a fierce but brief internal debate about whether to go or stay. Her sense of duty to her client prevailed.

"Okay. I'm on my way," she said. "But I want you to stay at the hospital until I arrive. Try to track down any doctor you recognize. Find out what you can and then call me. The only person to avoid is Ezra. Understood?"

"Yes."

Alex clicked off the phone and walked quickly over to the parsonage. Ted came to the door.

"What's happened?" he asked.

"There's a problem with implementation of the judge's order, and I have to go to Greenville."

"Now?" he asked with obvious disappointment.

Alex sighed. "Yes. I'm sorry. I'll call you later."

—

As Alex's car disappeared around a bend in the road, Ted lingered on the front steps. All that waited for him in the kitchen was a chicken salad sandwich, and he wasn't hungry. Closing the front door of the parsonage, he returned to the sanctuary. The large room that earlier had been bustling with activity was now completely quiet. He walked down the aisle and sat in front of the piano but didn't play. First, he needed to think.

Comfortable with spontaneity in music, Ted was much less impulsive in his personal actions. The sudden surge of attraction he felt for Alex Lindale when he saw her at the conclusion of the service had surprised him. It was the end of a Sunday morning church service, not the climax of a romantic dinner, yet she seemed to be at the same place in her feelings as he was. She knew he wanted to kiss her and made it easy. She kept the mood light, but it was a serious moment to Ted. It had been several years since he'd allowed himself a similar level of intimacy with a woman. His mind didn't offer any answers about the future, and he returned to the inner abode where he'd learned to dwell—a place called patience.

He bowed his head and offered a silent prayer for direction as to what to play. Immediately, Baxter Richardson and his family came to mind. He thought again about Maybeth Wells, a rose taken to heaven before it bloomed on earth. He opened a Bible to the Psalms, put his hands on the keyboard, and began. His thoughts shifted from himself to a family he'd never met and a man he didn't know. Resting the open Bible on the piano he began to play. Infused with sound, the words on the page became notes that permeated the atmosphere of the room and swirled upward like incense.

———

Once she was on the highway, Alex called Gwen, who agreed to check on Boris and Misha.

"I want to come home late tonight, but they need to be let out in a couple of hours," Alex said.

"Why don't I just hang out at your place until you get back?" Gwen asked. "I can be alone there as easily as I can here."

"That would be great. Make yourself at home. Feel free to eat or drink anything you can find."

During the long drive to Greenville Rena didn't call. Twice, Alex tried to reach her but landed in her voice mail. At the hospital she parked and walked through the main entrance. Inside the elevator her heart began beating faster in anticipation of the unknown. Several small groups of people were scattered about the ICU waiting room, but none of the Richardson family were present. Alex approached the male attendant, a familiar face from one of her previous visits.

"Is anyone from the Richardson family here?" she asked.

The young man nodded. "They went into the patient area a couple of minutes ago. It's already crowded, but you can ask the doctors if you can be present."

Alex's mouth went dry. "What are they doing to the patient?"

The phone on the desk rang, and the orderly answered it. Alex didn't wait. She pushed open the door to the ICU unit.

———

Rena stood on the far side of the bed. She felt detached. The other people in the room moved as if connected to wires. Their voices muted.

Their actions in slow motion. Baxter was already in a different realm. The overhead light shone brightly on his motionless form, and for a few fleeting seconds, Rena envied him. He was about to leave the world of pain while she remained to endure the struggle. She picked out a spot on Baxter's forehead and stared at it. Silently, she commanded the apparition that had stalked her to rejoin the figure on the bed. With each passing day, the events at the waterfall had receded deeper into the crevices of her memory, and her future happiness demanded that every connection she had with Baxter sink beyond the ability of anyone to rescue.

Ezra stood next to Baxter's head on the opposite side of the bed. Rena tried to avoid his sad eyes, but in the close quarters of the hospital room it was impossible. However, he held no immediate threat. The decision by the hospital administration to comply with Judge Holcomb's order had taken the fight from her father-in-law, and he'd aged years before her eyes. Every few seconds he stroked Baxter's hair. The gesture made Rena's skin crawl.

Beside Ezra was Dr. Berman and a doctor Rena didn't know. Jeffrey stood at the foot of the bed. He'd given Rena a solemn look when he entered the room, but she caught the hint of an unknown mockery in his eyes. Her brother-in-law was as complex as Baxter was simple. Rena wasn't sure what to say to him and kept her mouth shut. Total cooperation between her mind and her tongue was not guaranteed, and she didn't want to get herself into trouble with her words. There would be time to talk to Jeffrey, but she wasn't sure what needed to be said.

A nurse and a respiratory therapist were scurrying around getting ready. Rena fidgeted. It should be simple. Turn off the ventilator. But apparently the hospital rules and regulations required a meaningless protocol.

"Do you want us to give him any fentanyl?" the nurse asked.

"No, it's not necessary," Dr. Berman said. "Just keep the lorazepam at the current level."

The respiratory therapist spoke. "I'm reducing the inspired oxygen to 21 percent."

"That's fine," the doctor beside Dr. Berman answered. "Reduce the apnea, heater, and other ventilator alarms to minimum setting."

Rena shifted her weight from one foot to the other. The door opened, and Alex Lindale peeked into the room. Ezra glanced over his shoulder.

"What are you doing here?" he blurted out with indignation.

"I asked her to come," Rena answered. "She's here to help me through this."

Dr. Berman quickly intervened. "Why don't you stand beside Mrs. Richardson?" he said. "We're almost ready."

Alex squeezed past Jeffrey and joined Rena. The other people resumed their focus on the unconscious figure in the bed. The activity in the room reminded Alex of the preparation for execution by lethal injection. She tried to shake off the image. Baxter's death would be more merciful than the judgment he deserved.

"We're ready to remove the endotracheal tube," the doctor said.

Ezra blocked Alex's view of what the doctor was doing, but she kept her eyes glued to the steady rising and falling of Baxter's chest. The faint hissing sound slowly stopped, and the movement of Baxter's chest ceased with it. There was total silence for a few seconds, and Alex found herself holding her own breath. She'd never been in a room when someone died. It was an eerie feeling. Ezra put his hand on Baxter's shoulder and bowed his head. Alex could see Rena staring intently at her husband. She then sighed with relief. It was over.

The nurse moved a piece of equipment to the side, and Alex could see Baxter's face. He was wearing the pale mask of death. When the nurse resumed her position, Alex glanced again at Baxter's chest. There was still no sign of movement.

"There is independent respiration," the therapist said matter-of-factly. "It's weak but steady."

"Check the rate," the doctor replied.

Ezra raised his head. Alex's eyes grew bigger as she stared more intently at the motionless form in the bed. The words didn't match what she saw. Baxter was gone. He was as inert as a lump of clay. She glanced sideways at Rena, who took a step backward and collapsed before Alex could catch her. Her body hit a rollaway table with a loud bang and knocked it over. Dr. Berman and the nurse quickly came around the bed. Alex got out of the way and left the room.

She returned to the ICU waiting room and sat down. She didn't feel very steady herself, and the room became unnaturally warm. She put her head down toward her knees. A male voice brought her back up.

"Do you need some water?" he asked.

Alex looked up. It was the handsome young man who had been in the room.

"Uh, yes."

"I'll get it. In the meantime, breathe deeply and slowly."

In a few seconds, he returned with a plastic cup. Alex took a sip and began to feel more normal.

"I'm Jeffrey Richardson," he said. "You must be Ms. Lindale, the lawyer."

Alex nodded. "Thanks for the water. After Rena fainted, I felt a little lightheaded myself. Why did you leave the room?"

"All the medical personnel came rushing in to check Baxter and take care of Rena. I was in the way."

"That's the way I felt, too," Alex said. "I hope Rena didn't hurt herself. That was a nasty fall."

Jeffrey touched a place on the back of his head. "She has a pretty nasty bruise, but they were taking care of her."

Alex stood up. She was dizzy for a second, and Jeffrey reached out and held her arm.

"I'm okay," she said without pulling away.

"You still look pale. Maybe you should sit back down."

Alex plopped back in her chair. "Yeah. But don't stay. You need to go back to your family."

Jeffrey glanced back toward the ICU area. "Yes. I need to check on Rena, too."

After Jeffrey left, Alex finished the cup of water. The door opened and Dr. Berman entered the waiting room. Alex stood again. The dizziness had passed.

"Dr. Berman!" she called out.

The neurosurgeon came over to her.

"What can you tell me about Baxter?" she asked.

"That he's breathing on his own and otherwise unchanged."

"Were you surprised?" Alex asked.

The doctor tilted his head to one side. "Not really. Your suggestion in court was a good one. We would have eventually tried to wean him from the ventilator, and it's good to know he can breathe on his own. It will take time to know whether the additional strain of independent respiration will cause his overall condition to deteriorate. There are other mountains to climb. The greatest danger remains pneumonia."

"Is he still paralyzed?"

"For now. He may recover movement, or he may be at a permanent plateau. His long-term status may not be known for weeks or months; however, we will transfer him out of ICU in a day or so."

"Into a regular room?" Alex asked in surprise.

"Yes. His father wondered if Baxter could be taken home if a suitable environment can be created. I told him that's an option, but it would be very expensive unless an insurance company approves it as a cheaper alternative to continued hospitalization or care in a skilled nursing facility. It would require registered nursing care as well as a full-time attendant."

"I doubt money is a problem," Alex said.

"That's what Mr. Richardson indicated."

"How is Rena?"

"She's resting in an empty room. The ice pack they gave her should be enough to lessen the swelling of that contusion she suffered. She should be coming out in a few minutes."

"Does Dr. Draughton know what happened?" Alex asked.

"Not yet. I'll let him know. He's rarely—" The doctor stopped.

"Wrong?" Alex finished.

Dr. Berman smiled slightly. "Ms. Lindale, doctors can't admit a mistake in judgment, especially in front of a lawyer."

Awake, harp and lyre!
PSALM 108:2

AS SHE LAY on the hospital bed, Rena opened her eyes and stared at the wall in the darkened hospital room. She and Baxter were almost roommates. She wanted to close her eyes for ten seconds, open them, and find that her husband was gone. But it was no use. Baxter was alive. She put down the ice pack and felt the goose egg on the back of her head. It was now a very tender, chilled mound of flesh. She slipped from the bed and put on her shoes. A nurse entered the room.

"Are you steady enough to get up?" she asked.

Rena nodded. "I think so. Is anyone with my husband?"

"I don't think so."

Rena followed the nurse into the open area. The door to Baxter's room was open. Her father-in-law and Jeffrey were not in sight. She entered and closed the door behind her. The ventilator stood at the head of the bed and mocked her. The device had ceased its striving but Baxter had continued on without its assistance. She felt so tired, so exhausted, from the endless tug of war with the person who lay inert in the bed. She leaned over until her lips almost touched his left ear.

"Why don't you quit fighting?" she whispered.

At close range she could see the gentle rising and falling of his chest.

"It would be easier to let go," she continued. "It's not worth it to stay here. Go and be free."

The gentle rising and falling continued.

Rena clenched her fists. She wanted to pound them on Baxter's chest and scream at the top of her lungs. When healthy, Baxter was fairly sedentary. But in a paralyzed, comatose condition he demonstrated a resiliency and desire for survival beyond her ability to comprehend. Fuming, she turned and left the room without a strategy or plan of action.

She saw Alex when she exited the ICU area.

"How are you feeling?" Alex asked her.

Rena touched the back of her head and felt the huge bruise again. "Terrible. I'm still in shock. When I was lying down, I wanted to imagine that this was all a bad dream."

"Did Dr. Berman talk with you about Baxter leaving ICU?"

"No. Why would he want to do that?"

"He suggested transferring him to a regular room and then a special type of nursing home, but your father-in-law wants to bring him back to Santee and create a care center there with nurses and attendants."

"That won't work," Rena responded quickly. "Our house isn't set up as a hospital."

"Ezra may have been thinking about his house, not yours."

"Not there!" Rena's face revealed her alarm. "Uh, I wouldn't be able to check on him."

"Do you have another option?"

Rena bit her lower lip and thought for a moment. "We have a guest cottage on our property. Baxter and I lived there while they were remodeling our house. The cottage could be set up for him, and the medical people could come and go without entering the main house."

Alex nodded. "Would that be something you can talk to your father-in-law about directly or do I need to act as a go-between?"

Rena held up her hand. "You do it. He avoided me until right before we went into Baxter's room. I don't want to talk to him."

"By the way, what happened after you called me?" Alex asked. "You told me the doctors were going to ignore Judge Holcomb's order."

Rena looked away. "I don't know. I tried to find someone you could talk to, but no one was here. I left for a couple of hours, and when I came back, Dr. Berman told me they were going to shut off the ventilator in a few minutes."

"But I asked you to stay at the hospital and find out what was going on," Alex said sharply.

"I tried to find someone but couldn't take the pressure," Rena answered forlornly. "I had to get some fresh air. Send me a bill for your time."

Alex stared at Rena for a second before responding. She'd wasted a long trip for nothing. Her client's selfishness was understandable yet irritating.

"I'm going to ask Ken Pinchot about it tomorrow when I contact him about the arrangements for Baxter. It doesn't make sense that they would simply ignore the judge's order."

Rena looked past her. Baxter was standing casually by the door to the ICU area, watching them. He was wearing his favorite pair of pajamas and the bathrobe Rena had given him for Christmas.

"Well, I'm going back to Santee," Alex said. "What are you going to do?"

Rena shook her head, and Baxter disappeared.

"Find a hole where I can crawl in and die."

———

Gwen was dozing on the couch in the living room when Alex unlocked the door. She sat up and rubbed her eyes as Misha jumped down from the spot where she had been lying next to Gwen's leg and ran toward Alex. Boris entered the living room wagging his tail.

"How did the children behave?" Alex asked.

Gwen yawned. "No problem. I gave Boris extra treats so he would like me, and Misha and I speak the same language. How was your trip?"

Alex plopped down in her chair and gave her a quick version of the events at the hospital.

"What a mess," Gwen said. "I bet you're exhausted."

"The last hour in the car was a blur."

Gwen stretched. "I'd better be going home myself."

"Why don't you spend the night?" Alex suggested. "You don't have to sleep on the couch. The bed in the guest room is softer, and I'll fix coffee in the morning exactly the way you like it."

"Maybe another time."

"Misha wants you to stay."

"Perhaps I can invite Misha over to my place for a spend-the-night party."

Gwen reached over and stroked Misha's silver back. The cat arched her back in affirmation.

Alex called Ken Pinchot the following morning and found out that Rena hadn't deceived her about the events at the hospital. When Drs. Kolb and Berman communicated Judge Holcomb's decision to the hospital administrator, the woman contacted the hospital's lawyers and requested an opinion. There followed a series of e-mails and phone calls that resulted in the pulmonary specialist telling a colleague they were not going to remove the ventilator without additional clarification of the proper protocol from the court. Rena overheard part of that conversation. If she had gone into the meeting instead of calling Alex, she would have found out that everything was worked out.

"What does Mr. Richardson think about bringing Baxter back to Santee?" Alex asked. "Dr. Berman mentioned that he discussed it with you."

"He's exploring options."

Alex proceeded carefully. As long as Ezra held the durable power of attorney, she doubted she could win a tug of war over Baxter's immediate care.

"Have you considered turning the guest cottage at Baxter and Rena's house into a dedicated care facility?" she asked. "It would provide twenty-four-hour access for medical workers and allow all members of the family to visit whenever they wanted to."

"Ezra brought that up when we talked, but he wasn't sure about Rena's reaction."

"She's open to the possibility. We've already discussed it."

"Really?" Pinchot paused. "I'll contact Ezra and get back to you."

As soon as she hung up the phone, Alex called Rena in Greenville.

"How are you this morning?" Alex asked.

"Still in my hole. Do you have any news?"

Alex told her about Pinchot's positive response to moving Baxter to the cottage.

"The more I've thought about it, the more I like it," Rena said. "If I'm ever going to get over what has happened, I need to spend time with Baxter myself. I could have more opportunities to be alone with him if he's there at the house."

———

Two days later, Baxter Richardson returned to Santee. It was a different journey from the carefree drive he'd taken with Rena for a day hike in the mountains. His eyes were closed, and he had no sensation of the passage of time or distance. The seasons were changing and early winter was at hand. In the meantime, Baxter clung to life like an autumn leaf in an uncertain breeze.

The white guest cottage with green shutters and black roof had undergone a rapid transformation. Much can be accomplished in a short period of time if money is not an obstacle. Simple antiques had been replaced with modern hospital furnishings. The living room would be the main care area. In the middle of the room was a state-of-the-art bed surrounded by all the equipment needed to feed and care for a paralyzed, comatose patient. The kitchen was turned into the nurse's station and supply room. The bedroom served as the overflow area for everything else. Ezra hired a medical consultant from Charleston and paid for everything.

Rena watched the workers coming and going from the window of her house. She had to bide her time until the dust settled. While she waited, the seed of a plan to finish the job begun at Double-Barrel Falls began germinating in her mind.

The patient arrived via ambulance. Rena and Ezra stood on opposite sides of the driveway as the attendants rolled the gurney toward the house. Baxter's pale face appeared oddly white in the bright sunlight. His body didn't resist the small jolts as the gurney rolled across the pavement. When she saw him, it reinforced in Rena's mind the fact that Baxter wasn't really human. He was more closely related to a mass of cells inside a woman during the early weeks of pregnancy than a viable child about to be born, and just as Rena would have the right to discard those cells for her convenience, Baxter needed to be eliminated from her life. His stubborn presence kept her from going on into the future.

She held back and didn't go into the guesthouse until her father-in-law left. The uneasy truce that had brought Baxter back to Santee didn't extend to personal interaction. Jeffrey was out of town and wouldn't be back for a couple of days.

When she tentatively opened the front door of the cottage, Rena was greeted by a gray-haired lady wearing an old-fashioned, white nurse's uniform that exuded professionalism. The woman introduced herself with a firm handshake.

"Mrs. Richardson, I'm Clarice Hathcock, an RN who will be coming by several days a week to check on your husband." Ms. Hathcock handed Rena her card. "I live about five minutes' drive from here. If you need me, please don't hesitate to call."

Baxter was lying peacefully on his side with his face toward the door. His body was covered by a white sheet, and Rena could see the limp outline of his arms and legs.

"He was always on his back when I saw him in the hospital," Rena said.

"I'm sure they changed his position. We will be moving him on a regular basis to avoid problems. For people in comas, bedsores can lead to fatal infections."

A young female aide came into the room from the kitchen. Nurse Hathcock introduced her to Rena.

"There will be an aide here at all times. You don't have to do anything except come for visits whenever you like."

Rena nodded. "I might like to have some time alone with him."

"Of course. Just tell the person on duty to step into another room."

Rena retreated to the safety of the main house. As she walked in the door, the phone rang. It was Alex.

"Has Baxter arrived?" the lawyer asked.

"Yes."

"Would it be okay if I come by later?"

"What time?"

"About four-thirty. I also want to bring someone with me."

"Who?" she asked.

"Ted Morgan, the music minister at Sandy Flats Church. He's a friend of mine."

"Why does he want to come?"

"He's a musician and wants to play music on a portable keyboard in Baxter's room."

"Huh? That would be a waste of time. Baxter doesn't know what's happening."

"He's aware of Baxter's condition, but he wants to do it anyway. I'll stay in the room. You don't have to be there."

"Whatever, but you'll have to clear it with the nurse. Someone is with Baxter all the time."

"Alright. See you then."

———

Alex hung up and dialed Ted's number.

"You're in," she said when he answered. "I tried to sound casual, but it felt weird asking permission for a musician to play for a comatose patient."

"Did she ask you why?"

"No, and I'm not sure I could have explained it the way you did to me. The value of playing Bible verses as a way for God to touch a sick person is not something I've ever argued to a jury."

Ted smiled and put a clean glass back in the cupboard of his kitchen. "I'm glad you didn't have to use your lawyer skills. What time should I be there?"

"Four-thirty if the nurse on duty approves it."

"Should I meet you at their house?"

"No, come here a few minutes early and pick me up. We'll go together."

———

The idea that music could be the means God used to touch and heal someone was birthed in Ted's experimentation in translating spiritual concepts into their musical equivalents. It was a subjective exercise, but it was consistent with Ted's belief that in a perfect universe everything moved in harmony with the Creator. Ted's job was to intersect the expression of music that ran parallel with God-breathed prayer. When he did so, he communicated a depth of desire beyond his ability to express in words. It was a pure form of faith uniquely suited to the gift of God in his life.

He arrived in his pickup truck at Rachel Downey's office. It was fifteen minutes before Alex walked into the reception area.

"Sorry," she said. "I was doing paramedic duty on a woman's emotions. Let's go."

Ted's work truck didn't feature leather seats and the fancy stereo system looked out of place in the rugged interior. He'd wiped off the cracked vinyl seat with a wet rag before leaving the parsonage. The keyboard was in a black plastic case in the truck bed. When Alex slid in and closed the door, Ted handed her an envelope.

"Here's the bid for the work on the house. I went over there yesterday and changed a few things on the proposal."

"More money?" Alex asked.

"Not much," Ted replied as he backed out of the parking space. "And it will be even cheaper if you're willing to get some paint on the end of your nose."

"I don't have much experience as a painter."

"No problem. I can give you on-the-job training with an extra discount for the pleasure of your company."

Alex smiled. "As long as you promise not to get mad at me if I mess up."

"Put it in the contract, and I'll sign it."

"Done. Do you know the way to Rena's house?" Alex asked.

"Yes. I did a job last year in the same neighborhood."

It was a short drive from the downtown area to the neighborhood that featured several large, older homes.

"What are you going to play when we get there?" Alex asked.

Ted flipped down the sun visor as they turned west down a sunny street. "The beginning section is related to what I played the Sunday afternoon they took him off the breathing machine. From there it's less clear, but as I told you the other day, I've thought about the idea for years. This is just the first time I've actually tried to do it."

"Did you consider starting with an easier case?" Alex asked. "I mean, Baxter Richardson is barely alive."

Ted nodded. "If it depended on me, that would make sense. But I don't have the power to heal a sore throat. If something good happens today, it will be because God does it. All we have to offer is obedience and faith."

Alex glanced out the window. "No one can argue that Baxter doesn't need all the help he can get."

They pulled into the driveway and parked near the guest cottage. Alex called Rena's number.

"We're here," she said. Then she listened for almost a minute to Rena talk.

Flipping off the phone, she turned to Ted and reported, "Rena has already spent time with him today and doesn't want to come over again this afternoon. It's hard on her to see him like this."

"That's fine. I'd rather we be alone with him."

They knocked on the door of the cottage. Nurse Hathcock opened it.

"May I help you?" she asked.

Alex took charge. "I'm Alexia Lindale, Mrs. Richardson's attorney, and this is Ted Morgan, a local minister. We'd like to see Baxter."

"I have a list of approved visitors," the nurse replied. "Let me check."

She closed the door in their faces.

"This may be the hardest part," Alex said.

The nurse returned with a clipboard in her hand.

"I'm sorry, but neither of you is on the list. Mr. Richardson gave specific instructions about limiting visitors."

Alex took out her cell phone and hit the redial button. "If Mrs. Richardson says it's fine, may we come in?"

"Uh, yes."

Alex told Rena what they needed and then handed the phone to Ms. Hathcock.

"Here. She has something to tell you."

As the nurse listened, her eyes grew bigger. "To do what?" she asked as she looked at Ted and Alex with greater skepticism. "I've never had a request like this before. It should be cleared with the supervising doctor."

It wasn't clear to Ted and Alex what Rena said next, but Ms. Hathcock blinked and moved the phone away from her ear. The nurse's resistance evaporated.

"Yes, ma'am," she said and handed the phone back to Alex. "You can go in for ten minutes. Keep the volume on your instrument low."

Ted retrieved the keyboard from the back of the truck. In his other hand was a black Bible. As he entered the cottage, Baxter was alone. They stood side by side and looked soberly at the immobile figure in the bed. Ted took Alex's hand and bowed his head.

"God, help us. Amen," he said simply.

Alex motioned toward the kitchen and whispered, "The guards are in there."

Ted opened the case for his keyboard and took out the instrument. He didn't spend any more time staring at Baxter. He didn't want to waste his ten minutes. He plugged the keyboard into a wall outlet and turned it on.

"Where do you want me to sit?" Alex asked.

"Anywhere, so long as you can agree with what I'm playing."

———

Alex wasn't sure how to agree with musical notes, but she squelched any questions. She sat in a low-slung, comfortable chair that she suspected had survived from the days when Baxter and Rena had lived in the tiny house. The hospital bed blocked her view of Ted's face. Baxter was lying with his back to Ted and facing her. The music minister hit a few tentative notes then adjusted the volume of the keyboard. The instrument was capable of a wide variety of sounds, but Ted had apparently decided to choose straight piano. Alex could see an open Bible on the floor at his feet.

Ted began to play.

There was nothing remarkable about it. It was a simple succession of notes with basic resolutions every few measures. Alex wasn't sure what she'd expected, but given the seriousness of Baxter's condition, something with more musical pyrotechnics would have seemed appropriate. Ted played for a couple of minutes and then stopped to turn the pages of his Bible. Alex glanced toward the kitchen and saw the nurse peek out when the music ceased. Ted resumed, and Ms. Hathcock retreated.

He took up a different key and stayed in the lower octaves where he created a rumbling sound with a military stridency. The vibrancy of tone from the portable instrument was pathetic when compared to the grand piano in the sanctuary of the church, but there was potential in the notes the music minister coaxed from the machine. Alex listened more closely. Ted moved up the keyboard and then quickly dropped back down as if regrouping before going forward. Alex wasn't sure if it was her imagination, but she began to sense a purpose in the music. Ted was going somewhere. Alex glanced at Baxter. His face revealed nothing. There was no visible change.

Ted moved higher on the keyboard and continued playing with his left hand while he flipped through the pages of his Bible with his right. When he found the correct page, he hit several strong chords that made the hair stand up on the back of Alex's neck. She wasn't paralyzed, but the sound made her want to stand up and move her feet. She gripped the arms of the chair and glanced at Baxter. The decreasing light outside was making it more difficult to see, but it seemed that his right arm moved enough to disturb the sheet that covered it. She leaned forward and stared more intently. If Baxter Richardson were going to be healed, she had a front row seat.

Ted backed off for several measures before continuing with increasing intensity. His fingers moved effortlessly across the keyboard. Alex eased up from the chair so she could see the minister's face. His eyes were closed. The communication between his fingers and his heart was unhindered. It was amazing.

"Time's up!" The shrill voice of Nurse Hathcock shattered the atmosphere in the room.

Alex felt like she'd been slapped in the face. She plopped back into the chair. Ted played a few more notes and stopped. Baxter was unchanged. His breathing was so shallow that the sheet covering him didn't appear to move at all.

Alex stood up. "But he wasn't finished—," she began.

"You are for today," the nurse responded crisply. "And if you plan on coming back, it will be necessary that you obtain written authorization from one of the treating doctors. This has been highly disruptive to the atmosphere needed by a patient like Mr. Richardson."

Alex looked at Ted, expecting him to respond to the idiotic nurse. He was calmly unplugging his keyboard and putting it back in its case. Alex could not let the nurse's conclusion go unchallenged.

"That's ridiculous. The only atmosphere in this room was death. Couldn't you tell that the music was having a beneficial influence?"

The nurse's face became more stern. "I don't play an instrument, but I have been taking care of seriously ill patients for more than thirty years, and I've never heard of anything like this before."

"But just because it's a new idea—"

The nurse interrupted her. "Ms. Lindale, I'm not going to argue with you. The patient is my responsibility, and it is time for you to leave."

Alex was still fuming when she slammed the door of the truck.

"Why didn't you say anything?" she asked in frustration.

"Would it have made any difference?" Ted responded calmly.

"I doubt it, but at least you wouldn't have let her think she was right about her opinion. I could feel the presence of God in the room while you were playing. It was as strong as anything I've encountered at the church."

"That's good to know."

Ted turned left out of the driveway. Alex continued to vent her frustration.

"This was a lot of trouble not to accomplish anything. I thought you had a huge desire to play your music until Baxter Richardson was healed or whatever else you expected to happen. Then you meekly slink out without putting up any fight at all."

"Blessed are the meek, for they will inherit the earth," Ted said ponderously. Before Alex could explode, he added, "Listen. I'm upset, too, but I'm not going to let my emotions dictate what happens next. When things go bad in court, do you let your feelings tell you how to respond?"

"No. I try not to."

"It's the same for me. My job is to ask the Lord what to do next, not lash out at the nurse. There are plenty of people like her. Anything new is automatically viewed in a negative light. I have to deal with them all the time in church situations."

"What do you do?"

"I ask God to change them. If that doesn't work, I go over their head or around them. In this situation, one obvious step is to get permission from a doctor. The nurse is a stickler about rules. Whatever the doctor orders will be the law."

"But you don't know the doctors. If you contact Dr. Berman or Kolb and ask them to approve music therapy for Baxter, they're going to brush you off as a nut."

"Maybe. But they might listen to you. I may not be a music therapist, but they may be open to the idea. It can't hurt to try."

Alex sputtered. "I'm not sure—"

"I like the term 'music therapy,'" Ted continued with a smile touching the corners of his mouth. "It has a scientific ring to it. I can put together a list of my professional qualifications to send the doctors with your request. It won't be the first time my worldly accomplishments have served God's purposes, and I'm not hesitant about trotting them out for display if the cause is just. What do you think?"

"I'm not sure," Alex replied. "I need to think about it."

As they drove, Alex mulled over Ted's request. The sense of God's presence that had begun to permeate the room where Baxter lay in the bed was a hard argument to resist. Plus, she couldn't tolerate the thought of Nurse Hathcock having the last word. They pulled into the parking area for Rachel Downey's office, and Ted turned off the engine.

"Okay, I'll try," she said. "But I can't guarantee results."

Ted turned in his seat and lightly touched her shoulder. "You don't have to promise victory. I'm sure even the best lawyers don't win every case."

For nothing is impossible with God.
LUKE 1:37

RENA WAS STRUGGLING to fight her way out of a frustrating afternoon nap on a sofa in the living room when her cell phone rang. She glanced at the caller ID. It was Jeffrey. She debated whether to answer before finally pushing the talk button.

"Hello," she said flatly.

"Sorry I didn't make it by earlier," he began. "Is Baxter settled in okay?"

"Yes, if you can pretend this whole arrangement is normal."

"Yeah, I know it's rough on you to have him back home."

Rena had the beginnings of a headache and didn't want to engage in small talk.

"What do you want?" she asked.

"To follow through with my promises."

"Which one? You've broken every one of them."

"Didn't I give you money when my father gutted your checking account?"

"Yes, but you didn't help with the hearing in Greenville or let me know what is happening to the rest of my property."

Jeffrey kept his voice level. "It wouldn't have helped our long-term goals for me to show up in court in Greenville. My testimony wouldn't have made any difference, and it was while my father was out of town that I had the opportunity to investigate what he's done. Have you checked your bank balance recently?"

"I'm not using the joint checking account anymore."

"I'm talking about your new account."

Rena paused. "How did you know about my new account?"

"I told you to open it," Jeffrey responded patiently. "And I'm on the board of the bank."

Rena gave herself a quick internal lashing. She shouldn't have gone to a local bank. Nothing was secret from the Richardsons within fifteen miles of downtown Santee.

"Is your father on the board, too?"

"He came off a few years ago and doesn't know what you've done."

As usual, Jeffrey was a step ahead of her.

"Okay," she said. "I'm listening."

"I have the documents proving the transfer of Baxter's interest in several companies to a new holding company controlled by my father. Everything happened after the accident so this could only be done with the power of attorney."

"What businesses are you talking about?"

"Ones you don't know anything about and Baxter never investigated. It's all part of the group we discussed in Greenville."

"You mean the organized crime—"

"Don't ever say that!" Jeffrey interrupted sharply. "You don't know what you're talking about, and you don't know who might be listening."

"Is it safe to talk?" Rena asked.

"Yes, but develop a habit of avoiding comments you wouldn't want repeated."

"Alright, but how is this going to benefit me?"

"Remember, this is for both of us. I will give you information to pass on to Alexia Lindale so she can file the lawsuit against my father. I don't think it will take much to convince him to rescind his actions and return to the status quo. You saw how quickly he backed down about the checking account, and he doesn't want any of this other information coming out into the open."

Rena massaged her right temple with her fingers to fight off the headache.

"But even then I won't be able to do anything with Baxter's share of the companies. Everything will just sit there."

"My father will not be able to exercise control in these matters without Baxter's vote, and it will force him to cooperate with me. I want greater distributions of money to both of us than he would do otherwise. He likes to hoard everything; I'm more generous minded. So, there will be short-term benefit from greatly increased income that comes to you."

"How much?" she asked, her curiosity increasing.

"Enough to make the money Baxter gave you seem like a child's allowance. And if Baxter dies, you and I will be able to take things to a much higher level."

Jeffrey's plans sounded plausible, but Rena sensed something was missing.

"How do I know that you're going to follow through? I've been waiting weeks for this phone call, and all I have are more words."

Silence consumed several seconds.

"Are you still there?" Rena asked.

"Yes. I have some things to give you. Are you going to be at home tomorrow afternoon?"

"Tell me the time, and I'll be here."

"About three o'clock. I'll see Baxter and then meet with you."

———

The following morning, Alex left a message for Dr. Berman and then faxed a letter explaining in nonreligious terms what Ted wanted to do. She particularly emphasized Ted's musical training and mentioned Rena's support for the idea. An hour later the doctor's nurse called and promised an answer before the end of the day.

Shortly before 5 P.M., Alex was about to go home when Rachel's secretary brought a fax into her office. It was a brief statement from Dr. Berman approving music therapy for Baxter Richardson to be provided by Ted Morgan for up to thirty minutes a day. Alex called Ted.

"You've received the neurosurgeon seal of approval," she began. "If you could only bill the insurance company for your services, it would be a perfect world. I want to be there when you give the slip to Nurse Hatchet."

"Was that her name? I didn't pay attention."

"No, it was Hathcock, but I think she should change it. When do you want to go back to see Baxter?"

"I'm busy until tomorrow afternoon around four o'clock."

Alex looked at her calendar. She'd written *Vox v. Vox* in large letters beginning at 1 P.M.

"I have a hearing that starts at one o'clock. It's a preliminary matter and should be over by three unless it gets bumped down the calendar."

"If you're not able to go with me, should you call Rena and let her know what's happening?" Ted asked.

"No, there are people coming and going all the time. The important item is the doctor's slip. I'll fax it to the church in case we can't get together."

"Okay, thanks."

"What are you going to play?" Alex asked. "Will it be like the other day?"

"Probably, but with some differences. I've been thinking and praying about it a lot."

"I'd love to go with you. Call before you leave the church to see if I'm out of my hearing."

———

That afternoon Jeffrey left the cottage after spending five minutes with Baxter. The lump of flesh in the hospital bed couldn't hold his interest. His brother was taking up space and consuming assets without any tangible return. Things would be much more simple and direct if Baxter died, leaving Rena in control of his estate and Jeffrey in control of Rena.

He walked across to the main house. On the way, he passed a large tree where he'd tried to push Baxter out of a tree house when they were boys. His younger brother's cry for help had brought their grandmother from the house, and Jeffrey had been ordered to cease and desist.

Jeffrey and Rena had more in common than they realized.

Jeffrey stopped by his car, took out his briefcase, and rang the doorbell. Rena opened it.

"Come in," she said. "Did you see Baxter?"

"Just for a second. He's losing body mass by the day. I don't see that he can go on much longer like this."

Rena nodded. She'd not been over to the cottage all day.

"Let's go to the kitchen," Jeffrey suggested.

They sat down at a light-colored wooden table. Jeffrey opened the briefcase and took out a single sheet of paper. He handed it to Rena.

"This is a summary of the information your lawyer will need to file the suit. I have all the backup documentation, but I'm not going to give it to her unless my father tries to fight. I think a strong bluff will be enough to accomplish our goals."

Rena read the sheet. It was a list of companies with dates beside them and two lines of percentages. At the bottom was a list of ten people Alex didn't know. Most were men, but a few were women.

"What is this? It doesn't make any sense."

"Lindale will know what it means. Just tell her it represents recent changes in the ownership of the companies listed. The higher percentages were Baxter's ownership shares before the accident; the lower numbers represent what he holds now."

Most of the second column of figures were zeros.

Rena pointed at the names on the bottom of the sheet. "Who are these people?"

"My decoys. I don't want my father to get suspicious as to the source of your information. The men and women listed are employees who have access to information. If you have to reveal why you know something about the businesses, supply one or more of these names."

Rena raised her eyebrows. "But won't they get into trouble?"

"Yes. They'll be fired at the first opportunity. But every one of them is a person I want out of the company. They're loyal to my father, not to me."

Rena hesitated. Alex knew that Jeffrey was her contact. She wasn't sure the lawyer would cooperate with the subterfuge.

"I've done my part," Jeffrey said. "Are you going to follow through?"

"Am I still being watched?" Rena asked.

She had frequently looked out the window since returning to Santee but hadn't noticed anything unusual. The dark blue car was nowhere in sight.

"Guarded is a better word," Jeffrey responded.

He reached into the briefcase and casually took out a videotape.

"Watch this later. It will encourage you to cooperate with me for our mutual benefit."

"What is it?"

"Consider it a home movie. When will you talk to your lawyer?"

"I'll phone her tomorrow."

After Jeffrey left, Rena picked up the tape. It didn't have a label on it. She guessed it was probably from the previous year's Christmas party, but she didn't recall anyone filming the festivities. She had a small TV/VCR unit in the kitchen. She slid the tape into the player and turned it on.

The video began with a shot of the front of her house with the red convertible in the driveway. The date and time ran continuously across the bottom of the picture. As she watched, the side door to the house opened, and she saw herself coming outside. She got into the convertible and drove down the driveway. Whoever shot the film was in a vehicle that followed her through several stop signs and a traffic light until a truck pulled in front of them and cut them off. The video ended but the date and time stayed on the screen for several seconds.

Rena gasped and put her hand over her mouth.

It was the day she went for her joy ride down the coast toward Charleston. The surveillance film would destroy her alibi that her car was stolen while she'd gone for a long walk to the park. She went over to the VCR, ejected the tape, and threw it across the room. It knocked over a frame containing a photograph of Rena in her wedding dress and sent it crashing to the floor.

———

The following afternoon Ted called Alex at three-thirty, but she wasn't there. During the drive to Santee he repeated the same simple prayer over and over.

"Lord Jesus, let it be today."

He decided to stop by Alex's office. As he got out of his truck, Alex turned the corner down the sidewalk and saw him.

"I just finished my hearing in court," she said.

"Do you want to go with me?" he asked.

"Yes. I've done enough work for one day."

Ted got back in his truck and waited. In a moment Alex appeared and smiled brightly at him.

"Did you win?" he asked, as he backed the truck out of the parking space.

"I made progress," Alex answered. "Today was a major skirmish and I scored some points. But most cases aren't won in a day."

"That's how I'm looking at what we're about to do," Ted replied.

They rode in silence the few blocks to the cottage as Ted focused on what lay ahead.

"Give me the permission slip," Alex said. "I want to give it to the nurse."

"No," Ted replied with a smile. "It has my name on it. Be nice or I'll make you wait in the truck."

They parked in front of the tiny house. Ted got out and walked up to the door with his keyboard under one arm and the authorization from Dr. Berman in his hand. He prayed under his breath as he stood on the small stoop, knocked, and waited for Nurse Hathcock to appear. Alex stood beside him.

When the door opened, they saw a new face. She was an attractive, middle-aged woman with sleek black hair, dark eyes, and brown skin that suggested ancestry linked to America's original inhabitants. Ted and Alex introduced themselves, and he handed her the paper from Dr. Berman.

The woman glanced at it and said, "Come inside. I'm Sarah Locklear, the nurse on duty."

"Where is Nurse Hathcock?" Alex asked.

"Today is one of her days off. We work for the same agency, and I'll be filling in from time to time."

Alex and Ted went inside. Baxter was lying on his back.

"What is music therapy?" the nurse asked as she handed the slip back to Ted.

Ted set his keyboard on a chair. "I'm going to play for thirty minutes. The doctor hopes the music may stimulate a response in Baxter and help bring him out of the coma. You don't have to stay in the room."

"We won't be touching any of the equipment," Alex added.

The nurse didn't back away. "What if I want to stay?"

Ted had been taking the cover off the keyboard. He stopped and struggled for a gracious reason to exclude her.

"Uh, I won't be playing anything you might recognize. It's impromptu."

The nurse didn't budge. "That's even more interesting. Have you done this before?"

"Two days ago."

"I mean with other people who are sick."

Ted shook his head. "No, Baxter is the first person. I'm a minister at a local church, and I hope the music will be a way for God to touch him. I know it's different, but—"

An aide looked into the room from the kitchen. "Do you need me?" the woman asked.

"Go ahead and take your break," the nurse responded. "I'll be in here with these folks and Mr. Richardson."

"You're sure you want to stay?" Ted asked as he looked into the nurse's dark eyes.

"Yes, if it won't distract you. During the years I've taken care of sick people, I've seen many things happen that could only be explained as the hand of God."

Ted saw the sincerity in Sarah Locklear's eyes and instantly knew she was an ally, not an adversary.

"Okay," he said. "You're welcome to join us."

He looked for his Bible and then remembered he'd left it at home when he picked up the keyboard.

"I forgot my Bible," he said.

"I'll get mine," the nurse responded. "It's in the kitchen."

After the nurse left, Alex said in a quiet voice, "This is good."

Ted pointed upward and nodded. The nurse returned with a well-worn, brown, leather Bible, which she handed to Ted, who set it on a chair in front of him.

"Thanks," he said. "Let's pray, and I'll get started."

Ted bowed his head and offered a brief prayer. When he said, "Amen," he opened his eyes, but the nurse had an addendum.

"Lord Jesus," she said earnestly, "send your holy angels into this room and help us during this time of prayer for Mr. Richardson. May he be like the man at the pool of Bethesda who heard your command to rise up and walk. May he look into your eyes and find healing for his body, soul, and spirit."

Ted glanced over at Alex, who didn't try to hide her surprise. The nurse continued for a few more moments before stopping. Ted turned on the keyboard. He knew where he wanted to start. He turned the pages of the Bible until he found Luke 1:37—*For nothing is impossible with God.* The nurse had underlined the verse in thick pencil. He began to play.

Almost immediately, Ted could tell a difference from the previous session. There was a deeper awareness that the power of God was in the tiny house. He moved up and down the keys, producing notes that proclaimed the majesty and power of God. He glanced at Nurse Locklear. Her eyes were closed, and she was swaying slightly in her chair. Alex, her eyes also closed, was sitting quietly with her hands folded in her lap.

When release from the first scripture came, Ted turned to John 5—the healing of the man at the pool of Bethesda. The transition was smooth, and Ted began to watch Baxter's face as the notes bridged the gap between heaven and earth. Nothing changed. He continued to play. A faint sound from another place came faintly to Ted's hearing. He had often wondered what it would be like to hear the voices of angels singing. He kept playing as he strained to pull in the voice that lingered at the edge of his hearing. The sound grew slightly louder, but it was not possible to distinguish direction or words. It increased again.

It was Sarah Locklear. She was singing.

The nurse was an alto with a rich, deep timbre. Her voice followed Ted's fingers across the keyboard in vocal expression that communicated pure, unhindered emotion. The notes weren't as complicated as the inter-relationships Ted often created, but they tracked closely with the prompting he sensed from the Holy Spirit. For a second, Ted hesitated and wondered if he should try to follow her, but just as quickly he knew that there was only one conductor in the room. His name was Jesus. He was the head. They were the body.

Ted wasn't surprised when words began to come. The simple phrases complemented his instrumental petition and expanded its scope. Her voice was soft, yet distinct. In a different context, Ted suspected it could explode with power. Time passed. The thirty minutes prescribed by the doctor was irrelevant. Ted wasn't sure if it was fifteen minutes or fifty, but he knew when to stop. Sarah's voice quietly receded to the wellspring within her. In the silence of anticipation all three of them looked at Baxter.

He was unchanged.

Ted stood up and came close to the bed. Alex joined him. The sheet that covered Baxter's torso barely rose and fell. He was alive but remained wandering in the barren, waterless land between this life and the next. Nothing in his appearance gave indication that he'd responded to the anointed music that had filled his room.

"What do you think?" Ted asked the nurse, who was standing on the opposite side of the bed.

Sarah Locklear shook her head. "I'm not sure."

"Is there anything else we should do?"

"No," she said. "My heart is clear. The results are in God's hands."

Ted nodded. "You have a beautiful voice—"

"You don't have to say anything," the nurse interrupted with a smile. "It was a holy time."

"It was awesome," Alex added in a small voice.

"When are you going to be working?" Ted asked the nurse. "I'd like to come back when you are here."

"It varies. I don't have a regular schedule. I'll be back at least once every couple of weeks."

Ted took out his wallet and gave her one of his cards. "Please call me," he said.

"Okay. And I'll be praying about what you're doing."

"We're doing," Ted corrected.

The manifest presence of the Lord lingered with Ted as he drove down the driveway. It would take time to process what had happened with Sarah Locklear. Lost in her own thoughts, Alex didn't intrude.

The nurse returned to the kitchen and drank a cup of cold water. She had worshiped God in many ways ever since she was a little girl, but today a door had opened to an enormous room she hadn't known existed.

Left alone, Baxter Richardson opened his eyes.

*Coming Soon
from acclaimed novelist
Robert Whitlow...*

LIFE
EVERLASTING

Available Everywhere
January 2005

W PUBLISHING GROUP™
www.wpublishinggroup.com

Also Available from Robert Whitlow

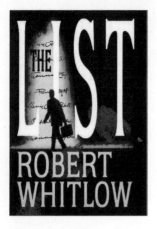

Renny Jacobson is stunned by his father's sudden death—and then by the terms of the will: For his only son, he has left nothing more than the contents of a safe deposit box and interest in a company no one has ever heard of—the Covenant List of South Carolina, Ltd.

When Renny, in rapid succession, encounters lovely Jo Johnston, meets the members of "The List," and discovers the staggering value of his father's mysterious bequest, his hope is resurrected. Renny accepts his inheritance and discovers there is more to the Covenant List than meets the eye—there is a power in the List.

Renny feels the power of the 140-year-old covenant—But when his life begins to unravel, he is forced to face the truth: the power residing in the List is not a force for good, but for unimaginable evil.

Attorney Kent "Mac" MacClain has nothing left to live for. Nine years after the horrific accident that claimed the life of his wife and two sons, he's finally given up. It seems suicide is his only escape. Now the question is death by pills or by bullet?

And then the phone rings.

Angela Hightower, the beautiful heiress and daughter of the most powerful man in Dennison Springs, has been found dead. The accused killer, Peter Thomason, needs a lawyer. But Mac has come up against the Hightower's ruthless, high-powered lawyers before. The stakes are high, but can Mac turn down a man whose life is on the line?

A Christy Award Winner!

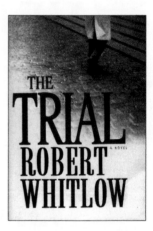

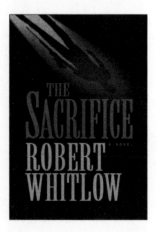

When Lester Garrison, a teenage racist with a shaved head and lightning bolt tattoos, is charged in a local shooting, Scott Ellis agrees to defend him.

While fighting for Lester's freedom, Scott volunteers as the advisor for a mock trial team at Catawba High School. To his surprise, the team sponsor is a teacher with a familiar face-Kay Wilson, the girl of Scott's high school dreams.

The darkness in Lester Garrison's eyes is not the only evil Scott faces. Frank Jesup, a student on the mock trial team, has his own problems threatening to explode. Ultimately, the stakes are much higher than Scott Ellis imagines, and the survival of many lives hinges on an unexpected sacrifice.

Visit www.robertwhitlow.com